BLOOD RACE

By Mark Olshaker

MARK OLSHAKER

BLOOD RACE

WILLIAM MORROW AND COMPANY, INC. / NEW YORK

Library of Congress Cataloging-in-Publication Data

Olshaker, Mark, 1951-
    Blood race / Mark Olshaker.
        p.   cm.
    ISBN 0-688-07109-0
    I. Title.
PS3565.L823B5 1989
813'.54—dc19   88-23016
                                                                      CIP

Printed in the United States of America

First Edition

1 2 3 4 5 6 7 8 9 10

BOOK DESIGN BY VICTORIA HARTMAN

For Ray Hubbard

AUTHOR'S NOTE

This is a work of fiction, and although it is based on actual events and persons, the specific situations, treatment, and dialogue are fabrications of my imagination.

Throughout my career, I have been fortunate in who my friends are, and this book is no exception. My deepest gratitude and admiration go to my editor, Lisa Drew, and my agent, Jay Acton, two people whose ongoing enthusiasm and guidance I have come to rely on. A. E. Claeyssens's friendship and wisdom, as always, influenced every stage of my effort as I tried to live up to the standard he has set. Larry Klein and Andrew Marin were also unending in their ideas, support, and encouragement throughout the writing.

I want to proclaim special thanks to my "panel of experts": David Kanin in history, Herman Hobbs in science, and Brian Mullin, Ray Mitchell, and my brother, Robert Olshaker, in medicine. They can take the credit for whatever I got right, but not faulted for the excesses and liberties I have taken in the interests of my story. Equally invaluable were the contributions of Carl Gover, Karen Hagemann, Mark Stein, and especially, Wolf Von Eckardt.

My wife, Carolyn, is always there to love, sustain, and inspire me. She is also my first-line editor and critic, as well as the springboard for all of my ideas.

And then there is Ray Hubbard, mentor, colleague, and friend, whose influences on my career and life have been equally profound. It is no exaggeration to say that neither this book nor that career would have happened without him. And that, among many other reasons, is why this book is dedicated to him.

—Mark Olshaker
Washington, D.C.

O, wonder!
How many goodly creatures are there here!
How beauteous mankind is! O brave new world,
That has such people in 't!

—Miranda,
in William Shakespeare,
The Tempest

The blood-dimmed tide is loosed, and everywhere
The ceremony of innocence is drowned;
The best lack all conviction, while the worst
Are full of passionate intensity.

—William Butler Yeats,
"The Second Coming"

BLOOD RACE

PROLOGUE

"This is the control," the white-coated director explained to the visitor. He plucked two squealing pink-eyed white rats from the racks of cages against the wall and placed them in two identical wire exercise wheels.

The visitor stood by, silently observing, boot heels pressed together and hands folded delicately in front of him. There was something strange and vaguely comical about this slight, practically diminutive figure in the shiny black uniform with its elaborate silver trim. It was as if some malevolent dollmaker had first tried to switch the head onto a more robust body and, having failed that, settled for dressing him up in some more awe-inspiring attire.

Still, the director had to admit, there was also something ominous and disquieting about the visitor that belied his mild and tedious features, something beyond the pasty complexion, the weak, watery eyes peering out from behind thick, rimless lenses, the fastidious little mustache, the thin, bloodless lips, and the receding chin, something unknown and unspeakable that filled him, a man of science, with a sense of almost primal dread.

The white rats scampered about the insides of their exercise wheels, spinning them faster and faster. Odometers attached by gears to each wheel clicked to higher and higher numbers.

"Now, at full speed, the one on the left, the blue-banded one, is running at fifty-three," the director stated dispassionately, "while the one on the right, the red-banded one, is doing only forty-four."

A young laboratory assistant with thick, dark hair stood by, holding a wooden clipboard.

"This is consistent with previous control tests on the same two specimens, which are both males of approximately equal size, musculature, and body weight," the director continued. He picked them

13

up by the soft fur on the backs of their necks and set them one by one in an empty glass tank on the table. The lab assistant placed a small metal dish of grain in the middle of the tank. Noses wriggling and whiskers twitching, the rats waddled tentatively toward the dish.

Gradually at first, then more assertively, the blue-banded rat began edging its red-banded neighbor away from the food. Each time the red-banded one tried to squirm its way back in, the more aggressive rodent pushed it away, then went back to greedily gobbling up the pile of grain.

The more timid rat uttered a squeal of protest. The blue rat looked up from its feast long enough to bare its fangs menacingly. The terrified protester turned on its haunches and scampered into the corner of the tank, where it curled into a quivering ball of white fluff.

"This corroborates the control demonstration," the director said. "Just what one could predict. Clearly Blue is the stronger and more aggressive of the two."

The young assistant dutifully registered the results. The visitor nodded ever so slightly but said nothing. His delicate hands remained clasped in front of his groin.

With a nod from the director, the eager assistant reached into the tank. The trembling rat was so traumatized it urinated in fright.

The director walked over to a refrigerator cabinet and extracted a small glass vial from one of the shelves. Then he picked up a syringe and proceeded to fill it from the vial. He pressed the plunger lightly with his thumb, shooting a tiny jet of colorless fluid into the air.

He walked back to the table where the assistant was holding the red-banded rat tautly. The young man had pulled the hind leg out to its full extension. The director sunk the needle into the exposed flank. The furry creature screeched in terror.

"We must allow a certain interval of time predicated on the individual's body weight," the director explained. "For a subject this small, it will not be long."

When several silent minutes had passed, the director dropped the red-banded rat back into the tank. The blue-banded one saw it and snarled, placing itself between the intruder and the metal grain dish.

The red rat landed with its feet squarely on the floor of the tank. Sniffing several times, it eyed its opponent with a clear gaze, no longer betraying any fear. It trundled over to inspect the empty dish. The blue defender firmly interposed its own body. It bared its tiny teeth defiantly and uttered a hiss of warning. Blue nudged the interloper out of the way, looking surprised when the learned behavior of fear did not materialize. Once, twice, three times the blue defender pushed its companion away, each time without result.

Suddenly the red-banded rat reared on its hind legs. There was a wild, inspired look in its eyes. It came down with front claws, grabbed hold of the blue-banded adversary, and sank its teeth into the other animal's shoulder.

The blue rat's eyes opened wide with surprise. It lurched backward in a desperate effort to free itself. But the newly emboldened red rat refused to let go. It dragged the blue one halfway across the tank, leaving a thin trail of blood from the deepening shoulder wound.

Finally it let go of its former tormentor, but only long enough to push the stunned animal over onto its side. The wounded blue rat squealed with pain and drew back, frightened and confused by the turn of events.

The inspired red rat charged again, this time going for its opponent's abdomen. Its jaws gaped wide to clench as much of the flesh as it could, clawing into the fur while its fangs held firm. The blue rat mewled in hideous agony, its legs flailing helplessly in the air.

The red rat ripped into the soft flesh of the blue rat's belly. Blood spattered across the glass walls of the tank. The red-banded rat burrowed its snout in among the intestines, then began working its way up the abdominal cavity.

Within moments it had found the pinkish white stomach, tore it open, and greedily devoured the undigested grain inside.

The visitor smiled with satisfaction.

ONE

Saturday, July 18, Oxford

Noon broke over the city of dreaming spires to find David Keegan gazing out across the rooftops, waiting for the ancient stones to speak to him and impart their wisdom. He stood by himself in the small vaulted cupola atop Christopher Wren's magnificent Sheldonian Theater, listening as the great bell of Tom Tower struck the midday twelve. His eyes traveled down to the gracefully arching Bridge of Sighs, linking the two quads of Hertford College and copied from the one in Venice. He was, this golden midsummer day, feeling every bit as forlorn as if he had been gazing at the original of this span, so named because it was the passage through which condemned prisoners were brought to their place of execution. He took little comfort from the fact that this was not medieval Italy but rather the fair and pleasant England of 1936.

He had been quite some time up in the cupola, and as he stared across the square, to the graceful tower of St. Mary's Church and the ornate dome of Radcliffe Camera, David felt similarly condemned, an emotion heartily encouraged by the several black-clad figures that came to collect him.

They all had turned out: Freddie Bascombe, their self-appointed leader; Tully Harkness and Hugh Marbury; Eric Wentworth and Harold Goldstein from the lab; Jack Seiderling and Tom Kent from Corpus Christi, whom he'd met first term and rowed with the following June during Eights Week. Some thought had been given to inviting to this august gathering a few of the more right-thinking dons, particularly David's tutor. But it was decided that they might have a somewhat chilling effect on the revels as well as on the participants' self-image of careless boys at play.

"Seven times 'round the battlements of Troy did Achilles drag Hector's body," Freddie Bascombe announced. "One time through the streets of Oxford will we drag David Keegan ere he parts."

"We Pilgrim Souls will chair you through the marketplace past all the sites that have become dear to your heart," Tully Harkness added.

"It feels more like the oxcart ride to the Place du Guillotine," David replied somberly.

They formed a solemn procession that wound its way down the rickety curving staircase and out by the side of the Bodleian Library. They trod past Blackwell's, where he'd spent tranquil hours browsing the musty shelves, in an incredible contrast with his life of the previous four years.

Each landmark they passed triggered a flood of memories: Sunday mornings, when every bell from every steeple in town rang out for what seemed forever, drowning one another out, competing like children for attention in a cacophony so uplifting that he always associated it with sunshine, even in the dead of English winter.

They turned at Balliol, where the debaters and intellectuals hung out. They rounded Martyr's Memorial toward the old Ashmolean, where the archaeological treasures took second place in David's mind to the beautiful Australian girl he'd first met there in the spring. They passed the Gothic splendor of Trinity, in whose gardens he had lolled away his Sunday afternoons.

Then he thought of the afternoon several days ago when he'd seen his few possessions packed up and carted away for the trip back across the ocean and the finality of his parting had settled in on him like a blanket of dry, rotting leaves.

The tour came to an end precisely as Tom Tower struck one. The Pilgrim Souls repaired to a public house of some local repute known as the Anchor and Crown, where a long wooden table had been set out in the back. The room was already overflowing when they arrived, and they had to elbow their way through the tide of boisterous humanity to reach their destination.

When pints had been served all around and he had called for silence with upraised hands, Freddie Bascombe stood at the head of the table. He spoke in the rich, carefully modulated accents of the British home counties. "Dearly beloved, we are gathered here together in the sight of God to mourn the passing of our colleague, one David Keegan of blessed memory, who is scheduled to depart this life before the cock crows thrice upon the morrow. We pray all benevolent and beneficent spirits to look kindly upon him as he ventures out."

Choruses of "Here, here!" erupted all about. The darts players in the back, used to such high-spirited undergraduate revels, paid them no heed.

Bascombe called again for silence. "For those of you whose brains are too pickled from grape or addled from indolence to recall the particulars of our departing colleague's history, let me refresh your memories. David came to us in the bloom of his young manhood just two years ago. Though only a callow youth in our old-worldly eyes, he had already achieved some recognition and renown in his home precincts. Long of limb, firm of sinew, fair of face, and determined of bearing, young David was—to use the hackneyed phrase of his countrymen—the all-American boy.

"Though we do not think of this gentle soul as possessing a warrior's temperament, David, as you know, completed his undergraduate course as a cadet at the colonists' imitation of Sandhurst, formally known as the United States Military Academy, where he distinguished himself in the biochemistry laboratory as well as on the playing field. So outstanding was his performance deemed, in fact, that the now Second Lieutenant Keegan"—he pronounced it *lef*tenant in the English style—"had his military obligation postponed and was invited to complete his scholarship here with us, under a stipend named—rather ironically under the circumstances—for Cecil Rhodes, rapist and pillager for empire." Freddie's eyes brightened. "May I have the proclamation?"

From the other end of the table Jack Seiderling produced a tightly wound scroll, which passed from hand to hand until it reached Bascombe. Freddie made a show of opening it with overacted flourishes. It had been carefully hand-lettered with elaborate illumination around the borders and gaudy seals at the bottom.

"My friends . . ." Bascombe cleared his throat noisily in another call for attention. "Whereas David John Keegan, member of Christ Church College, has shown himself to be of stout heart and good character; and

"Whereas said David Keegan has comported himself with academic distinction and gentlemanly grace during his tenure as Rhodes Scholar at Oxford University; and

"Whereas said David Keegan has endeared himself to all he has met these past two years; and

"Whereas said David Keegan is now departing this favored community, as well as this scepter'd isle; and . . .

"Whereas, before returning to America to take up his commission in the United States armed forces in the defense of the realm—"

"Thank God we're all at peace!" Eric Wentworth broke in.

Bascombe gave him a withering stare and went back to the scroll. "—said David Keegan is journeying to Berlin to compete in the Games of the Eleventh Modern Olympiad as a contestant in the decathlon; then

"Be it resolved, therefore, that we, his friends and elect members of the community of Oxford University, do hereby wish him well, godspeed, and that he do honor to himself, his country, and his own house.

"Given, this eighteenth day of July in the year of our Lord, nineteen hundred and thirty-six in the city and shire of Oxford, England, by—" He spread his arms wide to take in the entire assemblage.

"You'll show the Little Corporal and his master race whom they're up against," said Harold Goldstein.

David sensed the tears welling up in his eyes, the one thing he had not wanted to happen. "I—I don't know what to say."

"You don't have to say anything," Freddie said, clapping a heavy hand down on his shoulder.

"Just make us proud," Harkness said.

"I'll do my best not to disappoint you," David replied, trying to mask his emotion.

"Laddie, I'm assured of that," said Freddie. "You came to us a Yank, but you leave us an Oxford man. And if there be any in this assembly who can think of a higher accolade than that, let him remove himself from our company before another draft be downed.

"Gentlemen, I ask you to charge your glasses. And if I may be serious for one moment more, David, we leave you with the hope— in the words of the poet—that 'God bring you to a fairer place than even Oxford town.'"

Monday, July 20, Dahlem

Whatever the weekend had been for David Keegan, it had not been a good one for Miranda Wolff.

In that it was like many weekends these last several months. She'd begun arguing with her parents as soon as Karl brought her home from the ballet Friday evening. The tension had built steadily over the next two days, and the argument had gradually expanded from the subject of Karl Linderhoff to include the way she conducted everything else in her life.

By Sunday night she'd had about as much as she could take. That was when she threatened to move out and live on her own; it was what she wanted to do anyway. This in turn prompted her father to threaten to take a strap to her backside if she continued on this way, which instantly put an end to the entire discussion and sent Miranda storming to her room to throw herself tearfully across her bed and pound out her frustration on her pillow.

Now, on Monday morning, she sat at her desk, staring blankly out the window onto one of Berlin's loveliest parks, unable to stop thinking about it all. What hope was there for rational interchange when every argument—no, every simple difference of opinion—could end with the threat of punishment or retribution?

Not that he was a brute. Far from it. The fact of the matter was that Dr. Otto Wolff, trained at Heidelberg, student of Wittgenstein, distinguished professor of logic at the University of Berlin, was the most *proper* man she had ever come across. He had the most organized mind and the most carefully ordered worldview imaginable. But because of that, she supposed, he had extremely fixed (Karl would say "rigid") ideas on the way things ought to be. And if that worldview was ever violated by anyone in his control, there were consequences to be paid.

"I am twenty years old, Papa," she had protested. "I have a job, and I'm earning my own money. I have a right to think and do as I please."

"You have a responsibility to think and do as you've been brought up to, Fräuleinchen," he had sharply replied, "within a social order that has been established for the benefit of all." Even when speaking one to one, he could not resist the urge to lecture. "This, my dear, involves discipline. And if the individual proves incapable of providing discipline for his or herself, then it must be imposed from outside. For the social order to work to everyone's benefit, everyone—man, woman, and child—must uphold his or her responsibility."

The social order. How could he think like that? They must have had some individuality at one time—he and her mother—even to name her Miranda. Where had it all gone?

He stared at her for a moment, regarding her coldly, as if evaluating some piece of property he might buy. "You are fortunate to be both beautiful and intelligent. You always have been, ever since you were a little girl. The one trait leads you to be popular while the other leads you to be always questioning. And both you have always been. Just as you have always been rebellious and independent-minded. And with that combination, especially in a woman, there are always added risks of . . . compromise."

Everyone at the institute considered her a gifted, mature colleague. She knew she was doing interesting, important work. All of her and Karl's friends thought she was modern and attractive and fun to be around. But to her parents she would always be the strong-willed, rebellious little girl, always in need of correction and . . . "straightening out."

She stood up abruptly at the memory of the recent discussion, walked across her tiny office, and gazed longingly through the window at the world outside. All right, maybe she wasn't the proper young lady her parents wanted her to be. Maybe she was more interested in the way things actually were inside than in the pretense of how they looked. So what if she didn't like to attend teas with her mother's friends and didn't wear the right clothes? So what if she kept her blond hair long and loose and natural, unlike the sculpted, cared-for styles favored by most of the proper women of Berlin? She supposed there was something to be said for women like her mother, who could always get the seams straight on the backs of their stockings. That was one thing Miranda couldn't do or at least had never cared enough to try.

And then how could they complain about Karl? Who could be a better "prize" in their eyes? He was handsome, intelligent, always courteous to them. An Olympic athlete in the most challenging of all events, an officer in the Wehrmacht. And he was important enough to be requested by the Kaiser Wilhelm Institute (even if she had had some indirect hand in that).

"I know his type," her father had said. "I can see it in his eyes. He is what we used to call a rake or a cad. And I know of his reputation."

Dear Papa always knew what was best. Well, Miranda knew of

Karl's reputation, too. But that was all in the past. Karl was different with her. She knew he loved her and was devoted to her.

So what did her parents expect of her or of the two of them together? Were they so afraid she would lose her precious virginity and ruin her life? As if that were so important in this day and age. Is that what it all came down to? No matter whom she went with, they would never approve. No matter what she did she would never be right, unless she actually *became* like them. And that was out of the question.

Of course, she couldn't deny that Karl had been acting somehow—what was the word?—*strangely* to her lately. Distant, sometimes, as if he'd lost interest. That incredible fun-loving sense of humor and zest for life almost had disappeared. Sometimes she would wake up in the middle of the night thinking about it. Maybe it was just the pressure of preparing for the Olympics. She hoped so. Because if he really was losing interest or, worse yet, had become interested in someone else, she didn't know what she'd do. She'd die.

Oh, why was she always plagued with these doubts and negative thoughts?

Well, enough of this feeling sorry for yourself, she decided. *Time to get back to Dr. Hahn's work. That's what they're paying you for.* She sat back down at her worktable and spread out the sheets of equations in front of her.

Was it any coincidence, she wondered, that the two dominating men in her life were named Otto? Had she been drawn to the influence of one to escape the authority of the other?

Perhaps it was that. But the fact was, here at the Kaiser Wilhelm she had found her refuge. It was from here that she escaped the mundane outside world, with all its trivial problems and petty people. And here she entered the magic world of science, of physics. It was the land of dreams she had discovered long ago and was always led back to, like the little child searching for the fairytale castle in the clouds she'd once seen in the storybook. Well, here she could reach up into the clouds.

Forget everything else, she told herself. *Sink into your thoughts. Become them.*

The old feeling was returning, permeating every fiber of her body, penetrating every tiny square of her being. She could feel the eerie calm settling over her like a nimbus of starshine. This was a world of beauty and purity and mystical delights, where nothing that existed was evil or wrong. A world where questioning was the way of life and logic ruled. A world of forces and counterforces, embracing the balance and symmetry of nature and the fullness of time. This was a world of the eternal, of the pristine riddles and tantalizing enigmas of the universe.

She had arranged the equations into columns. So now . . . *Bohr says that the nucleus of an atom behaves like a drop of liquid. Fermi bombards uranium atoms with neutrons from a mixture of radon and beryllium, and what does he come up with? Radioactive products the chemical behavior of which leads him to suspect they're elements beyond uranium. "Transuranium" he calls them. And one product that's an isotope of uranium itself! The people at the Curie lab in Paris have done the same thing and come up with something that behaves like lanthanum. And lanthanum's atoms are just over half the size of uranium's, aren't they? That would mean a loss of thirty-five positive charges in the transaction. That doesn't add up. All matter and energy in the universe are conserved. Otto agrees it isn't possible and wants to repeat the Curie experiment here in Berlin.*

But possible or not, the Curie people had *come up with something; they* had *observed* something*. And nature always makes sense within itself if you can only figure it out. It all had to come together somehow. That is the rule of the cosmos. Fermi thinks that bombarding the atom with radiation elevates it into a higher, larger atom. But does that make sense?*

Symmetry. Balance. Logic. Nothing comes new into existence, and nothing is ever destroyed, only transformed from one thing to another. So what if the substance that behaves like lanthanum actually is lanthanum? *If the atom resulting after bombardment lost thirty-five charges and Bohr is right about the liquid drop nucleus, then why isn't it possible that the uranium atom has* split apart *to form two lower elements rather than been elevated to a new, higher element? That would be symmetrical. That would be balanced. That would be logical!*

And that would mean she was on to something that had eluded all the others. Even Otto!

Concentrate, Miranda. Stay with it. If you had an element that emitted two neutrons when it had taken up only one, then, in theory, such an element could sustain a nuclear chain reaction. She'd been thinking about this part for quite some time already. Now she had a place to fit it in.

She could sense it. She could feel it. The Great Rapture that Otto was always talking about, always dreaming about. She could feel her breathing grow shallow and quick. The inside of her mouth went dry, and at the same time, she felt the tingling, comforting moistness between her legs. The exhilaration of discovery increased and increased again.

She met Karl in the cafeteria at lunchtime. Abraham Behrman, the kindly white-haired chief of the biochemistry department, was with him. Karl was too reserved to do anything but take her hand in public. But as he often did, Behrman came over to her, smoothed back her blond bangs with his palm, and kissed her lightly on the forehead.

"My dear girl, you're radiating with some mysterious inner glow," Behrman observed. He looked from Miranda to Karl with an indulgent smile. "Have you two perhaps been meeting together in the lab this morning?"

Karl stammered something in denial to his boss and turned his head away slightly in embarrassment.

Miranda said nothing but only returned Dr. Behrman's smile with a radiant one of her own and felt the tingling again.

TWO

Tuesday, July 21, London

From Downing Street Number 10 looks like any other trim little Georgian row house, its dark brick facade protected by a simple black wrought-iron railing, its narrow, formal black door flanked by two equally narrow windows. But in the rear, where it looks out over the dignified expanse of Horse Guards Parade, the building transforms into a large Palladian mansion that was once a part of Whitehall Palace. Back there is a high-walled garden, with rolling lawn and lush flower beds, a privileged anomaly in this section of town, known rather more widely as the concrete and brick center of the government bureaucracy.

It was here that Stanley Baldwin, prime minister of England, was taking advantage of the unusually warm July weather and cloudless summer skies to entertain his official guests.

The party was well under way when Colonel Stewart Graham Menzies arrived, his presence the result not of an invitation so much as of a last-minute summons. It was only a brief walk from MI 6 headquarters at 54 Broadway, and Menzies wondered whether it was he specifically who'd been wanted or merely the person of the weekend duty officer, who, at the moment, he also happened to be.

Menzies surveyed the entire scene. Lords and ladies strolled along the flower beds. Liveried footmen and waiters with silver trays circulated unobtrusively among the crowd.

Menzies hadn't gone far when he stumbled into what must have been the foreign policy grouping. He stopped at the table set out with champagne glasses and canapés and made his way through assorted ministers and undersecretaries. In the shadow of an overhanging elm tree he recognized Sir Robert Vansittart and Warren Price from the Foreign Office. They were standing with Edward J. Acton from the Defense Ministry. In a business in which knowledge is power, they all were obviously trying to discern who'd been lately favored with more information about what. The three were busily engaged in a discussion of everyone's favorite topic these days: Adolf Hitler.

"The question as I see it," Vansittart was saying, "is when do we begin taking the chancellor at his word?"

"Depends on what you mean by that, old boy," said Price, who didn't seem to be sharing his companions' concerns.

"He's been acting rather self-confident of late," Vansittart stated. "And I just wonder, are there things going on in this new society of his that represent qualitative as well as quantitative leaps? Are there things that *der Führer* and *il Duce* can do under their forms of government that push them ahead of our 'tired democracies' in some strategic way?"

"What are you getting at?" Price frowned.

"What I'm getting at is this: Does Hitler have tools at his disposal that we don't know about, that make him willing to take these mad chances? Churchill, for one, believes he does."

"Churchill, for one, believes everything," Price came back. "If you listen to him, the Huns are already ahead of their World War armament level."

"If you listen to our own intelligence reports, they've already fielded and outfitted twenty-one infantry divisions and God knows how much armor so far." Vansittart noticed Menzies and turned to him conveniently. "Isn't that right, Stewart? It must be on SIS's mind as much as anyone's." Then, without waiting for a reply: "Winston says—"

"Winston's a hack and a has-been," Price insisted. "Twenty years later he's still trying to live down the Dardanelles, looking for another side action to resurrect a totally moribund and thoroughly repudiated career."

"But just look at the facts." Vansittart pressed on. He counted off on well-manicured fingers. "Hitler's rescinded the Weimar Constitution, he's effectively shut down the Reichstag, he's unilaterally abrogated the disarmament clause of the Treaty of Versailles and sent his soldiers into the Rhineland, and still we refuse to take him seriously."

"The fact that we failed to oppose him with force in a region which could readily be interpreted as part of his own territory hardly implies—"

"It hardly implies a damn thing except that Herr Hitler's taken our measure and knows what he's dealing with. You think it's any accident that he chose to invade the Rhineland on a Saturday morning? He knew that the British civil service wouldn't even bloody well notice it until business hours Monday. He did the same thing when he scuttled the disarmament clause last March. I shudder to think of his next Saturday surprise."

Vansittart had given his empty champagne glass to a waiter so he could use both hands to emphasize his point. "Look, these tense, intense people are going to make us look like a third-rate nation if we elect to continue haphazard, and they will want to do something with all this stored energy. These people are the most formidable proposition that has ever been formulated. Mark my words, they are in strict training now, not for the Olympic Games but for breaking some other and emphatically unsporting world records and perhaps the world as well."

Price took on the air of amused indulgence one might direct toward an overly insistent child. "I don't think you're being quite fair, Robert. There is no concrete evidence that Germany wants anything other than dignity and economic stability for itself and to get back into the community of nations."

"Then you ought to read the cables our own ambassador, Eric Phipps, has been sending back from Berlin."

"Who, if I am not mistaken, is your brother-in-law."

"Be that as it may, it doesn't change the situation—"

"Be that as it may, Robert, you have to understand the dynamics of the situation. I think all of us here realize that Versailles was not only bloody humiliating to the Germans but economically devastating as well. You can't blame them for wanting to put that humiliation and ruin behind them. That's exactly what Hitler's been working toward since he became chancellor. And look at what he's accomplished in just three short years. It's miraculous the way he's put that country back on its feet. No inflation, no unemployment—"

"No dissent, no civil rights . . . What about the Nuremberg Laws they passed last year? God help you if you're a Jew in that country today. They're throwing them out of schools, taking away their businesses—"

"For one thing, that's an internal affair, and it's none of our business. Plus you have to temper everything by the fact that the man's a rhetorical genius," Price responded. "That's his stock-in-trade. Once Hitler's secure in his power, all the ritualistic scapegoating nonsense will disappear, and he'll be able to concentrate on the real business of running the country. You have to separate out all the rhetoric and the anti-Semitic hocus-pocus from his real accomplishments. Look, you can say what you like about national socialism, Robert. But it's the new Germany, and it's bloody well working. All they're telling us is: 'How are the rest of you blokes doing here in the Depression? Well . . . we've got total employment and national pride, and no one is hungry anymore. We're tired of guilt and apologies. We want respect from the world, and we're going to get it!'"

"However they have to," Vansittart said. "What's the phrase I keep hearing? *'Heute haben wir Deutschland, Morgen die ganze Welt!'* 'Today we have Germany, tomorrow the whole world!' That's what worries me. And you can bet it's starting to worry the French, too."

"You can bet it is," said Edward Acton with a wry smile. "All you have to do is trace out the Maginot Line on a map to see what their game is. Look where it leaves off. If the Jerries have their eyes on the west, then force them up north. It's the Frogs' insurance policy. If the Germans invade, they have to come in through poor little Belgium, and that's sure to bring us into it. Or so they hope. Typically French," he added with a sniff.

"Ah, there you are, Stewart!" a deep and forceful voice called out. Menzies turned around to see the venerable Hugh Sinclair approaching, stately and magisterial of bearing. He wore the full-dress tunic of an admiral of the fleet. Menzies didn't think he'd ever heard him called by his proper name in all the years he'd known him. He had always been Quex to his close friends and Chief to everyone else, including Menzies since, as head of the Secret Intelligence Service, Sinclair was his boss.

He made a show of stealing Stewart away from the Foreign Office crowd.

"Something's come up," Sinclair imparted quietly when they were out of earshot. "And as I always say, royalty and prime ministers must never be taken by surprise." Well, he couldn't speak for Mr. Baldwin, but Menzies suspected King Edward had other things on his mind these days. Though it was still unbeknownst to the general public, it was well known in government and intelligence circles that the king had taken up with a two-time American divorcée and was apparently so committed to the proposition of making her his queen that he was willing to throw off the whole royal enterprise if Baldwin and the Commons wouldn't let him have his way. It was one of those torrid little affairs of the heart raised to the level of state crisis because of the personalities involved.

"We're meeting with the PM in the Cabinet Room," Sinclair explained as he led the way into the house.

They walked down the carpeted hallway and climbed the main staircase to the second level.

Perhaps it was no more than his awe and respect for the institution of parliamentary government, but Menzies never ceased to be affected by the Cabinet Room, if not always by the individuals who populated it. It was by his memory the largest room in the house, with brass chandeliers, fluted Corinthian columns, and white-paneled walls. The baize-covered table that ran the length of the room was itself symbolic of participatory government, being boat-shaped so that everyone around it could be easily seen and heard by everyone else.

"I shouldn't be away from my guests for too long," Baldwin said with some impatience. His private secretary nodded to emphasize the point.

"Yes, of course," Sinclair said. As if on cue, the white double doors swung open, and a footman directed Sir Arthur Hargreaves into the room. He was tall and distinguished-looking, with silver gray hair that glistened in the light. Menzies had never had any idea how old he was; could have been anything from forty to sixty. Though he'd come into MI 6 not long ago, Menzies didn't know him very well or exactly what he did. He was one of those denizens who haunted the new Scientific Intelligence Unit.

"Prime Minister, this is Sir Arthur Hargreaves of our SIU," Sinclair said. "We managed to obtain him on loan from the Cavendish Lab."

To Menzies, there was still something creepy about giving the scientists their own unit to run, the old joke about the inmates taking over the asylum.

"Well, Sir Arthur." The prime minister opened the meeting. "I'm a political man, not a scientist. All this talk about a secret weapon up Mr. Hitler's sleeve. Is is just blather, or is there anything to it? I gather that's the reason for this colloquium."

"In a way, yes," Sinclair replied. "Something's come to our attention that we felt you should know about."

Baldwin folded his hands together on the table. "Well?"

"Sir," Hargreaves simply began, "do you know anything about the science of atomistics?"

"I've known Rutherford vaguely since I was at Cambridge," Baldwin replied. "Isn't that what he does?"

"Yes, right. It has to do with discoveries he made about the potential for transforming atoms of one element into another through bombarding them with neutrons, one of his breakthroughs. And a number of the people Rutherford trained now lead the field, Enrico Fermi in Italy and Werner Heisenberg in Germany, among them, as well as Niels Bohr in Denmark. The modern science of the field goes back to Albert Einstein's theory of relativity. Are you at all familiar with—"

Baldwin waved him on.

"One of the theoretical principles of atomistics holds that vast amounts of energy should be able to be released from relatively insignificant quantities of matter. Physicists have been experimenting with radioactive uranium for this purpose for several years now with encouraging results. And perhaps the key center of this work is in Germany, in Berlin at a very prominent research facility known as the Kaiser Wilhelm Institute. There are a number of different departments: biology; chemistry; neurophysiology. The physics department—which Einstein founded, by the way—is under the direction of Professor Otto Hahn, who also studied with Rutherford, at McGill in Montreal before he took over the Cavendish. Hahn's team in Berlin gives all evidence of being the leaders in unlocking atomistic energy at this point." He paused briefly, as if for emphasis. "I'm sure you can appreciate the strategic implications."

The prime minister nodded.

"Now, one has to keep in mind that scientific intelligence is a new field. None of us is even quite sure what it is yet, or should be. But this definitely worries us. And we've recently identified a young woman at the Kaiser Wilhelm—a very young woman, actually—who works with Hahn. Her name is Miranda Wolff."

"And her significance is . . ." Baldwin led him.

"Hahn's brilliant, maybe the best of all. He seems able to integrate the breakthroughs made by all the others. It looks as if his work is going to point the way to the next step. And the next step could very well be the big one. But like Einstein, he's an academic. He needs to have someone around him with another type of brilliance, the kind that can make the leap from equations on paper to practical application, the kind of person who can conjure up, within the realm of his or her own imagination, a new kind of reality and then figure out how to make that reality happen. Those people are extremely rare. They come along maybe once or twice in an entire generation."

Menzies looked at Hargreaves. "Your opinion of this woman . . . I'd like to know its source, if I may. Does she give speeches? Has she published?"

"Not as yet. Though when she does, I would expect the impact to be every bit as great as Einstein's first article in the *Annalen der Physik*. Our information comes to us by way of Dr. Leo Szilard, a Hungarian Jewish émigré, an expert in thermodynamics who was himself a gifted student of Einstein's. He's now here in London, where he considers himself a sort of spokesman for the entire European scientific community. A few years ago, though, he taught for a time at the University of Berlin, where Fräulein Wolff's father is also on the faculty. With that connection, it was not difficult for her to gain early admission after excelling in her *Gymnasium* studies. She quickly became Szilard's prize pupil. He introduced her to Hahn, who immediately recognized her brilliance. She got through her degree in record time and then went over to Hahn full-time. Within two months he told Szilard—and this is a quote—" Hagreaves read from his notes. "'She's the one with the flash of intuition that's going to provide the crossover. I'm sure of it.'" The scientist looked up from the paper. "We have confirmation of this opinion from a very gifted visiting student called Herman Hedberg who worked with her before returning to England. I assure you, sir, she holds promise of being the genuine article."

"How can someone so young and inexperienced figure so prominently in this proposition?" Baldwin asked bluntly.

Hargreaves shrugged. "An interesting question. First of all, one has to appreciate the fact that even though the team is extremely important in scientific inquiry, nearly all the critical breakthroughs—those moments that sweep everything that's come before them out of the way and change the course of history—come not from the team but from the individual. Second, we're not dealing with a field in which age or experience necessarily comes into play. In physics new discoveries involve the abstract permutation of numbers and equations rather than judgment based on accumulated empirical experience over the course of a long career. It's more a question of some kind of innate but transcendent ability; divine inspiration, if you will. Einstein was no more than twenty-one or twenty-two, working as a Swiss patent examiner when he came up with the notion of special relativity. By the time Newton was twenty-three, he'd discovered the principles of gravity and invented differential calculus. It's a special breed."

Hargreaves paused again, this time for a longer interval. "Not much is known about Miranda Wolff other than what I've already told you. But we've got to find out more. And if our suspicions are correct, then we've got to get to her."

THREE

Shivering in the cold morning drizzle, David Keegan huddled with the other tourists at the base of Stintfang Hill, in front of the great baroque facade of St. Michael's Church. He watched the stevedores on the docks below him tying up the SS *Manhattan*, nine days out of New York. He had left England yesterday afternoon on the Dover–Calais ferry and had taken the overnight train through Brussels to be here in time to meet the ship.

As it turned out, he'd given himself plenty of time—it wasn't only the Italian trains that ran on time these days—and so had several hours to wait as the *Manhattan* slowly made its way up the Elbe into port. He'd had yet another stretch alone with his own thoughts.

The rain and wind were an unpleasant welcome, even colder than the greeting of the immaculately dressed border guard who had come into his carriage at the Dutch-German frontier, demanded his passport, and icily inquired as to the purpose of his visit. David decided he was probably being too sensitive. The guy was only doing his job. When David answered him in fluent, perfectly accented German, he suddenly loosened up considerably and welcomed him as a returning brother. After all, this was the country of Goethe and Schiller, of Beethoven and Kant.

More important, it was the country of his grandparents. The Keegan side was all solid Irish and English stock. But his mother's mother and father had left a little town on the edge of the Black Forest to set their stake in the New World. Throughout the trying times of the Great War they never lost their pride. And with all their love for America and what they had been able to achieve there, they never lost their affinity for the old country and the old ways.

David had never been here before. Throughout his time in England he had purposely avoided it, setting the Olympics as his special goal. But he had always felt a powerful bond. German was the language of science. And he was proud that it was also the heritage of his family.

He felt as if he'd come home.

He pulled the collar of his trench coat closer around his neck. He had to admit this was pretty goddamned lousy weather. Back in Pennsylvania it would have been warm and beautiful. And when he left Oxford, it had still been in the midst of one of those glorious English summers.

Oxford. He couldn't believe how much the place still possessed him. When he'd reached Hamburg, the medieval spires rising above the glass-smooth waters of the Alster momentarily tricked his mind into thinking he'd never left.

What was it exactly that was plaguing him? The tangible end of youth? The end of the two-year lark? The daunting prospect of going back and finally taking on real responsibility, of taking up his commission and having other men depend on him? Whatever it was, he couldn't worry about it now. Just as he had at the Point, just as he had at Oxford, he had a job to do, a job that would require all his concentration and stamina.

David hadn't wanted to stand out from the rest of the crowd while the ship docked, looking for all the world like an American. So he waited until he saw the gangway come down. Then he quickly climbed down the hill and ducked into a men's room in a small *kneipe*, a seaman's pub. When he emerged, he was dressed just like the other 382 men and women—all in dark blue blazers over white flannels, each man with a red, white, and blue banded straw boater, each woman in a white linen cap pulled rakishly to one side—waving and throwing streamers from the deck of the "Largest Steamer Ever Built in America."

But despite his costume and no matter what he did, David could no longer fade completely into the crowd any more than the United States could any longer fade into the background of world politics. Only one power had emerged stronger and more exultant and triumphant from the ashes of the Great War. Only one power had emerged better off and more influential than it had gone in. And David John Keegan, late of Oxford University, honors graduate of the U.S. Military Academy, promising scientist, athlete, and commissioned officer of the United States, had been proclaimed among its finest representatives. Whatever he may have thought of himself, this handsome soldier-scholar, with the shy, boyish smile and the physique that was made for the revealing brevity of a track suit, fitted the bill perfectly for a nation desperate for reasons to rejoice.

The dock was thronged with people. The mayor of Hamburg and other officials stood waiting on a raised platform decked with bunting. Five-ringed Olympic pennants flew from every available flagpole. A municipal German brass band was playing as the American Olympic team marched proudly down the gangway. David blended into the ranks as soon as the flag and banner carriers stepped onto the dock. For official purposes, he'd been told to make it look as if he'd come over with the rest of the team. Avery Brundage was very big on form and appearance.

He scanned the faces of his teammates for one in particular but was distracted from his efforts by the voice of another.

"Keegan! David Keegan!" He heard the familiar call from somewhere near the middle of the throng. He looked around and saw Tom Quinn's welcome face inching nearer amid the sea of hundreds of other faces. It renewed—for the moment, at least—that comforting feeling of being home.

"I can't believe it's really you," said David.

"It's me all right. You didn't think you could get rid of me that easily, did you?"

"So how's active duty treating you? What have I got to look forward to?"

"Fort Bragg ain't exactly Oxford University."

"That's what I was afraid of."

They had met six years before, their first day as plebes at West Point. They had been assigned as roommates during that first horrendous summer in "Beast Barracks." And they'd stayed roommates and best of friends throughout the grueling four-year ordeal that turned them—in the popular expression of the day—into "officers and gentlemen." In the four years they spent at the Point, David seemed to excel in everything: science; athletics; leadership. His grace and bearing appeared effortless. People said he was a natural. But if Tom didn't appear to be quite as gifted as David, not quite as much of a student, an athlete, a "leader of men," that fact never seemed to get in the way of their bond. Tom had a natural buoyancy, a resilience, a sense of humor that never allowed him to take himself or anyone around him too seriously. That quality had gotten them both over many a rough time in those four years. Only Tom knew of the private fears, the insecurities, the gnawing doubts that continually picked away at his friend. Tom good-naturedly accepted his position in David's shadow. And only David realized how much Tom had contributed to his success and sanity.

For his own part, in his assigned capacity as "leader," David had constantly pushed Tom, trying to get him to be everything he could. Perhaps it was no more than his wanting someone else to share the burden of the limelight and the high profile, to take some of the heat off him, but he dragged Tom into everything he did, pulling him along in his wake, and wouldn't let up until his roommate also made the Army track team and got on the honor roll.

It was a foregone conclusion that David would make the Olympics. His track and field skills had been as important as his biochemistry in winning him the Rhodes. But when he received the letter the month before saying that Tom had also made the team—as a member of the four-hundred-meter-relay team—he felt a sense of elation that he had never really generated for himself. Having to be the all-American boy all the time could grow very tiresome.

Avery Brundage, former track and field man, millionaire real estate and construction magnate, chairman of the American Olympic Committee, and self-proclaimed protector of all that was holy in amateur athletics, was up on the speakers' platform, slashing his arm through the air. "Sport transcends all political and racial situations!" he was saying, to the great delight of the cheering crowd, which probably couldn't understand a word he was saying, and to the mayor, who could.

"I can't listen to this again," said Tom. "Anywhere we can get a drink around here?"

"I know just the place," said David.

They went back to the *kneipe* David had discovered. It was crowded—a real mix of people, all locals—but they found a tight wooden booth toward the back. The girl who came to take their order was tall and buxom and had dirty blond hair. She was a little too imposing for David's taste, but from the admiring expression on his face, Tom apparently found her quite acceptable. When she smiled back at him, David knew his roommate was once again in love.

David ordered two dark beers in German. The waitress nodded and disappeared into the crowd.

"You could really lose yourself in those knockers," said Tom. "Miss the Olympics completely if you weren't careful."

"I see nothing's changed," said David. "So tell me. How was the crossing?"

"Eventful. You know Harold Smallwood, the sprinter from USC? Came down with appendicitis."

David shook his head. "Bad luck. Is he okay?"

"Apparently. He says he's going to compete. But Chuck Middleman, the hurdler from Pitt . . ."

David nodded.

"Broke his leg on a trampoline. But he's come over here to cheer us on, cast and all. I mean, that's the American way, right? Oh, I guess the big news from the trip is about your friend"—Tom paused—"your, ah, *former* friend Alison Prescott."

He had known the name would come up sooner or later. It had to. She had to be on that ship. How could she not have been, after winning a silver medal in freestyle swimming four years ago in L.A. and capturing the hearts of America in general and one young cadet in particular?

David's mind traveled back to the first time he had laid eyes on her, back at the beginning of those games. Ali was an absolutely gorgeous brunette whose stunning figure cried out for attention whether it was showcased in her competition gear or wrapped up in the bland and traditional cut of the Olympic uniform. It was no surprise to anyone, least of all David, that she'd been dabbling in the movies ever since her Olympic triumph.

What they'd shared back then had been brief, David remembered, limited strictly by the duration of the Los Angeles games. But it had been intense. There had been an instant mutual enchantment and a feverishness of passion that he had never known before or since nor had any realistic hope of knowing again. And on the last day, when the games were over and the flame was finally extinguished, it was all he could do to withstand her tearful entreaties to remain with her in California and give up his commission at the Point. What was so great about being a soldier boy? After all, it wasn't as though he didn't have alternatives. He was a young scientist of tremendous promise. Everybody said so. UCLA, Cal Tech, any of those places would be thrilled to have him.

He had known from the beginning of the anguished conversation that he would choose honor and duty over desire or even glory. He didn't know if she understood that. He wasn't sure he fully understood it himself. But he couldn't escape it. And when he stared across the small hotel room at her tear-streaked face and the words finally escaped his lips, he'd felt as if his world had suddenly gone empty.

That was the last time he'd seen her or spoken to her, though a day hadn't gone by in four years that she was not in his thoughts.

Tom must have seen the faraway look in his eyes and was determined not to let him wallow. "She's everything you remember. But the story goes on."

"What do you mean?"

"During the trip Brundage caught her and her friend Eleanor Holm one too many times carousing with the press boys in the first-class lounge."

"Eleanor Holm? The backstroke swimmer."

"Right. The really cute one. She's actually become Eleanor Holm *Jarrett* since the last Olympics. So Avery's had them both spanked and sent to bed without supper."

"What are you talking about?"

"He's thrown them off the team."

"You're joking!"

"Would that I were, matey."

"How can he do that? They're both shoo-ins for gold medals this time."

"Were." Tom corrected him.

"But how did it happen?"

"Well, Eleanor was caught drinking. The stories about Ali are even more tantalizing. You can imagine that she and Avery have hated each other from the word 'go.' She's so glamorous and charming and flirty, and he's got a terminal case of flagpole up the ass, not to mention the fact that he tried to have her amateur status yanked away two years ago when she went out to Hollywood. So he's had it in for her all along."

"What a jerk."

"And they say Hitler's a dictator!"

*   *   *

By the time they left the beer hall, the formalities on the platform had ended. Various coaches with clipboards were shouting in all directions and conducting team members to the buses that had magically appeared for the short ride to the *Bahnhof*. David and Tom had just opened their packets of instructions and color-coded tickets when they crossed paths with a tall, lanky, light-skinned black man who seemed, in the midst of the confusion and turmoil, to be surrounded by an aura of calm.

"Hey, how ya doing, Jesse?" David greeted him.

"Fine." He smiled. "Smooth as silk."

David watched him from behind as he walked over to his assigned bus. There was something beatific, something otherworldly about Jesse Owens, both on the field and off. He was modest and easygoing and seemingly devoid of ego. He let his magnificent legs and his unyielding heart do the talking for him.

The past of every great man, even one as young as James Cleveland Owens, is the stuff of legend. He was a natural in the true sense of the word. Everyone on the American team knew his story. He was born in Alabama, where he spent most of his childhood picking cotton. His mother moved him as a teenager to Ohio, where he could go to high school. One day the track coach saw this totally untrained sharecropper's son sprinting across the grass and asked him to run a trial hundred. When he crossed the finish line, the coach looked at his stopwatch, realized there must have been some mistake, and promptly took the instrument to the local jeweler for repair. The watchmaker completely disassembled it but could find nothing wrong. It had been working perfectly.

"I can't wait to see him run again," Tom Quinn said.

"Me, too," said David.

These were to be the greatest and most elaborate Olympic Games in modern history, an international spectacle no one could ever forget, the first time the German capital had ever played host. The games were supposed to have been held there in 1916, but they'd been canceled because of war. This time it would be different. There would be more than twice as many athletes as had competed in Los Angeles four years before. The color-coded packets they'd each been given detailed every aspect of their lives during the Olympic Games. With the legendary German efficiency their hosts were leaving nothing to chance. There was also a glossy, official *Olympic Magazine*, printed in English, on every seat.

As they settled onto the train in the Hamburg station, Tom asked, "Do you want to see if we can find Ali?"

"Not yet," David said. "Give me some time."

"Sure." Tom studied his packet as an overt way of changing the subject. "Well, it looks like we've got each other as roommates," he declared. "I guess the Germans really have thought of everything in their planning."

"What do you mean?" David asked.

"They must have known no one else could put up with you."

For a time the train tracks followed the course of the Elbe. The journey carried them through black-green forests of towering fir trees and past quaint fairytale villages with charming cobblestone streets and "Hansel and Gretel"-inspired thatch-roof wooden cottages. This was a timeless land, a land of folk stories and traditional ways and music that haunted the air.

But David began to notice something else. The farther away they got from the port city of Hamburg, the fewer of the white Olympic flags, the banners which had virtually lined their route of arrival, could be seen. Out in the countryside the five interlocked rings had given way to the swastika, the symbol of the National Socialist party. From staffs at every village square, from the balconies of every town hall, from towers at every train platform, hung the same ensign—a lean black spider on a field of blood.

Tom was watching the same sights out the window. He broke into David's reverie. "The Germans seem to think they're going to do real well this time."

"Why?" David replied. "They had the third largest team in L.A., and we still wiped the floor with them."

"I don't know. Maybe they're starting to believe this master race stuff. You heard about the boycott stuff, I guess."

"Yeah, something about it, I think."

"The AAU wanted the American team to stay away because of Germany's treatment of the Jews and the things the Nazis have been saying about Negroes being inferior."

"Not so loud," David warned.

"You're starting to sound like Brundage. 'Remember, ladies and gentlemen, we are guests in this country, and we must at all times comport ourselves as the finest representatives of America.'"

David grabbed him by the arm, whispering, "Come on, Tom, I'm serious. Watch what you say."

Tom gave him an upraised palm in mock defense. "Don't worry about me, buddy boy. I'm open-minded. Remember, I've got Sam Stoller and Marty Glickman on my relay team." He sat forward. "Hey, ever wonder if you have any Jewish blood in you?"

"No."

"If maybe that's why your mom's folks left?"

"No."

"It's possible."

"It's also ridiculous even thinking about it. What do people's religions have to do with how fast they can run or how far they can throw?"

"Don't ask me," Tom protested. "But how many Jews were in our class at the academy?"

"I have no idea. I've never thought about it."

"That's just my point. They try to hide it because they know it'll be held against them. It's almost as if they have to live underground in certain places."

This time it was David who wanted to change the subject. "So at any rate I guess the boycott didn't work, or else we wouldn't be here."

"Yeah, old Avery held them off all right. Just about single-handedly. The guy's got balls of iron. Said the stuff about the Germans discriminating against Jewish athletes was all poppycock. Made it sound like anyone who wanted to stay away was betraying the country; same thing Hitler's been saying about the Jews right along. Brundage even got the Nazis to call back some of their Jewish athletes who'd left for other countries to become ringers for the German team. Show the world everything was okay. Like that high jumper, Gretel Bergmann, who went to England, or Helene Mayer, the fencer from California."

"Yeah, we could have used her, too. But you have to admit Brundage's right in a way," David asserted. "Politics has no place in athletics. Once you let the two become intertwined, the Olympics become a mockery."

"A noble sentiment. But I wouldn't exactly call Brundage nonpartisan, though," Tom countered.

Tom picked up the *Olympic Magazine* and began leafing through it. "Ah, here's a little item from the man himself."

"Brundage?"

"No. Hitler. 'Our athletes will inspire the entire German *Volk*. They will lead us to our destiny.' That's got to get the old competitive juices flowing."

The train journeyed forward, precisely on schedule, past more quaint villages and more rural stations and more flags, carrying them deeper and deeper into the heart of the New Germany, on toward the lengthening shadows of the German night.

FOUR

Saturday, July 25, the Tiergarten

If anyone ever needed to get in touch with the head of the Abwehr the first thing in the morning, he didn't have far to look. Early each day, seven days a week, regardless of the weather, Admiral Wilhelm Franz Canaris spent an hour riding his horse through the lovely wooded trails of the park that occupied the central part of Berlin.

When he pulled up in his chauffeur-driven Mercedes at five minutes to seven this morning, Obergruppenführer Reinhard Heydrich of the SS was waiting for him at the stable doors.

"I took the liberty of arranging for a horse with the hope that you'd allow me to accompany you," Heydrich said as Canaris got out of his car.

The chief of military intelligence nodded his assent. "It would be my great pleasure," he replied, his voice straining with politeness.

They went inside the stable and walked down the straw-covered aisle, past the long row of stalls. The two men were very much a study in contrast—one, the venerated symbol of the old order; the other, the rising star of the new. Canaris, gentlemanly, white-haired, and approaching fifty, was a genuine naval hero from the Great War and the embodiment of the German professional military tradition. Heydrich was tall and well built, with starkly chiseled features and an imperious bearing. Cultured in music and the arts, he was also an excellent horseman and a viciously proficient fencer, in all, the physical and intellectual model of Aryan perfection. At thirty-two he was already the SS equivalent of lieutenant general and head of the Berlin Gestapo. And whereas Canaris had come by his status for dauntless courage commanding a U-boat through countless perils, Heydrich had come by his for murderous efficiency in stamping out the rival SA during the Night of the Long Knives just two years before.

He was well aware of his nickname, the Blond Beast, and did nothing to discourage its use.

But there was one additional factor that threatened the uneasy truce between the rival divisional chiefs. For a time at the beginning of his career Heydrich had served under Canaris in the Reichsmarine, demonstrating tactical flair and administrative brilliance, until he was unceremoniously cashiered out for compromising the virtue of a shipyard director's daughter. The burgeoning National Socialist party was not as concerned as the navy with the niceties of protocol and conduct unbecoming. He found a ready home there, and when the Nazis came to power two years later, Reinhard Heydrich's career was made.

Now he was an equal of his former commander. Soon, he was sure, he would be giving him orders.

Heydrich was tired this morning. He had been out most of the night observing and personally supervising the roundup of a group of Gypsies into "protective custody." Ordinarily he wouldn't have bothered with the fieldwork himself, much as he enjoyed it. But alarming reports had been coming in of late, hinting at the haphazard, hit-or-miss nature of current arrests of dissidents and undesirables. There was even talk that officers had been letting some mothers and children go free in exchange for certain considerations. Heydrich felt it was always best to deal with these matters before the situation got out of hand.

They left the stable. Canaris rode along at a stately canter, his head erect, his body rising and falling in perfect unison with the fluid motions of his horse. Despite his fatigue, Heydrich set out at a full gallop, but he quickly had to rein his animal back in when he realized that Canaris had no intention of competing with him.

The Abwehr chief rode in total silence with his eyes fixed straight in front of him. He seemed to be implying that he could wait out all these upstarts who had taken over the country, no matter how long it took. Heydrich was not a man to question his führer's judgment. But he seriously wondered if Hitler had made the right decision in appointing the old war-horse to so sensitive a position. Canaris wasn't a party man and never had been. Therefore, he could never be completely trusted.

Finally, as they approached the side of the lake, Heydrich sidled up close to Canaris and made his move. "Knowing how busy you are during the day, I thought I'd take this opportunity to discuss a matter of some importance."

Heydrich maintained an even pace with Canaris. "While the Olympic Games will undoubtedly be the triumph of the German *Volk* that our führer has inspired us to achieve, I'm afraid they will be something of a trial for those of us charged with the unenviable task of maintaining the security of the state during this period."

"I have no doubt that you are well equipped for such a duty," said Canaris.

"We try to be," Heydrich said with a practiced obsequiousness whose true meaning was never lost on the listener. "But with the influx of visitors from all quarters, it will be difficult to perform our tasks with the completeness we would like."

"I wouldn't worry," said Canaris with a slight smile. "Your reputation for completeness is known throughout the Reich."

They turned and crossed a small stream that fed into the lake, putting Canaris slightly in the lead. He leaned back to regard Heydrich out of the corner of his eye, as if never wanting to let the SS officer completely out of his sight.

"You honor me with your kind words."

Canaris suddenly pulled his horse up short. The animal stopped abruptly, scattering pebbles along the bridle path. For the first time the admiral stared directly at his riding companion. "As you say, my dear Heydrich, let us not waste any more of each other's time. Tell me what it is you require of me."

"Very well," Heydrich said, circling his horse to face Canaris. "I want access to dossiers your department maintains on every known or suspected subversive in the government or military. I want copies of reports your agents have filed on foreign operatives who might have reason to use the Olympics as an opportunity to infiltrate the country. I want sufficient numbers of your men detailed to my office for assignment to watch specific visitors whom we will have designated as potential threats during the time of the games. And I want a directive to go out from you today instructing that all orders regarding security and intelligence during the games are to come from me and me alone."

"Does it not occur to you that we are the hosts of an assembly of *friendly* nations gathered in the spirit of peaceful competition? And that we are pledged to demonstrate our culture and civilization rather than our paranoia?"

"If you wish to believe so, that is your privilege. But make no mistake, my friend, the Reich's enemies are everywhere, waiting impatiently for a moment of weakness or inattention. We have but to give them the one opening they need, and then everything that we have worked for, that is our destiny will be destroyed." He turned his head to pierce Canaris with his gaze. "I am director of Reich Security. I will do whatever I have to to make certain that does not happen, and anyone who stands in my way will face the consequences."

Just then a large gray rabbit darted out from the wood in front of Heydrich's horse. It must have been scared out by the pounding of the hoofbeats. Like a hunter instinctively locking in on his target, Heydrich instantly reached down to his side, plucked his Walther 7.65 from the black leather holster on his belt, and drew aim.

"Are you insane?" Canaris shouted. "You can't be shooting off a pistol in the middle of a public park!"

Heydrich suffered a split second of hesitation at this remonstrance. He glanced over at Canaris, then replaced the gun in its holster. He locked his sight back on the rabbit. It had darted out of the way and was just about clear of the path. Once it got back into the trees, it would be lost.

Quickly he jerked the horse's reins sharply to the left and dug his heels into the animal's flanks. Within a second the horse had overtaken the rabbit. And as it made one desperate leap toward the safety of the wood, Heydrich lurched forward on his mount, bringing the horse's front hoof down squarely on the rabbit's skull.

He pulled tight on the rein. The horse came to a sudden stop. Now he could relax.

He took a moment to catch his breath. "I hope we understand each other now," he said.

"I believe we have always understood each other," Canaris replied icily. He spurred his horse, which took off across the grassy field. Together horse and rider cleared a high bramble thicket with a grace and form which would not have been out of place on the Olympic team.

Heydrich watched the jump, then lashed his own horse fiercely with his riding crop. He charged off in the direction of the thicket, determined to take the obstacle even higher and faster than his former commander had.

Döberitz

It had taken most of the night to get things sorted out in the Olympic Village, about a half hour's bus ride from Berlin. It was already dark by the time the American men arrived. At the village they had been greeted by yet a third German brass band (the second being at the *Bahnhof* in Berlin) and the blond heads and smiling blue-eyed faces of a detachment of Hitler Youth. Each young boy held a blazing torch above him, giving the area around the entrance gate the look of a pagan religious rite.

The Americans arrived at the same time as the Italian team. Most of its members were freshly back from the military expedition to Ethiopia, where their tanks and planes had managed to crush the massed resistance offered by Haile Selassie's tribal spears.

The French team didn't show up until about one-thirty in the morning, apparently the result of some bureaucratic slipup. But the Germans were so eager to show their hospitality and have everything go according to plan that they trooped the band and the Hitler Youth out once again to welcome them.

The Olympic Village really was a complete planned city, nestled into the birch forests nine miles west of the stadium. One hundred and sixty cottages of brick and stone housed twenty or more men each, with dining halls, a library, a hospital, a dental clinic, a theater, swimming pools, and natural lakes.

"There's only one thing missing here," Tom said.

"I know," David replied. "We might as well be back at the Point. I wonder where they put all the girls."

"They've carried them away to some secret breeding farm to mate with the finest examples of German manhood."

"I think you've been seeing too many movies."

They had finished breakfast in the dining hall, and Tom had gone out to practice his sprints on the running track when a man in a German army uniform came over to the table where David was sitting.

"Lieutenant Keegan?"

"Yes?"

"Captain Wolfgang Fürstner, deputy in charge of the Olympic Village." He extended his hand. "A pleasure to meet you." He was handsome, just about the same size as David, and spoke with an upper-class German accent.

David rose to his feet. "I'm very pleased to meet you. But how did you know who I am?"

"With your long list of accomplishments, you are already something of a celebrity here. I have personally followed your career and admired your exploits for quite some time. Plus we are well aware of your heritage and therefore take particular pride in welcoming you. We think of these Olympics as a homecoming for all the sons of Germany. So I wanted to find you as soon as I could, let you know that your comfort and good feeling are very important to us here, and offer my services in any way I can."

"Thank you. I appreciate that."

"Of course, I have an official automobile at my personal disposal. Perhaps you would allow me to show you some of Berlin's many interesting attractions."

"It's very kind of you. . . ."

"If you are well rested after your journey and before you begin your intense training regimen, perhaps this evening would be convenient for you, Lieutenant."

"Thanks. I'd like that. But it's David."

"Very well, then . . . David. Around seven. I'll wait for you in front of the dining hall."

David had made up for himself a chart which he carried in his pocket. It laid out, very simply, the entire challenge before him—the most grueling, formidable test of skill, endurance, and courage in all athletics:

DAY ONE	DAY TWO
100-meter dash	110-meter hurdles
Running broad jump	Discus throw
Shot put	Pole vault
High jump	Javelin throw
400-meter run	1,500-meter run

Next to each event he'd marked down the "World Decath Record" and his own "Previous Personal Best." He'd also set out the general outlines of his training regimen and left room for notes. Shot put and discus were going to be weak; he'd never been very good at those. On the javelin he'd be good enough. It was like throwing a football. He wouldn't gain any ground with it, but he wouldn't lose any either. He'd always had a flair for pole vaulting, but so much of that sport was split-second luck and timing. He'd just have to hope it all came together for him on the afternoon of August 8. His strongest events would be the four runs, although he hated practicing for the hurdles. There was too much chance of injury. Most important were the four hundred meters, which closed out the first day, and the fifteen hundred, at the end of the second day. The last one, particularly, could be a killer. It was nothing more than raw determination and grit, at a time when all logic said you had nothing more to give. And that was what David pinned his medal hopes on.

He'd come close to a bronze in Los Angeles, but not close enough. He'd been strong and fit, but that was only half of it. He had been too young and inexperienced, and now he knew it. The decathlon had as much to do with mental discipline as physical performance. The conventional wisdom was that you needed a full Olympic decathlon before you really knew what you were doing.

David got in a couple of miles of roadwork on the shaded paths that crisscrossed the Olympic Village. Running was one thing he had to do every day to keep up his stamina. The other skills he would work on selectively to try to reach his peak just at the right time.

After the run he spent the rest of the day wandering by himself around the village. He went over to watch Tom practicing his baton pass with Sam Stoller, Marty Glickman, and Ralph Metcalfe. They looked good. Then he watched Jesse Owens jump. He stayed away from Glenn Morris, the leader of the American decathlon team and one of the favorites to take the gold. No sense spooking himself.

He walked over to the area of the field where the German team was training. The atmosphere was completely different. The Germans were highly organized and disciplined, with coaches shouting out directions and trainers with notebooks keeping records of results. As each man completed his exercise, the time or distance was reported back to a man in the center who kept the overall tally.

He found himself a vantage point on a rise overlooking the field. It was close enough to see what was going on but not too close to seem as if he was spying. Anyway, everything was supposed to be openness and sharing at the Olympic Village. The Olympic committees were encouraging athletes from different countries to work out and practice together. The whole setup was supposed to promote international camaraderie and understanding.

Actually, it was good to see some of these guys again, even at a distance. He recognized most of them from previous meets, either in England or the States. They hadn't been the greatest athletes he'd ever seen, but most of them had been pretty friendly and outgoing, especially when they realized he spoke their language.

David settled in on the grass for this surprisingly organized program of events. First came the hammer throw. Then the shot. Then the javelin. These Germans weren't bad. A lot better than they'd been in L.A. just four years earlier.

A few minutes later the runners and hurdlers took their places. David's mild surprise turned to amazement. He rough-timed them on his wristwatch. He looked from the dial to the finish line and back again. These guys were really good. He'd run against most of them before, and they hadn't been like this. Could these be the same men he had seen at L.A., at Ann Arbor, at Princeton, at Oxford? They were methodical and serious. The Germans really were going to be a threat.

He realized he had started to sweat. He felt slightly light and queasy in the stomach, the way he got before most races, even though the first competitions were more than a week away and his event was almost two weeks off.

He tried to get hold of himself, to put the whole thing in some perspective. This was only a game. The attack of nerves seemed foolish and misdirected and unworthy, considering the previous generation of competitors had expended their efforts and spent their young manhoods at the Marne, at Ypres and Verdun. Was it possible that responsible governments of feeling, intelligent men would ever lead their people into another battle like the Somme, where twenty thousand young soldiers had died in the first two hours and where it was said the river had run red for days? If nothing else, the World War had taught mankind a lesson in human folly that was inconceivable to repeat. Maybe that was what the Olympic spirit was all about.

Was that, perhaps, why athletics had become so important to him? Was the competition of the game merely a surrogate for actual combat and genuine struggle? Was that what this attack of nerves was all about?

Ever since he could remember, David Keegan had always had two callings that pulled him with equal strength: biochemistry and military "science." In one were the foundations of life; in the other, the foundations of death.

He had essentially escaped from it, mostly put it out of his conscious mind during his two idyllic years at Oxford. But now, he realized, he was facing his old demon once again: In spite of everything he had forced himself to face, and everything he had pushed himself to do in his twenty-four years on earth, he had yet to be truly tested.

FIVE

Except for competing in his own events, there was no reason a resident of the Olympic Village ever had to leave if he didn't want to. Even the practice facilities were duplicated there, though most of the athletes preferred taking the bus ride over to the stadium to get the feel of the actual competition.

Eventually, David knew, the monastic segregation of the village would begin getting to the men, and they would inevitably seek their comforts on the outside. But for the first few days, at least, the Olympic Village provided a serene and inviting haven with most of the comforts of home and a lot more variety.

Patterns developed quickly. An hour or so before the first dinner serving, athletes and coaches began assembling in the dining hall. When David and Tom arrived, there were already a fair number of people sitting around talking, playing cards, introducing each other to fellow competitors they'd managed to meet during the day, and trying to get to know as much as they could about their counterparts from distant lands. For the great majority this was their first experience away from home, and the German Olympic Committee seemed determined to make this a memorable time for all of them.

Since the Americans and Germans were fielding two of the largest teams, it was natural that their athletes would gravitate toward the long tables near the center of the hall. David and Sam Stoller were listening to Tom rate, in ascending order, the attributes of all the women on the American team. The fact that Ali was no longer officially on the squad made the exercise somewhat more diplomatic.

When the appraisal was complete and the differences in opinion had been negotiated away, the three men let their attention wander over to the German table. Several chessboards had been set up. A group of German athletes on one side of the table had taken on a group of French on the other.

The symbolism seemed apt to David. Chess was a representation of war, of kings and knights, castles and peasants, the aggressive, competitive drive channeled into a controlled board game. The Olympics had been designed by the ancients to serve the same function, the community of nations transferring their warlike urges to a field of athletic rules and controlled contests.

Suddenly voices were raised, immediately followed by a clattering crash onto the table and floor. A flying rook hit Sam Stoller in the arm. All other conversations halted, and all attention turned in the direction of the clamor.

One of the Germans was standing on his side of the table, glaring at his French opponent. The hand that had just upset the chessboard was waving menacingly in the air.

Someone was saying in German, "Calm down. It's only a game."

David knew he had seen the man before at other meets. He was a hurdler. First name Rolf. Schmidt was his last name, David thought. Not much of a standout, but a nice, quiet, good-natured kind of guy. David wondered what the French fellow had done to provoke him.

"Well, so much for international cooperation and goodwill," Tom muttered as the room waited to see what would happen. French and German athletes eyed each other warily.

Rolf lurched toward the Frenchman. Just then he clutched his hands to his chest. He let out a loud, wheezing gasp. His whole body convulsed. He pitched over the ruined chessboard, then collapsed onto the floor, gashing his forehead on the back of the wooden chair as he fell.

David rose instantly and ran forward. A crowd of the German's teammates gathered around. An air of panicked frenzy had taken over. Instinctively David pushed his way into the group. He knelt. He pushed Rolf over onto his back. He gripped his hand around the victim's neck and squeezed hard, feeling for a pulse. Nothing. He ripped open the shirt. Buttons popped in the air. He flattened his ear against Rolf's chest. Still nothing. The face was turning blue.

Hurriedly, David rolled Rolf onto his belly and assumed a kneeling position at his head. He placed his open hands on the center of Rolf's back, rocked forward and pressed hard. Then he rocked back and pulled the victim's arms into the air. He repeated the procedure over and over again, trying to force air into the German's lungs. *Come on!* he silently intoned. *Breathe!*

David had no idea how much time had gone by, but someone tapped him on the shoulder. He looked up. A medical team had arrived and had taken up its positions.

David gave way, lying on his back with his knees up to catch his breath. He closed his eyes and tried to blot out everything.

When he opened them again, Rolf and the medics were gone. Members of the German and French teams helped David to his feet.

Charlottenburg-Wilmersdorf

"That was quite a heroic effort from all reports I've received," Wolfgang Fürstner said as the car headed through the Charlottenburg streets. "You have the admiration and deepest thanks of all of us. I only wish I could have reported a more favorable outcome."

"I wish I could have done more," David said. "I wish anybody could have."

"You did all that was possible," Fürstner assured him. He shook his head sadly. "It is always a pity when something like this happens. And a particularly poignant tragedy when it is an athlete . . . in the prime of his life and conditioning."

"Then it was his heart?"

Fürstner nodded. "They believe so. I'm sure a postmortem examination will be conducted by the proper authorities."

That seemed a strange way to refer to doctors, but David said nothing. He just wanted to forget about the whole thing, at least for a while.

"I hope it doesn't cast too much of a pall over the games," Fürstner commented. "After all the effort that has gone into them, that would be such a shame. But let's try to think of happier things. I'll show you what still remains of the old Berlin."

They cruised slowly down the Kurfürstendamm. It was a graceful, treelined boulevard flanked by solid, impressive buildings. The ground floors held one outdoor café after another.

On the wide streets, bright lights canceled out the nighttime darkness. Cafés and broad sidewalks teeming with people reminded

David of the best of New York and Paris rolled into one. There was excitement here, electricity, the seductive lure of the forbidden.

David still thought it odd that the deputy head of the entire Olympic Village should single him out for such hospitality and personal attention, even if he was a Rhodes Scholar and military officer. There were other military men on the team, and a lot more with a stronger chance at a gold medal than he had.

That didn't seem to make any difference to Fürstner, though. He seemed friendly and interested in everything David was doing and, like just about every other German he'd met, very eager to please. David felt relaxed and comfortable with him.

"We're going to one of the best clubs in town," Fürstner said. "It's not far from here."

He steered the car into an alley and parked it against an empty wall. "These days no one will bother a car with an army number plate," he explained.

They got out and walked the short distance back to the Kurfürstendamm and merged into the endless tide of humanity. They crossed the intersection with the Joachimstalerstrasse. "That corner is the Café des Westens," Fürstner pointed out. "It used to be the place for all the artists and intellectuals in the old days."

A pack of young brownshirt troopers came down the street toward them. The oldest in the group looked no more than eighteen. They were marching more or less in step, considering they'd obviously had more than a few beers apiece, and they were singing in unison at the tops of their lungs:

> Raise up the banners!
> Stand rank on rank together.
> Storm troopers, march on,
> With steady, quiet tread. . . .

It was a military song of some sort—rousing, with a deep, passionate, soul-stirring quality that instantly insinuated itself into David's psyche, as if it were tapping into some noble yearning that had been there all along waiting to be awakened.

Fürstner must have seen it in his eyes because he nodded with recognition as soon as the brownshirts had passed. "It's called the 'Horst Wessel Song,'" he said. "Written by and named for one of the early martyrs of the National Socialist movement. He was killed in

Berlin six years ago, but his name and memory have been venerated. You'll probably be hearing it a lot while you're in Germany. It's one of the führer's favorites."

"I can see why," David said.

They passed a place called the Katacombe. Its sign was out, and the doors were boarded up. David had noticed several places like it along the length of the avenue. "The master of ceremonies there, he didn't like the National Socialists much," Fürstner said. "He made it part of his act every night. It has been closed since last year."

He thrust his hands into his pockets and shrugged slightly. "Hitler has done many wonderful things for us since he took over. But I must admit that I sometimes miss all the free culture of the Weimar days, decadent though it might have been." David looked around. This whole scene looked pretty free and decadent to him. He could only imagine how wild it must have been before the Nazis came to power.

"See how clean the streets are," Fürstner said as they continued walking. "It used to be you couldn't walk down the Ku'damm without falling into a pile of garbage or tripping over a derelict lying drunk in the gutter. National socialism has changed all that."

There was something strange about Fürstner, David had to admit. As closely as he could gather, the German had been the one who'd really been responsible for the Olympic Village. Everyone said it never could have happened without him.

But for some reason—and this was where the story got hazy—he had suddenly been replaced as the man in charge by someone else, a Lieutenant Colonel Werner von und zu Gilsa. And this just a few weeks before the start of the games. With all the foreign dignitaries coming, maybe they wanted someone with a higher rank to show the flag. But in that case they would have found some old retired general somewhere instead of a lieutenant colonel. No, somehow, it didn't all add up.

Well, it was none of David's business. He was sure the Germans could take care of themselves. All he wanted to do was concentrate on doing as well as he could in his sport and having good memories when all the games were over and he went back to "real life."

"Ah, here it is!" Fürstner said. He clapped David on the shoulder and guided him toward a brightly lit storefront bearing a large flashing sign: KABARETT ÉCLAIR.

Inside, David tried to take in the entire scene at once. The Éclair was a curious mix of elements. A jazz band consisting of black musicians at one side of the curtained stage played loud and brassily. Toward the back of the room he noticed one or two men in the severe black uniform he'd learned was that of the Gestapo. They seemed to be enjoying themselves along with everyone else. The waitresses scurrying between the tables were done up in cutaway formal coats and black fishnet stockings, like Marlene Dietrich in *The Blue Angel*. And large panels of the wall were covered over with white canvas dropcloths.

"Murals done by an artist from the Bauhaus," Fürstner explained. "Very modernistic, no longer in favor. In fact, the entire Bauhaus School was closed down several years ago."

The other unusual thing David noticed was the telephone on every table, like the ones brought out for big shots at restaurants in Hollywood movies.

"So that you can call anyone you see at another table who strikes your fancy. Much more sophisticated this way, don't you think?"

"I guess so," David said, shaking his head. He'd certainly never seen anything like this in England.

"There used to be a famous comedian called Willi Zweig who worked here. Very funny, very incisive. Gave everyone in power a hard time. He was one of the things that made this place. I don't know what happened to him."

The waitress came over to take their order. She was blond and rosy-cheeked with absolutely incredible legs. David found himself staring at them, but when he looked up, embarrassed, her expression made him realize she was used to it.

"Two pints of Pils to begin with," Fürstner instructed, managing to lean back and pat the young lady's shapely behind as she passed. "Oh, by the way," he said, calling after her, "whatever happened to Willi Zweig?"

She stopped. "He's not playing here anymore."

"I know that. Where is he playing?"

"Elsewhere."

"Yes." He persisted, beginning to grow impatient with her. "Where?"

She took a step back toward the table so she would not have to shout. "Oranienburg," she said, and walked away.

At this Fürstner just nodded, as if he had been caught up short. Something almost imperceptible seemed to drain from him, and

David thought it best not to pursue the matter. There was a moment of awkwardness in which it seemed the entire mood of the evening had shifted into a minor key. Fürstner sensed this and broke it by asking, "So what do you think, Lieutenant?"

What David thought was that this all was an incredible spectacle, and on the training regimen he'd been following, just the thought of all these gorgeous girls running around in their fishnet tights made his manhood rise. With the forced celibacy the International Olympic Committee insisted upon and with the start of the games approaching, David knew this was the last opportunity he might have for quite some time. It was kind of awkward, though. Any other time or place, and he would have abandoned his companion right here at the table.

"Where do you get them all from, Wolfgang?"

Fürstner smiled with indulgence. "All German girls are beautiful, David. It's one of our great natural resources."

There was a drum roll and downbeat from the band. All eyes fixed on the stage. The curtains parted.

Twelve women stood frozen still, heroically posed, grouped around an ornate chariot and two rearing plaster of paris horses. All the women were bare-chested. In fact, they were completely naked except for laurel crowns in their hair and matching leafy coverings on their most vital areas that still left almost nothing to the imagination. Oh, and the two actually in the chariot had tiny feathered wings sprouting from their milky white shoulders. David sucked in his breath.

An appreciative hum of recognition arose from the sophisticated audience.

"It's an interpretation of the victory sculpture on top of the Brandenburg Gate," Fürstner explained. "We passed by it on our way into the city."

After holding this tableau for several beats, the actresses began to move. Actually, gymnasts would have been a better description of them because as the music struck up, they immediately began romping and cavorting about the stage, doing somersaults and backbends and tossing flowered garlands among themselves. When the woman holding the chariot reins suddenly jumped out and landed at the foot of the stage in a deep split, David thought he would melt inside.

"She's nice, isn't she?" Fürstner said.

"Ah . . . sensational," David spluttered.

The lead actress rose to her feet again and pirouetted, the muscles of her glistening buttocks contracting enticingly. David was sitting close enough to observe the nipples standing up firm and straight on her prominent breasts. Apparently she was enjoying this as much as he was.

"I'd thought the Nazis had closed down all this stuff. How do they get away with it here?"

Fürstner smiled again. "They call it *Freikörperkultur*. It means something like 'free body culture' or worship of the healthy body, which the Nazis officially approve of." He pointed in the direction of the stage. "And that's what this is supposed to be." Then he gestured in the other direction. "So when the Gestapo come in, they turn a blind eye and just enjoy the show."

The act concluded to a thunderous round of applause. A few lascivious whistles emanated from the back of the room. The band shifted back into a Dixieland beat, and the waitresses in fishnet reappeared.

Fürstner picked up the receiver of the telephone in front of him. "Backstage, please," he ordered, winking at David. The rest was whispered in a colloquial German dialect, and David couldn't make it out.

He was still in the process of catching his breath when the performer he had just admired so passionately came out from the stage door and began making her way through the congratulations of the admiring crowd. She was now wearing a short red kimono, tied with a black sash at the waist, which still managed to show off her bountiful chest and endless legs to full advantage.

"Ah, Lorelei!" Fürstner called out. As she came closer, he stood up. David awkwardly followed suit.

"Wolfie! They told me you were here." She turned toward David with eyes twinkling. "And who might your extremely handsome companion be?"

"Lorelei Bremmer, may I present Lieutenant David Keegan from America."

She extended her hand. David took it in both of his. "Ah, would you join us?" he managed to get out.

"Thank you. I'd like that," she said.

They sat down. Lorelei pulled her chair close to David. Fürstner ordered her a glass of white wine.

"Wonderful performance!" Fürstner declared. "Truly inspiring."

"Did you like it, Lieutenant?"

"David, please."

"All right, then. Did you like it, Lieutenant David?"

"Yes . . . yes, very much."

"And David knows whereof he speaks."

"I do?" He nearly spit out his beer.

"He's an athlete, you see. Over here to compete in the games. Decathlon."

Lorelei seemed to take a special liking to this fact. "I thought that was the body of an athlete—tight and trim and highly trained, like a thoroughbred racehorse." She ran her hand lightly over David's bicep and purred, "Tell me about the decathlon."

He gulped. "Well, it's ten events over two days, and it's supposed to represent the kind of all-around competition the ancient Greeks actually took part in."

Lorelei grimaced theatrically. "You enjoy this?"

"I'm not sure that's the right word for it," David said.

"Why do you do it?"

"Sometimes I wonder. But I do know it's something I want as much as I've ever wanted anything in my life."

"They have this for women, too?"

"*Nein, Fräulein Bremmer.*" Fürstner broke in. "It's the one medal that shows who the real men are. The man who wins it is considered the greatest athlete in the world."

"Then that must be what you are," she said to David with a smile of satisfaction.

From there the conversation grew even easier and more animated. Lorelei wanted to know everything about David: his time at West Point; Oxford; previous track meets; what it was like to grow up in the far-off United States. She crossed her legs tightly, and the kimono fell open to the tops of her thighs. He could feel her bare flesh grazing his own thigh under the table. That he had this effect on women, especially beautiful women, still surprised him.

All the while Fürstner kept ordering more beer and wine. David and Lorelei sat closer and closer together. Was it just the casual and accidental placement of her hand, or was she purposely stroking the inside crease of his leg?

For the first time since he'd left Oxford, David felt totally relaxed—relaxed, that is, except for the thrill of the conquest rising up inside him. Tomorrow the training would begin in earnest. But for tonight, at least, he could forget his responsibilities and concerns and revel in the magic that Berlin still offered to those bold enough to embrace it.

In fact, tonight he could forget everything but the enchanting creature sitting there next to him with her arm around his shoulder, giggling at his small talk and whispering little secrets in his ear.

David didn't know how much time had gone by until Fürstner looked at his watch. "I suppose we ought to be going." David reluctantly agreed. Lorelei started to offer a pouting protest.

"Can we offer you a ride somewhere?" He turned quickly to Fürstner. "If—if it's okay with Wolfgang, that is."

"By all means," the captain said. "I'll go get the car."

"I'll just have to nip by my dressing room for a minute and change," Lorelei said. She wrapped her hands around David's arm. "You come with me and help."

He turned toward Fürstner. "Perhaps I should . . ."

"Go on," the German advised.

Lorelei marched off toward the stage door. "I'll be waiting for you."

"I'll stay fifteen minutes in the alley," Fürstner said. "And if you haven't come out by then, I'll assume you've gotten lucky. Then you're on your own getting back to the village. I'll make sure the guards know to let you in. See, it does pay to have friends in high places."

"Are you sure about this?" David whispered.

"Absolutely."

"I don't want to cut in on anything you've got going."

"Don't be silly. Our relationship is strictly one of friendship. I've known her parents for years."

Fürstner was turning out to be an even better friend than David had thought.

David knocked on the dressing-room door and was both slightly relieved and disappointed not to find her standing there naked and waiting to pounce on him. Instead, she had already changed into a fashionable but relatively modest street dress that still did no shame to her voluptuous figure.

"Are you ready?" she asked brightly. David nodded.

Just then there was a knock on the door. It opened, and the young man who'd been tending the stage door came in carrying a large bottle tied with a bright red ribbon.

"From a secret admirer, I think," he said.

She took it from him, and he left.

"Does this happen very often?" David asked.

"Not so often that I ever grow bored with it," she said. "It's already cold. It would be a shame to waste. I know. Before we go out, let's just have one sip to toast our new friendship." She handed him the bottle. "Would you do the honors?" She brought over two glasses from her dressing table. "To your success!"

He took a sip. A feeling of calm and warm contentment instantly pervaded his being. A kind of surreal quiet enveloped him. He started feeling slightly dizzy. The room began to spin. Lorelei's form blurred before him.

Her concerned face looming above him as he lay on the floor was the last thing he remembered seeing as he blacked out.

When he awoke, he was alone. He was no longer in Lorelei's dressing room, but in a dark, windowless chamber with only one solid door leading out. And he was no longer lying on the floor but was tied hands and feet to a straight-backed wooden chair which was growing increasingly uncomfortable by the minute.

SIX

He came to consciousness gradually, prodded into wakefulness by the cramping in his thighs and the throbbing pain at the base of his spine.

The room was small. There was no other furniture in it. He was thoroughly bound. One rope around his shoulders was tied through the slats in the back of the chair; another was looped around both his wrists, holding them wide apart. A third, tight across his pelvis, held him down into the chair. And a fourth across his ankles tied his feet to the chair's front legs. Maybe this was Lorelei's idea of some kinky love game.

Lorelei! She had set him up. Right from the start. Coming over to the table after her act, showing all the interest in him, luring him back to her dressing room—it all had been part of the setup. There was no other possibility. Fürstner must have been in on it, too.

He directed his mind back through everything that had happened. He remembered the last-minute champagne that arrived just as they were about to leave. It had to have been the champagne. He'd poured two glasses, one for himself and one for her. Why did it affect only him? She must not have drunk hers, only pretended to sip it.

A sharp pain jabbed between his shoulder blades. It traveled down his arms to his wrists crossed behind him. How could he have gotten himself into this? How could he possibly have let Wolfgang Fürstner lead him straight down the primrose path . . . and into this? He'd bought the whole bill of goods about why the German had singled him out. How could he have been so naive?

So Fürstner and Lorelei Bremmer had been working together. For what, though? And how did he fit into it?

Keegan, you are such a simple, trusting son of a bitch, he thought with disgust. *How could you let yourself get into this? Well, that's all past history now. What can you do about living through it?*

His pulse quickened as he tried to think logically. Whoever put him here would obviously be back. And their intentions would not exactly be kindly. At best they'd be back to interrogate him, but about what he couldn't imagine. He had to do something as quickly as possible. Or at least try. If he somehow got out and lived through it, then he would deal with Wolfgang and Lorelei. Revenge. It was one of the purest emotions he knew of. He hoped the anger would sustain him, give him the strength he needed.

Do something! He prodded himself. *Anything is better than nothing. Play the cards you're dealt, not because you want to but because you don't have any choice. Think logically, strategically, just the way you were taught at the Point. Eliminate the variables, and then act. There's only one way out—through that door. You don't know what's on the other side, but it doesn't matter because you have no choice. But to get there, first you have to get yourself out of this mess. . . .*

He struggled to lift himself off the seat just enough to move the chair. Painfully he inched the chair across the floor until he was about a foot from the wall. He didn't want to make any more noise than he had to and alert whoever was out there. It would be unavoidable soon enough.

He took a deep breath, filling his lungs as completely as he could. Then he let it all out, contracting his stomach muscles until he was sure his chest was empty. He held his breath in that condition. There was a slight amount of slack, not enough to free himself but something to work with.

He positioned himself precisely with respect to the wall. Then he shifted his weight on the balls of his feet and at the same time leaned his head and chest forward to throw himself slightly off-balance. Timing was everything. And he'd get only one chance.

Just as he was beginning to tip forward, he jerked his head and shoulders violently to the left, toppling the chair over. A split second after it had begun its fall, he got his head out of the way and whipped his shoulders around in the other direction, causing the left upright of the chair's back to smash into the wall as chair and occupant crashed to the floor. He closed his eyes and steeled himself for the shock.

He landed on his shoulder and side, trying to tumble as much as the chair would allow to protect himself from the fall. He came to rest on the floor. His shoulder and hip hurt; they had taken the brunt of the impact. His lip was cut, and his nose was bleeding. Other than that, he seemed to be in pretty good shape. More important, the force of the collision with the wall had shattered the wooden upright. When he let out his breath, the rope was loose enough to let him maneuver his left hand and wrist.

He didn't have much time. Someone would have heard the sound. Feverishly he began working at the knot that held his wrists in place. He could use only one hand, and his fingers kept cramping. His thumb felt as if it were going to break at the joint.

He managed to pull his wrist over far enough to reach the splintered broken end of the wooden upright. Feeling his way, he angled the knot onto its jagged point. Gradually he was able to grind it down onto the point and work the wood up into the fist of the knot. As he rotated it back and forth, he felt it slowly loosen.

That should do it now. He lifted his knotted wrist off the spindle. He felt with his other hand. It was loose enough now to work with his thumb and forefinger. He pushed and pulled, pushed and pulled the end of the rope until it came undone in his hand. Both hands were finally free.

He slid down in the chair to free himself from the shoulder rope. Then he untied the one around his ankles. The remaining rope across his lap was more difficult, but with his hands free, it finally gave way, too.

He stood up. Now the next problem.

He tiptoed over to the door. He reached out and tested the knob. Of course, it was locked. Well, that was that. He'd just have to sit here and wait for them to come for him, plus face punishment for breaking up their furniture. End of the adventure.

Maybe not! He studied the door for a moment. It opened into the room, so the hinges were on this side. If the pins weren't wedged in too tightly . . .

He tried the lower one first. It slid out easily, the lubricating grease blackening his thumb. Now, if the top hinge would just come out the same way . . . He walked back across the room and brought the remains of the chair to stand on. He climbed gingerly onto the shaky apparatus, holding the top of the doorjamb for support. He formed the thumb and fingers of his other hand into a claw and clamped it over the top of the pin. He pulled straight up. Nothing happened. He gripped tighter and pulled again, slowly, with all his strength concentrated. This time it came.

He climbed down again. The only thing holding the door closed now was the lock itself. He gripped the empty lower hinge and pulled it as far as he could from the doorframe. He managed almost an inch, far enough to insert the greasy metal pin into the crack. He took the other pin and inserted it just above, then slid it up higher, creating a wider crack.

He picked up the shattered upright from the floor and examined it. Solid oak. Only the angle at which it had struck the wall had made it break. Used the right way, it ought to be as strong as the door itself. He pried the narrow, splintered end into the crack. He leaned into it, pressed forcefully against the other end, and rocked it back and forth. He heard the door creak, as if the very fibers of the wood were groaning. *That's it. Come on!* Back and forth again.

Then suddenly it split loose, ripping the bolted lock mechanism out of the doorframe. Quickly he grabbed the door on both sides before it could crash to the floor. He moved it to the side and leaned it against the wall. Then he picked up the oak chair part. It was his only weapon.

Stealthily he slipped to the other side of the door. He found himself in a short hallway, almost like an anteroom. There was another door at the opposite end.

He approached it slowly. He put his ear up close to the surface. He couldn't hear anything on the other side. He put his hand on the doorknob. He twisted it delicately. It turned. This one wasn't locked. He took another deep breath. Okay, this was it. Risk everything.

With one hand he gripped his oak club tightly. He raised it above his head, ready to strike. The other hands gripped the doorknob.

In one motion he turned it and lunged through the door.

He quickly looked around. He was in an ornate sitting room full of rich period furniture. Portraits in gilt frames adorned the walls. Cut-glass chandeliers hung from the high ceiling. And in the middle of the room a tall gray-haired man, his long legs crossed, looked up from the newspaper he was reading just as David was about to strike.

"Oh, good, you're here."

David stopped short. He took a step back and held his pole up defensively. "Who are you?"

The gray-haired man put down the newspaper and stood up. He started to extend his hand but then caught a glimpse of David's up-raised club and apparently thought better of it. "Arthur Hargreaves is my name. And I will assume you to be David Keegan." He spoke with an upper-class English accent. He would have been right at home in Oxford.

"Where am I? What's going on?"

A somewhat pained expression came over the gray-haired man's face. "Yes, of course. Well . . . Where to begin? It's a bit difficult. Some of the other people were dubious and insisted upon a sort of initiative test. By your presence here, I'd say you passed."

"A test for what?"

The newspaper was the *Times* of London.

"Yes, well, that is the point, isn't it? Do put that stick down if you wouldn't mind. No one's going to hurt you."

"You knock me out, tie me to a chair, and force me to risk my neck breaking out as if I were Harry Houdini, and then you tell me know one's going to hurt me?"

"Reasonable question," Hargreaves allowed.

"Now, why don't you just tell me exactly what's going on before I crack your fucking skull open?"

The gray-haired man let out a long sigh. He walked over to a carved, inlaid secretary desk and picked up a dark file folder. He opened it and handed a photograph across to David.

David took the picture from him. It was of a tall, well-built young man of about David's own age. He had medium dark hair and a square jaw. He was wearing a track suit and stood in the empty concrete bowl of a large stadium.

"Does this man look familiar?"

"Vaguely," David replied.

"Can you place him?"

"A German. I've run against him."

"When was the last time?"

"Last spring. At the Cambridge Invitational. I won."

"Good. Do you happen to remember his name?"

"Karl somebody. Karl Lindermann."

"Linderhoff, but close enough. I'm pleased you remember him. And the fact that you won means he'll remember you as well."

"Just what is this all about?"

Hargreaves raised his hand in a conciliatory gesture. "Bear with me, please. We've been looking for possible . . . connections between the two of you. We noted that you both were also at a track meet at Michigan State University on May twenty-fifth, 1935—a meet, coincidentally, where your teammate Jesse Owens had a rather memorable afternoon."

"A lot of people were at that meet." He handed back the photograph.

"Even so, it provides us with a scenario. You'll find you two have a good deal in common. Like yourself, Linderhoff is an army officer—"

"And just who are the 'us' and 'we' you keep talking about?"

"Section Six of His Majesty's Military Intelligence Service." He made the pronouncement gravely. "I myself am assigned to the Scientific Intelligence Unit. Let's say you've just been recruited."

"I'm an American," David protested.

"An American *commissioned officer*. And lest you be concerned, this has already been cleared with your superiors. You are, in effect, on loan to us for the duration."

"The duration of what?"

"We'll get to that in due course," the Englishman replied.

"If this was all arranged the way you say, why did you have to knock me out and tie me up and scare the shit out of me?"

"As I told you, you're young, you're inexperienced, you're an unknown quantity. Not the optimum situation. It was thought that since there was no time for specialized training, we had better make sure in whatever minor way we could that you were tough and resourceful enough to meet the demands that might be placed upon you. As we've seen, you've certainly done that so far. Also, of course, we couldn't very well simply approach you on the street without arousing suspicion. And we are assuming that all telephone lines into the Olympic Village are tapped."

The Olympic Village, David thought. "What does Wolfgang Fürstner have to do with this?"

"Who? Oh, yes, the German chap you were with last night. We don't know much about him. Should we?"

"Then how did you get to me?"

"We followed you into Berlin. That part wasn't difficult. It was quite clear you were out for a bit of naughtiness before getting down to serious business. Not that I blame you; we're not Puritans here. Then, when we saw you making friends with the performer from the cabaret, we knew we had something to work with. We timed it just right, sent in the bottle of champagne, and let chemistry do the rest. We thought you as a student of science would appreciate that little touch."

David rubbed his throbbing shoulder. Yes, he was most appreciative. "So Lorelei wasn't in on this either?"

"The cabaret girl?" Hargreaves looked down his nose in disdain. "Hardly."

"Then how could you be sure she wouldn't drink the champagne, too?"

"And what if she did? Quite clearly that was part of the plan. How else could we remove you from the premises without arousing her suspicion?" He glanced at his wristwatch. "She should be awake by now, having found no remaining trace of you. Probably thinks you're something of a cad, but *c'est la vie*. Oh, well. She didn't seem the type to develop a long-term relationship with, anyway."

"I generally like to be able to make those decisions for myself," said David tersely.

"All's fair in love and war, I'm afraid. And this is war of a sort, make no mistake about it."

"It's not my war. So let me out of here." He made for the door opposite him.

Hargreaves made no move to accommodate him but merely continued in the same tone. "The point is, the Olympic Games are our best—perhaps our only—opportunity, and you're the best available candidate. You are in this country legitimately as an athlete in the same event, so the relationship will seem normal. You're of German heritage and speak the language fluently, so you won't seem out of place to your hosts. You're in excellent physical condition, have had tactical and survival training at West Point—"

"I'm not interested. I came here to compete in the decathlon, and that requires all my effort and concentration."

"—and you're under military discipline, so you can't refuse us." Hargreaves seemed to brighten at the recall of this last detail.

"Why are you so interested in this Karl Linderhoff?"

"We're not, actually. It's his girl friend we care about."

"His girl friend?"

"That's right. Linderhoff is simply the cleanest and most direct way of getting to her without, as I mentioned, arousing undue suspicion. That's another reason you fit into our plans: You understand science."

"So who is this girl friend?" David asked warily.

"Her name is Miranda Wolff. She works in the physics section of the Kaiser Wilhelm Institute of Science in Dahlem, not far from here."

David was growing impatient. "Then why don't you get someone over there to take care of her for you, whatever it is you want done?"

"I thought I had made that clear. A scientist or anyone on the inside, even if we could tap someone, would be suspect."

"I'm not a physicist. I'm a biochemist. In fact, what I really am is a biochemistry *student*."

"In a perfect world you'd have the scientific background of Albert Einstein, the looks and charm of Clark Gable, and the intuition of Sherlock Holmes. But unfortunately, Mr. Keegan, this isn't a perfect world. Believe me, we've gone over this rather intensively back at the home office. You're the best we can do."

"I'm touched." David rubbed his wounded shoulder again. "You haven't given me a whole lot of reason to trust you so far." He gripped his wooden stake at both ends. "How do I know you're really who you say you are?"

Hargreaves remained maddeningly unflappable. "A good question. Shows that you're thinking even in the midst of stress, that you're skeptical and wary. All part of the initiative test. Which brings us back to your earlier question of where you are. I didn't mean to put you off, you see." He crossed the room toward the door. "Be so kind as to follow me if you would."

The gray-haired man opened the door and led him down a long corridor. They came to the end, and Hargreaves opened a door. David looked around. It led into another large room of similar decor, equally rich-looking, same high ceiling and chandeliers, but this one was outfitted as an office. At the far end a prominent carved walnut desk, flanked by two overstuffed leather visitor's chairs, faced the doorway. And behind the desk were the most notable features of the room: a Union Jack draped around a walnut and brass flagpole and a framed oil portrait of His Majesty King Edward VIII.

"You're in the British Embassy," Hargreaves announced, "specifically in the office of the ambassador." He spread his arms wide to take in the scene. "All this by way of demonstrating to you the official sanction of this project. And to prove that we're on the level . . ."

As if on cue, a panel door in the wall behind the desk opened. A small middle-aged man with thinning hair and a mustache appeared. His belly curved out in a good-natured paunch, but his eyes were small and serious and intense.

"May I present His Excellency Sir Eric Phipps, ambassador to Berlin."

Phipps came over and shook David's hand heartily. "Pleased to meet you, Lieutenant Keegan. Glad to have you aboard."

Both men looked down at the wooden stake David still clutched tightly in his hand. David looked up at Phipps awkwardly.

"From what everybody tells me, you'll be giving our boys a good run for their money at the stadium next week, not to mention these Germans here."

These Brits were amazing, David thought. The world could be coming down in flames, and they'd still remember to compliment you on your choice of neckties.

Sir Eric kept David's hand and subtly began walking him over toward the door. Hargreaves followed along. "The prime minister is very high on this, so if there is anything else I can do or any way I can be of assistance, you know that you have but to ask."

"Thank you, sir," Hargreaves said, reassuming custody of their guest from the ambassador.

He led David back down the corridor. "Believe me now?"

David said nothing.

"Good. Then let's get down to business." He ushered David into another office, this one small and functional. Hargreaves motioned him to take the one armchair in the room, then sat himself on the edge of the metal desk. "Now, let me tell you something about this Fräulein Miranda Wolff."

He gave David a brief grounding in atomistics and told him how every piece of evidence pointed to the young, brilliant Wolff's being one of the key components in the equation, "the one that could take the edge away from them and give it back to us."

"Why are you so concerned?" David challenged him. "Science is an international community."

"I'm afraid the Germans are shutting it down rather rapidly."

"You're the ones, not the Germans, who are going around kidnapping people." David thought about how he'd misjudged Wolfgang. "I like it here. I feel at home. The Germans all have been extremely friendly to me. All they want is for people to understand them."

"Look, we know about your grandparents, and I don't mean to offend your heritage," Hargreaves said, "but have you heard of a man called Carl von Ossietzky?"

"No."

"You should have. He's a writer and journalist who won the Nobel Peace Prize last year. They've been burning his books over here for three years now. Not just him, either. Freud, Marx, Einstein, Thomas and Heinrich Mann. Incidentally, Ossietzky couldn't claim the prize himself. Do you know why?"

"Obviously I don't," said David contemptuously.

"Because he's being held in a type of detention center the Germans euphemistically refer to as a concentration camp to cover up its true purpose, where he's apparently being systematically tortured to death. This is what the Nazis think of peace. All because he also wanted people to understand them."

"Is there any proof of this?" David challenged.

Hargreaves shook his head. "Proof? No. But let's say we have strong reason to believe. The proof, as you call it, will come in time. It always does."

David sat silently for a moment, confused, unsure of what he was supposed to believe. The things Hargreaves was telling him sounded unreal, like the typical enemy horror stories he'd read of from both sides during the Great War, the things his grandparents had been taunted with, blamed for.

"Don't feel bad if all this seems strange and unbelievable to you," Hargreaves said. "People in my own government find themselves unable to grasp it."

David had no response. Finally he said, "So let me make sure I've got this straight. You want me to hang around and make friends with this Karl Linderhoff so I can get to know his girl friend."

"That's right. Develop a relationship with her."

"What sort of relationship?"

Hargreaves shrugged. "I leave that to your imagination."

"And once I develop this relationship with her, I'm to get her to confide in me, and figure out if she's everything you think she might be."

Hargreaves nodded.

"What then?"

"We'll face the next part if and when we get to it. For now the main thing is to get this critical information to us."

"Then am I to assume that after I perform this chore of intelligence gathering for you, I'm off the hook?"

Hargreaves paused for what seemed like a long time. "I can't promise you that, I'm afraid. But we can talk about that later."

"We can talk about it now," David insisted.

Hargreaves sighed and frowned. "Right, then. If we determine that it is strategically advisable to deprive Germany of her services and secure them for ourselves—and I include our cousins across the big pond, of course—then we shall probably enlist your aid to that end. That's it."

"You mean, then I'd have to figure out a way to get her out of Germany and into your excited little paws?"

"We'll give you all the support we can," Hargreaves stated, trying to sound upbeat. "Now we'd better get you out of here before you're too badly missed. There is a taxi waiting downstairs to take you back to the Olympic Village."

"And how do I get in contact with you?"

"Take two glasses of orange juice at breakfast instead of your normal one. We'll take it from there."

It gave him a chill to think that they already knew this much about his personal habits. "That's all?"

Hargreaves gave him an expression of mild disdain. "We are in the spy business, after all. Give us some credit for technique." He stood up and gestured David to do the same. "I'll walk you out."

"One other thing," David said when they were halfway down the sweeping staircase. "What if this Miranda Wolff refuses to leave with me?"

"That presupposes that you have determined there is legitimate reason to think she is, in fact, valuable, and we have decided to go ahead with phase two of our plan."

"And if I so determine, and you so determine, and yet she still refuses to leave?"

Hargreaves clapped a fatherly hand around David's sore shoulder. "Well, then . . . we're all professionals here, one way or another. In that case, dear boy . . . we'll have to deal with the situation as it arises, now, won't we?"

SEVEN

Sunday, July 26, Döberitz

Wolfgang Fürstner rushed over as he saw David walking across the path back toward his dormitory room. "Where have you been? I waited half an hour outside the Éclair. Then I figured you had gotten lucky, so I left. But when you weren't back by the middle of the morning, I began to worry. I was almost about to send out the security police."

"I'm okay," David said quietly, trying unsuccessfully to mask his weariness. He forced a smile. "Thanks. And thanks for everything last night."

Fürstner glanced at his watch. "Almost noon. You must have had quite a time with her."

David hesitated a moment. "I . . . Yes, I guess I did."

He began absentmindedly massaging his shoulder. He winced at the initial touch. Before he realized what he was doing, he saw that Fürstner had noticed.

"My God, Keegan! What did she do to you? I hope you've got something left for the competition."

Monday, July 27, Dahlem

Karl Linderhoff burst into Miranda's office without knocking. "Let's go. Get your things together."

She looked up at him from her desk. "But I'm working."

"It can wait. I want you to come with me."

"Where?"

"To the Olympic Stadium. To watch me practice. The weather's beautiful, and it's about time you came out."

"Dr. Behrman is letting you out this early?"

"Better than that. He's coming along to watch and insists you come along as well. Says he'll clear it with Dr. Hahn."

"I didn't know Dr. Behrman was interested in sports."

"Human kinetics is what he says he's interested in. A fancy name for how the body moves. But I'd say he was just as interested in you."

"Hmmmph," Miranda declared.

Karl took her hands in his. "Everybody loves Miranda."

"And Miranda loves Karl," she whispered, as if imparting a special secret; as if to reassure both herself and him. She felt an internal shudder, and it made her want to touch him. She had begun to feel that way more and more lately, as if the life-force within her could no longer be held back. So often now it felt as though something were bursting inside her and needed to get out. What social virtue could there be in denying one of the elemental forces of nature, a power no more or less basic than the attraction of magnetic poles or the orbit of an electron about a nucleus? *Papa would say I'm just being independent and rebellious.*

She stood up, pulled her hands away from Karl's grasp, and ran her palms across the surface of his chest. She circled her hands around to his back; then, as they dropped playfully to his buttocks, she pulled him to her until their bodies met. Sometimes, lately, the feeling inside her was so strong, she could hardly contain herself.

"Not now," he said sharply.

She withdrew in surprise, like a little girl who'd just had her hand slapped. He was acting that strange way again. It frightened her that his mood could change so abruptly.

"What's wrong?" she asked. "What did I do?"

"Not during training."

"It hasn't stopped you before."

"This is different. This is the Olympics. The whole world will be watching. Each of us has a responsibility to ourselves and to our führer to do the best we can—no, to do *better* than we can, to transcend our bodily limitations by the sheer force of will."

Why did everyone have to be so serious about this business? Did Karl realize he was letting the life go out of himself? It was so tiresome. "That was very inspiring."

"It's nothing to joke about," he snapped, and for one horrifying moment he reminded her of Papa. "The future of the fatherland depends on what we're doing. You must try to show more respect."

"I have one father already," Miranda snapped, placing her hands squarely on her hips. "I don't need another."

"Come along," Karl responded, still sounding like a stern parent. "Dr. Behrman will be out by the car already, and we shouldn't keep him waiting."

But when he saw her lower lip form into a delicate quiver and her large liquid eyes growing wide, he relented. "Besides, I've arranged to practice with one of the Americans. They're the best. I hope I can pick up some pointers. His name is David Keegan. He speaks good German. I think you'll like him."

Döberitz

The confirmation came in a sealed envelope inside a good-luck telegram personally delivered by an attaché from the American Embassy in Berlin. Everyone on the American team got a copy of the inspirational message from the ambassador. Only David's contained the additional message, typed out in the uneven block capitals of military orders.

> TO: LT. DAVID J. KEEGAN, USA.
>
> THIS IS TO CONFIRM THAT PURSUANT TO YOUR COMMUNICATION FROM SIR ARTHUR HARGREAVES, UNTIL FURTHER NOTICE YOU ARE TO COOPERATE FULLY WITH, FOLLOW ANY INSTRUCTIONS, AND OBEY ALL ORDERS GIVEN YOU BY DULY AUTHORIZED AGENTS OF HM GOVERNMENT, MILITARY INTELLIGENCE SECTION SIX, REGARDING ANY AND ALL MATTERS ON WHICH YOU ARE ADVISED.
>
> PLEASE DESTROY THIS COMMUNICATION AFTER READING.
>
> AUTHORIZATION AND VERIFICATION CODE: MARVEL-ABLE-RACOON-KING-TWO-TWO-EIGHT-FIVE-ONE.
>
> FROM: C. DANIEL CLEMENTE, USA, MILITARY INTELLIGENCE COMMAND. FT. DIX, N.J.

He still couldn't believe what the Brits had asked of him and that the U.S. Army had agreed. For David, these Olympics had been a magic dream for so long, a distant goal shimmering against a golden horizon. No matter what he'd done—at West Point, at Oxford—he'd never let this target out of his sight. Not a day had gone by in six years that he hadn't worked out, that he hadn't trained. Los Angeles had been the warm-up. Berlin was the main event.

Winning in the Olympics took everything you had to give and then that much more again. Nothing could distract you. And now he was being asked to shift his concentration away from the thing that at the moment was most important in his life to get involved in some sort of bizarre spy mission against a friendly country, a country that had certainly been friendly to him. Everything he'd sweated blood for could go up in smoke. It just wasn't fair.

Grunewald

With the German propensity for running words together to form new words, the Olympic complex was known as the Reichssportfeld. It had been designed and built especially for these Olympic Games. But it was also clearly built for all time, with a solidity that would last a thousand years and stand as a monument to a time when the German people had the courage, foresight, and discipline to accomplish such great things.

When David and Tom got off the shuttle bus from the Olympic Village, a group of women from the American team was already on the Maifeld, the vast grassy area behind the giant, classically styled stadium.

"Hi, girls. What's cooking?" Tom greeted the women.

"We're what's cooking," Ruth Wilfort informed him.

"We've missed you ladies over at the village."

"Not as much as we've missed you," Ruth stated matter-of-factly.

"And you can keep *our* Olympic Village," Helen Stephens declared. She was a Missouri farm girl, slim and lean, with angular features and as tall as most of the men on the team. She ran for the sheer pleasure of it and was the hope of the women's hundred- and four-hundred-meter relay squads.

"You can take it and shove it," her teammate Ruth added. It was the first time David had seen any of the American women since they'd landed in Germany.

"We feel like we've been in jail the last two days," Helen said.

"I thought they were supposed to be making a big deal over you all," said Tom. "We have to take a half hour bus ride to get here, and you're all just a short walk away in a nice little house."

"Right," Ruth said. "It's completely surrounded by a high wrought-iron fence that the better brought-up girls say reminds them of a convent school, and the rest, a prison."

"You can come over and share our room anytime you like," Tom offered. "And I know I speak for my friend Keegan as well when I make the offer." David nodded his head emphatically.

Helen paid him no notice. "The food stinks, the rooms are tiny, there's no heat, and you can complain till you're blue in the face." And Ellie and Ali get to stay in some fancy hotel, drink and hobnob with society, and have the time of their lives, while Eleanor's husband sits home alone in California."

"Poor Artie Jarrett. She must be some handful," said Helen. "I'll bet he's not the first man whose heart she's broken. And she's an angel compared with Alison."

Tom smiled noncommittally. David said nothing.

"They're the lucky ones," Ruth said. "They know how to use their talents. Did you know Alison's been hired by International News to cover the games?"

"Is that so?" Tom said.

"And I don't think it was for her great skills as a reporter."

"I wouldn't know anything about that," he said, glancing at David.

"It doesn't exactly hurt to be gorgeous," said Helen. "I heard she's been hanging around with Lindbergh and his wife, who're over here as Hermann Göring's official guests. She was all tears and remorse when Brundage suspended her, and look at her now."

David practiced the shot put, his weakest skill, while Tom ran wind sprints.

"You chose the wrong event," Tom told him.

"How do you figure that?"

"All I have to do is run as fast as I can and make sure I don't drop the baton. You have to be good at ten different things."

Plus baby-sit some four-eyed child physics prodigy whom no one knows what to do with, David thought.

He perched the sixteen-pound ball against the crook of his neck and reared back on his right foot. He had pinned so much on this chance at the Olympics, he had put in so many overused pain-filled hours over so many years that the thought of having it all jeopardized by something on the outside that had nothing to do with him made him almost sick to his stomach.

He pushed forward and let the shot fly.

He saw Karl Linderhoff coming toward him from the far side of the field. With him were two other people—an older, balding man and a young woman. Karl had said last night he was going to try to bring his friend Miranda, and David had responded with a cautiously noncommittal "Very good. I'll look forward to meeting her." David liked Karl; he was a genuinely nice guy. He'd been friendly and easy to approach and thrilled that a member of the American team seemed interested in him and wanted to be his friend. David hated to be using him this way.

"David!" Karl called out in English. "Just where you said you'd be. And I see you've already worked up a sweat."

"Karl." He hefted the shot from hand to hand. "Maybe you can teach me how to throw this thing."

"May I present Dr. Abraham Behrman of the biochemistry section of the Kaiser Wilhelm Institute."

That sounded like a Jewish name, David thought. So they couldn't be treating the Jews as unfairly as some people said.

David extended his hand. The older man smiled and grasped it formally, bowing slightly as he did so.

Karl continued. "And Fräulein Miranda Wolff of the physics section."

David introduced Tom and the women runners.

With the introductions it had taken David a moment to focus on the particulars of Karl's female companion and have her register fully on his consciousness.

"Miranda, David is the American I've been telling you about," said Karl, "though his grandparents on his mother's side are from Württemberg."

David took the time to look closely at her. She had straw blond hair that swept down past her shoulders. She had enormous blue eyes, framed by long, delicate lashes, that reminded David of a clear sky at dusk. She had high cheekbones that were lightly freckled and a cute, perfect nose—also freckled—which turned up at just the right point. And when she smiled—a dazzling, radiant smile that lit up her face, that brought out her deep dimples and showed just the tiniest suggestion of gleaming white teeth between her sensual lips—David instantly decided he had never seen a more beguiling creature in his life.

She wasn't tall, but her legs were proportionally long and perfectly shaped. She was wearing a plain white pullover sweater and a simple navy blue skirt that came to just above her knees. Neither article fitted tightly, but both conformed to her slim figure as if they had been fashioned for no other purpose than to pay it homage. At the same time she wore her clothes artlessly and utterly without self-awareness, as if either she didn't know how she looked or the entire subject was too unimportant to be concerned with. There was something oddly touching about her only concession to decoration or vanity—a small, little girl's locket on a gold chain that hung down between her breasts, which were just prominent enough to show through the sweater.

"'Miranda,'" said David, trying bravely to be casual. "That must be an unusual name in Germany."

"She is an unusual young woman," offered Behrman.

"I think my parents fancied themselves quite literary and exotic in their younger days," Miranda sweetly explained. "They named me from *The Tempest*, though I'm afraid that's exactly what they've considered me ever since."

And suddenly David found himself washed up on Prospero's magic island.

Tom went off "to play with the girls." Since both he and Helen Stephens ran on their respective four-hundred- and hundred-meter-relay teams, he claimed to be obsessed with racing her "man to man." In fact, David suspected, she had become only the latest object of his fixation and his interest was more in the "man to woman" line. So far she had refused, protesting with her characteristic rural sweetness that she didn't want to embarrass him and make him doubt himself.

David spent the remaining hours of usable daylight practicing with Karl. To begin with, David hurled the shot and Karl measured the distance. Meanwhile, Miranda and Dr. Behrman sat a short distance away watching, he in a folding chair one of the ubiquitous Olympic aides had dutifully provided, she, childlike, next to him on the grass. She held herself up on one outstretched arm and hand, her feet tucked under her and the hem of her skirt raised midway up her smooth, bare thighs to protect it from staining. At one point David noticed she had taken off her flat single-strap shoes and was wriggling her toes around in the grass.

David wondered about Dr. Behrman's interest in observing their rudimentary practice. But he couldn't very long get his mind, or eyes, off Miranda.

"Try again," Karl called out. "Your rhythm is good. I think you'll get it this time."

David blinked for a moment and realized Karl was talking about the metal sphere he held in his hands. He stepped back to the starting spot, went into the crouch, cocked his right arm back, and pushed the shot forcefully off his palm.

"Not bad," Karl announced. "Almost thirteen meters."

Not good enough, David thought. No matter what he tried, he couldn't seem to get it. "You try it now," David said, walking toward him. "Let me watch how you do it."

Amiably the tall German took the ball from David. He walked over to the starting spot. David observed him carefully. Karl held the sphere in front of him with both hands, as if trying to sense the perfect equilibrium. Then he raised it to shoulder level, closed his eyes, and rubbed his cheek intimately against the smooth metal surface.

For a split second David felt an uncomfortable and embarrassing pang at the thought of the ball's being replaced by Miranda's cheek. He stole a glance over at their small audience. Dr. Behrman continued to watch the proceedings intently with apparent satisfaction. Miranda noticed David looking at her and instantly offered her enchanting child-woman smile.

Karl shifted his weight a few times, then set up for the release. He reared back, sighted down his left arm to his target area, pushed off with a grunt, and sent the sphere flying. He held himself in check at the end of his follow-through, watching to see where it would land.

"Fifteen-point-two-five meters!" David exclaimed. "That's incredible for your first throw, for any throw."

The German smiled modestly. Miranda, seeing David's reaction, broke into enthusiastic clapping. Dr. Behrman also looked highly pleased by what he had just seen.

"Where did you learn to throw like that?" David asked.

Karl shrugged. "I've been practicing."

* * *

The next event.

David scanned the perimeter of the Maifeld and approximated a course of four hundred meters. "Call it when you're ready," he said.

"You're the guest," said Karl, deferring.

"Okay. On your mark. Get set. Go."

They both took off, two highly conditioned bodies launching into action. On the basis of the less than ideal surface and the corners they would have to turn, David calculated the race would take a little more than a minute. He paced himself accordingly. He settled into a comfortable stride. He was sure Karl would do the same. The real competition would come in the last hundred fifty or two hundred meters. But as soon as the German was up into his full running stance, he broke forward into an all-out sprint. He quickly went several lengths in front of David.

He's going to be sorry he did that, David thought. *This is where our longer track and field experience and superior coaching really make the difference. I can teach him a few things about competitive strategy.*

Suddenly David had a pang of conscience as he ran. It was one thing to help a competitor from another country with technique. There you could only do so much. You either had it or you didn't. But strategy—that was something different. That could actually change the outcome. If he said anything, would he be giving another team an unnecessary leg up on his own people?

He thought about it for several seconds, breathing rhythmically with the regular cadence of his run. *Competition is one thing, but let's not forget the overall Olympic idea. If you believe it's worth participating at all, then you have to believe that the single most important reason is to use athletics to promote harmony and understanding. That's what the Olympics are all about. That's why the American boycott failed. That's why those kinds of movements will always fail.* If he could help someone else, then he ought to try, just as Karl was genuinely trying to help him with his own weaker skills. And anyway, on the basis of L.A., the Germans were absolutely no threat in the decathlon, much less anything else on the track and field side. *The whole world will be watching. Why not at least help them look respectable on their own turf?*

The course was half over when they reached the middle of the straightaway. By that point Karl was easily eight or nine lengths ahead. Now was the time to make a move. As nice a guy as Karl was, now was the time to make the German regret his show-off start and teach him something in the process.

David kicked hard and put on a burst of speed. Instantly the gap between him and Karl began to close. It was natural; he had kept it all in reserve and Karl had already used himself up.

But just as David caught up, Karl shot forward again.

David couldn't believe it. He poured it on, all he had, and got to within a length of Karl. He was really straining, but he was matching the German stride for stride.

Then, without so much as a glance in David's direction, Karl shot ahead once again. His strides were easy, regular. . . . Only they were fast as hell.

David felt a jab of panic in his gut, the kind he often got when he knew he had lost. Had he miscalculated, held too much back? No, he was running at top speed now, racing conditions, giving it all he had. And Karl was still lengthening the gap between them with every step.

There were only about fifty meters to go now, and Karl was moving at the same lightning pace he'd maintained the entire race. It defied logic. How could he have anything left? Even Jesse Owens didn't run that way, and he was a sprinter.

David pushed himself for all he was worth. He worked his arms as if to pull himself forward. He sucked in as much air as his lungs could hold and forced it all back out with every breath. Every muscle in his body strained against nature. He pushed the ground behind him faster and faster with every step.

Yet it wasn't enough.

Karl crossed the finish line a full ten meters ahead of him. David's chest was bursting from exertion. Karl looked as though he'd just finished a moderate-speed workout.

"That was a good race," he said. "You set a fine pace. But you shouldn't have let me win. It will only make me feel stupid when we get to the real competition and you show the crowd how you actually run."

They continued walking the edge of the Maifeld together.

"I didn't set any pace at all," David protested, breathing hard. "And I didn't—" He stopped himself for a moment. "I didn't purposely let you win. I'd never do that. You, uh, ran a smarter race than I did."

Karl looked at him not unkindly but skeptically. "No one runs a smarter race than the Americans. The whole world knows that."

That is true, damn it, David said to himself. *The Americans are supposed to be the decathlon champs. They dominate the sport. So what's going on here? Have I fallen off that much? Did I get that fat and lazy at Oxford that a second-level athlete from a second-level team can beat me without even breathing hard?*

But then he thought back to the Cambridge Invitational track meet the previous spring. He remembered it vividly. He and Karl had both run in the fifteen hundred meters. They'd drawn only one lane apart at the starting line. It had been a well-run race: good pace; perfect track conditions. He remembered thinking while they were running what a determined athlete this German fellow had been. A fierce competitor, like so many of his countrymen, never giving up, no matter what the odds. David could read it on his face as he passed him at about the eight-hundred-meter mark.

But pass him he did. He had passed Karl Linderhoff and all the others and gone on to win by ten meters. No matter what Karl would have done, no matter what strategy he would have used, no matter what pace he would have set, he hadn't had it in him to beat the field he was running against. He hadn't had the innate, natural ability to win against competition of that class.

That had been only six months ago. Yet today Karl had whipped him soundly.

Behrman and Miranda came over and joined the two athletes as they continued walking. The old biochemist had a look of pride and satisfaction on his face, as if Karl were his favorite son or he somehow shared in the younger man's victory. The young woman, beaming, threw both arms around her boyfriend and rested her head lightly on his shoulder as they walked.

Then she withdrew one arm and wrapped it around David's sweaty waist. He went momentarily rigid with the surprise of her touch. She must have sensed this because she smiled up at him and, still clutching Karl, pulled him in toward the two of them. The gesture was totally spontaneous, so full of naive charm and innocent affection that David suddenly felt himself jaded and unworthy and terribly old.

He cast a glance down in her direction, and his heart felt as though it were sinking into his gut. He had matched himself against

Karl twice today, and twice he had come off second best. He wasn't used to losing, and he couldn't deny it had shaken him.

Now he looked for a fraction of a second into the endless depth of Miranda's night blue eyes. Absolutely fetching, so completely full of life, she would be his next challenge.

And he didn't even dare stop and think to himself just exactly how he meant that.

EIGHT

Wednesday, July 29, Döberitz

"I'd like to see where you work," David had said to Karl at breakfast, trying to sound casual. "I've heard so much about the Kaiser Wilhelm Institute. It would mean a lot to say I'd been there."

"Then you'll come have lunch with me there this very day," Karl replied. "You can get there easily on the *U-bahn*, the underground train. Then afterward we'll both go over to the Reichssportfeld to practice again."

Like all the other athletes, even the native Berliners, Karl was living at the Olympic Village during the games. Because of the importance his country had placed on the competition, he had to report to his assignment at the Kaiser Wilhelm's biochemistry section only half a day for the duration. The rest of the time he was to concentrate on fulfilling the destiny of the German people.

"I must be off now," Karl said, rising from the table. "But remember, I'll expect you at the institute at noon sharp."

"Perfect," David said to him. *Perfect*, he said again to himself. All very easygoing. Like one of those new weekend get-togethers in the mountains where single people try to meet each other. Just make your plans openly over breakfast with whomever you want.

The ambience of the village and the atmosphere with which it was infused were helping him with his unwanted assignment. To be honest, David had to admit that the Olympic Village concept here did work amazingly well. The German hosts had proclaimed it a place where young men from all over the world would, for a few weeks, live communally and get to know and understand one another in a spirit of cooperation and respectful competition. The fact of the matter was that was exactly what was happening. Even though each team had its own assigned place in the dining room and its own national foods provided for it, one didn't have to stay there or limit oneself. On this particular morning, there were easily men from eight different countries at the table with David and Tom and Karl. Signs were posted of meeting times for athletes in the same event to get together and compare notes. Members of the German Olympic Committee were always around, arranging introductions between the various teams. Photographers constantly set up and snapped pictures of people who shared no common language practicing, playing, singing, and laughing together. Everybody was friendly and outgoing, ready to take you into his heart.

God, what Lorelei Bremmer must think of him. He'd managed to suppress that memory for a while. One way or another he was going to have a lot of amends to make when all the dust finally settled.

David went back to his room to study the package he'd received in the same post that had brought his letter of "congratulations." It was a physics textbook, sent in response to his request for the latest material available in a field which was not his.

Karl had told him to arrive at the Kaiser Wilhelm promptly at noon. David spent a good deal of time calculating the time it would take him to get there by the efficient German public transportation. Then, if he had figured it properly, he would just "happen" to get there a little bit early and have some time to spare.

By midmorning he was on his way down the winding path to the main gate. Not far from the dining hall he saw that a small crowd had gathered up ahead. He heard commotion. There seemed to be some jostling back and forth, as if a fight had broken out.

He got closer and saw three men struggling to hold a fourth. The man being held was thrashing around, cursing, and trying to free himself. Orders were being shouted in three or four languages.

David edged his way into the crowd. The screaming man was Horst Müller, the top German long-distance runner. He hadn't done very well in Los Angeles. But the rumors around the village were that he had a real shot against the Finns, who had dominated the five- and ten-thousand-meter events ever since the modern Olympics had been instituted.

Müller's eyes were bulging with a mixture of terror and rage. No matter what the other men did, they couldn't hold him still for long. Two more men grabbed him around the legs, and he still managed to thrash madly.

"What happened?" David asked.

"Don't know," someone in the crowd answered breathlessly. "He just . . . cracked. Someone crossed in front of him in line in the dining hall. That was all. No one else even noticed it. Suddenly he just went wild, crazy. I don't know what did it to him. Maybe the pressure."

David realized his own heart was pounding.

Together the men had managed to wrestle Müller to the ground and pin him there. Just then David saw Wolfgang Fürstner and two of his uniformed assistants running up the path from the administration building.

"Hold him there if you can," Fürstner ordered. His face was grave. "I've called for a doctor." He noticed David. "Keegan. What happened? Did you see it?"

David relayed the story he had just been told.

Fürstner shook his head in obvious shock and distress. "Nothing like this has happened here before. And now two incidents in less than a week!"

A doctor arrived on the scene. He knelt next to Müller and opened the small black satchel he carried with him. "Keep him as still as you can." The men holding Müller strained to comply. The doctor removed a large-bore syringe from his bag. He held it firmly, aimed it downward, then jabbed it straight through the athlete's pants leg, into the large muscle of his thigh. Müller bucked in protest. He grew suddenly rigid, convulsed; then, in a few moments, his body went slack and relaxed.

Tentatively the men holding him loosened their grips.

"It's all right," the doctor assured them. "He'll sleep now."

Fürstner studied him, lying peacefully on the ground. "Thank God. I thought we were going to have another situation like—like Rolf Schmidt. Such a pity, though," he said, shaking his head. "One of our top competitors. A very gifted young man." He turned to David. "I'm sorry this happened, and sorry you had to see it, especially with your experience with Schmidt last week. I promise we will make it up to you and your memories of Berlin all will be pleasant ones. I've called Security. They'll be along soon to take him." He shook his head sadly again. "I hope he is still able to compete. Such a pity. Perhaps it was the pressure."

Yes, the pressure, David thought. *The pressure. It's getting to all of us.*

Central Berlin

The headquarters of the Schutzstaffel, or SS as it was commonly known, was at 8 Prinz-Albrechtstrasse, not far from the park where Wilhelm Canaris rode every morning.

Whenever he could, Reinhard Heydrich spent his mornings at a different athletic pursuit.

After he had completed the day's initial round of paper work, when he was not otherwise engaged, Heydrich would repair to the gymnasium room in the building's subbasement for a vigorous work-out with the dueling foils. His opponent would be whoever volunteered. More often than not, however, a partner was not forthcoming and had to be recruited, for the *Obergruppenführer* had a fierce reputation as a swordsman and was widely known to prefer fencing with foils not covered with protective tips.

His opponent of the morning, a young intelligence adjutant called Helmut von Tannenberg, was just wiping the line of blood away from his jaw with a white cloth Heydrich had considerately provided, when the door to the room opened. Heydrich turned from the calm satisfaction of studying his handiwork to see who had the audacity to intrude upon his respite from the pressures of responsibility.

It was his secretary, Helene Siemons.

"If I might speak with you a moment, Obergruppenführer . . . Another incident has just been reported to this office by the assistant commandant of the Olympic Village," she stated. "I believed you would want to know about it."

Dahlem

The Kaiser Wilhelm Institute for the Advancement of the Sciences was built on a tract of rolling farmland the old emperor had donated in 1912 in an elegant suburb of Berlin. The organization had been set up the following year by Max Planck and Walther Nernst with the hope of attracting the top scientists available and placing a strong, confident Germany in the forefront of both theoretical and applied research. The minds working here today, they reasoned, would fuel the next generation of German industrial and technological progress. And so on, and so on. They succeeded beyond their loftiest expectations, beginning with their recruitment of a chief for the physics section, a man already acknowledged as the greatest theoretical physicist in the world: Albert Einstein.

The World War had robbed Germany of its confidence, and the new regime dedicated to restoring it had robbed it of Einstein and many of his colleagues, but the Kaiser Wilhelm Institute continued to exert its incredible influence over the entire range of scientific investigation.

The main building was a strange agglomeration of architecture. It was three stories high with a sloping roof that went up one story more. The traditionally styled brick facade was interrupted by a classical Greek pediment supported by four false columns. A large round tower rising from the right corner of the building was capped by a conical, pointed dome that resembled—unintentionally, David supposed—the kaiser's famous helmet.

As David approached the institute on his way from the *U-bahn* station, he felt as if he were making his first pilgrimage to a shrine. This place was already legendary. In so many fields this was where the new ground was being broken every day.

He was still shaken by what he'd witnessed at the Olympic Village. He couldn't get the image of the wild-eyed Müller out of his mind during the entire train ride. But he had a job to do here now, so he would have to try.

As he'd planned, he arrived at Dahlem forty-five minutes "too early" for his appointment with Karl. He presented himself at the guard station in the lobby. A uniformed guard checked his name on a list, then handed him a badge, with his own name typed out and Karl's name as sponsor. "You will please wear this at all times in the institute. It is valid until August fourteenth. You will surrender it at that time." He pointed to a logbook lying on the counter. "Please sign in here."

As soon as David was out of the guard's view, he followed the signs to the physics section. He walked briskly, yet deliberately enough to observe the names on the closed office doors and the occupants beyond the opened ones.

There was Otto Hahn's office and laboratory on the left. David stopped and peered through the opened doorway. The professor was standing over one of his radiochemistry worktables, holding an instrument that looked like a pair of forceps. He was gray-haired, with strong features, large, slightly protruding ears, and a full gray mustache. Rutherford had worked with him in Montreal and thought the world of him. But those in a position to know seemed to think there was a potentially more important prize right here on this floor. David took a deep breath and continued walking.

Miranda Wolff was in her office, a tiny cubicle near the end of the corridor. She was sitting at her desk, hunched forward, with her palms together, clasped tightly between her thighs. Her eyebrows were deeply knit, and her lips pursed, as she studied a sheet of paper flat on the desk. From time to time she raised one of her hands to brush a wisp of blond hair out of her face, then immediately returned the hand to where the other remained. She looked for all the world like a little girl concentrating on some impossible homework problem.

He knocked on the open door. Miranda looked up, startled. "Oh, hello," she said, and broke out into a dimpled smile. She self-consciously withdrew her hands from between her legs. David pretended not to notice.

Summoning all his studied and well-rehearsed casualness, he said, "Hi. I came to meet Karl for . . . and I hope, you, ah, too, for lunch. I, ah, wanted to leave myself plenty of time, but I guess I left too much. Your public transport is much more efficient than . . . So I thought I'd look around . . . and I'd, uh, look you up since I had the time."

All right, don't overdo it. Keep it real.

"I'm very happy to see you, David," Miranda said. "And happy you came to see me. Please come in." She motioned with her hand, then with her eyes seemed to apologize for the fact that there wasn't much to come in to. There was a brief moment of awkwardness. "Perhaps we should go out and walk instead," she suggested.

Perfect, David thought again. *If we're seen walking together out in the open, there's a presumption of innocence. God, I'm already thinking like a spy*, he said to himself. In a perverse way he found it rather appealing. There was a comforting unreality about it, almost like some complex and extended game. "I don't want to take you from your work," he said.

"Don't worry." She smiled.

She stood up, grabbed her handbag, then led him out of the building and down into the park behind it. It was a beautiful place and reminded David of the equally beautiful backways of the Olympic

Village. Germany was a very easy country to fall in love with. He glanced over at Miranda walking beside him. And so were its people.

"I enjoyed seeing you practice your sport the other day," she said, her hands clasped in front of her like a schoolgirl.

"Thanks. I'm afraid I wasn't much more than a pacesetter for Karl."

"Karl thinks very well of you. He likes you so much."

David loved the way she walked.

"Quite clearly you are the one Karl thinks the world of," he said to her.

Miranda wrinkled her perfect little nose in reaction. "He doesn't always act like it," she confided sadly, "especially these last few weeks. He loses his patience with me all the time. That never used to happen before." She looked up at David with her big, imploring eyes. "Often, now, he acts as though he wished I weren't around."

"It must be the Olympic fever."

"He's been in the Olympics before. I was only sixteen during the last ones, and I didn't know Karl then. But I wonder if he was like this." She sounded genuinely distressed. On the other hand, twenty-year-olds, especially beautiful ones, think the world revolves around them, and any slight or hurt becomes a major emotional crisis. The beautiful, impassioned, unbearable image of Ali on the night of their parting took hold in David's mind.

"It's different this time," David said. "You all are the hosts instead of us, and you're putting on the largest and most spectacular games in modern history. It's perfectly natural that the pressure should get to him a little bit."

The pressure. Yes, the pressure. Suddenly David thought again of Rolf Schmidt upsetting the chessboard, of Horst Müller thrashing on the ground, and his blood froze. Miranda stopped walking and looked at him apprehensively, as if she were afraid she'd said something wrong.

He diffused her concern with a smile. "The older gentleman with you the other day . . . Dr. . . ."

"Dr. Behrman. Abraham Behrman." Miranda's eyes lit up. "Yes, what a dear, sweet man he is. So gentle and kind. Like a wise old grandfather."

David started fishing. "From the looks of things, Karl isn't the only one to be quite fond of you."

"Yes, I love him very much. He always has time for me whenever I want to talk, no matter how busy he is."

David watched the play of her sparkling eyes reflecting the sun and couldn't imagine anyone ever turning her away, even if the führer himself were on the phone.

"He is a very important man around here." She continued, gesturing back toward the building as if to underscore the point. "I think he's very important everywhere."

"What exactly does he work on?"

"Growing, I think."

"Growing?"

"I'm not sure exactly. I don't know too much about biology. But he's been trying to find out why people like dwarfs and midgets don't grow up right and why other people grow to be seven feet tall. It is involved with the hormones, I think he said."

"Yes, that would make sense."

"So, can you imagine all the good it's going to do for the world if he finds what he's looking for?" she asked excitedly. "All those poor unfortunate people God has turned his back on will be helped."

"I was kind of surprised to see him at the sports field watching Karl."

"I was, too," Miranda admitted. "I didn't know he was interested in sports. Maybe he was just going along for Karl's sake, to give him support. He's very sensitive that way."

"Then you know him through Karl?"

It only took a subtle shaking of her head to make her blond mane cascade about her face and shoulders. "No, it's the other way around, actually. Dr. Behrman is close friends with my director, Dr. Otto Hahn, and with Dr. Leo Szilard, my teacher at the university. So I suppose he took an interest in me because of that." She lowered her eyes demurely but then allowed herself a mischievous grin. "At least at first it must have been."

"And Karl?"

"Karl I met through my best friend, Karen Hagemann. Karen and I grew up together, and Karl's family moved next door to her. As you know, Karl is in the Wehrmacht—the army. He has a very good position, I think. He came to visit me here one day when he had leave, to pick me up after work, and I introduced him to Dr. Behrman. Dr. Behrman liked Karl immediately. Everyone does. He's just that way, you see, which is why I find so troubling how he is acting lately toward me."

David began idly wondering if they'd slept together. No, probably not, a girl from that background. Well, maybe. *She is supposed to be independent and modern, and Karl says her parents think she's headstrong and rebellious. She wants to have done it. Yes. She could have. But her eyes say no.* He tried to put the entire irrational consideration out of his head before it drove him crazy.

"So Dr. Behrman asked me about him, what he did. And then the next thing I knew, Karl told me he had been . . . what do you call it, lent by the army?"

"Detailed," David offered.

"That's right. He had been detailed to work for Dr. Behrman here at the Kaiser Wilhelm."

"Interesting."

"Yes. It made me very happy. Now I get to see him every day. At least I did until these Olympics got started." She pouted, but her pout didn't stay for long.

David fought with himself not to come on too strong. "Did Dr. Behrman mention anything to you about why he wanted Karl to work in his lab?" He wasn't sure he was succeeding.

Miranda considered the question for a moment. "No, I don't think so. Just that he had been looking for someone like Karl a long time."

"Does Karl enjoy working here? Other than the obvious advantage of being able to see you anytime he wants?"

"I think he does. Yes, very much. He says that Dr. Behrman is doing very important work, which will be a source of glory for the entire country in the years to come, and that he feels proud to be having a small part in it. It will be good for his military career. And I am very happy for him, especially since I had a little part in making it happen."

"More than a little, I'd say." Karl Linderhoff was a very lucky man, no doubt about that.

David had steered the conversation carefully, planning and pacing each step as he would a race. "Well, enough about Karl and his work. Tell me about yourself and what you do."

She looked at him helplessly and shrugged again. "I was born in Heidelberg and lived there till my father got his position in Berlin. I went to school, and now I work here. I live at home with my parents. I don't think there's anything to tell."

Other than the fact that you are reputed to be brilliant, and I can see for myself that you are blond and willowy and dazzlingly beautiful, that you combine your sweet innocence with a deeply powerful sensuality that even now makes me want you as I have never wanted another woman before you, in spite of my growing bond with your friend and the false pretenses under which I sit here, that makes you embody and personify for me as nothing else can the vibrant and exciting and passionate spirit of the new Germany that everyone here keeps talking about. . . . But these are not things that would occur to you, my dear. And that in itself is part of your fascination and charm.

"I'm, ah, sure there's a lot to tell." David groped for words. "Especially working at a place like this. I'm sure I wouldn't understand it, but I'd be fascinated to know what you do."

She had stopped and stooped to pick a yellow flower that particularly interested her. She held it in front of her with both hands as they continued strolling. She peered down intently at the petals, as if trying to discern their internal structure. He would have loved to know what she was thinking.

"I try to figure out how nuclei of atoms are put together and what would happen if they came apart," she said simply, almost reading his thoughts.

Then she turned and walked in the direction of a massive old oak tree. It was almost completely dead. Its branches were gnarled and twisted and there was a gaping, rotted-out cavity in its trunk.

"Doesn't this tree look like an old man?" she commented. "An old scientist, maybe. I've always loved it, ever since I first came here. Those two knots are his eyes, and that big hole is his mouth. To me, everything in nature has a personality. My job is to find out as many of those personalities as I can."

"That's all?" He gently prodded her. "What were you doing when I interrupted you?"

Miranda's eyes brightened, and she grew even more animated. Suddenly, subtly the child before him had transformed into an adult; more than that, into something ageless and wise beyond human experience. Still holding the flower, she clasped her hands behind her. This had the effect of innocently thrusting out her breasts and giving an exuberant bounce to her stride.

"Well, it just seems to me," she began, "that the breakup of some of these atoms may be triggered by the same particles that they, in turn, emit when they disintegrate. Now, if these disintegrations produce more than one of the triggering particles, a chain reaction is clearly possible. Of course, you'd have to choose your atom very carefully. Some elements have particular isotopes that give off radioactivity and some that don't. Most atoms would be too stable. But if you could get the right atom into the proper unstable state and shoot this other particle at it, we can easily imagine how much heat, how much energy would be released each time. In fact, we can calculate it. Here, I'll give you an example," she said.

She handed him the flower, then reached into her handbag and pulled out a small notebook and pencil. "I carry this with me wherever I am," she explained, "in case I have an idea." Then, with her tongue pressed between her teeth in concentration, she proceeded to write down a set of equations on the notebook page.

David studied them, long enough the commit them to memory for later analysis. They were neat and elegant, symbolic mathematical representations of a world of scientific magic that only she could see. "What's to stop this chain reaction?" he asked.

"Maybe it's when you exhaust the target material. Or"—she held up her finger—"maybe it's not until you use up all the atoms in the entire universe." She turned to him and smiled enigmatically. "It's one of the great mysteries of existence."

He needed to learn more, but seeing her handiwork in front of him, he could already tell that Hargreaves was right. She was the real thing. Her mind was a prize beyond any calculation. "That's fascinating," he said to her.

"I'm glad you think so," she replied, putting the notebook away.

"By the way, I've wanted to ask you: Didn't Einstein work here?"

"Yes, that's right. He was the first director of the physics section."

"Did you know him?"

"No, he left long before I came here."

He took a chance. "I wonder why. Did it have anything to do with his being Jewish?"

He held his breath, waiting for her reply. When it came, she was completely relaxed and natural. The ageless seer was gone, and the child-woman had returned in her place. "I wouldn't know much about that."

Central Berlin

When Wolfgang Fürstner arrived at Prinz-Albrechtstrasse, Frau Siemons directed him right into Heydrich's office. Ordinarily the

Reich security chief preferred to have his visitors wait awhile in his reception room, absorbing the "ambience" of his ever-widening domain, so that by the time he was ready to see them, the strategic advantage, as he called it, was already with him.

But the nature of his business with Fürstner did not allow such luxury. Today he would have to gain the advantage by sheer force of personality. Never mind, though. As always, Reinhard Heydrich was up to the challenge.

"Heil Hitler." Fürstner greeted him as he stepped with military bearing up to the desk.

Heydrich stood and thrust his hand up vaguely in return of the salute. "It was good of you to come see me so promptly," he said with his usual icy civility. "Please sit down and make yourself comfortable."

Fürstner rested his cap on his crossed knees.

Heydrich riveted him in place with his piercing gaze. "Captain, as chief of the Berlin Gestapo, I am most concerned about the incident this morning involving one of our runners."

"As are we all at the Olympic Village. It was most regrettable. We are striving to make an excellent impression on our guests, in accordance with the führer's inspiration and orders. And I know that I speak for Kommandant von und zu Gilsa as well as myself in saying that we deeply regret that anyone had to witness this unfortunate display."

"Yes, yes, of course," Heydrich responded, apparently busying himself with a file on his desk. "In that regard I understand you were the first German official on the scene."

"Yes, that's right."

"Do you think you could provide me with a list of those individuals who either witnessed or participated in the incident this morning?" Despite the grammatical form, it was not a request.

"I'm sure I could do that," Fürstner stated.

Heydrich nodded and offered his brittle smile. "I was sure you could as well. Now, the most important message I want to leave you with is as follows: "If this, or anything like it happens again during the games—"

"I do not anticipate that it will, Obergruppenführer," Fürstner assured him.

Heydrich's thin lips drew tightly across his mouth. "If it should,

Captain, I wish to be informed personally. Do you understand what I am saying to you?"

Fürstner nodded tensely.

"Any time of day or night, it doesn't matter. My secretary has been instructed to give you direct telephone numbers where I can be reached. Furthermore, the details of any future incident—should it occur—are to be contained and any witnesses are to be questioned immediately."

"I understand, Obergruppenführer."

"We are both professional soldiers, Captain Fürstner, and let us be plain with each other. Our athletes are not simply individual competitors trying to do their best in their respective categories. Each one of them—man or woman—is a single combat warrior for the fatherland, and the Reichssportfeld is the no-man's-land between the nations."

Fürstner returned his gaze and swallowed hard. "I understand, Obergruppenführer."

Heydrich maintained the intensity of his scrutiny as he spoke. "We have had two incidents since the Olympic Village opened. That is two incidents too many. And I must tell you, the Reich regards this matter with the utmost seriousness."

And it was already well established throughout the Reich that what Reinhard Heydrich considered with utmost seriousness quickly became a serious matter indeed.

NINE

Grunewald

From the new Olympiastadion _U-bahn_ station, Karl and David walked down the stately Olympischer Platz, past teams of workmen putting the finishing touches on the double avenue of flagpoles that would provide a dramatic approach to the sports field site.

"My stuff is in a locker on the north side of the stadium," David said. "Opposite the pool. We can cut across through it."

The Schwimmstadion adjoined the main stadium on the north side. As the two men crossed onto the deck area, the diving tower stood directly before them, cutting across the sky, six stories high, a series of concrete shelves projecting from an ultramodern glass elevator tube. David had never seen anything like it. At the other end of the deck from the tower, monumental flights of steps led down to water level, where they were lapped by the gentle pool currents. The scale was incredible, and the setting was impressive. It almost looked to David like photos he'd seen of the Oberammergau Passion play. Altogether the swimming complex looked like a stage for some grand aquatic drama.

A fair number of people were in the water, taking advantage of the warm weather. In the half of the pool roped off for practice laps, David noticed the red, white, and blue suits of the American women. He squinted into the glare of the water's surface. He recognized Eleanor Holm and—

He stopped. An electric surge jolted through his body. He caught Karl by the arm. "Hold on a minute. You're about to see something you'll never forget."

As they stood on the deck watching, Ali Prescott glided swiftly from one end of the pool to the other. Her path was absolutely straight, as if she were guided by some primeval homing instinct. Her long, slender arms continuously reached above her head to pull her through the water, and her legs maintained an even kick that was both elegant and erotic. A clear, straight wake followed her progress like a royal train, moving out in perfect symmetry until it had dissolved into nothing but rivulets by the time they reached the sides of the pool. When she reached the end of the swimming lane, she flipped over into a reverse of her direction, as if by magic, all in one lithe, seamless motion. Like the best of natural athletes, she made the expenditure of so much energy look both effortless and spontaneous.

In the last four years there were a lot of things about Ali that David had not been able to put out of his mind. But there were other things that no one who had seen her in the last Olympics in Los Angeles would ever be able to forget. What Jesse Owens was to the poetry of the track, Alison Welles Prescott was to the ballet of the pool.

Here in Berlin in 1936 she was no longer nineteen, but she was still very much her own woman. That was what had gotten her into trouble with Brundage. David watched in rapt fascination the rehearsal for a performance that would never take place.

She completed her last lap, then stood in the shallow end of the pool and climbed slowly up the stairs like Venus rising from the sea. The collaboration of water and the newly emerged sun made her whole body glisten, a body that was made for swimsuits. She pulled off her swimming cap and shook out her golden brown hair. She sexily wriggled her shoulders and hips as silvery droplets of water flew in every direction.

Then she noticed David, and their eyes met and locked.

From the very first David had found her tremendously exciting to look at, in the water or out of it. And now, four years later, he found the sensation in no way diminished. Maybe she would take his mind off the Miranda problem. No, that wasn't the way it usually worked. Especially not during training. More likely it would only recall what they had been to each other during the last games. Each of them had intensified the obsessions of the other, like two tuning forks vibrating precisely in phase.

And his relationship with Ali had been quite different from what he had been asked to do with Miranda. Anyway, the comparison between the two women really wasn't fair. It was like comparing the old apples and oranges or "before" and "after" photographs. Because if Miranda was just now poised on that tantalizing frontier between adolescence and womanhood, Ali had firmly and long ago set out her own territory in the new world.

She sauntered over in his direction, still dripping onto the concrete deck. It was one of his most primal images of her, and he found it incredibly sexy.

"Hello, David," she said quietly.

"Hi, Ali," he replied, trying to keep the trembling of his body from betraying him.

"Long time, huh?"

He nodded. "Real long time."

"Lotta water under the bridge."

He watched her drip.

She took both his hands in hers and slowly planted a firm kiss on his lips. David savored the sensation of her wet nose against his.

"How's our Oxford soldier boy?" she asked.

"Fair to middling," he said. He couldn't believe she was finally standing in front of him again, face-to-face. Alison Prescott, the motivating spirit of his young manhood, wild and flamboyant and full of life. Ali Prescott, who was just the other side of dangerous. The kind of girl you dream about, especially during four years' worth of long, lonely nights at West Point.

"You look good," he said, and felt the words failing him. "What am I talking about? You look great."

"Thanks. You don't look so bad yourself." She flashed him that dazzling smile that momentarily erased the past four years of his life.

"Ali, I wanted to tell you yet how sorry I am to hear about what happened. I really mean it. After what you did in L.A., you'd have been a shoo-in for the gold here."

"I've got nothing to prove," she retorted. "And now I'm getting paid for being here. I don't know if you heard I got a job."

"I did. And I also saw a picture of you in yesterday's _Berliner Tageblatt_. At Hermann Göring's house with Lucky Lindy."

"Lindbergh's sweet. So handsome and so shy. The opposite of Göring. The air marshal's like a great teddy bear. Fascinating man and absolutely charming."

David felt instantly jealous. What other woman could make him envy Charles Lindbergh and Hermann Göring in the same breath?

"Tough life." He sighed. "DANCING TILL DAWN, I think the head-line said."

"Not quite dawn," Alison pointed out slyly. "About two A.M. they all decided they wanted to see me swim."

David suddenly realized he had forgotten Karl standing next to him. Or at least, he had been. David turned his head to see. Karl was standing several paces back, looking pale and nervous. Miss Prescott really did have an incredible effect on men, if that was what it was.

David called him over. "Ali, this is Karl Linderhoff, who's doing the decathlon for the Germans."

Ali flashed the famous smile. "Hey, you're cute, too," she cooed, stroking her hands along Karl's forearm. "Maybe I'll marry you and swim for the Germans."

Karl forced a smile but seemed strangely rigid. Women like Ali could be very intimidating.

Then David remembered what Miranda had said: "Often, now, he acts as though he wishes I weren't around. That never used to happen before."

Or was it just the stress of training?

Ali was huddling herself tightly to keep from getting chilled. "I'd better get out of this wet suit," she said.

"Yeah, you'd better. You don't want to catch cold." There was an awkward pause. What he'd wanted to be was caring and protective and gentlemanly, to say that he bore her nothing but the best feelings and that the memory of their time together was precious to him. Instead, he sounded to himself hollow and self-serving and forced.

The fact of the matter was that on every level women like Ali could take care of themselves. They related to men, but they didn't depend on them. Alison Welles Prescott didn't depend on anyone but herself. And both of them knew it. Both of them had always known it.

She was standing there shivering, but he didn't want to let her go.

"I was thinking maybe I ought to do a story on you now that I'm a journalist," she said. "It's a natural, with all your credentials and as cute as you still are." She touched the side of his face with her wet palm. "We'll have to get together so I can interview you."

"I'll be seeing you around, then," David said, trying to be as cool as he could.

"You can count on it, soldier," Ali replied, the delicious promise implicit in her fiery eyes.

She gave him a sort of mock salute, the kind you might see in a production number from a Busby Berkeley film, then headed off—still dripping slightly—in the direction of the women's locker room. David watched her from behind, in subtle and alluring detail—the provocative lilt of her walk, the way her hips moved from side to side above her finely muscled legs—just as he had watched her four years before, just as he had watched Miranda an hour or so ago. That was the problem with being in training. It made you obsess.

He turned back to look at the huge swimming pool. The afternoon sun was knifing through the gentle ripples, glinting off the bodies of the swimmers still doing laps. Then he turned toward Karl, who remained standing several paces off. Ali had inspired him.

"What do you say we take a swim ourselves before we start practicing? I could stand some loosening up before we start running hard, and that water sure looks inviting."

Karl held up his Wehrmacht equipment bag with an apologetic shrug. "I'm sorry, I didn't bring my suit."

"That's okay. I know they have suits we can borrow. And towels. I checked. You, of all people, should know that no detail gets past the Germans."

"Well, if you want to, I suppose we could go in for a little while." But he seemed to be straining for air. Sweat had beaded on his forehead.

"Karl, are you all right?" David asked.

"Yes, fine. Let's go."

"Are you sure?"

"Yes. Let's go."

They were alone in the locker room. David had hung his clothes in the locker and was just about to pull on his trunks. Karl still sat naked on the narrow wooden bench. David noticed a freshly healed cut about two inches long on the edge of his hip, just where it joined the buttock. It seemed a strange place to find a wound. He was going to ask if it was a Prussian dueling scar, but in view of its placement, he wasn't sure Karl would find the humor.

"I'm sorry. I can't do it. I can't go through with it," the German said with resignation.

David's fist closed instinctively, crumpling his trunks into a little ball. He looked down at Karl with concern. "What are you talking about?"

"I can't swim," he declared.

David was incredulous. "You don't know how?"

"I do know how. I learned when I was a child, like everyone else in Germany; the States, too, I suppose. I just can't do it. I thought that I would be able to bring myself to do it . . . here, with you. I thought that whatever my fear, some sort of pride would take over that would not allow me to shame myself in front of you. But I can't go through with it."

"Why, Karl?"

"I'm frightened—no, that is the wrong word. I am terrified of the water. I always have been, ever since I can remember." He continued to look down, hands clasped in front of him, arms resting on his knees.

Finally he looked up with pleading eyes. "No one else knows this, David." He glanced furtively down the aisle, to make sure no one else was listening. Then his eyes returned to the floor.

"It's—it's nothing to be ashamed of," David said. "We all have our demons to face. I'm not crazy about heights. The first time I had to jump with a parachute, I thought I was going to have a heart attack."

"But you can control it. This is irrational, I know. It is something every child can do. But it is beyond my power to control." He pounded one fist into the other. "I am weak. It is a flaw in my character. The führer has taught us from the beginning that we can triumph over any obstacle, any adversity simply by the rigid assertion of the will. This holds true for any German citizen."

"Karl, I think you're making too much out of this," David counseled him. He didn't know what else to say.

"And I am not merely any German citizen. I am an Olympic athlete, carefully chosen and rigorously trained, charged with the sacred duty of representing my country."

"And you're going to represent it pretty damn well, from everything I've seen so far."

Karl wrung his hands between his knees. "I am an officer in the Wehrmacht. I have been trained to suppress my fears, to overcome them through the triumph of my will." When he looked up, there were tears in his eyes.

He ran his hand anxiously through his hair. David noticed small tufts clinging between his fingers. David tried to look closer. There were thinning patches all over his scalp. Had Karl put himself under such stress that his hair was falling out?

David sat down next to him on the bench and looked into Karl's eyes. He wanted to say something, to reach out to him, somehow to show that he cared. He wanted to let Karl know that he understood, that there was no difference between them so great that it could not be bridged. Beneath him, the edge of the narrow bench dug uncomfortably into his bare buttocks. It was as if the stripping off of clothing had also somehow removed a last protective layer of inhibition, as if this exposure had laid bare not just his body but his identity as well.

He felt suddenly very vulnerable, for himself, for the two of them together, for what they had already become to each other and what violence might be done to that in the coming days.

They sat silently, naked and alone, for several minutes. Then David stood up and tossed his swimming trunks back into the locker. "Forget about all this," he said, trying to sound upbeat. "Let's go do some running." He grabbed Karl heartily by the arm. His hand grazed along the angle of the elbow. Instead of being rough and bumpy, it was velvety smooth. "Smooth as a baby's ass," his father would have said.

David took a closer look. Altogether Karl had the smoothest skin he had ever seen on a grown man.

He had not looked up, nor did he move from his fixed position on the bench. David sat down again, and this time he put his hand on his friend's smooth bare shoulder. "Karl," he said softly, "whatever they've taught you, whatever miracles you've accomplished, none of us can be a superman."

TEN

The Tiergarten

"Do we have to send you a bloody telegram before you'll get in touch with us?" Arthur Hargreaves demanded as they walked along one of the many pleasant, tree-shaded gravel paths of the Tiergarten. "I didn't relish the idea of sending you a letter and having it sit in your mailbox until you picked it up. You knew the signal. Why didn't you use it?"

"I thought it was supposed to be for me to contact you when I wanted," David replied.

"That's right," said Hargreaves with annoyance. "So why hadn't we heard from you yet?"

"I had nothing to report," David said, and continued walking.

Ahead, children ran and played, mothers pushed prams and strollers, young couples walked hand in hand, all taking advantage of the splendid August weather, so welcome after the stretch of unseasonable cold and dampness.

Hargreaves caught up with him. "Have you made contact with Miranda Wolff?" he demanded.

"Yes." David thrust his hands into his pockets as he walked.

"And?"

"And nothing. I'm still working on it. I told you that already."

"Is the boyfriend turning out to be a problem?"

"No, not at all. He's a terrific guy."

"You've been able to maintain his trust?"

"Yes."

"Good, that's the way it seemed to us, but I'm relieved hearing it directly from you."

David felt a sudden chill as he thought of himself constantly on display. Whoever was checking his orange juice each morning was not being idle the rest of the day.

Hargreaves knelt to retrieve a child's wooden top that had spun out of control and into the side of his foot. A young boy in shorts with reddish blond hair ran over after it. He smiled and bowed from the waist as the Englishman placed the toy back in his outstretched palm. Hargreaves turned back to David. "Well, then, what's she like?"

"She's very unusual."

"We know that. It's why we're interested in her."

"She's not like anyone I've ever met."

"How is she different?" Hargreaves pressed him. "Please be more specific."

How specific could he be in terms that would mean anything to Hargreaves? Would he understand if David talked about that certain selective naïveté mixed together with a strange worldliness, an élan and freshness of spirit which he himself no longer possessed, if in fact he ever had? Or was he simply interested in knowing whether her grasp of atomistics was as advanced and strategically "useful" as his scientific brethren had supposed?

After a moment David simply said, "She's totally wrapped up in her work."

"Yes, of course. We knew that as well. But as far as—"

"I don't mean just putting down equations on paper and solving mathematical problems. I mean . . . in the truth and beauty of it. That's all."

Hargreaves ruminated on this soberly, nodding his head slightly as he did. "Yes, yes. I believe I see what you're saying. I would very much like to have her."

"So would I," David said.

Hargreaves regarded him with the mixture of disdain and mirth reserved for those who cannot seem to manage to keep their business and personal lives straight. "We have no objection. We're interested in only one aspect of this little drama. So there's nothing stopping you."

At least nothing you would understand, thought David.

They continued up the path to the wide, tree-shaded goldfish pond. David watched the fat, well-fed goldfish darting up to kiss the murky surface of the water.

Hargreaves came up behind him. "Well, I'm gratified things are going so swimmingly between you," he said. "Have you made your determination yet?"

"Not completely," David responded. "I'm still just getting to know her. There are a lot of things I still don't understand."

"We're all in the same boat, I'm afraid. Look, I don't want to tell you how to do your job—"

"Your job." David corrected him. He quickened his pace.

"Whatever." Hargreaves kept up with him. "At any rate I need not remind you that we are in something of a time-critical situation. Once the Olympics are over, you lose your cover for being here."

"It's not a cover," David said sharply. "I need not remind *you* that *I'm* here legitimately."

"Which is one of the reasons you're so valuable to us," Hargreaves allowed. "But please keep in mind, if you haven't been able to do anything by the time your franchise is over, we will have to make other arrangements."

"What are you talking about?"

Hargreaves shrugged, suddenly playing coy. "If, by the time you're to leave, you've not determined her strategic value, then we must assume the worst—or best, depending upon your definition— and take appropriate, albeit extreme, measures on our own."

David's eyes grew wide with outrage. "You're out of your minds! All of you! How can you even be thinking that?"

"We're none of us children here." The Englishman laid his hand flat against a stout white oak, almost leaning against it, as if he were using the tree's solidity to bolster his own impact. "You know, Keegan, aside from everything else I told you back at the embassy about understanding science and speaking fluent German and being in the Army, there was another reason we selected you."

"And what might that be?" David asked resentfully.

"That you are now an Oxford man."

"Oh, come on now."

"And all that that conveys. We thought—we hoped you were one of us. That you valued our way of life and would know instinctively that there is always a price to be paid to preserve it."

"You're the one talking about appropriate measures, not I."

"Look, I'm not happy about this either. I just want to get back to Cambridge and the lab. But we all give king and country what's expected of us. And in this one we're on the same side. So then, when do you plan on going the rest of the way?"

"What's that supposed to mean?"

"Anything you like," said Hargreaves with plain annoyance. "Just answer the question."

David spun around to face him. "I don't know," he said angrily. "When the time seems right. When I get her drunk. When we share some quiet moment together and the music is just perfect. What do you want from me? I just met her."

"We have only a couple of weeks at best," Hargreaves said tersely.

"What you want is miracles. And I'm afraid I can't deliver."

Hargreaves shifted tone again. "Where's that celebrated American confidence and pluckiness of spirit we keep hearing so much about on our side of the pond? You're a boy. She's a girl. Et cetera, et cetera. Use your imagination."

"Your persistence is getting tiresome," said David.

Hargreaves put his hands up in front of him and scowled. "So sorry, old stick. Quite right you are. Above all else, we wouldn't want to be tiresome now, would we?"

David felt his anger grow to the flash point again. "Just lay off me, okay? I've got enough problems of my own without yours."

"Yes, I keep forgetting. I shouldn't be distracting you with all this state security stuff. You've got your precious running and jumping and hurling and whatever all else you do to think about. And you're worried about the Olympics."

David stopped abruptly. "I am actually."

"How do you mean?"

"I don't know. There's something strange going on."

"Strange? How so?"

"The German athletes. I've been watching them. They're good this time. Very good."

"That's very inspiring. They say they've been working hard. I gather they made a rather dismal show of it in Los Angeles four years ago. And it's logical that they'd want to come off well in their own games."

"It's more than that," David said. "I've run against a lot of them before. Man for man, they're going beyond their abilities."

"What about Karl Linderhoff?"

"Him, too. When you first mentioned his name to me and asked if I remembered him, I said I did. I remembered *beating* him."

"Yes, I recall that," the Englishman said.

David looked at him straight on. "Well, I can't beat him any longer."

"You can't? Yes, I see what you're saying." Hargreaves stroked his chin as he walked, then stuck his finger up in the air in front of him, as if he'd just thought of something. "I guess you're going to have to practice more, aren't you?"

"Don't you see? It's not just me. There's been an unexplained death at the village. Someone else has gone berserk."

"Lamentable. I grant you that. But not our problem. You can't worry about the whole world. Now, let's talk a bit more about Miranda."

David sighed in frustration. "There's nothing more to say."

"Ah, but there is," said Hargreaves, suddenly much more agreeable. "I don't want you to think we're placing the whole thing on your admittedly athletic shoulders without giving you any support."

"What are you talking about?" asked David, still annoyed.

Hargreaves reached into the pocket of his suit jacket and produced a small envelope. "Monday evening's program of the Berlin Philharmonic. Wilhelm Furtwängler's going to be conducting an all-Beethoven program. Tickets are impossible to come by. People will kill for them. No one would turn down your invitation. You've got three here—best seats in the house—but you're going to be using only two as it turns out. Something's going to come up unexpectedly at the last minute for the third member of your party."

Hargreaves noticed David's reaction. "Not to worry, old chap. Nothing sinister, if that's what you're thinking."

"I still don't know what you're talking about," David complained.

"We feel badly about the burden we've asked you to take on, and we want to try to make it up to you."

"I'll bet you do," said David.

"Just to help you break the ice. We think you should get out more," Hargreaves said, "and I know you're shy, so we've arranged for you to have a little date."

Dahlem

"I don't like the looks of this," Abraham Behrman announced. He ran his fingers through his thinning white hair. "Switch off the lights, please."

Rudolf Kiesel walked over to the switch by the door.

Behrman flicked on the tiny bulb of his ophthalmoscope, bent over, and held it up to Horst Müller's eye. The athlete, strapped down on the examining table, jerked his head reflexively at the intrusive brightness.

Behrman squinted intently into the instrument for several seconds. "Heightened visual sensitivity commensurate with marked hypertrophy of the optic nerve. We'll have the lights again." The younger man dutifully switched them back on. "Now look at this," Behrman said to him. He handed over the ophthalmoscope to Kiesel and picked up a rubber-headed hammer. He aimed carefully, then tapped Müller sharply just below the knee. Müller's knee jerked as violently as his head had just a moment before.

"Don't you see what I'm saying? These physiologic responses are directly analogous to the emotional outbreak as it was described at the Olympic Village. And remember, when you stop to consider this presentation, that this man is still under heavy sedation!"

"So what exactly are you saying?" Kiesel challenged him.

"Only that the total spectrum of psychomotor effects is beyond our control or understanding at this point, and to go any farther would be foolhardy."

Kiesel leaned against the wall with his arms folded across his chest. His white lab coat, unlike Behrman's, was crisply starched so that the lapels creased under the pressure of his crossed hands and wrists. "We are now just beginning to venture into the area of greatest promise."

Behrman regarded Müller's prostrate form, then turned back to Kiesel. "We are now venturing into an uncharted wilderness whose only signposts will be madness and death."

"Every advancement in the progress of science ventures into an uncharted wilderness. And every scientist is a pioneer."

The older man shook his head. "I don't like it. We're coming up with results we did not anticipate and could not have anticipated. I would like to examine Rolf Schmidt's body as soon as possible. There may be a connection, a clue. In the meantime, I say we go back to the animal studies."

"That's impossible," Kiesel countered. "We're too far along. There is an objective. There is a timetable. The administrators will not want to jeopardize it."

"Timetables are arbitrary. Science does not work according to a schedule. Tell that to the administrators!"

Kiesel took a step forward and faced the distinguished scientist across the table. "Let us both be sensible," he said. "Certainly there is risk, as we both can see. But that is inevitable. You, of all people, have always been aware of the risks. With so much at stake, with so many potential benefits for everyone . . . Such a brilliant continuation of your life's work . . ."

"I will be the judge of how my work is to continue," Behrman declared, "or *if* it is to continue."

"Look at what you have already accomplished."

"Yes, look," said Behrman sardonically.

"You do not realistically think you would be allowed to terminate it at this point, do you?"

"And how could I be stopped from doing that?"

Kiesel turned, took several paces toward the wall, and rubbed the back of his neck in frustration. When he spoke, he seemed almost at a loss for words. "I cannot believe that I am hearing the great Abraham Behrman speaking. When I was in medical school, you were already a legend. Stories had grown up about each of your breakthroughs, things you'd discerned that ordinary mortals had failed to grasp. You were my inspiration, do you hear me? Long before I entertained any hope of ever meeting you, much less working with you, you were already a god."

"Only God is a god," Behrman said solemnly. "And it is always at our peril when we lose sight of that."

Kiesel would not relent. "It would be unthinkable to abandon so much progress this close to the end, when we have come this far."

"It would be unthinkable to continue blindly along." Behrman corrected him. He placed his hands squarely on the examining table, by Horst Müller's shoulder and hip. The runner gave out a low moan, then opened his eyes briefly, long enough for both men to register the confusion and the terror.

"Perhaps we have already come too far," Abraham Behrman stated, shaking his head.

Döberitz

All during the taxi ride back to the village, David kept thinking about what Hargreaves had said. But whatever the ultimate good of what he was supposed to be doing, he was being asked to compromise his integrity to accomplish it. So how could any good ultimately come of that? He was being used, just as he'd been asked to use Karl to get to Miranda. He had established a trusting relationship with Karl. Karl had confided things to him David was certain he'd never told to anyone else. He was betraying not only a trust but a genuine friendship.

But there was something even worse. If he did what they were asking of him, he could also be betraying a life.

The Brits were deadly serious about what they said they were going to do. And when he'd realized that, David hadn't been completely honest. He'd said he needed more time. The fact of the matter was he already knew. Miranda was everything they thought, maybe more.

Yet if he told them, if he admitted how successful he'd been in the first part of his assignment, there were only a limited number of options.

So if he out-and-out lied to them and said she had turned out to be an interesting but minor lab assistant, that might get her off the hook and they'd leave her alone. But what if then she did come up with something that— Could he morally do that? On the other hand, morally could he place in jeopardy the life of an innocent girl?

Karl. Miranda. Hargreaves and his secret service friends. David had a different story for each of them now, and none bore even a receding relationship to the truth. His betrayal was complete. His duplicity went across the board.

He needed time to think. But as Hargreaves kept reminding him, time was running out. The question was, How could he possibly act in conflict with his own conscience and still keep his soul?

He couldn't and wouldn't. That was all there was to it.

That felt good. For about three minutes. Then he managed to remind himself that there was, in fact, a larger issue involved, a higher ethical standard even than his own feelings and comfort or his undeniable attraction to a young German girl with golden hair.

When he joined the military, he had given himself over to a greater authority. Whether he agreed with or even understood the ultimate purpose of his assignment, he was still a soldier. He was only following orders.

And that in itself was an extremely noble and honorable thing to do.

ELEVEN

Friday, July 31, Near Paderborn, Westphalia

When Rudolf Kiesel was still a medical student in Bavaria, he joined a small and loosely organized political group then floundering on the rightist fringe. It seemed to have potential, though, inasmuch as its leadership had recently been taken over by a highly strung former army corporal and renamed by him in globally inspiring style—the National Socialist German Workers party. Kiesel had joined the group not because he was particularly political himself— he never had been—but simply because he craved a sense of belonging, something this energetic and eager young man not blessed with high birth or brilliant family connections had been unable to achieve in the stuffy and class-conscious halls of university and medical school. He had toiled in physical labor to earn every penny of his education; it only made him a source of derision to most of his classmates. To them he would always be an outsider. But these National Socialists—outcasts themselves—had been happy to accept him into their midst.

He had long ago concluded that it was the wisest and most percipient decision he had ever made. It was an observation he reaffirmed yet again as he approached the fortified guard tower of Wewelsberg Castle, recently restored by the faithful to all its medieval splendor.

And there was something else. Early on Kiesel had had a realization that would stand him in good stead for the rest of his professional career. The logic was simple, direct, and unassailable. This was a new age they were living through, an age of science. To succeed, simply to survive, the government had to control that science—in all its myriad aspects and phases. In his own case, the government was the party. And the party needed men whose understanding was profound and whose loyalty to the party was unquestioned.

Rudolf Kiesel, Doctor of Medicine, met both those qualifications.

He produced his credentials for the spit-shined SS guard. The young man with ice blond hair snapped to attention and a sharp Hitler salute upon realizing with whom he was dealing. Then Kiesel proceeded across the polished oak drawbridge, past the gleaming portcullis, and into the mammoth stone fortress where he was to see another Bavarian—the former chicken-farming failure who, like himself, had had a vision of the future and who, like himself, had been able to transform that vision into personal triumph.

Heinrich Himmler, *Reichsführer-SS*, understood the value of myths. He understood how people drew strength from them. That was why he had painstakingly patterned his beloved Schutzstaffel on the order of Teutonic Knights. That was why he had spent a fortune of reichsmarks to rebuild the towering castle of Wewelsberg. And that was why he returned regularly to these ancient Westphalian hills and forests.

Everything contributed to the sacred myth. The dining room Himmler fashioned at Wewelsberg measured 145 feet by 100 feet and was lit by torches. There the elect of the SS gathered with their leader at a great round table taken from the Arthurian legend, seated at high-backed leather chairs, each of which held a silver disk bearing the occupant's personally devised coat of arms. A flight of stone steps led to the crypt just below, where urns containing the ashes of fallen brethren reposed on pedestals of solid rock. They were purposely positioned so that those assembled could watch the smoke of the funeral pyre rise through vents in the ceiling and thereby witness the spirits of their comrades ascend into Valhalla. It was from there that the blood oaths of the holy order were pledged.

The great headquarters complex on Prinz-Albrechtstrasse in Berlin served as the administrative center of the SS. But the brooding castle at Wewelsberg was definitely its spiritual home.

Himmler had his personal sanctuary in a great room high in the eastern barbican of the castle. He had chosen the location carefully. From one window he could look out over the glorious Westphalian countryside. From the other he could look in toward the castle's inner ward. Together they symbolized his unique position in the Reich as the man whose vision had to be, at the same time, out toward the rest of the world and ever introspective toward the true goals and aspirations of his movement.

Like most other adornments of the castle, Himmler's desk was a massive object of carved oak, chosen to inspire awe. It stood near the end of the room on an imposingly raised platform, in front of a torch-flanked open fireplace that was taller than the tallest perfect specimen of SS manhood. This was where he sat, intimidating by the sheer scale of his surroundings. Beside him, in the position of honored trust, stood his handpicked deputy, Reinhard Tristan Heydrich.

The double iron-studded doors at the opposite end of the room swung open. Kiesel looked around, gaping, taking in the impressive scene. His reaction was typical, just as Himmler had planned it. He walked with measured step, lest he somehow show disrespect to the formidable spirits that haunted the air or the equally formidable personages who loomed tangibly before him.

"Dr. Kiesel," said Himmler, rising. "It was good of you to come to see us. I'm sorry to ask you to come so far from Berlin. I know the journey cannot have been pleasant."

"Not at all, Reichsführer," Kiesel replied, still tentative in his bearing.

"Of course, you know Obergruppenführer Heydrich," Himmler said with a magnanimous wave of his hand.

"Yes, of course."

Heydrich nodded severely.

Himmler came around from behind the desk, stepped down off the platform, and beckoned Kiesel into one of the two large visitor's chairs covered completely in zebra hide. Unlike Heydrich—the perfect Aryan specimen—the man who had founded the SS was short and myopic, with undistinguished features. He therefore made it a habit always to wear his full black Death's-head Order uniform in the presence of guests and to spend much of the meeting standing above them while they sat.

"So then," he announced, polishing his thick, rimless spectacles with his handkerchief, "we have brought you all this way. What can you report to us?"

"Behrman wants to terminate all research immediately," Kiesel stated grimly.

Heydrich blinked almost imperceptibly in surprise at what he had just heard. "Because of Herren Schmidt and Müller?"

"It confirmed fears he already harbored, I believe."

"This is a very serious matter," said Himmler with studied calm. He drummed his fingers contemplatively on the leather desktop.

"Yes, Reichsführer," said Kiesel. "And I immediately tried to dissuade him from such an action. I said two casualties are not an excessive number in a program of this scope. But he says that the respective conditions we have seen in the men are of unknown origin. We don't know why Schmidt died and why Müller is reacting this way. Therefore, he is of the opinion that we have no choice but to go back to animal studies until we can understand the physiological mechanism and take medical action against it."

Himmler's receding chin set into a deep frown. He ground one fist into the other palm to control himself. "I haven't felt completely comfortable with him ever since I saw his demonstration in the laboratory some months ago. What he did with the rats was inspiring, no doubt about it. He took a weak and ordinary rat and before my eyes transformed it into a killer. I appreciated that. It showed great promise. But there was something about the doctor himself that left me worried." With his hand he seemed to grope momentarily for words. "A certain lack of spine, if you will. A certain failure of emotional rigor."

"He is a brilliant scientist," Kiesel said.

"He is a Jew."

Kiesel sat rigidly straight in his chair. "Yes, Reichsführer."

Himmler rested his hands delicately in his lap. He turned first to Heydrich, then to Kiesel. "Well, what are we going to do about this? The next two weeks are critical. If we fail there, all our dreams are for nothing." He rehooked the spectacles behind his ears and bore in on Kiesel. "The question is, Can you convince Dr. Behrman of the greater good for the nation in continuing his work during this vital period?"

"I'm not certain," Kiesel replied. "He is a difficult man in many ways. He considers it unethical to jeopardize human life through unknown procedures and says as well that he is now concerned about long-term outcomes."

"I am more concerned with short-term outcomes at this point," Himmler said.

"I knew this would happen!" Heydrich broke in, slamming his fist on the edge of Himmler's desk. "Jews cannot be trusted under any circumstances. We have been foolish and deluding ourselves to entrust a project of this magnitude and importance to a Jew."

Himmler waved him off with his hand. While it was certainly well intentioned, he knew full well the real reasons for the outburst. Heydrich had been haunted for years by rumors of Jewish blood in his past. And while the Gestapo's Office of Racial Purity had cleared him, the whispers and innuendos continued. In all other things, Heydrich was unassailable. This was the one whip that Himmler continued to hold over his strong and ambitious lieutenant.

"As you well know, I don't like dealing with Jews any better than you do," Himmler calmly explained. "It is our sacred mission to rid the world of these subhuman vermin." His voice grew cold and sharp. "And ultimately that is precisely what we will do. But it is not as if we have a choice in this particular matter, my dear Reinhard. We didn't assign Dr. Behrman to this research. He does not even know it is being sponsored by the SS." He turned to Kiesel. "He happens to be the leading expert, if I am not mistaken."

"Yes, without question," Kiesel confirmed. "He is the great pioneer of the field."

"Of course. And we initially became interested because his work with dwarfs gave promise of aiding us in our destiny as the master race, a destiny we are this moment on the verge of proving to a skeptical world. Now, gentlemen, let me remind you of a little of the historical background." He rose to his full height and stared directly into the eyes of the other two men. "I went to the führer himself more than a year ago and made the recommendation to him that the *Übermensch* program go forward. That is the reason—the sole reason—he was willing to make the kind of personal and national commitment to the Olympic Games that he did. You may remember that when he became chancellor, he was not in favor of Germany's hosting the games. *Übermensch* changed that. It was why the party took over the German Commission for Sport and Recreation and why Captain Hans von Tschammer und Osten was appointed *Reichssportführer*. It was why the great stadium and the village were built. I recommended all this. I put myself on the line. But before I did that, I needed to have at my disposal all the pertinent facts."

That was Himmler's other great insight. A great organization drew its strength and identity from myth, but it survived on detail. Heinrich Himmler was the Reich's master of detail.

"Among those facts were an understanding of the medical challenge being faced and the resources we could devote to it. Now you say Dr. Behrman wishes to terminate the research at this most critical juncture."

"Yes, Reichsführer."

He waved his hands in front of him. "That is simply out of the question. He is concerned with jeopardizing a few expendable lives. What he is doing will jeopardize *Übermensch* itself. No matter what, we cannot allow that to happen."

"Of course not," said Kiesel, sitting up even higher in his chair. "That is why I contacted you right away."

"With or without Behrman, the project must not be halted. So the question comes down, like most questions in science do, to a simple equation. Yes? If Behrman refuses to continue his work and therefore himself becomes expendable, can you carry on the work without him?"

Kiesel's expression was bleak. All he had worked for was in danger of coming apart. "Not at this point, no," he replied honestly. "Like most medical breakthroughs in the early stage, the work is largely empirical. It is based on instinct. And Abraham Behrman is the only one—probably in the whole world—who possesses that instinct."

"Then the matter is settled," said Himmler simply. "If the program cannot be carried forward without Behrman, it *must* be carried forward with him. Whatever it requires, that is what we must do."

He stood up and extended his limp, clammy hand. "I cannot thank you enough for coming, Dr. Kiesel. The next several weeks will tell if all that we have worked for these past years will come to pass."

Still holding on to Kiesel's hand, the *Reichsführer* looked him squarely in the eyes. "Together we will fulfill our destiny," he said to him.

TWELVE

Saturday, August 1, Central Berlin

Arthur Hargreaves was staying at the fashionable Hotel Adlon at 1 Unter den Linden. He was registered under his own name, ostensibly a well-heeled British tourist in Berlin for the Olympics. As a result, he'd been supplied with a block of tickets to the stadium and swimming events, none of which he planned to attend.

On Saturday morning, when nearly everyone else in the city was consumed with anticipation of the opening ceremonies, Hargreaves was in his room, listening to the radio. That was when he decided he'd better have a quick pop around to the embassy.

This little journey turned out to be more logistically complex than he had figured upon. As soon as he emerged from the Adlon's front door, he discovered the entire length of Unter den Linden was wall to wall with humanity. The beaming doorman reported the police estimate at half a million for this one avenue alone.

It's worse than the bloody cup final in London, Hargreaves thought.

"Why here?" he asked. "What's everybody standing around for?"

"The procession to the stadium," the doorman proudly explained. "Everyone is hoping to catch a glimpse of the führer as he passes by in his automobile."

Hargreaves thought of the crowds that thronged in front of Buckingham Palace days before every coronation or royal wedding and that erupted into a deafening cheer just to see the king or queen step out onto that balcony for a wave. He had never really understood the mentality of crowds, the mass psychology of the pack. But he did know that it didn't take much to sway them in one direction or the other. That had always worried him. It was probably why he had no interest in sitting in a stadium with a hundred thousand other people to watch the Olympics.

Taking a cab through this mob was out of the question, even if he'd been able to find one. So Hargreaves walked to the embassy.

When he got there, the duty officer took him up to the communications room. It was a tiny compartment, like a closet. Hargreaves heard the door lock behind him, then settled into the leather chair in quest of a comfortable position. Within a few moments he heard a buzz, so he picked up the receiver.

Stewart Menzies had been put in charge of the London end of the operation. This being a weekend, he was at home. The MI 6 duty officer in London patched the call through to Menzies's home, where the colonel's ever-attentive wife called him in from the garden.

Don't Englishmen ever do anything else on Saturday mornings? Hargreaves wondered.

"Hello, Arthur, is everything all right?" Menzies asked through the static of the connection.

"Yes, good, other than the crowds and all the Olympic bother. But I'll tell you this, the longer this little intrigue goes on, the more nervous I become."

"I agree," said Menzies. "I have the feeling that something big is in the offing, which does make it all the more important now that our friend David not tarry. Our opportunity here may be small and diminishing before our eyes. The entire atomistic unit could be put under military wraps at virtually any time, and then we lose our access completely."

"Yes, look, Stewart, on that subject I'm afraid I had to go a bit rough on Keegan," Hargreaves reported, "time being of the essence and all."

"And how did he react?" Menzies asked.

"Not unexpectedly, under the circumstances. Though he did go somewhat round the twist when I suggested we might have to take matters into our own hands if he couldn't deliver the goods." Hargreaves paused. "I feel bad about it. He is a nice chap."

"Is he measuring up, though?"

Hargreaves shifted his position in the chair, still trying to find a position that didn't make him feel so claustrophobic in this little cubicle. He pictured Menzies comfortably at home, a sea away in the pleasant outskirts of London. "He's making the old school try. I think he's trying to do the job up right for us. But he's quite preoc-

cupied by these damn Olympics, very worried about his performance."

"Because of the distraction from his training?"

"I suspect so. It fits right in with the psychological profile we
developed on him: nervous overachiever, always afraid someone's
going to overtake him or show him up to be a fraud. Never satisfied
with himself. With his stellar record—West Point, Oxford, biochemistry, fluent in languages, all the track medals—it would be
more of a surprise than not if he were anything else."

"Well, when you're trying to hook a fish, it's the bait that's in the
position of the most stress," Menzies pointed out.

"And you have to remember, after all, he's only twenty-four."

"And Miranda Wolff is only twenty."

"I wonder if this extreme is really necessary," said Hargreaves.

"I leave it to you," Menzies replied. "You're the scientist. How
important is Miranda Wolff—to them and to us?"

Hargreaves sighed. "That sort of thing's always a bit sticky. How
important is the electromagnetic field? Not important at all until it's
discovered. Then after that, once you learn what to do with it, it's
vitally important."

"Well, then, what's your best guess?"

Hargreaves sighed again, longer and louder this time. "We'll have
to wait and see what David tells us, but I'd have to say, potentially,
very important. I'm not saying she's the one critical key to atomistic
power, although she could be. Think of her more as a link in a
chain. Once that link is removed, even though there are a number of
others, the chain is no longer as strong and doesn't stretch quite as
far as it used to. And owing to her youth and attendant lack of
sophistication, her inexperience, and the fact that she's not yet really
accepted as a member of the scientific establishment, she is the most
accessible link in that chain for us. That's one of the reasons we
keyed on her. To remove Hahn, for example, would be a much more
formidable proposition without achieving any better results, probably not nearly as good, candidly."

"We had considered that," Menzies said. "Removing Hahn, instead, I mean."

"Yes, I'm sure. But Miranda's definitely the one for us. If she is of
sufficient caliber that her removal from the Berlin scene would deal a
crippling blow to the German atomistic effort, I can tell you that it
would also give a tremendous infusion of insight and inspiration to

our own effort. She'd be able to put us on to things we're probably not even dreaming about."

"Then you've answered the question. I'm more concerned with practical matters at this point. For example, Arthur, how do we know Keegan is trustworthy? His German heritage is only one bothersome aspect."

"Yes, quite," Hargreaves said. "But his past history gives one a high degree of confidence. According to the psychological profile we worked up, he should cooperate even if he doesn't fully appreciate or empathize with the overall goals of the mission. Obligation is important to him. At the last Olympics he had a rather intensive fling with that swimmer Alison Prescott. She wanted him to leave West Point and stay with her, but in the end he opted for duty."

"Let's say Keegan does come back and confirm what we suspect about the Wolff girl, and we therefore proceed to phase two."

"Yes, all right," said Hargreaves. "But I do wonder if perhaps we should have had professionals for this."

"A professional would probably give us a *higher percentage* but for a *lower-preference* outcome," Menzies observed, "meaning, we might have a better shot of removing Miranda from the scene over where you are, as you suggest, but that would be the end of it. There'd be very little chance that we could also convince her to come over to our side. For that you need to develop trust through a personal relationship, which is where David comes in. Now, with David, since he doesn't really know what he's doing and is improvising every step of the way, we have a *lower percentage* of success for the first—the lower-preference—outcome. But we have a higher percentage for the *higher-preference* outcome, which is not only to remove her from the scene in Berlin but also to get her to work for us at the Cavendish."

"This is quite edifying," said Hargreaves dryly.

"Of course, the *odds* of the higher-preference outcome's working out as opposed to the lower-preference one are considerably lower overall. So I suppose we have to factor that in."

"So where does that leave us?" Hargreaves asked.

"With David Keegan," said Menzies with assurance. "For better or worse, the die has been cast."

"I'm afraid so. You know, the groves of academe are looking more inviting to me by the minute."

"So we're going to have to light whatever fire under him that we can."

"I may have to show up at those bloody games after all," Arthur Hargreaves grumbled.

Menzies tried to console him. "I suppose we'll all sleep a little better once young Miranda's safely on our side of the Channel, helping out our fellows."

"'And a little child shall lead them.'"

"The prophet Isaiah."

"Yes. But another prophet's line keeps running through my mind."

"Who is that?" Menzies asked.

"Rutherford. 'Some fool in a laboratory might blow up the universe unawares.'"

THIRTEEN

Grunewald

The focal point of the entire Reichssportfeld was the Marathon Gate, a broad opening in the stadium flanked by two heroic towers of marble. Physically it connected the stadium directly to the massive Maifeld behind it. Symbolically it connected the giant concrete showcase to its sources of ancient heritage and modern glory, for the Marathon Gate was on the route through which the Olympic flame, carried by runners all the way from Olympia, would triumphantly arrive at the games and into the imagination of the entire world. It was the gate through which Adolf Hitler would do the same.

Nothing in David Keegan's experience had prepared him for the spectacle and splendor, the sheer scale of the opening ceremonies here in Berlin. He and Tom were standing in the Maifeld, huddled with the rest of the American team in their sportive red, white, and blue uniforms. It was the first time they'd worn them since the *Manhattan* had docked in Hamburg more than a week ago. The flags of the participating countries flapped against their poles high on the rim of the stadium. Excitement and tension were growing to a fevered pitch. All around them the best athletes from fifty other nations around the world stood together, straining to hear the directions of their coaches and German Olympic officials, awaiting the call that would bring them into the stadium, already packed with a hundred and ten thousand screaming, cheering fans, to begin the greatest massed spectacle the world had ever seen. Thousands of other spectators and fans packed the stands along the west wall and spilled out onto the grass.

"You know something?" said Tom. "Hitler really knows what to do with crowds."

Suddenly a massive shadow descended over the field, like the sun in eclipse. David looked up to see directly above them the great zeppelin *Hindenburg*, as big as three football fields, gracefully cruising the overcast skies. The giant airship, too, carried through the twin visual themes of the day. Immense red, white, and black swastikas were emblazoned on its huge tail fins. And it towed an enormous white banner of Olympic rings.

A thundering and spontaneous cheer rose from the crowd as they took in this sleek and dazzling proof of German technical might.

"It's a flying hotel." Tom had to shout, even though David was less than a foot away. "I read it can go from Frankfurt to Lakehurst, New Jersey, in forty-nine hours. That's twice as fast as the fastest ship on the ocean."

"It is amazing," David said. "Everything's amazing here."

"Here's something else. Did you know the Germans have even gotten rid of mosquitoes for the Olympics? Not one lousy mosquito in the whole of Berlin. They've been spraying every possible breeding place for a year. It's absolutely incredible. These people are capable of anything."

Dahlem

Rudolf Kiesel had been in bed when the call came through. It was from Martin Gillhausen, the overnight lab technician in the biochemistry section of the Kaiser Wilhelm Institute.

"I think you'd better come over right away, Doctor," the young man had said.

"What is it?"

"Horst Müller."

"Yes?"

"He's gone."

"What do you mean, he's gone?" Kiesel demanded. A sickening feeling was rapidly invading his stomach.

"I think it would be best if you would come over and see for yourself. Ordinarily I would have called Dr. Behrman. But of course . . ."

"Yes . . . of course."

When he arrived at the institute, Gillhausen was waiting for him in his office.

"He just left his room," Gillhausen reported. "The one next to the animal lab."

"Wasn't it locked?" Kiesel asked.

"Yes, but it was a simple keyhole lock, more designed to keep people out of a room than in one. We have no need for high security here. He must have slipped something in between the door and the jamb and pried it open."

"That would take a lot of strength," Kiesel observed. "And where did he go from there?"

Silently Gillhausen led the way through the slightly opened wooden door and into the small-mammal lab. Inside, the rats in their cages were still shrieking madly, scampering up and down the wire mesh walls as if desperately trying to escape from what they had witnessed.

In the center of the bank of cages that lined one wall, two stood out prominently. Their doors were open, and they were empty.

"He must have got into them," said Kiesel. "They might still be in the room. But with the door left ajar, they could be anywhere in the institute by now."

"I don't think so," Gillhausen said. He walked with Kiesel over to the shiny wooden counter along the opposite wall. There, amid a disquieting array of broken glass containers and vials, lay two furry white bodies, already stiff from rigor mortis. Blood was matted thickly on the fur, which stopped abruptly at each neck. From there, Kiesel could see nothing but two black, gaping holes surrounded by jagged rings of flesh.

It didn't take a doctor to realize from the nature of the wounds that the heads had been bitten off.

Grunewald

Throughout the Maifeld a ruggedly beautiful woman with sharp blue eyes and dark, wild hair was seen everywhere, popping up in all corners. She wore a bulky knit sweater and mannish khaki slacks, she traveled with a small retinue, and she never stopped barking out orders in German to her scores of cameramen and assistants positioned at all vantage points.

"Who's that?" Tom asked in admiration.

"Leni Riefenstahl," said David, equally admiring. "She's an

actress. Karl says she's Hitler's favorite filmmaker. She did a film for him of the 1934 Nuremberg rallies called *Triumph of the Will*."

"That sounds pretty big-cocked, especially for a woman."

"Apparently he liked it so much, he made her the . . . I don't know . . . the official director here. She's going to be making a movie of the games. Preserving them for all times."

"Think a woman can handle something that big?"

For a moment David watched her ordering the entire German team into the configuration she desired, then positioning her crew to capture them on film. "I'd say she can handle anything."

Tom spotted Dean Crowell, the men's relay coach. "What are we waiting for?" he asked.

"Hitler's entrance, they tell me," said Crowell. "Nothing happens till the big man arrives."

"I'm going to go see if I can find out anything," David said to Tom.

"Don't any of you jokers go getting lost now," Crowell warned. "Brundage'll bust a gut. I want everyone in place when they tell us to march in."

"Don't worry," David said. "They can't start without us."

"Right, Keegan. People have been making a big deal over you too long. Aside from the fact that it isn't true, don't forget that over here we're the *Vereinigten Staaten*. We're the last team alphabetically."

"All right then. They can't finish without us."

Central Berlin

Heinrich Himmler was standing at his desk when Reinhard Heydrich reported to his office.

"Tell me everything you know," the *Reichsführer-SS* instructed him.

"Müller got out of his room and left the Kaiser Wilhelm Institute," Heydrich said urgently. "Probably early this morning. Certainly before dawn. I've just been able to begin piecing it all together."

"He simply walked out?"

"Essentially, yes. But not before chewing the heads off two live rats."

Himmler raised his eyebrows. "Interesting. That certainly demonstrates a competitive spirit. Do we take a chance allowing him to display it publicly, I wonder?"

Heydrich said nothing.

"Then what?"

"Then he disappeared. No one can find him."

Himmler took off his glasses and methodically began the characteristic gesture of polishing them with his handkerchief. "I don't like this."

"Nor do I, Reichsführer." It was unusual for Heydrich to call him by his title.

The telephone rang. Himmler picked it up and listened silently for several moments. "Thank you," he said, and put the receiver down. "He's surfaced."

"Where?" asked Heydrich.

"The Olympic Stadium."

"I should have known. What do they say?"

Himmler repeated the information. "He is wearing his uniform and, from all reports, seems to be in control of himself."

"Has he said anything to anyone?"

"No, he's said nothing at all. Not one word."

"No reports of incidents?"

Himmler shook his head.

"I have security men all over, including several plants in Leni Riefenstahl's crew."

"The führer's motorcade is heading to the stadium."

"I have a car waiting with motorcycle escort," said Heydrich. "I'm on my way. I'll get there before he does."

Himmler replaced his glasses. "Good. Things are out of control. I don't like being out of control."

Grunewald

David made his way through the huddled masses of the Maifeld, over toward the earlier teams in the alphabet. In German the Egyptians were first. David saw them milling about in their maroon fezzes and waistcoats. There were the French in their blue jackets, white trousers, and (of course, thought David) blue berets. The Englishmen and women all were topped off in straw boaters, just as he would have seen at the Henley Regatta.

Before long he spied the German team, attired in sleek gray uniforms and precise, military visor caps. They looked like a miniature army, ready to be led into attack.

He looked all around. Was it possible he might not be here? David felt a clutch of panic in his gut. "Karl!" he called out.

"David!" came the reply. "I'm so happy to see you." The two men who would soon be using everything they had to wrest victory from each other now threw their arms around each other's necks.

"How are you?" David asked. "I was worried that I hadn't seen you at the village for several days."

"You shouldn't worry," Karl assured him. But there was some strange formality, some stiffness in his voice. "I had some work at the institute that couldn't wait, I'm afraid. I am supposed to be free every afternoon, but it's difficult when you serve two masters. But I'm all right. Just a little nervous. And you?"

"A lot nervous," David confessed. "How is Miranda?"

"Good."

"Is she here?"

"Yes, she insisted."

"I'm glad she did." Somehow, he had to get to her.

They were still holding on to each other, each man's hands clutching the other's forearms. "Karl," David said softly so that no one else around would hear, "now that the games are starting . . . no matter what happens from here on out, promise me that nothing will come between us."

Karl nodded.

"Say it."

"Yes. Always."

There was some commotion behind them. David realized that everyone was being arranged into neat, even rows. That could mean only one thing. He had to get back to his own team.

Just as he was about to head back, something caught his eye. He hadn't seen Horst Müller at the Olympic Village or practicing at the stadium since that day last week when the security police had carried him off in manacles. He seemed tense and jumpy here, springing up and down in place, like a prizefighter having just climbed into the ring. His eyes were distant, and he didn't say anything to anyone.

But here he was, smartly dressed in his national uniform, standing proudly with the rest of his team, waiting to parade before his leader and the world.

Despite the numbers of people packed into the Maifeld, it was an orderly crowd and no major disturbance was anticipated. Therefore, the Reichssportfeld security director had dispatched only one dog patrol.

Its handler let the German shepherd do as it pleased, following the animal with slack leash as it sniffed its way about the expansive lawn. Dog and man worked as a close team, conditioned to pick up on the other's subtlest signals. As long as the dog remained relaxed, so did his handler.

From time to time, people bent down to pet the dog, which was bred and trained to be just as docile and affectionate to friendly entreaties as it was to be ferocious to hostile actions. The shepherd licked the hands or legs of whoever stroked its smooth dark fur, and the handler stood by accepting compliments for such a noble and friendly animal.

When they reached the area where the German team was waiting, the dog seemed to sense it was among its own people. It circled proprietarily around the perimeter of the group, keeping the various team members together as if asserting the ancient purpose for which it was bred.

Suddenly the dog grew tense. It stopped rigidly, uttering a low growl. The handler looked down at the animal, then up at the object of its animosity. It was Horst Müller, the leading distance runner, and he was staring back at the dog with the same intense wariness. Like the dog, he looked as if he were about to strike. The handler was sorry the dog had done this to the celebrated athlete. He would have to go over and apologize. He hoped Müller wouldn't take offense.

There was no logic for the shepherd to pick out one member of the national team like this. There were just some people dogs didn't like. But dogs often sensed things that people couldn't. The handler would have to sort it out quickly before it developed into a scene. He didn't want to do anything that would call undue attention, especially with the führer about to make his entrance.

But then he saw Obergruppenführer Heydrich striding across the field, and he knew the decision was no longer in his hands.

It was incredible how everything was totally under control. By the time David made his way back to the American team, the German security people had cleared a wide path down the center of the Maifeld, just as Moses had parted the Red Sea. David, with the other

Americans, was pressed back toward the west side of the field near the stands where it opened up to the road.

He heard the ground-shaking cheer before he saw anything. Then he heard the motors. Then he saw people running, chasing, followed by a procession of black, open-top Mercedeses. The crowd was wild, already in an incredible frenzy. The figures in the cars were indistinguishable at first, but soon he could make them out.

In the first three cars were Count Henri de Baillet-Latour, president of the International Olympic Committee; Dr. Carl Diem, secretary of the German Commission for Sport and Recreation; and Dr. Theodor Lewald, president of the German Olympic Committee. They waved with restrained dignity to the multitudes and waited in their cars as the rest of the motorcade came through.

In the fourth car was Air Marshal Hermann Göring, fat and smiling, resplendent in his sky blue uniform. He smiled broadly and waved a gold baton. His picture had been in the local newspapers all week. Then came another man, smaller and slighter, with straight, greasy black hair. He was not smiling, but rather looked nervous, as if he weren't used to being out of doors. David wasn't sure who he was, but he heard the name Rudolf Hess whispered behind him.

When the next car turned onto the Maifeld, the roar from the crowd was like being inside an airplane engine. It seemed to rock the very concrete foundations of the stadium. The car pulled to a stop right in front of where David and Tom were positioned. And not twenty feet away David could clearly see standing in the back of the Mercedes, the chancellor and president of Germany and the leader of the National Socialist party, Adolf Hitler.

Unlike Göring, who was decked out to the teeth, Hitler was wearing a cap and simple brown uniform of a storm trooper, with jodhpurs and jackboots. A black leather buckled strap crossed his chest and joined the one at his waist. His only decoration was the ribbon denoting his award of the Iron Cross, which he had won for valor as an enlisted man in the Great War. In response to the cheering, he put up his right hand in a Nazi salute. Typically it was so casual as to seem more like a friendly wave.

Hitler stepped down onto the car's running board. Just then, above the constant din, David heard a shout from the crowd in the stands right behind him. It was a high-pitched woman's voice.

"Mein Führer! Mein Führer!" she called out. "I want to have your baby!"

Hitler turned to see where the shout had come from. As he did, he ended up in David's direction. David took in the entire figure. He saw the straight black hair combed forward over the high forehead. He saw the thick, square mustache covering a straight upper lip. He had seen the picture thousands of times before. But this time it was in the flesh.

Their eyes met. David found himself looking directly into the eyes of the leader of the German people. And in that split second an incredible sensation came over him. In that surreal rupture in time he was completely captivated, completely caught up and absorbed into a personality, a force, a power far larger than himself—a force more overwhelming, more compelling than anything he could have predicted or imagined. For an incredible eternity it was only the two of them alone in the world. In the brief moment that they stared into each other's eyes, David knew he would have done anything this man asked of him. He would have laid down his life. He would have walked through fire.

By the time Hitler turned away and began walking with his retinue across the Maifeld, David's heart was pounding. His mouth was dry, and his throat was tight and burning. His palms were wet with perspiration. He didn't know what had come over him. He had no idea what had made him feel that way.

As he watched Adolf Hitler walk off through the Marathon Gate, David felt an unnamed terror touch his soul.

The teams had been organized into straight ranks for the procession into the stadium, and the first countries had already made their ways through the Marathon Gate. Reinhard Heydrich stood next to the banner of the German squad as if he were forming some sort of honor guard to escort them. Though he appeared to look straight ahead, he never for long took his eyes off Horst Müller, standing in the middle of the team. He had breathed a sigh of relief when the führer and his entourage had walked past without incident.

The signal came for the German team to begin marching. The banner carriers picked up their poles. The drillmaster called out the first cadence.

It happened so quickly Heydrich did not even notice at first. But when he looked again, Horst Müller was lying flat on the ground. The rest of his teammates were scattered in confusion around him.

And by the time Heydrich made his way into the center of the group, he could see no expression at all.

The remainder of the opening ceremonies became a blur to David, a collection of images and sensations piled one upon the next until they challenged his ability to absorb any more.

There was the stirring evocation of national pride as Richard Strauss, living national treasure of Germany, conducted a chorus of three thousand voices in "Deutschland über Alles" and the "Horst Wessel Song." There was the old Greek shepherd, Spiridon Loues, hero of 1896, the first modern Olympics. Dressed in the white tunic and black stockings of his national costume, he presented Hitler with an olive branch from his homeland as he said, "I present this to you as a symbol of love and peace. We hope that the nations will ever meet solely in such peaceful competition." And there was five-year-old Gudrun Diem, adorable as could be in her short white dress and ankle socks, Carl Diem's granddaughter, running up to Hitler with a bouquet of local flowers as more than a hundred thousand people cooed approvingly.

And somewhere in the stands, David knew, Miranda was watching it all.

There was the incredible march past the official box by each nation in succession. The crowd thundered as the arms of the Austrian team members shot up in a collective Nazi salute. The small Bulgarian team did them one better, saluting, goose-stepping, and then dipping its flag to the red cinder track as it marched by. Perhaps the crowd did not realize that this last gesture was not for Hitler but for the Bulgarian king, who sat next to the chancellor in the box of honor.

The French were equally respectful, thrusting out their right arms in a motion that could have been construed as the traditional Olympic salute but that was met with a "Heil!" in unison from the crowds, which roared out its adulation. Perhaps never before that moment had the love and outpouring of warmth between the two countries been greater. The grinning, joyous Italians were also favorites with the Fascist salute they had originated.

There were brave little Haiti and Costa Rica, whose single athlete each had to be both flag bearer and marcher. Yet no country marched with greater pride and dignity.

For David, the most thrilling—and poignant—moment came during his own team's march past. Avery Brundage led them, and Alfred Jochim, the great gymnastic champion, carried the standard. During the 1908 London games the American flag bearer had declared, "This flag dips for no earthly king." Despite the jeers and protestations of the crowd, Jochim was not about to alter that proud tradition. As they marched past the chancellor's box, the 383 men and women removed their straw hats and placed them over their hearts. More than one patriotic tear was seen to be shed as the band struck up "The Star-Spangled Banner."

But that was not the reason David would remember the moment as long as he lived. At the final crescendo he happened to glance up to the press box just in time to see Alison Prescott, beautiful as always in a lavender dress, collapse in a torrent of sobs as the last members of her team filed past.

It occurred to David at that moment that she had never cried that way for him.

There was more. Weeks before, a flame had been kindled amid the swirl of mist and myth atop an ancient mountain in Olympia. From torch to torch it had been transferred across the face of Europe. Now, with stunning precision, the last of 3,075 runners emerged to the triumphant fanfare of trumpets through the Marathon Gate. He was lithe and blond and dressed all in white, a perfect German, a perfect symbol for all humanity. He ran with exquisite grace across the red cinder track and climbed the stone steps all the way to the top of the stadium, where the giant brazier waited to receive his fire. When he touched the core and it lit up with a sweeping whoosh, Adolf Hitler advanced to the microphone and declared, "I announce as opened the Games of Berlin, celebrating the eleventh Olympiad of the modern era."

The smoke of the Olympic flame wafted in the air, ascending toward a modern Valhalla. At that moment thousands of doves of peace were simultaneously released into the Berlin sky.

That evening, in a festival entitled "Pageant of Olympic Youth," written and organized by Carl Diem, ten thousand young dancers dominated the Maifeld. The ceremony was held at dusk, when the mood of myth and spectacle was strongest in the air. David watched the dancers, boys and girls alike, in their brief and tight-fitting white costumes. Their precision, their regimentation were striking, as if they had been well-drilled soldiers. The program climaxed with the fifteen-hundred-voice chorus swelling into the "Ode to Joy" from Beethoven's Ninth Symphony.

Then later still, as night dissolved into morning, each athlete among the thousands no doubt lay upon his or her bunk and contemplated the challenge that lay ahead, praying for victory, agonized by dreams of failure and defeat. David thought about them all and what they must be thinking at this very moment: Jesse Owens and Ralph Metcalfe and Sam Stoller and Marty Glickman. Helen Stephens and Ruth Wilfort. Glenn Morris in his own event. And Tom Quinn in the bunk next to him. And Karl. He couldn't forget Karl.

And then, effortlessly, inevitably, no matter how he tried to keep his mind on the contest to come, there was the enticing image of Miranda Wolff. He couldn't get her out of his thoughts. Who was she, this beautiful Rhine maiden? This Valkyrie. This fair, blond vision conjured up from somewhere deep in the mythic German past. And what was he going to do about her?

Suddenly he found himself thinking back to the question he had asked Arthur Hargreaves that morning at the embassy: *"What if this Miranda Wolff refuses to leave with me?"*

Hargreaves's response came hauntingly back to him.

FOURTEEN

Sunday, August 2

"Ich rufe die Jugend der Welt." "I summon the youth of the World."
It was a quotation from the great German poet Friedrich von
Schiller, and it was boldly engraved on the sixteen-ton Olympic bell,
the centerpiece and paramount symbol of the Berlin games. It hung
from a massive beam of Bavarian oak, which in turn was mounted on
a soaring tower high above the west wall of the Maifeld, where it
commanded the entire Olympic site. Merely casting such a huge and
flawless bell and then raising it to its enormous height and balancing
it there required a staggering feat of engineering, one more reminder
to a marveling world of the ingenuity of the German people and the
intensity of the German will.

Every morning and every evening the great bell tolled in perfect E
minor pitch, officially signaling the start and the completion of the
day's contests.

This first day of competition was still cloudy and bleak. Once
again the humidity was uncomfortable, and a cold wind blew across
the Maifeld and into the stadium. Yet once again the giant concrete
bowl—the largest arena on the planet—was jammed full. More had
been turned away than were able to get tickets. The passion and
pride and enthusiasm of these Germans were overwhelming.

The decathlon wouldn't begin until Friday, but David wanted to
be at the stadium from the very start. It was important to begin
absorbing the rhythm of the games. He hoped to reach his physical
and psychic peak at just the right moment.

Already there was activity all over the place. The strikingly beautiful Leni Riefenstahl was everywhere, her cameras occupying every
conceivable vantage point. Her staff had even dug a trench at the

end of the long jump pit. Still other cameras were set at the various finish lines along the track, poised to record close races.

People went busily about their tasks. More than anything else, it reminded David of a colony of ants. He loosened up on the grass sidelines as his teammates and the other athletes began collecting across the red cinder track for the first round of the men's hundred-meter trials.

David tried to take in the entire scene. He watched as Jesse Owens, on the edge of the track in front of him, calmly and methodically stretched out his long arms and legs. Owens was one of a kind, a singular person. David had never met another athlete quite like him. There was a perfect, supernatural serenity about him that David knew he himself would never achieve. Nothing fazed Jesse. He showed none of the agitation or skittishness common in sprinters, none of the nervousness of the beginning of a meet. It was as if he had been born into this setting and drew his peculiar kind of energy from it.

Looking up into the stands, David thought of another singular personage, noticeable by his absence from the box of honor. He recalled with an icy chill another peculiar kind of energy, the personal, private, one-on-one effect this man had had on him right here, not twenty-four hours before. Could it be some dark recess in the racial memory of his German heritage coming back to haunt him?

It was more comfortable to go back to thinking about Jesse Owens and the magic of his running. Owens and Metcalfe and Matthew Robinson were definitely the American sprinting hopes, and everybody knew it. But David had seen the Negroes on the team referred to as "black auxiliaries" in the German press, as though the Nazis couldn't imagine them as full-fledged Americans. The suggestion was that the United States had brought in subhuman savages from Africa to bolster its Olympic showing. "It is true that a cheetah can run faster than a man," David had read. "However, that fact does not make it into a man." This in spite of the fact that most of the Negroes on the American team were college-educated.

Tom was right. The Nazis really did seem to be serious about all the master race nonsense. David hoped even more now for a tremendous showing to prove to the world what America was all about. And yet all the German people he'd met had been so friendly. He just couldn't square that with these official pronouncements of prejudice and discrimination.

The Olympic hundred-meter dash may be the most glamorous of all the track and field events. It is quick, dramatic, and decisive. Its winner can properly lay claim to being the fastest person on earth. David walked over to the team bench to check the roster of trial heats. Jesse wouldn't be running until the last one—the twelfth.

The runners for the first one were digging themselves toe holes in the cinder track with the little silver trowels that the German Olympic Committee had given each of them as a souvenir. Having to go through this ritual for every heat was going to take some time. Before every large meet there was always talk of allowing adjustable starting blocks for the sprinters, but so far it hadn't gone anywhere. Maybe this large a field would finally convince the Olympic authorities.

As the runners crouched down to assume their starting positions, a huge cheer went up for the local favorite, Erich Borchmeyer. He was an enormous dark-haired German with broad shoulders and massive legs who seemed better built for the hammer throw than for sprinting. But as the gun sounded, he broke out to an early lead and easily took his heat. When his official time of 10.7 seconds was posted on the scoreboard several moments later, another roar of approval went up from the enthusiastic crowd. As Karl Linderhoff had suggested, these people seemed to know they were playing out their destiny here in this world arena.

But Borchmeyer's triumph was short-lived. Frank Wykoff trimmed a tenth of a second off his time in the next heat with a 10.6. A hush of surprise came over the crowd. From the sidelines David felt his soul stirring. Even though it was only the trials, America was on the board. And Wykoff was white! What would Hitler say about that?

But the thing about athletic records, especially the minute gradations of track and field competition, is that they are made to be topped. No sooner had the American bench begun to savor the lead they knew would undoubtedly remain with them than Martinus Osendarp of Holland bested all the previous times with a 10.5!

The competition would be ferocious, David realized. On top of that he had Miranda and the damn British intelligence service to worry about. Right from the start he had resented their intrusion. But now, for the first time since he'd met her, he even found himself resenting Miranda . . . her very existence . . . her unbreakable connection to his life.

God, it was amazing and terrifying to think what a simple footrace could do to a man. Any man he knew would be thrilled, beyond thrilled to have that lovely creature for himself. So what was going on? Is this what had happened to Karl? Is that what Miranda was complaining about when she said that he had stopped paying attention to her? Had it already happened to David? He had always told himself he competed because of what it did for him inside. Had he already been swept up in the frenzy here and sold his soul to the dream of Olympic glory?

The next many heats went by in an abstract parade of repeated images: runners assembling at the starting line and digging their toe holes, getting set in their stances; the crowd expectant, urging on its particular favorites; the starting gun firing; the runners dashing down the track; one of their numbers breaking the tape with his outthrust chest. Ralph Metcalfe of Marquette won his heat impressively, and David and his teammates again took heart.

By the final heat of the first round David could tell that the crowd was growing restless and impatient. All the runners had merged into one. Even the race officials looked bored. What could one more race show them that the previous eleven hadn't?

Jesse Owens sauntered up to the starting line as if no one else had raced that day, as if no one else were racing against him now. He seemed totally self-absorbed, unmindful of the clock, ready only to merge himself for those crucial seconds with the natural forces of speed and dexterity.

Herr Miller, the stocky, jovial starter in an immaculate white suit, held the .380 pistol high in his right hand. In measured cadence he called out, "*Auf die Plätze . . . fertig . . .*" The explosion of the gun shocked the stillness of the air.

What happened then stunned everybody.

As soon as the starting gun sounded, Owens was up and away from the field like a bullet. He seemed not so much to move forward as to disappear and materialize from point to point in a perfect, graceful rhythm that reminded David of a living series of timed motion photographs.

Within a split second the entire crowd was on its feet. There simply were no other runners in the race. Suddenly the entire pattern of the morning came into sharp focus. All the other heats had been necessary merely to serve as a backdrop for Owens's singular genius.

Jesse's coach, Larry Snyder, had been standing next to David and snapped his thumb down on his stopwatch as soon as his man burst across the finish line.

"I don't believe it!" David said to him when he saw what Snyder's watch had recorded. But Jesse Owens had caused people to doubt their instruments before, and when the official time was posted, the scoreboard read out 10.3 seconds. The stadium had been transformed into a community of believers.

At lunch Jesse was still serene and easygoing. He ate well and laughed easily. And then, in the afternoon, he made the crowd forget the experience of the morning with a performance that replaced all memories which had preceded it. Metcalfe and Borchmeyer each won their heats with impressive times of 10.5 When his moment came, Jesse blasted down the dull red track in an unbelievable 10.2! The crowd exploded. Only the slight following wind prevented his time from being declared a new world record.

And this was only the trials!

Let the Germans throw their best at us, thought David. *We can take on any comers.*

As impressive as the stadium was, it was only one of several Olympic sites. Yachting was being held up north at Kiel, on the Baltic coast. A rowing and canoeing course had been laid out at Grünau. Boxing, wrestling, and weight lifting were to take place in the impressive Deutschland Hall. Fencing events were scheduled for the tennis grounds. And just south of the stadium complex, in the Grunewald Forest, the first event of one of the most interesting competitions was getting under way. The modern pentathlon is a grueling five-day program that is the most overtly warlike of all the Olympic sports, with each contestant portraying a mythical soldier escaping through enemy lines. The pentathlon had been invented by the Swedes for the 1912 Stockholm games, and they had never failed to take at least the top two places in each Olympics since then.

The first of the women's events here in the stadium was the javelin. It would be a pleasant and relaxing change of pace, David thought, after the tension of the men's hundred-meter trials. Four years ago Babe Didrikson had dominated the event. This time all the potential medalists were European, so there wasn't even the pressure of cheering an American girl on to victory. On the other hand, there was something quite beautiful about watching the slender spears gliding against the sky.

Herma Bauma, the Austrian champ, dominated the first round and broke the old Olympic mark. Some of the electricity of the previous races returned to the stadium. The crowd picked up even further as Luise Krüger, a German, did almost as well. Wouldn't it be something if the Germans could take a medal? It had never happened before since the beginning of the modern Olympics, but weren't these the Games of Destiny?

But then the powerful Pole Maria Kwasniewska came forward. She set off with a forceful run and a powerful release, and her throw exceeded that of even the prodigious Bauma.

Yet still the Germans had hope. Tilly Fleischer took her place in the lane and began her loping run toward the throwing line. With her vivacious smile, she was a particular favorite of the partisan crowd.

As soon as she released, everyone watching could tell that she hadn't risen to the occasion. A wave of disappointment swept over the crowd. There was something tentative, incomplete about her throw. David genuinely felt for her. *An attack of nerves*, he thought. The pressure must have gotten to her.

Yes, the pressure must have gotten to her. The same pressure that had got to Horst Müller. The pressure that threatened his friend Karl. The thought caught him up short.

On the sidelines between rounds, he saw Luise and Tilly huddling quietly together. They weren't talking so much as communing together, as if transferring energy between themselves.

Whatever they were doing had its effect. In the second round Krüger came out with a hurl of 43.29 meters, putting her firmly ahead of Kwasniewska. Then Fleischer came up to the line again. She paused for a moment, collecting her concentration and directing it all back to the center of her being.

She began her run. She reached the release line and sent her javelin flying. The stadium was silent. Time stopped. The wooden spear soared through the air for what seemed like forever before implanting itself with a firm thud into the lime-lined grass. The officials raced out with their tapes. The numbers went up. Forty-four-point-six-nine! A new Olympic record. Fleischer of Germany was in the lead!

The exuberant crowd immediately launched into a rhythmic chant of "Til-ly! Til-ly! Til-ly!" It was several moments before the competition could continue.

But the Austrian, Herma Bauma, was still threatening. One superior throw in the final round could dash all German hopes, as they'd been dashed so many times in so many Olympics past. It would take a superhuman effort from Fleischer or Krüger to give Germany a medal. From what he'd seen in Los Angeles, David just didn't think either woman had that kind of talent or consistency.

Luise Krüger didn't disappoint. She maintained her numbers in the third round and pulled ahead of the Pole. David and Tom looked at each other in astonishment.

Then it was Fleischer's turn again. "She can't do it this time," David said to Tom.

"But wouldn't it be something if she did?" he replied.

She did. Like Jesse Owens before her, Tilly Fleischer topped the untoppable, making history twice in two tries. When the tape was pulled away from her upright javelin, firmly impaled in the grass, the scoreboard proclaimed an incredible 45.18.

The crowd was stunned beyond belief. A German woman had broken the great Babe Didrikson's 1932 Olympic record. A low rumble built into an incredible cheer that rocked the concrete foundation of the arena as the reality of what had happened quickly set in. At the awards ceremony immediately following the event Tilly Fleischer stood beaming from the top tier of the three-tiered victors' platform, the gold medal around her neck, an olive wreath crowning her head, and her right arm outstretched in a Nazi salute while the loudspeakers boomed out "Deutschland über Alles." Half the stadium sang along as two swastika flags were hoisted into the breeze. On the second tier stood Luise Krüger, equally proud, wearing the silver. For the first time in the history of the modern Olympics Germany had won a gold medal. And it was the first one awarded here in Berlin, in these Games of Destiny.

David had a more personal interest in the next event, the men's shot put. It had always been the weakest of his decathlon skills. Jack Torrance, a great oak of a man, had held the world record for two years now, and everyone on the team was anxious to see him repeat and give the United States its first medal of the games.

But something was wrong. Torrance couldn't do anything in the first round, a training injury several days earlier at the Olympic Village keeping him well below the top of his form. In his place Sulo Barlund of Finland led briefly with a good throw of 16.03 meters.

But when the final results were in, Barlund was second to Hans Wöllke of Germany and his new Olympic record of 16.20. His countryman Gerhard Stöck was third.

The Americans were not even in the running.

The Germans had repeated their female counterparts' twin triumph and moved decisively—for the first time ever—to the head of the pack. Once again the two swastika banners rose above the stadium as the victors bowed their heads to receive their medals. After "Deutschland über alles" had been played, the wildly euphoric crowd burst into a spontaneous round of the "Horst Wessel Song" which stopped the proceedings for several minutes.

There was one more aspect to the achievement that did not go unnoticed: an additional spectator among the thousands to cheer on his compatriots. During the final round of the shot put Adolf Hitler had slipped into his box above the victors' platform. And at Wöllke's final throw the leader of the German people could be seen pounding his rolled-up program excitedly on the rail in front of him.

When the awards ceremony was completed, there was some commotion around the victors' platform.

David turned to Tom. "Can you tell what's happening?"

Tom strained to see over a sea of heads. "I don't know. Someone in a gray uniform's just pulled the two Germans aside."

"Yeah, it looks like they're leading them away."

"You don't think they've been arrested, do you?"

"For what? For winning?"

"I don't know." Tom shrugged. "Who knows how they do things here in Germany?"

There was more confusion and murmuring throughout the stadium as Wöllke and Stöck solemnly marched off and disappeared into the concrete entry tunnel. But a few moments later they reappeared, entering Hitler's box with enthusiastic waves to the crowd. Before the assembled multitude the chancellor gestured, summoning the victorious athletes to him. They stepped forward. He extended his hand to each man in turn for the official congratulations. With the other hand, he clapped each one firmly on the shoulder, as if they were reunited brothers. The crowd went wild.

"He's turned the stadium into a temple of Aryan supremacy," said Tom.

The games were delayed briefly while Fleischer and Krüger made their way up to the box for the same honor. Again the concrete bowl rang with the stirring strains of the "Horst Wessel Song," carried aloft by fifty thousand eager voices.

And the German leader magnanimously showed the same treatment a few hours later for the "Flying Finns"—Ilmari Salminen, Arvo Askola, and Volmari Iso-Ollo—who swept the ten-thousand-meter run, leaving Don Lash of Indiana, the best of the American distance runners, far behind.

"I don't know what's happening to us," said David in despair. The faces of his teammates mirrored his gloom.

In fact, the only hopeful American note of the afternoon session was the qualification of Johnny Woodruff, the dynamic black freshman from Pitt, in the eight-hundred-meter trials.

But when Woodruff came back to the bench to receive the backslaps and congratulations of his teammates, something suddenly occurred to David. Another chill rippled through him.

"I just thought of something. . . ."

"What's that?" asked Tom.

"Germany's been doing so well. . . ."

"Yeah," he said glumly. "What about it?"

"Everything's been going their way. But the one place it looked like they were *going* to do well, in the eight hundred trials, Horst Müller didn't run."

"You're right," said Tom, stunned. "And he *was* the one legitimate German hope. Where is he?"

David and Tom both replayed the events and images of the day in their minds. Though both distinctly remembered seeing him at the opening ceremonies yesterday, neither of them could remember spotting Müller in the stadium anytime today.

It was not until late in the evening, with dusk settling over the field, that the Americans finally rallied. But when they did, it happened in spectacular fashion. Out of an impossibly crowded field of more than fifty contestants, Cornelius Johnson of Berkeley took the high jump gold with an Olympic record 2.03 meters. The competition was so tight that Dave Albritton of Ohio State and Delos Thurber of USC tied for silver and bronze just inches below Johnson. Overshadowing the astounding German victories earlier in the day, it was the first clean sweep of the games.

Three American men stood together on the victors' platform, and three American flags went up the winners' masts. For the first time in the games "The Star-Spangled Banner" was heard across the Reichssportfeld.

But also for the first time in the games no proffer of congratulations or good wishes came from the official box. Some in the stadium said it was that the hour was growing late and affairs of state had grown pressing. But to David Keegan and his teammates another scenario suggested itself. Realizing early on that America's "black auxiliaries" were bound to win, the führer had quietly stolen away before he would have had to acknowledge their achievement publicly.

The great Olympic bell that had summoned the youth of the world tolled, signaling to them the end of the first day.

Döberitz

Back at the Olympic Village, David was feeling tense, agitated. He sat in the dining hall watching the Germans stuffing themselves with food and felt queasy just looking at them. It wasn't just Karl, as it turned out. All the German athletes seemed to have incredible appetites.

At dinner he saw Dean Crowell, one of the American coaches, just leaving the dining hall. David hurried over to him.

"Can I talk to you a minute?"

"Why not?" the coach replied. "What's up?"

"I'm not sure."

They strolled from the dining hall over to a lounge room that was empty. David knew Crowell pretty well since he was the coach for the four hundred relay, Tom's event. They took seats around a coffee table in a comfortable grouping in the corner.

"Quite a day, huh?" said Crowell, obviously wondering what was on David's mind.

"Yeah," said David. He said nothing else for several moments. After he had collected his thoughts, he began. "Coach, does it seem strange to you that the Germans are doing so well?"

Crowell's eyebrows knitted together. "Strange? How do you mean?"

"They've never won a single track and field event since 1896. You were in Los Angeles. You've seen them at other international meets. They didn't do squat. And now look at them."

Crowell leaned back in the easy chair, stretched his arms out behind him, and put his feet up on the padded ottoman. "As surprising and impressive as it is, winning those two events in the first day—"

"Four medals in two events," David put in.

"All right—even four medals—is not exactly conclusive of anything."

"It's more than just that," David protested. "There's a whole pattern. You must have seen their guys practicing around the Olympic Village. They're terrific. Man for man. Better than they've ever been before. I timed myself against one of them, a guy I'd beaten several meets in a row. And this time he whipped the shit out of me. I don't even think it's just the Olympics, Coach. What about Max Schmeling? How'd he knock out Joe Louis in New York?"

Crowell pulled his body back to an upright position and crossed his thick arms in front of him. "So what are you saying, Keegan? You saying the Jerries aren't playing fair? That they loaded up Schmeling's gloves? That they've doctored the measuring tapes or slipped in light equipment? Maybe they slipped Jack Torrance or Don Lash a Mickey Finn before they went out. Maybe that's what your Jerry friend did to you at the village. Is that what you're suggesting?"

"I don't know," David glumly admitted. "I'm just telling you what I've seen. Coach, you have to admit that the Germans are doing better all across the board."

"Okay," Crowell responded. "So what?"

"And there has to be a reason."

"Fine. What is it?"

David leaned in toward him. "What do *you* think?"

Crowell uncrossed his legs and crossed them again in the other direction. He frowned and rubbed the end-of-the-day stubble on his chin. "What do I think? Let me get back to you."

FIFTEEN

Monday, August 3

First thing in the morning there was a knock on David's door. He opened it to find Dean Crowell standing in front of him.

"Tom's not here," David told him. "He's already gone out to practice."

"I'm not looking for Quinn," Crowell stated. "It's you."

"What's going on?"

"Brundage wants to see you. Now."

"What for?"

"I'm sure he'll tell you. Let's go."

Crowell led him out of the dormitory, across the wooded path, and into the administration building. They came to a room David hadn't even known existed. There was a conference table and some lounge chairs. The sole window looked out over the lushest part of the forest.

Avery Brundage sat by himself at the end of the table. "Good morning, Mr. Keegan. Please sit down." He gestured to Crowell. "Close the door."

David sat down at the table at the farthest point from Brundage. Crowell continued standing near the closed door.

"How are you getting along here in Berlin?" the chairman inquired. "Everything to your liking?"

David shrugged. "Sure." What was he getting at? There was always a veneer of rather stiff cordiality about Brundage that seemed to hide something seething just below the surface.

"Good. As you might imagine, I'm very busy," said Brundage. "So let me get right to the point. Coach Crowell tells me you've become concerned with the performance of certain athletes in these games, specifically the German athletes."

So that was it. Crowell had gone right to the top. Brundage himself was getting involved. And he was the one guy David could think of who had enough influence to get to the bottom of this. To Brundage the sanctity of amateur athletics was a religion. Instantly David's spirits brightened.

He told Brundage everything he had noticed, just as he had done with Crowell the night before. Without mentioning Karl specifically, he related the two-man race between them and the practice heats of the German team he'd observed before that. The chairman listened without saying anything, a deepening scowl etched across his broad face.

When David had finished, Brundage brought his two hands together on the table and interlocked the fingers. "Let's not mince words, Mr. Keegan. You're a bright and observant young man. That much is clear to everyone. Even though you've been overseas for the past two years, you are undoubtedly aware of the . . . controversies that have been attending these games. A number of countries, including our own, threatened boycotts. There was much idle talk about so-called persecution of certain minority groups in Germany. And with our cooperation the German authorities have gone to great pains to avoid any possible taint of implication from these charges. A tremendous amount of time and effort and resources has gone into making these the greatest Olympic Games in history. Our German hosts have dedicated themselves to setting the standard that all future games will strive to live up to."

"Yes, I can well appreciate that," said David amiably. "I've been very impressed."

"I was hoping you would be," said Brundage. He unclasped his hands and balled one of them into a tight fist. "This is the message I want to impart to you this morning. And it goes equally for any of your friends or fellow athletes who might have similar ideas. I will not have anything occur which *in any way* might jeopardize the success of these games. I will not tolerate any accusations of unfair play or bad sportsmanship leveled by anyone under my authority. With all that has preceded us here to Berlin, nothing could bring a cloud over this event faster than to have it torn apart by charges and countercharges of impropriety. I have been in close contact throughout with Count Henri de Baillet-Latour, president of the International

Olympic Committee, and he is utterly convinced of the Germans' good intentions."

David protested, "But that doesn't prove—"

"Prove? You have no proof of anything, because there is nothing to prove. If there were no possibility of a national team improving from one Olympics to another, there would be no point in holding them. That is their excitement. What is the point of holding a football game if the outcome is preordained?"

"I'm not just talking about special, isolated cases, Mr. Brundage."

"Germany itself is a special case, Mr. Keegan. It has risen from the ashes of military defeat and economic despair to take its rightful place among the world's leading nations. I suspect its new vigor in athletics is but one aspect of it, a very important aspect, which we are going to do nothing to tarnish."

"I'm not suggesting we are," said David with exasperation.

"Mr. Keegan, have you been shown any discourtesy or unkindness by anyone since you've been in Berlin?"

David shook his head.

"I'm gratified to hear that," Brundage stated. "I was concerned, you see. Because it would be unfortunate if any charges of unsportsmanlike conduct leveled by you were taken in the wrong way or if you were perceived to have an ax to grind or something to prove because of your German heritage, however well covered it might appear to be by your Anglo-Saxon surname. That sort of behavior would put us all in a bad light. I don't think any of us would want that, would we?"

"Of course not," David said. "But that's not what I'm talking about. There's been a death at the Olympic Village. And you must know what happened to Horst Müller."

"Very regrettable," Brundage commented. "Yet it only underscores how nothing worthwhile in life is achieved without sacrifice. Not freedom, not progress, not personal accomplishment. That spirit of sacrifice and dedication is what the Olympic movement is all about. I was proud to hear the way you tried to save that German boy's life, but whatever you did, he has literally sanctified these games with his death. That should be a sobering and chastening sentiment to us all."

David felt the old anger once again welling up within him, physically rising from the pit of his stomach to his throat. Brundage was monomaniacal. People could die, and he wouldn't jeopardize his precious Olympics.

Brundage's voice remained calm and even. "Mr. Keegan, no one denies your accomplishments and the pride your country may take in you, least of all I. And no one wishes you greater success in the decathlon this coming Friday and Saturday. As a former Olympic athlete myself I know the pressure you are under. But let me also tell you this, Mr. Keegan. If you insist on casting unfounded aspersions upon our German hosts or are perceived in any way to embarrass the American team or the American Olympic Committee, I will personally have you packed up and out of here so quickly it will make your head spin. There will be no recourse, no appeal, Mr. Keegan. I am the law. And if you doubt my will or my ability to carry this out, you have but to try me as others have before you. Check with certain of your friends on that score."

"I was not brought up to take kindly to threats," David commented.

"The particulars of your upbringing are no concern of mine," Brundage stated. "Oh, and one other matter, Mr. Keegan. It has been brought to our attention that you have been spending not inconsiderable portions of your time away from the Olympic Village, making 'forays' into various parts of the city."

David felt as exposed and naked as he had in the locker room with Karl.

"I will only add that it would be extremely unwise either to squander your precious training time or to make a nuisance of yourself to our German hosts."

Who was watching him? A new, even more immediate sense of jeopardy permeated David's being.

"Have I made myself plain, Mr. Keegan?" The Olympic chairman gestured for Crowell to open the door. The audience was clearly over.

David walked by himself back to his dormitory, wishing a plague on all their houses. He had told his story to Arthur Hargreaves, who thought him nothing more than a neurotic athlete, overwhelmed by the task that had been placed before him and deathly afraid of losing. He had told his story to Avery Brundage, who considered him an annoying, sanctimonious meddler with an ax to grind and something to prove.

Well, there was probably some reality in both those descriptions, David admitted to himself. He was what he was. But that didn't alter another set of realities: He had seen what he had seen. And now he was truly alone.

Grunewald

The weather on Monday was still dull and gloomy, matching David's mood. Heavy showers intermittently raked the stands and infield, turning the grass into patches of swamp.

And Germany continued to win. David arrived at the stadium in time to see the German carpenter Karl Hein establish a new Olympic record for the gold medal in the hammer throw. His teammate Erwin Blask finished a strong second for the silver. It was an event the United States had never lost before, yet the best ranking any American could muster was a dismal fifth.

David's arrival coincided with that of another spectator. Hitler had an uncanny ability to sense when his countrymen were about to triumph. Next to him as honored guests in the box today were Max Schmeling, former heavyweight boxing champion of the world and the führer's symbol of German supremacy, and Leni Riefenstahl, his beautiful artisan of film. But while Leni herself sat next to him, her platoon of cameramen were busy recording Germany's victories from every angle, in all its spectacular aspects.

A young girl clad all in white held the olive crown above Karl Hein's bowed head. He straightened up, and while his country's national anthem was sounded yet again, he looked straight to Hitler's box and gave his leader a firm Nazi salute. Then the two winners were led off as the other Germans had been the day before. David watched and waited to see them emerge in the box of honor. Instead, Hitler himself left the box for several minutes. The word was that Baillet-Latour had politely suggested that the chancellor make his selective congratulations less public. This, apparently, was his way of complying.

Amid the frequent downpours, which did nothing to diminish the dedication and enthusiasm of the capacity crowd, the afternoon of games progressed through the trials of the steeplechase, the eight-hundred- and the four-hundred-meter hurdles. In none of them could the United States capture its dominance of years past. Meanwhile, through radios, newspapers, and film, the whole world looked on.

But then with one brief event the tide turned. For David there were two overwhelming impressions of the afternoon, and they were tied inextricably together, twin images that would remain with him as long as he lived.

The first was the race itself, the finals of the men's hundred-meter sprint.

Six runners had survived the trials and made it through the endless series of heats. Now they stood across the starting line of the rain-soaked track, digging their toe holes in the soggy earth. In the first lane, Jesse Owens, the standout American thus far. Next to him was Borchmeyer, the German who had surprised everyone, who still might surpass all others. Next to him, Hans Strandberg of Sweden. And next to him, Martinus Osendarp of Holland, who had briefly held the Olympic record the previous day. Then Frank Wykoff. And on the outside in lane six, America's other black rocket, Ralph Metcalfe.

The stadium was electric with anticipation. Osendarp paced nervously around his assigned place, continually checking his toe holes and rubbing his hands on his shorts. The remaining five stood calmly by, betraying no recognition of the magnitude of one another's skills or the challenge they faced.

The flags that ringed the arena were still on their poles. There was no wind in any direction to call a winning time into question.

Herr Miller raised his pistol in the air. "*Auf die Plätze . . . fertig . . .*" The gun sounded, and the runners were off.

Owens was gone like a flash. But Metcalfe stumbled coming out of the starting holes or slipped on the wet track. The others sped past him. *Bad luck*, David thought. He hoped he wasn't injured.

At thirty meters the pack was still together, breathlessly matching stride for stride. Behind them Metcalfe hung in bravely.

Then, in his gracefully fluid way, Owens began to pull ahead. He gained with every step, his speed devastating. He could have been a comet, a hurricane, any of the relentless forces known to nature. Within yards he had the track to himself.

Except for Metcalfe. He refused to let his horrendous start defeat him. With head down and arms churning, he barreled down the track toward the others. He knifed through the pack with fewer than twenty meters left, kicking his way past in pursuit of the unreachable leader. Wet cinder splattered behind him.

Jesse Owens crossed the finish line in a blur. In spite of the deplorable condition of the track, he broke the tape at 10.2 seconds, shattering the Olympic and world records. Ralph Metcalfe finished one meter behind.

Martinus Osendarp was so thrilled to come in third that he turned around and joyfully sprinted back down the track.

The crowd, which had been as a Greek chorus in these games, echoing the triumphs and disasters of its heroes, took up the chant of "Yes-sa Ov-enz! . . . Yes-sa Ov-enz!" as if it had been an ancient tribal memory reemerging into the light of consciousness.

"Yes-sa Ov-enz! . . . Yes-sa Ov-enz!"

It grew steadily, by degrees, until it seemed to ripple the earth and rumble through the concrete and pulsate through the brain of every human being within the confines of Berlin.

"Yes-sa Ov-enz! . . . Yes-sa Ov-enz!"

This proudly partisan crowd, conditioned by years to its own supremacy and the ultimate degradation of all racially inferior beings, took the black sharecropper's son powerfully and enchantedly to its heart.

Eventually the cheering died down. The victors ascended the platform, and the medals were presented. Owens broke out into his infectious grin. The crowd went wild again. Though they didn't know the words, they hummed along with "The Star-Spangled Banner," as if wanting to share this moment with Jesse Owens in any way they could.

The second image of the afternoon was far simpler than the first but no less shattering in its impact.

As soon as the national anthem was over, Owens relaxed his stance. All eyes were still on him. He turned in the direction of the official box and met Hitler's eyes with his own. Then the twenty-three-year-old runner bowed formally in respect to the all-powerful chancellor of Germany.

Hitler appeared to freeze for a second. He recovered and acknowledged Owens's gesture with an equally formal salute. Then he turned decisively away from the young athlete, as if any further contact would contaminate him. The crowd murmured, and the officials around Owens waited to see if Hitler would invite him up for a private audience and congratulation as he had with Hein and Blask moments before. But David and Tom already knew the answer to that. He had made his position on the "black auxiliaries" clear the day before.

David ran into Karl as he was waiting for the bus to take him back to the Olympic Village. They greeted each other and embraced as the old friends they had become.

"I have to go back to the institute for a while," Karl reported.

"But I'll see you tonight for the symphony," David said.

"Of course. I wouldn't miss it. And I know how much Miranda is looking forward to it. You have seen how excited she gets."

"Good," said David, again conjuring up the exquisite child-woman vision in his mind. He wondered how the evening was going to work out. Hargreaves had told him it would end up just being the two of them. He hoped with all his soul that the Englishman hadn't been jerking him around and wasn't planning anything "unpleasant" as far as Karl was concerned. No, that was ridiculous, David told himself. The "pressure" was definitely getting to him, too.

"So we'll meet at seven up in the main foyer of the institute?" Karl asked.

"Yes, seven, that's right," David confirmed.

"Good. We'll see you then." The German offered a friendly wave and turned away in the direction of the *U-bahn* station.

Suddenly David called after him. "Karl!"

He stopped. "Yes?"

Even now David wasn't sure what he wanted to say. Maybe he should tell him to forget it, that it was nothing, just that he was really looking forward to seeing him and Miranda tonight. But something was gnawing away at him, and it would continue to gnaw away at him until he got it off his chest. And he knew Karl was the only person he could share it with.

Karl looked at him quizzically. "Is anything wrong?"

David began, "You were here for the men's hundred meters."

"Yes. Very impressive. I have never seen anyone run like your Jesse Owens." He pronounced the name with the hard *V* sound, the same as the chanting crowd.

"But the way Hitler treated him . . ."

"Yes? What about it?" Karl sounded as if he hadn't noticed.

A pained expression came over David's face. "After the way he'd treated the German winners . . . after the way he'd treated the Finnish winners, it just seemed wrong to me the way he slighted Jesse and Ralph, to all of us. You said it yourself. It was probably the most spectacular single performance ever seen in the Olympics. And yet Hitler ignored it. He went out of his way to ignore it."

"The führer does not need me to answer for his actions," said Karl. "He knows his own mind very clearly . . . as well as the minds of his people."

"But does he?" David protested. "I remember when I was a kid growing up in Pennsylvania after the war, all the taunts and mistreatment and hate I suffered through because my family was German. I was only six when the war ended, but I'll never forget wondering why other kids hated me for something like that. I hadn't done anything to them. I was born in America. But my grandmother and grandfather still spoke with a German accent, and that was all it took in that climate. When I got to Germany, I thought, *Well, I've finally arrived home.*"

"Everyone has been nice to you, I think. They've welcomed you as a fellow German."

"Yes, you know that. I'm not saying they haven't. But that's what makes this all so painful and difficult to understand. The Olympics are supposed to be a time of friendship and tolerance and respect. That should be their whole point."

"Among people who share common goals and heritages," Karl added.

"With all you've got going for you in this country now, with all the German people have been able to accomplish, why do your leaders have to single out the Jews or the Negroes or anybody else? What have you got against them?"

Karl listened patiently, nodding his head once, as if he had heard all this before. Without unkindness, but with his eyes clear and focused, he said, "How can you criticize our supposed treatment of anyone with what you do to your Negroes in your South or your Orientals in your West? We have read in our newspapers that last year eighteen Negroes were lynched in your country, and eight more have been lynched so far this year. Is that a lie we have been given?"

"No, probably not." David sighed. "But it's not the whole story. You're taking it all out of context."

"Am I?" Karl asked. "Tell me, do you allow Jews to attend your finest schools or belong to your finest clubs? Do your upper class or your aristocracy invite them to their social gatherings? Here, in Germany, there is no hypocrisy among us. We did not create the differences between the races. The Almighty did that, just as he created the differences between the animals as you go higher and higher up the scale. There is no reason to suppose the differences stop when you reach man. Our scientists have confirmed that for us. We have an ancient destiny to fulfill as a people and as a race. Our führer has led us to it. And nothing must be allowed to debase the purity of the German blood or the immortal spirit of the German *Volk.*"

Now, finally, David was beginning to understand how men like Adolf Hitler worked. Truth to the Nazi leader was no more than a commodity, to be used and manipulated toward any desired end. Offer just enough of this commodity for a person to seize hold of. Insinuate these ideas into the thoughts of a people with a proud heritage and a heavy burden of recent history. Direct their resentment, and tie it together with their loftiest ideals. And who was to say that had the history of the last twenty years been reversed, he could not have just as easily taken hold in England or America? It could just as easily have been David saying this to Karl. His own childhood proved that. David could not deny the lynchings. He could not deny the segregation and the bigotry. He could not deny the hatred that had been visited upon him in the schoolyard and the neighborhood as an innocent six-year-old.

There is a certain emotional comfort to be had in the embracing of moral absolutes. There is a certain painful maturity in denying them yet refusing to lose all hope. Looking at Karl, David wondered if he had any better fix on truth or destiny or hope than the hundred thousand other people who had screamed and shouted and cheered along with this afternoon.

Karl put his hand on David's shoulder. "We should not be talking about this," he said heartily. "It doesn't matter. Politics has no place in athletics."

"I'm not sure that's what you've been telling me," said David sullenly.

"Certainly not between similar people like us, who share the same heritage, the same outlook, the same aspirations." There was something cold and aloof, almost derisive in the way he said it. David was shaken. Could this be the same person with whom he'd formed such an instant bond? All he knew for certain was that as of this moment he wanted to win the decathlon more than he'd ever wanted anything in his life. And if he couldn't win, he just wanted it to be another American who could.

Dahlem

Things were going well for Miranda. The problem Dr. Hahn had set out for them to tackle was coming into focus. She could feel it, like a warm flush of satisfaction starting to settle over her. She could almost sense it within her grasp. The answers she hungered for were close by. They tantalized her, just out of reach. They teased her, like phantom shapes glimmering on the distant horizon.

She could visualize the atomic particles in her mind's eye—little bluish globes, bouncing into one another, bursting to tell their secrets to anyone who truly wanted to listen.

She was floating within this universe of her imagination when she was startled back into the concrete world by a knock on her open door. It was Karl. She could tell by the sound. She had been lost in her thoughts. It must be time to stop work. She looked up at Karl. He had on his Wehrmacht dress uniform.

"Why are you wearing that?" Miranda asked, rising to kiss him.

He reacted coldly, as though he had more important things on his mind. "There has been a change in plans," he stated.

"What do you mean?"

"I just now got a call. I'm to appear at the British Embassy this evening."

Miranda blinked in surprise. "What for?"

"A reception the English are staging in honor of the Olympics. As I'm an athlete from the host country and a military officer, I've been asked to represent Germany. Frankly I believe that my particular event also has something to do with it," he explained haughtily. "The British have no hopes in the decathlon, so I would not be an embarrassment to them."

Miranda's lips formed into a pout to register her disappointment. "And am I to go with you?"

"No. It's an official function. The invitation is for me alone. No escort."

"But what about our plans with David?"

"We will have to disappoint him."

"We can't do that," she protested. "It's not fair at the last minute like this."

"'Fair' is irrelevant," said Karl offhandedly. "We must fulfill our duty."

"But he went to so much trouble to get the tickets, I'm sure."

Karl shrugged. "That is unfortunate, but the way it is."

"But how is he going to feel when you tell him you're breaking the date?"

"He will understand. He's a soldier, just as I am. In a situation like this, personal feelings must be ignored."

"No. That is wrong," said Miranda emphatically. "Personal feelings must never be ignored."

"That is a woman talking. When duty requires it, we have to forgo individual pleasures. This is a great honor. I have been asked to represent my country."

"I haven't," said Miranda.

Karl's eyes narrowed. "And what do you mean by that?"

"I don't mean anything by it," she said casually. "You go to your English party, and I will go with David to the symphony."

"It would not look right for you to be seen in public alone with him."

Miranda folded her arms across her chest. "So you want me to sit home? Is that it? What are you worried about? He's your friend. And our guest."

"Even so, it would not please me for you to go alone with him."

"I am so sorry, Lieutenant. But when duty requires it, we have to forgo individual pleasures. In a situation like this, personal feelings must be ignored."

Karl's face was growing red. "You and I have a relationship."

"Yes," she shot back. "And you should trust me in it."

"It's not a matter of trust. It's a matter of what is proper, of what other people will think."

"I don't care what other people think."

"Miranda!" said Karl sharply. "Get your things together. I'll take you home."

"You will not," she said with growing defiance. "I'm going to wait here for David."

"You're trying my patience."

She couldn't believe what she was hearing. Had the gentle, caring, understanding Karl completely disappeared? Who was this auto-cratic creature who had taken his place?

"I'm waiting," he said firmly.

"I'm not a child!" she said back to him.

"Then stop behaving like one."

"Now you sound just like my father."

"And you sound just like the spoiled little girl you are. Whenever it's convenient for you, you just crawl into your little shell and forget about the world outside. All you know and care about is your science."

"That isn't fair, and it isn't true!" she declared.

"You have no understanding of discipline or propriety."

What could be more disciplined than science? she thought angrily.

"You're too independent and freethinking for your own good."

Miranda didn't know whether she was more indignant or hurt. "I thought you liked that . . . admired that in me."

"When it is appropriate."

"How long have you felt this way about me?" she asked, her lower lip quivering.

Karl didn't answer. Instead, he said, "You always had to be different. You were never interested in the League of German Girls, the way your younger brother, Hans, is in the Hitler Youth."

"No. And he's given my parents none of the trouble I have, has he?" She stood up. "What's happening to you, Karl? You always took up for me against my parents. You agreed with me about how unreasonable they were. I defended you and our relationship and told them they were wrong about you. Now you sound just like them."

"Maybe they knew the only way to handle you." He began tapping his foot, perhaps unconsciously. "Now I'll tell you one more time, Miranda. I don't want you going out this evening without me. I'm taking you home."

She came around from behind her desk and stood facing him. "What gives you the right to talk to me that way?" she shouted.

"Keep your voice down," Karl warned her. "The door is open, and you're creating a scene."

"I'll do what I want!"

"You'll do as I tell you."

"I will not!"

She saw his arm rise. She felt the impact on her cheek immediately, the pain a split second later. Instantly tears welled up in her eyes, and she brought her hand up to the side of her face.

"How—how could you?" she wept. "Just get—get out of here. Leave me alone."

Without saying anything, Karl turned and walked out of the tiny office. But as he did so, he reached for the doorknob and pulled the open door closed behind him as if she were a child confined to her room until she had learned how to behave.

Miranda pounded her fist down on the desk in anger and humiliation and frustration, then sank back into her chair, sobbing.

SIXTEEN

Central Berlin

Heinrich Himmler quickly climbed the steps of the Reich Chancellery, acknowledging the smart salutes of the storm troopers who flanked the two sides of the entrance. The impressive building on the Wilhelmstrasse always gave him a feeling of peace and confidence. It was constructed of pale yellow stone and designed to last a millennium, like the thousand-year Reich it symbolized.

Inside he strode purposefully down the monumental main corridor. He came to the gleaming black marble pediment that marked the entrance to the führer's study. On either side of the twenty-foot-high double doors stood black-helmeted, white-gloved members of the Leibstandarte-SS, Hitler's personal bodyguards.

Rudolf Hess, the deputy führer, came from the other direction. "The führer wanted a nap when he returned from the Olympic Stadium," Hess reported. "Now he's just finishing up a light repast."

Himmler nodded, his hands folded characteristically in front of him. He could imagine the nature of the führer's light repast. Probably some carrot sticks, some dry toast, and one of any number of unidentifiable substances referred to by his chef as health foods. Hitler was the total antithesis of the gluttonous, epicurean Göring.

A nap and a light, boring repast, yet highly representative of the dull, quotidian personal life of the man they all acknowledged as their leader. To his *Reichsführer* Heinrich Himmler, all of Hitler's personal tastes were middle-class, banal, unflamboyant, and utterly predictable. All in all, an extremely uninteresting individual. But it was also completely beside the point. Because as far as Himmler was concerned, Adolf Hitler was not so much an individual as a primal force, a force which would fulfill Germany's historic destiny, a force

162

which embodied the heart and soul of the National Socialist movement.

Himmler stood by the door with Hess, staring at the great red and black swastika pennant hanging from the wall. It made his heart swell with pride. National socialism had not started with Hitler. Its true origins were lost in the mythic past of the German consciousness. Wagner had understood this. Neitzsche had understood this. And soon an entire world would understand it.

Hitler's profound insight into the workings of the human mind, the manifestations of the will, the deepest longings of the German *Volk* were what set him outside commonplace experience and marked his intersection with the infinite and all-powerful imperatives of history. To Heinrich Himmler, Adolf Hitler was at the same time more and less than an individual human being. Adolf Hitler was the instrument of destiny.

Here was a man who could speak to all the greatest of his land. Here, too, was a man who could speak to all the angry, frustrated little failures and say to them, "The fault is not within you. It is beyond you. But not beyond your control. If you set your lot with me, I promise that you will triumph. *We* will triumph. All of us. Together. And together we will show the rest of the world."

Heinrich Himmler, former Bavarian chicken farmer, a quiet, diminutive, nearsighted, and balding man just two months short of his thirty-sixth birthday, had long ago set his lot with Adolf Hitler. As a result, he was the second most powerful man in Germany. And the future shone forth ahead of him with unbelievable brilliance.

"I'm dining with an English guest," said Hess. "The Duke of Hamilton. He seems a reasonable sort of man whom I believe I can win over to our cause."

"Best of luck," said Himmler without commitment. The idea of Rudolf Hess's carrying out even the simplest exercise in diplomacy struck him as absurd. Hess was Hitler's lapdog, a dull and thick-headed peasant whose only lasting claim to greatness was that he had served time with Hitler in Landsberg Prison after the Beer Hall Putsch and had acted as his personal secretary, transcribing the manuscript to *Mein Kampf.*

Other individuals on his own staff gave him greater worry.

Reinhard Heydrich approached from down the corridor and offered his somber, narrow-lipped greeting to the other two men. Just then the doors to the study swung open. Himmler jealously wondered if the timing had anything to do with his handsome deputy's arrival.

Hitler came toward them from somewhere in the far reaches of the cavernous room. He appeared to be in good spirits, clear-eyed and well rested from his nap and obviously buoyed by what he had witnessed this afternoon.

"It was quite a show at the stadium today," he said to his three visitors. "I must confess that athletic competition never much interested me. But our athletes' performance these past two days has been nothing short of inspiring."

"And were it not for their auxiliaries, the Americans would be presenting no competition at all," Heydrich remarked.

It was clearly just the right thing. Hitler nodded his head in delight. "The Americans should be ashamed of themselves, letting Negroes win their medals for them. Unbelievable. Do you know, after that fellow Owens won the race . . ." He looked to Hess. "Which one was it?"

"The hundred meters," Hess replied.

"Yes, whatever. In any case, would you believe that right after this race, Baldur von Schirach, the Reich youth leader, suggested it would be good for our image to be photographed with this Owens." As usual, Hitler continued his narrative without the prompting of others. "I said to him—no, I take that back—I shouted at him, 'Do you really think that I will allow myself to be photographed shaking hands with a Negro?'"

The three high-ranking visitors nodded their heads in approval.

Suddenly serious again, Hitler demanded, "Why did we not win that race?" It was a technique he had perfected to keep his associates off-balance.

"We firmly expected to," Himmler stated. "However, our principal hope for that event, a young man called Rolf Schmidt, died unexpectedly of a heart attack at the Olympic Village a week ago, Saturday."

"Well, when one soldier falls, another will always be there to take his place. We shall prove that our young Aryan men and women are more than a match for anyone in the world, just as we did this past spring when Max Schmeling defeated the African whom the Americans had representing them in New York."

"Yes, exactly," Himmler said. "And I'm pleased to be able to report equally good news and stunning successes on the current score."

"Please sit down, gentlemen," said Hitler.

When he had taken a seat opposite the fireplace, Himmler crossed his legs, leaned forward, and continued. "Your faith in the *Übermensch* program has been vindicated, and your personal inspiration has borne a rich harvest. So far the results have been highly gratifying and justify all the time and resources we've devoted."

"I would expect nothing less," said Hitler, clapping his hands once and then balling the right one into a triumphant fist. "I had proclaimed to the entire world that our athletes would be the best. I am both pleased and relieved that you backed me up."

"There was never any question in my mind," Himmler stated modestly. "We have already begun receiving press reports from around the world. Clearly everyone is both surprised and impressed by our outstanding showing this time. In fact," he went on, "in the first two days of the games, after the hundred-meter dash, each targeted event has been won"—he glanced down at his notes—"with the exception of the eight-hundred-meter run."

"And what happened there?" Hitler asked, his manner suddenly more subdued.

"A full explanation is not yet available, I'm afraid. We had an excellent candidate in that event, a very powerful specimen by the name of Horst Müller."

Hitler's eyebrows raised slightly with impatience. "And so then?"

Himmler sighed, removed his glasses, and began rhythmically polishing them with his handkerchief. "Shortly before the commencement of the games Herr Müller's behavior became increasingly erratic. He began displaying symptoms of mental instability, including a particular incident at the Olympic Village. Fortunately Obergruppenführer Heydrich contained the matter before it could pose a serious threat."

Hitler nodded his approval in Heydrich's direction. "And how do our future prospects look?"

"Equally promising," Himmler stated.

"Good. Now, on to even greater glory! I want you to report to me every day."

"Of course. Among other events, we have high hopes for the crowning achievement of the Olympic Games—the decathlon. It is a title that carries with it tremendous prestige. The man who wins this series of competitions can easily be thought of as the greatest physical specimen in the world. So clearly success in this event could be extremely important in our program."

Whenever any mention of superiority or domination over the rest of the world came up, Hitler's eyebrows raised and his ears seemed to perk up. "We have good prospects for this, my dear Himmler?"

"Excellent prospects, my führer," the SS chief replied.

"I'm very sorry to hear that," David said when Miranda told him Karl would be unable to join them for the evening. "But I guess when duty calls, you have to respond. And it is quite an honor." So the Brits had come through after all.

"Karl was sure you would understand," said Miranda lightly. "I'm not sure I would. My father says I'm immature and have no sense of responsibility. Maybe he's right."

You have absolutely everything you need, David thought.

"So I'm afraid it will be just me this evening if that's not too disappointing."

David smiled. "We'll manage to bear up under the circumstances." He gazed at her and tried to read her reaction, but it was impossible. She looked lovely and innocent and seductive. She had her blond hair swept back and pinned behind her head, where it cascaded down the back of her neck in what, for her, would pass as a formal style. She wore a simple knee-length cotton dress of baby blue under a white knit cardigan to protect her from the chill of the Berlin evening.

"You look beautiful," David said.

"Thank you," she replied, smiling shyly and demurely lowering her eyes.

David sprang for a taxi from the institute to the symphony hall; it seemed to impress Miranda. She would have been even more impressed, he figured, if she'd known that the British were willing to put out an essentially unlimited supply of reichsmarks if it meant winning her.

The Philharmonie was a cavernous hall that had been built about a hundred years before as a roller-skating rink. The vast amount of florid decoration that had been used in transforming it for music had not quite eradicated the feeling of an overadorned warehouse. It was

Wilhelm Furtwängler's performances which were relied upon to make the Philharmonie over into a palace of artistic expression.

Miranda's eyes radiated with the reflected glow of the hall's huge chandeliers, and she sparkled with the excitement of a young girl being taken to her first adult dance.

The box was small and intimate, with only a few velvet armchairs. It was lined with velvet drapes and very romantic, she thought. It was out of direct line of sight of the other seats but with an excellent view of the orchestra. The program was to consist of Beethoven's Triple Concerto in C, to be followed after the intermission by the Third Symphony. She was still mentally reeling from the horrible and unexpected confrontation with Karl, and she'd been trying hard all evening not to let David see how tense she was.

For some strange reason the music reminded her of David. She glanced over at him when he wasn't looking. He was charming and upbeat and very handsome. But it wasn't in any kind of studied or cultivated way, not like the young men she'd known from school. And he didn't seem terribly aware of or concerned about his good looks; it made him all the more appealing.

She didn't know what it was about David. It was somehow as if she'd conjured him from deep in her own subconscious memory, or was it rather from her own imagination and desires? Just as she searched for the subtle secret that would release the energy and power of the atoms, so in her imagination had she been searching for the force that would ultimately release the energy and power raging within herself. She couldn't get David out of her mind.

Was that what Karl was afraid of? Did he have reason to be? Could that possibly have anything to do with why she was so devastated by his reaction—because it had the ring of truth to it?

Oh, what was wrong with her life? she wondered in despair. She felt the fragile buoyancy of her mood slipping helplessly away. Why did she always keep messing everything up? Was it the rest of the world, or was it she? How could it be everyone else? Why couldn't she be the daughter her parents wanted her to be? And what had she done to make Karl change and start treating her the way he had?

Why couldn't life be more like science, where everything was elegant and tidy, where all the elements were rational, and where there was a solution for every problem if one could only figure out how to pose it?

By the end of the concert's first half even Beethoven hadn't been able to bring her out of her gloom.

Under another set of circumstances, this could have been his dream date. But by intermission David was feeling nothing but increasing frustration. They left the box and walked out to the café and bar in the foyer, where they mingled with the cream of Berlin society.

Here he was with Miranda—alone—in a situation that clearly impressed her. She seemed relaxed with him. She was obviously having a good time. He could easily tell that by her manner and the wide-eyed expression of delight on her lovely face. If there were going to be an opportunity, an opening for him, this would be it. Yet he couldn't figure out how to reach her.

"Are you enjoying the concert?" he asked. *Come on, David*, he chided himself. *You can do better than that.*

She smiled. "Yes. Very much. Beethoven has always been my favorite composer."

"It's too bad Karl couldn't be here with us." *Yet another brilliant bon mot.*

"Yes. I'm sorry he had to miss it."

"Would you like a drink?"

"No, thank you. I'm fine."

"Some wine perhaps?"

"No, thank you."

Okay, so the girl doesn't drink. What does she do? Try something else. "Oh, I've been meaning to ask you, have you been able to see any of the Olympics?"

"I was there yesterday. And I plan to be there on Friday and Saturday when Karl . . . and you . . . play in the decathlon."

A strange way of putting it, but he had to keep remembering that English wasn't her native language and sports wasn't her first love. "I hope you won't cheer too hard against me."

She smiled again, in an innocent way that made him want to protect her and possess her all over again. "Don't worry."

He tried another tack. "Have you ever been to England or America?"

"No," she said sadly. "I've never been out of Germany except last year, when I went to a physics conference with Dr. Hahn in Vienna."

"Would you like to see other places?"

She nodded. "Very much. Karl has told me all about America, at least the part of it he's seen. And England, too. He's been both places to race. I don't think he liked England as much as the United States."

A lot of Germans didn't, David thought. At least that had been true among the German Rhodes Scholars he'd known at Oxford.

"I'd love to be able to show America to you," he said. Was he getting any closer?

Her face glowed, wistfully, it seemed to him. "That would be very nice. I would love that some time."

How about next week then? Deluxe tour, all expenses paid by His Majesty's Secret Military Intelligence Service. Say, right after the medals ceremony for the decathlon? Have your bags packed and sitting on the curb in front of the Kaiser Wilhelm. I'll have someone from the embassy around to pick them up.

"How is your work going?" he asked.

Her face brightened again. "Very well. I suppose I'm very fortunate to be able to do something I love so much. I think we may be close to something exciting."

All the more reason to get her out of here right away, he thought nervously. *But this is getting nowhere. I'm sure Hargreaves's boys must be tailing us.* And pretty soon—like tomorrow maybe—they were going to want to know how much longer his "fact-finding" mission was going to last.

How about another strategy? he thought as he stared into the depths of her blue eyes. Should he turn on all his masculine seductive power and try to charm the pants off her? Maybe a roll in the hay was just what she needed. It sure as hell was what he needed. But this wasn't just some undergraduate conquest, he kept reminding himself. There was a lot more at stake than just his wounded male ego. If he played it wrong, that could be the end of the tether right then and there. Ultimately, though she had no way of knowing, he was playing for her life.

"He thinks too much: such men are dangerous," Shakespeare had Julius Caesar saying. Well, the Bard had gotten Lieutenant David John Keegan's number all right.

He was driving himself crazy. He couldn't figure her out, this enigmatic *Fräulein*. What buttons should he press? What rang her bell? She was warm and friendly and charming, and there was always that hint of deep sensuality just waiting to be brought to the surface. She seemed continually capable of delightful surprise. But she was still very much the alluring yet quiet schoolgirl, sensitive and reserved, and it seemed that every exchange, every bit of dialogue between them came at his initiative.

David noticed her staring upward, where the flickering of the chandeliers twinkled like stars against the darkness of the high ceiling. Without prompting this time she said, "I think Beethoven could have been a great physicist if he'd wanted."

"Why do you say that?" David asked.

"They say that mathematics is the language of science. Maybe that's true. But I think anyone who could write music like that has to understand the wonder of how the universe is put together."

"And for the most critical part of his creative life, he couldn't even hear what he was composing." She was so beautiful.

She brought her eyes downward and even with his own. "He could hear it the way it's important to hear it, just as I can see the centers of atoms too small for the most powerful microscope."

She was still so mysterious and elusive. There were realms of her mind he could not begin to fathom. She was a vital prize to Britain's strategic scientific enterprise. Yet, when he gazed at her, all he could think of was a poem by Yeats he had read the year before at Oxford: ". . . Only God, my dear,/Could love you for yourself alone / And not your yellow hair."

And so it went until the chimes sounded for the beginning of the second half of the concert.

Beethoven's Third Symphony is known as the *Eroica*. David knew it as nothing so much as the epic challenge that brought music into the modern world. And just as Miranda was convinced that the composer must have understood the universe, David became certain, while listening to it, that he must have understood the human soul equally well. The music was transcendent. This was the Olympics and war and sexual conquest and all the triumphs and tragedies of heroic struggle pulled together.

He kept glancing over at Miranda during the first movement, looking for clues to *her* soul, but she maintained an impenetrable curtain around her emotions. During the second movement—the celebrated funeral march—he finally noticed some reaction. A tear glistened poignantly at the corner of her eye, suspended for a moment between her long lashes, then trickled down the side of her face. It was a powerful point in the music, and David was moved to see her respond so intensely.

Emboldened by this tiny crack in her protective shell, he leaned over and covered her hand with his. She continued staring straight ahead, and the tears continued to flow.

Like a little girl, Miranda wiped her nose with the edge of her sweater sleeve. David pulled his chair close to hers and put his arm comfortingly around her shoulders. He felt her body shudder. He retrieved the handkerchief from his pocket and silently passed it to her. Then he took her by the hand, gently but firmly. "Come on," he whispered, leading her out of the box.

"I'm—I'm so sorry," she sobbed when they were out in the corridor. "This is just horrible of me. I've ruined everything."

"No, no, you haven't," he assured her. He led her to the wall and almost leaned her against it. He took the handkerchief back from her and began daubing it tenderly on her wet face. Even in the subdued and shadowy light he could make out the reddening blotches spreading across her cheeks. And even in the murky light he couldn't help noticing how lovely she still was.

Ernest Hemingway had written something about never being able to know the depths and totality of a woman's beauty until you'd seen her in tears. David was now more convinced than ever that Miranda Wolff was the most beautiful woman he had ever seen.

"I'm sorry," she repeated through her weeping. "I'm an absolute disgrace."

"Just be quiet," he said to her. He put one hand around her waist and with the other, brushed her hair to the side. He kissed her on the forehead and then on the cheek, tasting the salty residue of her tears. He casually wondered if he would always remember her now by that taste. "I'll take you home," he said.

"No. Please don't," she said. Her watery eyes were pleading, larger than he had ever seen them. "Not yet."

David found a café a short walk from the Philharmonie. They went to a small booth in the back.

"Now, tell me what's bothering you," he said, reaching across the table and clutching her hand.

"Oh, I don't know. It's all so silly," Miranda replied through her sniffles. She was still red-eyed, interlocking her fingers and twisting her hands nervously about each other. "I guess . . . It's—it's Karl."

David was only half surprised. The powerful music hadn't triggered any long-buried traumas. It had merely evoked something immediate and close to the surface. What else would it be at her age?

So he was being cast in the role of hand holder while she moped about boyfriend problems. Though he knew he had no right to be, he also realized he was more than a little jealous. Okay, how had Karl slighted her, and how had Miranda managed to get her nose so far out of joint? Still, he encouraged her to go on. If the problem was this serious to her to make her react this way, then the least he could do as a friend was to try to help her feel better.

"He's different lately." She began haltingly. "I'm sure of it. And I don't know what to do about it."

They had already had this conversation walking in the park beyond the Kaiser Wilhelm Institute. But as she continued talking, his attitude quickly changed.

"He hit you?"

Miranda nodded.

"Has he ever done anything like this before?"

She shook her head.

David felt his stomach turning. It seemed strange and almost perverse to him, that with all the killing and savagery of the past twenty years—from France and Flanders to Africa and Ethiopia and Spain—this tiny act of violence loomed so great and monstrous in his mind.

"Karl is the kindest and most gentle man I have ever met," she said. "And at the same time, one who could always make me laugh."

David had to admit that was one aspect of Karl's personality that he'd never seen. "He's never given you any indication of being capable of this kind of behavior? You've never been afraid of him before, when he was angry or upset?"

She wiped away a tear. "No."

David searched for some explanation, for something to say to her. "Are you certain?"

"Uh-huh. Yes. Karl would never do anything like that." A sudden note of resentment crept into her voice. "My father is the only man who's ever struck me . . . or threatened to."

Wasn't her father a professor of something? David couldn't conceive of the type of man who'd beat the charming child Miranda must have been.

"I will tell you something," she said softly, as if making a confession. "Sometimes with Karl, I would do things, say things . . . see how far I could push him before he'd hit me or do something like that."

David watched with inordinate fascination as she casually played with her shoe under the table, dandling it effortlessly on the tip of her toe. "Why?" he asked.

She shrugged. "I don't know. To test him. To test myself. To prove to myself that he wasn't like my father, that whatever I did, he wouldn't punish me or hurt me. And no matter what I did, he never would react. Ever. He just isn't—wasn't that kind of person." She stirred a spoonful of heavy cream into her coffee and watched it swirl. "And . . . with him like this now, I feel my world . . . that everything is coming apart."

"What else?" he asked.

Miranda gave him a quizzical look.

"Is there anything else different about Karl?"

She looked down at the table and hesitated. "I don't know quite how to say it. But I think"—she bit her lower lip until it went white—"I think he has lost his—his desire for me."

A new pang of disappointment and jealousy instantly swept over David, as powerful as it was irrational. Staring across the table at her in the café's lambent light, he simply could not countenance the idea of another man physically possessing or enrapturing this creature.

He blurted out, "You mean you have stopped—"

She blushed deeply. "No. We've never done anything like that."

He was flooded with equally irrational relief. "Then I'm not sure I quite understand what you're saying. If you've never—"

"No, we haven't," Miranda confirmed, "though I suppose all men try to get all women to do it. Isn't that the way it is?"

David tried to nod noncommittally.

"What I'm saying is that he has stopped trying to get me to agree to it. And as gentle as he has always been, that is still unlike him."

"Well, it could still be all the pressure of the Olympics," David suggested.

"No," Miranda asserted. "It isn't just that."

"What makes you so sure?"

"Women can tell these things." For a moment the little girl was gone, and she embodied all the wisdom and experience of the ages. The tears began welling up in her eyes again. "Oh, David, I'm so sorry to be acting like this." She clutched her fingers tightly around his, as if this grasp were the only means by which she could continue hanging on. "I don't know what I'm going to do. You're the only one I can talk to. You're the only one I feel close to." She tried to blink away her tears, which glistened on the ends of her lashes. "I'd just like to run away somewhere and never come back."

Suddenly an inspiration came to David. He'd been waiting for his opening all evening. And whatever it was, he would have to take it. He was no longer an Oxford gentleman out on the playing field. This was real life, and he was a spy. He had to employ whatever means were available to him. He could hate himself for it later, but he had to use all his resources to play on her weakness and confusion and vulnerability.

Surprise attack was always the most effective strategy. That's what he had been taught back at the Point.

"Miranda," he said, holding her hand in both of his, "why don't we go away somewhere together?"

Her eyes opened wide, as if she'd just been slapped again. "What did you say?"

"As soon as the decathlon's over." He had to work fast, get her commitment before she regained control. "I know just what you're feeling. Believe me. Let's get away from all this. Anywhere, as long as it's away from here. Somewhere out of the country." Then his British friends could take it from there.

It was what the SIS boys called a cold pitch, and Hargreaves had told him that it was sometimes the only course available. He could ruin it all here, but it was a chance he had to take. David held his breath. It hinged on so many things—what she really thought of Karl . . . what she really thought of him . . .

"You're a grown woman now," he added, trying to strengthen the pitch. "You're independent. It's 1936. You can do what you want and you don't have to listen to what anyone tells you."

He watched her eyes and tried to imagine what was going on behind them. A dreamy, faraway look came over her face. She could have been floating above the clouds. *Come on, Miranda. Do this for me. Pack up your troubles in your old kit bag.*

Then he couldn't tell what had happened exactly, but he could see reality and rationalism clicking into gear. "I couldn't do that," she stated quietly.

His heart sank. "Why not?"

"Well"—she groped for the words—"because . . . I have responsibilities . . . my family."

"You said yourself how unhappy you are with them."

"But they are my family. I can't just pick up and leave."

"We're just talking about going away for a little while," David said with increasing desperation.

"And what about Karl? How would that look?"

"Do you really care?"

"And . . . and I have my work. That's the most important thing of all."

No matter what he suggested, she set up another roadblock. "Miranda, this is not a climate for scientists to work in."

"The people have been so friendly to you," she replied, her agitation growing. "You said it yourself."

"They have," David said. "But there is something deeper going on."

He thought he detected a flicker of comprehension in her eyes.

"You mean with the Nazis?"

"I don't know. Maybe."

But then it was gone. "It doesn't affect me and what I do," she said. "Politics has no place in science."

But then only a moment later she pleaded, "Help me, David. You're the only one who can."

David was pretty much quiet for the rest of the evening, and Miranda felt bad that she'd ruined things with her outburst. She hoped she could trust him not to let it get back to Karl. She was confused by his sudden suggestion about going away with him and didn't know what to make of it.

What was he saying? Did he want her? Was he making a commitment or suggesting one? Or was he only offering to help her out of her unhappiness? How could she go?

But there was a part of her that wanted to say yes to him, that wanted to passionately. And that was the most frightening thing of all.

She did feel something special for him. She couldn't deny it. Something deep and primal and as elemental as the atom. Something that she knew she'd never felt for anyone else.

Ultimately, that was probably why she had said no; not because of social convention, or what her parents might think, or even love for

Karl. There was something uncomfortably natural and logical about David's request. She had said no because of the suddenness and intensity of her feelings. To have said yes would have meant calling her entire life into question. And that was something she just couldn't do.

David took her home in a taxi and walked her up to her front door. He told her that he hoped he would see her again soon. But whether he actually meant that or was just trying to be polite and save her from further embarrassment, she couldn't be certain.

After the way she'd behaved to him, she only hoped he wouldn't hate her.

Grunewald

It was the third night in a row that her husband had stayed over at the laboratory, so Esther Behrman had finally given up and gone to bed early. She was already asleep when a faint banging sound gradually crept into her consciousness.

It grew steadily louder and more insistent as she awakened. It was coming from downstairs. She turned over and looked at the clock next to the bed. Why would anyone be knocking at this time of night? Unless Abraham had finally decided to come home tonight and as usual had forgotten his key.

She got out of bed and put on her bathrobe. The banging on the front door continued with obnoxious regularity. Could he have been drinking?

"Just a minute. Just a minute, I'm coming," she called out. Her daughter, Jessica, just back from the university, came out of her room and watched from the top of the stairs.

Esther put her hand on the doorknob, ready to rebuke her absentminded husband for upsetting her life this way. When he was involved with one of his experiments, that was all he thought about. She had long since stopped trying to understand what it was he did. She was just glad he'd finally come home.

But when she opened the door, she was confronted by two men in identical black leather trench coats and a third wearing the dark uniform of the Gestapo.

Esther let out a gasp.

"What is it, Mama? Who's there?" Jessica called from the top of the stairs.

"Frau Behrman?" the first man said.

Esther could only nod through her fear.

"Your husband, Herr Dr. Abraham Behrman, sends word that he is involved in an assignment of utmost importance which will require his full-time presence at another facility. He regrets the inconvenience and the distress this might be causing you. We have been instructed to collect any personal belongings he might need while he is away."

"Why hasn't he come to get his own things?"

"I am told that he cannot be interrupted from his work."

"But where is he?"

"I'm sorry. I don't have that information."

"When will he be coming back?"

"I'm sorry. I do not know."

"How can I get in touch with him?"

"I'm sorry. Now, could you please direct us to Dr. Behrman's bedroom and study so that we may get what we need?"

Jessica came down the stairs. "Who are you?" she demanded. "What gives you the right to come in here like this in the middle of the night?"

But the intruders stood their ground. "It would be a most serious mistake for either of you to impede us in any way," the first man warned. "It would also be a serious mistake to repeat or give out details of this visit. Your husband urgently requires your cooperation."

SEVENTEEN

Tuesday, August 4, Döberitz

All through the night David couldn't stop thinking about what Miranda had told him. While Tom slept peacefully in the bunk just a few feet away, David tossed and turned, knowing all the while that each missed hour of sleep this close to the competition would cut into his performance and concentration. And aside from everything else, there was the burden of not being able to share his secret with Tom.

There had been a moment last night when he felt he'd almost reached her. She seemed just about to confront what he was saying to her, until its import closed in and overwhelmed her. She was almost willing to consider his suggestion and face what was going on in her life and around her. But that would have meant thinking like an adult and taking on grown-up responsibilities. Quite clearly Miranda wasn't altogether ready to do that. It was far easier and less troubling to retreat into the comfortable excuse of work and family. Even if, in reality, her work could be done anywhere. Even if, in reality, her family was cold and insensitive and sometimes brutal. They still provided a constant in her life which she apparently still needed. And then there was Karl.

David had decided not to go to the stadium today. As exciting and stimulating as that atmosphere might be, especially if the Americans did well, it was also a monumental distraction at this point. Instead, he would stay at the village, practicing, trying to turn himself inward and prime himself for the decathlon, which was now only three days away.

It was again cold and drizzly as he walked over to the dining hall. The Berlin weather had become a perfect expression of his mood.

He went into breakfast with the first sitting, purposely staying off by himself at the end of the table.

As soon as he had finished eating, David went to the bank of telephones just outside the dining hall. He went all the way over to the end where no one else was talking. He picked up the receiver quickly, before he lost his nerve.

In German he asked the village switchboard operator to connect him with the Hotel Bristol. When the hotel's operator came on the line, he was efficiently connected with his desired room on the first try. This wasn't England. In Germany all the systems worked.

One, two, three, four, five rings. He decided to hang up, as much in relief as disappointment.

"Uh . . . Hello?" announced the distant voice. Ali Prescott had obviously been sound asleep.

"Hi. It's—it's David."

"Oh . . . uh, hello, David. Sorry. I had a late night."

And a lot more fun than mine, I'll bet, he thought. "I'm sorry to wake you."

"No, that's okay." The life was already coming back into her voice. She was incredibly resilient. David had always found that women like Ali had an amazing ability to recover quickly from awkward situations.

"What's cooking?" she asked him.

"Well . . . how about letting me grant you that interview we talked about at the pool the other day?"

"Huh? Oh, that. Right. Yes, good idea. That would be nice. When did you have in mind?"

"What about tonight? Say, around dinnertime? You pick the place."

"Hmm. Training finally getting to you? Sounds a little like the bum's rush to me. But I guess now that I'm a journalist, I should take advantage of such a willing subject."

"Great," said David, overwhelmingly relieved. "You've made my day."

"Already?" She sounded amused. "Then maybe you'll return the favor by making my night."

How could she possibly sound that seductive and enticing at this hour of the morning? It was as if the last four years hadn't taken place. With girls like Ali in the world, how could he be unhappy?

"All right. Why don't you meet me at the Café Kranzler on the Ku'damm at eight-thirty?"

"Fine. But could we make it a little earlier?" David asked.

"Oh, that's right, I keep forgetting. You're in training, aren't you? Okay, make it seven-thirty then. We'll make sure you're in bed early tonight," Ali promised.

Dahlem

Miranda didn't sleep all night. In the morning she felt irritable and cranky, and for the first time since she could remember, she didn't look forward to going into work. It didn't get any better during the *U-bahn* ride to the institute, and it didn't get any better once she had sat down at her desk.

No matter what she did, she couldn't concentrate. How could she think about unlocking the abstract problem of nuclear physics when there was a more immediate problem to unlock?

So after about an hour's worth of accomplishing nothing—of pacing and tearing up papers and staring out the window—she got up and went over to the biochemistry section. As always, Miranda had to have answers. And there was only one person she could think of who might be able to give them to her. One person whom Karl looked up to. One person who knew and understood him. One person who knew and understood her.

Dr. Behrman's office door was closed. She knocked tentatively. There was no answer. She knocked again, a little more stridently this time. Still no response.

Hesitantly, like a child about to go where it knows it's not allowed, she put her hand on the doorknob. It wasn't locked. She opened the door a crack and peered through it. Dr. Behrman wasn't at his desk. She opened the door wide enough to stick her head inside and look around. She still didn't see him. Gaining in both courage and curiosity, she opened the door the rest of the way and walked into the office.

Dr. Behrman wasn't there. She walked over to his desk, looking for some evidence of how long he'd be gone. There wasn't any, so maybe he'd just stepped out for a moment.

She decided to wait for him, as if petulantly refusing to believe that he could be anywhere else when she wanted to talk with him.

She plopped herself down in his large, comfortably battered desk chair. If he came in, he wouldn't mind if he found her sitting in it.

She waited for quite a while, hoping that each shuffle of footsteps in the hall was his. She knew she wouldn't be able to concentrate until she had this business with Karl resolved in her own mind.

Maybe something in his desk would say where he was, whether it was worth waiting. A calendar or a date book perhaps. It wasn't very nice to snoop through other people's things. She had hated it when she was a teenager and she'd found clues that her mother had gone through her drawers, looking for private writings and other secrets. But she wasn't doing anything mischievous or devious here. She just wanted to find out where he was.

Slowly she pulled open the top drawer. There was the usual mass of rubber bands and paper clips. There was a book of stamps and a couple of old bank receipts. Other than that, nothing but the kept refuse of a man who obviously didn't much care for record keeping or the little personal details of life.

She carefully closed the drawer and pulled open the next one. Right on top was a calendar, the kind on heavy paper with one month per sheet. It was a free one, given out at Christmas by one of the scientific instruments companies. Miranda had been sent the same calendar last year.

She scanned down to today's block. Nothing written down, nothing that would give any evidence if he were coming right back. She replaced the calendar and fished around in the drawer, looking for other clues. Now she really was no better than her mother. But she continued to look anyway, having no idea what she hoped to find.

Nothing else looked particularly interesting. There were mostly old requisition forms for various materials and lab equipment signed by Dr. Behrman and countersigned by the institute's supply officer. There was a stapler and a small photograph of his daughter that was mounted in a leather presentation case. She was a very pretty girl, Miranda thought.

Then she found one more sheet of paper that kind of surprised her, knowing Dr. Behrman as she did. It was a typed list. She looked closely at the entries. Each was a sport played in the Olympics. It again reminded her that there must be a side to Dr. Behrman that wasn't readily apparent, interests he held that he didn't talk much about. Unless he was only involved because of Karl's participation. That would be very nice indeed. After all, it had surprised her when he'd left work to go to the stadium and watch Karl practice. Maybe Karl had actually given him this list of sports he thought would be most interesting.

Suddenly she heard footsteps outside the door. Miranda guiltily shoved everything back in place and managed to get the drawer shut before the door opened.

It was Karl. She sucked in her breath with surprise.

"What are you doing here?" he demanded.

"I'm waiting for Dr. Behrman," she replied defensively. "Do you know where he is?"

"Why do you want him?"

"I just do. Is he here today?"

"No." Karl regarded her as if he'd just caught her stealing cookies. Or state secrets.

"Do you know if he'll be here tomorrow?"

"Little girls should mind their own business," he warned.

"Stop treating me like a child!" she snapped.

"Dr. Behrman doesn't owe you an explanation. None of this has anything to do with you."

"Oh, it doesn't? Maybe you don't remember how you got here."

Karl planted his fists firmly on the desk and leaned in toward her on his knuckles. "And what is that supposed to mean?"

"It was my relationship with Dr. Behrman that got you your job."

"It was me that he offered the job to," Karl countered.

"Because he knew me."

"That was only how he met me. Being a friend of yours had nothing to do with my qualifications."

"Friend of yours . . ." It sounded so distant and impersonal. After all they'd been through together, this was what Karl now thought of their relationship.

Almost every moment since yesterday afternoon Miranda had been thinking about what it would be like when she saw him again. Would he immediately rush over to her and beg forgiveness for being such an insensitive boor? Would he tell her tearfully that he had no idea what had possessed him to hit her and that she was the most important thing in the universe to him? None of that would have erased what happened. But it would have been what she needed to get through it. It was what she would have hoped for as a woman.

Instead, there was more hostility, more wariness, more veiled accusations. He was the same defensive, almost maniacal entity she had encountered the day before. Not a word about hitting her. Not an ounce of remorse.

She never imagined she could be so hurt by someone whose unquestioning love she had once taken for granted. She had the urge to lash out, to get back at him, to strike him as he had struck her.

"How did your evening go?" she asked sardonically.

"Just as it should have," he answered formally.

He didn't bother to ask about hers. He stood rigidly with his fists still on the desk surface and watched her until she left the office.

Döberitz

It had been a good day for the Americans, as Tom breathlessly reported as soon as he got back to the Olympic Village.

Buoyed by his telephone conversation with Ali, David had had a good day practicing. He ran hard and fast, getting his timing back, trying through his exertion to banish everything else from his mind. He knew he never could have achieved that level of concentration if he'd gone to the stadium, but he was sorry he'd missed firsthand the inspiration of his teammates' triumphs.

David's rival from Navy, Joe Patterson, had looked for a while as if he'd take the four-hundred-meter hurdles, staying with Glenn Hardin of Mississippi until near the end. But then he'd faded back to fourth behind John Loaring of Canada and Miguel White of the Philippines. It was nice to chalk up another American gold medal. But David was haunted by the idea of the Annapolis man's falling off so fast. Men from the service academies always received more than their share of attention, and if David fell off the same way in the decathlon, the two defeats would only compound each other in the public's mind.

He repeated the prayer of every soldier on a mission where others are counting on him: "Dear God, please don't let me screw up."

Jesse Owens had continued to distinguish himself. He set new world records in each of his three trial heats for the two-hundred-meter sprint. Mack Robinson and Johnny Woodruff also won, so the final the next day promised to be an American blowout. Later in the day Woodruff won the hard-fought eight-hundred-meter run. Maybe things were finally coming around for the United States.

"But it was the long jump that you really should have seen," Tom recounted. "With those long, gangly legs and the way he'd been wiping out every other record in sight, we figured Jesse had it in a cakewalk, right?"

"Yeah," David admitted as he propped himself up by the elbow on his bunk. "So did he?"

"Listen," Tom said, practically bouncing on his own bunk. "What none of us figured was that on his first two attempts he'd overstep the takeoff, and the jump would be disqualified. I'm watching; I can't believe it. I don't know what's wrong. It looks like Jesse doesn't either. One more false start like that, and he's out of it. You can imagine the Jerries licking their chops at that prospect. So anyway, between rounds I see Jesse off talking to Lutz Long, the German jumper who's already qualified. They're gesturing and moving around, and Long's pointing to a spot on the ground, and I can't tell what's going on between them. Anyway, Jesse makes his final attempt and qualifies easily. We all breathe a sigh of relief. It's a terrific jump. The two hundred trials have hardly affected him. The guy's unbelievable. Everyone else makes his jumps in this round. No one can touch him. I figure he's got it cinched. Gold medal number two. Then guess what happens."

"I can't imagine," said David.

"Hitler comes into the stadium. The crowd goes wild. It's as if a current of electricity has gone through the German team. The next guy who comes up is—who else?—Lutz Long. Long takes off like a rocket. An incredible jump. I've never seen anything like it. The crowd can't believe it either. The führer is beaming up in the stands. Things are looking bleak for Jesse and the Americans. Then, on his next try, Jesse starts his run. You can tell he's blocking out the whole rest of the world. He has a terrific takeoff. He sails through the air. He just hangs there. It seems like hours. Then he lands in the pit. *He clears twenty-six feet!* Twenty-six feet five and five-sixteenth inches, to be exact."

"You're kidding!" said David. "That's never happened before."

"Not until today. Everyone is stunned. Hitler's face drops. They give out the medals, play 'The Star-Spangled Banner.' Then Jesse and Long walk off arm in arm, like the best of friends."

"Isn't that something?" said David, and wondered what it would be like between him and Karl by Saturday evening.

"Then Hitler calls Long in for one of his little private chats. That's so he doesn't have to congratulate an American—much less a

Negro American. Then I run into Jesse afterward as we're getting on the bus to come back here. I ask him what was going on between him and Long. And he tells me, Long had been watching him and had figured out what was wrong with his takeoff. He pulled him aside and explained it, told him to mark a place mentally on the ground behind the takeoff line and to jump from there. Jesse realized what he was doing wrong, and he's such a great athlete he was able to correct it right on the spot. But he tells me flat-out if Long hadn't helped him, he would have missed his third jump and been out of it. Long has to realize this, right? He has to know that Owens is his only serious competition, the only thing standing between him and the gold. Yet he helps him. This blond poster boy for Aryan supremacy helps a foreign Negro to beat him while Hitler watches. You know something, David?"

"What's that?"

"I just can't figure these Germans out."

Central Berlin

"What went wrong today?" the chancellor and führer of the German people demanded as the *Reichsführer SS* strode through the double doors of his study. Hitler was on his feet, pacing impatiently behind his giant carved desk.

"There are many variables in sports," Heinrich Himmler explained. "We firmly expected to win the long jump, for instance—"

"Expectation and performance are not the same!" Hitler thundered. "You promised me victories!"

"And we have had many so far. There will be more. We are very confident."

"John Woodruff, Matthew Robinson, Jesse Owens. Always Jesse Owens! It's disgusting the way the crowd fawns over him. Three American winners. Only one of them is even white! That should be a warning for all of us throughout the civilized world. The only thing I am confident about is that today will henceforth be known in Olympic history as 'Black Tuesday.' This is a disgrace, and I will not—I cannot accept it!"

Himmler knew that when the führer had worked himself up to this level of invective, there was no stopping or calming him. There was nothing to do but wait for the storm to pass.

"Is no one with me?" he roared. "Do I stand at this crossroads of destiny all alone?" Now he was wagging his finger at Himmler the way he wagged it at the crowds in his outdoor party rallies. "Because let me tell you, if I have to, I will. And the rest of you will be judged by history accordingly. Do you understand that, Reichsführer?"

"Yes, of course," said Himmler with the proper measure of humility and control. "There is no question that today did not go as we had hoped or anticipated. But if I might just urge a little patience, I can assure you that the *Übermensch* program is still progressing right on schedule."

"And I can assure you that my patience on this matter is limited," Hitler stated. "The world must see what the German *Volk* is capable of. And they must see it now. Do you hear me? I demand victory! In all things victory! At all costs victory!"

Grunewald

Miranda remained troubled throughout the day. So on her way home, instead of riding through to the Zoo station near her home, she got off at Fehrbellinerplatz.

She'd never been to Dr. Behrman's before. He was one of those people whose life centered on their work. And the small part of it that was left over he managed to keep completely separated. He just seemed to belong in his laboratory.

It was a nice, traditional-looking house on a proper and well-maintained street. She walked up and rang the bell. As soon as it was answered, she got a bad feeling.

The woman who opened the door looked as though she were carrying around a heavy burden. From her features she might have recently been smart and elegant-looking. But now she was tired and gaunt and drawn. Her mouth was set in a tight, straight line, and her eyes betrayed the wariness of someone who expects to be hurt. Miranda had seen it before—in the eyes of those forlorn little dogs that pulled the vendors' carts along the Tiergarten, cowering under the prodding of their masters' whips. It was a level of casual and commonplace cruelty that made her want to cry.

As a young girl she had always felt a degree of kinship and identity with those unfortunate animals. And now she instantly felt the same bond with the woman who faced her, uneasily clutching the half-opened door.

"Frau Behrman?" Miranda asked.

"Who are you?"

"My name is Miranda Wolff. I work at the Kaiser Wilhelm Institute."

She thought this would ease the woman's apprehension. Instead, she seemed to flinch at the words.

"What do you want?"

"I would like to speak with Dr. Behrman if you please."

"He's not here."

"Do you know when he might be expected back?"

The fear in the woman's eyes became even more palpable. "Why are you asking me this?"

Miranda was feeling very uncomfortable. She felt perspiration forming at the backs of her knees and other awkward places. "I'm sorry to trouble you. I was only hoping to have a few words with him. If there would be a time that would be more convenient, I could return later—"

The woman broke down. Her voice cracked. A flood of tears streamed from her eyes. "Why are you people doing this to me? I don't know where he is, where you've taken him. I don't even know what he's doing for you. I told the man. He didn't tell me about his work. He never mentioned it to me or my daughter. Are you checking up on me? I haven't said a thing. I swear it! Just tell me, please. I beg you. When is he coming back?"

Miranda looked on with a feeling of helplessness. Then she took a deep breath and said quietly, "Frau Behrman, do you think I could come inside for a moment?"

The Tiergarten

As soon as Miranda returned home, she went into the parlor and told her parents she needed to talk to them. Otto Wolff looked up from his easy chair, reacted calmly, and asked her if the matter could wait. Since she had arrived home late, she had already altered the normal course of the evening. Dinner had had to be delayed, and it was not a good idea to upset established order without compelling reason. But Professor Wolff was a reasonable man. And when his daughter said she wanted to talk before eating, he acceded and told her to go into his study.

Professor Wolff's study was central in its position within the flat and central in its prominence in family affairs. It was to the study that Miranda had always been summoned for all solemn and ceremonious occasions—when she was to be commended, or counseled, or called to account for her actions, or punished for them. She'd lost track of how many times she'd left that room in tears.

As usual, her father took his place in the wing chair facing the fireplace. Her mother, Hannelore, stood next to him with her folded arm resting on the high back of the chair. It could have been a formal portrait.

"So you're telling me Professor Behrman is away from his office," Otto said.

"He's *disappeared*, Papa."

"And how does this matter concern you?"

She hadn't told him why she'd gone to see Behrman. That would only confirm her father's opinion of her as an irrational and emotional little girl. "I'm worried for him," she explained. "His wife doesn't know where he is. She hasn't seen him in days. The Gestapo came to collect some of his things and told her not to ask any questions."

Otto Wolff's eyes narrowed. "The Gestapo? Is Professor Behrman in trouble with the law?"

"That's not possible," Miranda declared. "Even the men who came said he was on an important mission for the government."

"If the Gestapo told her not to ask any questions, why did Frau Behrman tell this to you?"

"She was very upset. She doesn't know what's going on. She and her daughter are all alone. She had to talk to someone. I was there."

"And why were you there?"

Miranda sighed in frustration. "Because no one at his office could tell me anything. So this seemed logical."

"What seems logical at first glance is not always logical in fact," Professor Wolff intoned.

Miranda shoved her hands into the pockets of her jumper. "Papa, no matter what you say, something very strange is happening."

"What does Karl Linderhoff say about this?"

"He either doesn't know or won't tell. He's treating me like a child. He says it is none of my affair and I shouldn't be putting my nose where it doesn't belong."

Professor Wolff raised his eyebrows. "Perhaps I've underestimated him."

It figured, thought Miranda. The only time her father would agree with her boyfriend was when it meant siding against her.

"Papa, I need your help," she pleaded. "We have to do something."

"What is it you want?"

What it was she wanted was for him to be a father—not a teacher, not a judge, not a disciplinarian. She wanted him to acknowledge the fact that she was troubled and tell her he would take care of it, take care of her. "I was hoping with all the people you know that you could talk to someone . . . I don't know. I just thought if I came to you, there would be something you could do."

"I'm gratified you chose to come to me," he said sternly. "I had become disturbed that at your age and with your disposition you had little respect for the opinions and values of your elders. Now it is understandable that you would be concerned about Professor Behrman if you enjoy a good relationship with him, and I commend you for that concern. But that does not necessarily mean we should insinuate ourselves into situations where we might not belong."

"What do you mean, Papa?" Miranda asked.

He put his hands together in front of him and placed his fingers together into a pyramid. "Let us look at this logically. There are two significant and possibly interdependent factors to consider: one, that he may be pursuing work that is important to the state and, two, that the Gestapo is involved."

Miranda stood there with her heart sinking, realizing what was coming, waiting for her father to look at it "logically" for her.

"If, in fact, Professor Behrman is away from his home and office pursuing business for the state, then he is acting of his own free will. He has made the decision based on the needs of his work as to who should know where he is and what he is doing. And if he has chosen not to confide his plans to his wife—or to you—it is not for you to interfere. If, on the other hand, he has come under the scrutiny of the Gestapo for . . . other reasons, then it would be a disloyal and possibly illegal act to interfere."

"But we can't just do nothing," Miranda protested.

"Don't contradict your father," Hannelore Wolff interjected. It was the first thought she had contributed to the discussion, but it followed the same disheartening predictability that the rest of the conversation was taking.

"Professor Behrman is a Jew if I'm not mistaken," Otto stated.

"What have you got against Jews?" Miranda questioned.

"Nothing," her father replied. "You should know that. I've always taught you and Hans that each person should be judged individually, on his own merits and flaws."

"Then I don't see what this has to do with anything."

"Only that the Jews are currently a suspect group in our society, as a matter of national policy. That is not my preference, opinion, or doing. That is merely the way it is. With the disarray that has plagued this nation for the past fifteen years, it is one of the prices which must be paid for order and stability. And logically speaking, it is therefore a foolhardy endeavor to interpose oneself in a situation involving a Jew and the state authorities."

"So I should just sit back as if nothing's gone on?"

"This is not your affair, Miranda. There is nothing to gain, and you can only hope to get yourself into trouble by pursuing it."

"And bring your family in," Hannelore added.

"What about Dr. Behrman's family?" said Miranda. "They didn't ask to be brought in. Yet there they are, and they're sick with worry about him."

"Didn't you hear what your father said, Fräuleinchen? You have neither the experience nor the judgment to be getting yourself involved with this. If you simply attend to your work and your own family responsibilities instead of butting into other people's, you'll have more than enough to keep you occupied."

Miranda sighed again and shifted her weight impatiently. Her fists dug deeper into her pockets. "Thank you for that sage advice, Mother."

"I don't have to listen to that kind of insolence from you!" Hannelore shot back. "You may think you're smarter than anyone else, but you're still not too old or sophisticated for a good whipping, you know."

Yes, I know, Miranda thought sullenly. *Papa has made that more than clear to me. Though you would never even think of dealing with Hans that way, and he's more than three years younger than I. He's also captain of his soccer team at school, president of the debating society, and group leader in the*

Hitler Youth. He does what he's supposed to and brings pride to the sacred Wolff name. The fact of the matter was that her father had never considered science a proper field for a woman to pursue, so nothing she did would ever be right in her parents' eyes. But verbalizing all this could do no more than force the issue in this extremely "logical" family. Because another point of logic Miranda had picked up over the years was that the whip hand had to be exercised from time to time, if for no other reason than to assert the precious right to maintain it.

So she merely said, "I apologize for my disrespect, Mother."

"Very well," said Hannelore severely.

"All right, then," Otto announced. "I consider this matter resolved. "Let us go into dinner."

Miranda ate her meal in silence. Her tense jaw and constricted throat protested every mouthful. It was like chewing cardboard and swallowing plaster. She played with her fork and pushed the food around on her plate as she had done years ago when she didn't like what she was forced to eat.

Everything was wrong. Karl was turning into something ugly and threatening. Dr. Behrman was gone. Her parents would not help. Worse, they had forbidden her to become involved. But that didn't alter the reality of what was happening around her. And now she was truly alone.

Wilmersdorf

From the sidewalk terrace of the Café Kranzler one could sit for hours and watch the whole world go by. The treelined Kurfürstendamm teemed with activity all hours of the day and night. To David there was no more exciting street anywhere in the world.

He didn't know how long he'd been sitting there at the streetside table by himself. The café itself was already nearly full. Of course, Ali was late. He'd known she would be. It wasn't just her dizzy disorganization, although that was part of it. But when she needed to do something or be somewhere, her timing could be as precise as it was in the pool. No, she just had to make an entrance. Well, that was okay, David allowed. He just hoped she would show up. She would, though. Unless she was acting superior or punishing him for four years ago.

At this very moment a baseball exhibition staged by two U.S. pickup teams had filled the Olympic Stadium. The Europeans had never seen anything like it, and they thronged in to be a part of it. Who would have believed there could be such fanaticism for something so inherently American in the very heart of the old country? Not even the terminology translated. David had seen the printed program. The bases had become "locations," the pitcher was referred to as the "thrower-in," and center field was dubbed "middle outside." There were a lot of contradictions in this country that he just couldn't figure out.

Ali breezed in a few minutes later, seemingly pulling along a small hurricane in her train.

"Sorry I'm late," she tossed off, kissing him square on the lips as she took his hand and guided herself into the proffered chair all at the same time. There was still that instinctive fluidity to her every motion that David could only marvel at.

She sat back and looked up at him. "Is that your Olympic jacket?"

David looked down at himself. "Yeah. It feels funny after two years to be back in uniform, even this one."

"I feel like burning mine," said Ali.

"Don't," said David lightly. "You never know when it might come in handy."

"I can't imagine. Avery Brundage has seen to that."

So was it to be just another round of small talk and avoiding the main issue? In a way David couldn't believe that they were sitting here together. He recalled the closing ceremonies in L.A., when the Count de Baillet-Latour had called upon the youth of the world to assemble four years hence in Berlin and when all David could think about was seeing her.

"You know, I've always dreamed about this," he said. "The next time we'd have dinner together . . . if it would ever happen. Who knew it wouldn't be until another Olympics?"

"Where else would it be?" said Ali. "We're both competitors. Neither one of us can stand to give in or to give up on anything. Even each other, I suppose."

"I suppose not," said David quietly.

The waiter brought the bottle of Gewürztraminer David had ordered and poured it for them.

"Okay . . . so what's it like being a movie star?"

"I'm not exactly a star yet," she said, "or even a starlet. Though

God knows I've been trying my damnedest. The problem is, no matter what I want to do, all anybody wants me to do is swim. If I give in, I'll be typecast forever. I won't be able to do anything else. So I've been holding out."

David wondered if it was the only thing she'd ever held out on. Such different concerns they each had in their lives now. Such different worlds they each inhabited.

"I was hoping the Olympics would give me the exposure and fame I needed. The world's attention is all right here on Berlin these couple of weeks. Even though I'd still have been swimming, I thought this would give me some power with the studios. Now I don't know."

"I think you're still getting a fair amount of exposure and fame. More than any of the rest of us, for sure. Except for maybe Jesse."

"That's sweet of you. Make the best of a bad situation, isn't that what they say? I guess a girl uses her charms and her ingenuity however she can. So, what about this interview now? Think you'll make a big story for the folks back home?"

"Actually, there's something else I'd rather have you do," said David.

Ali flashed a sly grin as she sipped her wine. "Then you did lure me here under false pretenses. David, in your shy, reserved way, you always were a wolf."

"No, it's not that," he said, though God knew, he wished it were. "I'd still like to have you do a story—or at least the *research* for one—but on someone else?"

"Who?" Ali asked.

"Karl Linderhoff."

"Who? Oh, you mean that big blond stiff you introduced me to at the pool?"

"That's not really being fair to him. But yes."

"Whatever for?"

David leaned into the table. "Ali, there's something strange going on, and I can't get anyone to believe me."

"Something strange with him?"

"With the whole German team. Or at least with a lot of them."

A light seemed to go on behind Ali's eyes. "Tell me what you mean."

He told her the careful but steady accretion of small details and bits of evidence as well as the larger inexplicable but alarming incidents: the death of Rolf Schmidt; the crazed agonies of Horst Müller. He even touched on Karl's recent behavioral changes and his treatment of Miranda without getting too specific.

"I didn't know about the two athletes you mentioned," said Ali. "Yes, maybe I did see something in the paper about Schmidt; I'm not sure. But I noticed it, too, watching the games as an observer this time. And it did strike me as kind of funny that the Germans are doing so well, particularly in things they've never done anything impressive in before."

"Exactly."

"So what is it you want me to do?"

"You're the toast of society. Everybody likes you. You're also a journalist now with press credentials, so you can go around asking questions without arousing any suspicion. I'd like you to check into Karl's background, get the specifics on his past performance, any clues to what's going on with him now. Say you're doing a feature story for a large German community in the Midwest or something. That will at least give us something to go on, someplace to start."

"I don't know, David. I'm not really a journalist, you know, regardless of what my press pass might say. I'm actually just another pretty face."

"You're a lot more than that," David said. "And you always have been." He gazed at her tensely. "You'll do it for me, won't you?"

Her eyes clouded over. "You know I will."

"Terrific," he said, trying to mask his relief.

The waiter came back and set menus in front of them.

"What would you like to eat?" David asked.

"Oh, I don't care," she said. "Something quaint and local." She appeared to scan the list of entrées for a moment. She looked up wistfully and said, "You know something? Under the right circumstances we really could have gotten it together." She paused, then added, "Maybe we still can." She closed her menu and for a little while watched the throng of humanity parading down the Ku'damm. "Just tell me one thing, David," she said. "If we were back in L.A. and it was that last meeting between us and you had it to do all over again, would you still leave me for West Point?"

"Yes," said David.

Ali nodded in acceptance. "But have you ever regretted it?"

"Every day for the last four years," he replied.

EIGHTEEN

Wednesday, August 5, Lubars

The *Gymnasium* Karl Linderhoff had attended was on the northern edge of the city. Ali had gotten the name from the German Olympic Committee press office. The people there were only too happy to provide foreign journalists with any minute detail about their athletes, especially those, like Herr Linderhoff, who were expected to bring "new heights of glory to the fatherland."

The headmaster of the school, a funny little man by the name of Herbert Falkensee, was equally solicitous. Ali quickly got the impression that Ruthenberg *Schule*, as the place was called, was something of a second-level institution in the German educational hierarchy, so it was exulting in the attention that its one star alumnus was bringing it.

"Did he show such outstanding promise even when he was in school?" Ali asked after Herr Falkensee had ceremoniously ushered her into his private study.

"Well, yes, he certainly did," the headmaster stated in impressive English. "He was quite an outstanding student. No, actually, quite an outstanding athlete, I believe. Memorable. Yes, truly memorable. The best soccer player we've ever had. No, runner, I think it was . . ."

Ali herself had taken the time to peruse all of the athletic and academic plaques that adorned the walls in the hallway outside the school's main office. She found a testimonial for every imaginable type of achievement. There was even a plaque for perfect attendance. The track and field events were broken down individually, to give more students the opportunity for recognition. Clearly this was the type of school that wanted to make everyone feel like a hero. But she found Karl's name only one place, and that was on a list for the high scorers in some sort of biology exam.

As a next step Ali asked Falkensee if the school had anything like a school newspaper.

"Yes, yes," he replied, adding that Ruthenberg Schule was very complete in the academic and social experience it gave its students. He proudly escorted her down the hall to the library, where he pointed out an entire shelf of tattered and badly inked newsprint sheets, obviously run off in the school's print shop. He stayed with her, to serve personally as her translator, assuring her that he would continue to be at her service throughout her stay at the *Schule*. And if her undoubtedly busy schedule permitted, he would be honored to arrange luncheon as well.

Ali made a strong show of her appreciation for all his hospitality but begged off from the lunch, thanking him profusely for his indulgence and many kindnesses, tremendously grateful that he understood the time pressures of a working journalist. There was no way she was going to eat the slop they dished out to a bunch of mealymouthed little blond boys, she had already silently resolved. Her loyalty to David went only so far.

With Falkensee as her guide, it didn't take her long to find—or, rather, not find—what she was looking for. Karl had begun at Ruthenberg in 1924, when he was twelve. Ali searched through each issue from then until he graduated in 1930. Every year offered a complete list of all the athletic champions and team members the school had fielded. Karl Linderhoff's name appeared in no major category.

At first she thought to wonder if he had possibly changed his name. But no, that wasn't it. He did appear in occasional pictures and in two or three junior varsity shots. So there was definitely no mistake on that score. The simple fact was that Karl Linderhoff had not been an exceptional athlete anytime during his school career.

What he had been, interestingly enough, was something of a class clown and comedian. That was definitely a surprise after the dour face he'd presented at the swimming stadium. The newspapers all through his later years in school kept referring to his sense of humor, how funny he was, how easy to get along with, all that sort of thing. He had the humorous roles in the school plays, with reviews to prove it.

The other surprise was that Karl was portrayed in the papers as

an emerging ladies' man. Aside from being funny, there were
hints—school publications can't come right out and say it—that his
amorous appetite was close to insatiable.

Interesting fellow, this Karl Linderhoff.

Her next stop was the offices of the *Berliner Illustrierten Zeitung*. As
a fellow working journalist she was graciously accorded all the
courtesies of the newspaper. The fact that her rather provocatively
posed picture had recently appeared in the publication only
smoothed her way even further. The managing editor, a Herr
Eberhardt, came out from his glass-paneled cubicle and greeted her.
He was obviously as smitten as Herr Falkensee had been. Yessirree,
the sheer blouse and tight skirt had been an excellent idea.

And when she explained that she needed to do some research for a
piece she was writing on some of the German Olympic athletes, he
escorted her across the newsroom to the morgue and made it clear to
the mousy librarian behind the desk with her hair in the cliché bun
that Miss Prescott was to have at her disposal the full resources of
the paper, including herself as a translator.

The *Zeitung*'s coverage of track and field events was impressively
complete. Looking through newspaper clippings took considerably
longer than perusing high school yearbooks, even with the help of
the card index the librarian provided. But she was determined to do
the job for David and to prove she really could be a legitimate journalist in the process.

Each clipping was pasted on heavy paper and arranged in a file
folder by subject matter. The clippings were further broken down
by year, so that she had to start from scratch on each subject year by
year. By the time she'd gone through two complete cycles, her head
buzzed from the woman's droning reading.

But she also found that she had started to get into the rhythm of
what she was looking for, just as she had got used to the rhythms of
athletic training. It gradually became easier to pick out the right clipping without having to go through an entire file and then to have the
librarian quickly pick out the salient details.

Before too long she could see the pattern.

For as far back as she looked, Karl's name appeared nowhere in
the lists of competitors for any of the major track and field meets,
not even as a loser. A little more than a year before, he started appearing with regularity. The first mention was the Michigan State
meet in May 1935 at which Jesse Owens had made such a splash. He

was also at the Cambridge Invitational in the spring, but he hadn't won either of them.

Then, suddenly, he began winning every decathlon in sight. The articles started touting him as the strong German hope for the '36 Olympics, which even on the face of it was a joke, since in that sport the Germans couldn't even tie their shoes up to the standards of the Americans and the Scandinavians.

But there was no mistake. Linderhoff had become a sensation. The same kid who was remarkably unremarkable in school suddenly burst forth onto the international track and field circuit. It didn't add up. Ali had sacrificed enough of her own youth to training to know that Olympic-level proficiency doesn't come overnight. And anyone who'd spent as many agonizingly tedious hours as she staring at the rippling blue bottom of a swimming pool didn't believe all that bull twaddle about the führer's inspiring his followers to new heights of greatness. *All the inspiration in the world ain't no substitute for years of practice and hard work. And even that assumes you've been born with the God-given gift to begin with.*

No question about it, this Karl Linderhoff was a strange young man. Just how strange, Ali decided to find out for herself.

Dahlem

While they were sitting together in her living room, Frau Behrman had told Miranda a story. Many years before, when she and her husband had been courting, he had given her a small gold locket that had belonged to his late and beloved grandmother. Upon receiving the gift, Esther noticed that the clasp was broken. Abraham, always the absentminded scientist, had never even looked.

Knowing that it would take him forever to tend to the problem, Esther herself took the locket to a local jeweler. When she got there, instead of having the neck chain fixed, on an impulse she decided to have it fitted with a key chain instead. When it was ready, she placed her own photograph inside and presented it back to her husband.

Abraham was overwhelmed, she recalled to Miranda, practically overcome with emotion. Now the keepsake represented the two women he had loved the most in this world. Deathly afraid of losing it, he swore he would never carry it in his pocket. Instead, it would always remain in his desk as a good-luck charm to inspire him in his work. And wherever he went, from university to university, from laboratory to laboratory, the key chain locket went with him, always occupying a position of security at the back of the top drawer of his desk. It was the one physical totem of his life, the one icon that held metaphysical meaning for him.

If Abraham had undertaken his "new assignment" of his own volition, the locket would definitely be gone from his desk. It was the first thing he would have retrieved, Esther told Miranda. He wouldn't have thought of going to work somewhere else without it.

If, on the other hand, God forbid, he had left under different circumstances, the locket would still be there. Esther Behrman had to know. She couldn't sleep nights thinking about it. If it were gone, she would rest at least a little easier. If it were still there, she had to have it back. She would do anything if Miranda would return it to her.

Miranda knew there wasn't much she could do for this woman. So this small comfort took on the dimensions of a sacred trust.

This was what she thought about as she walked down the corridor of the biochemistry section. The matter of Karl's unpleasant behavior toward her now seemed so petty. Some people had real things to worry about.

As she came to Dr. Behrman's office, she looked around carefully to make sure no one saw her. Then she turned the knob, opened the door, and slipped inside.

The room looked considerably different from the last time she'd been here, just a few days before. She blinked with disbelief.

The shade of the single window was pulled down. All the books were off the shelves. The top of the normally cluttered desk was bare. On it, and on the floor around it, were large cardboard packing boxes.

Each had the same marking, written large with a dark crayon: "K-208." She had no idea what it meant. That wasn't the way rooms or departments were designated at the institute.

Nothing was as it should be anymore. Miranda wanted to cry. But she had come for a purpose, and that was what she had to think about. She sat down in Dr. Behrman's chair and pulled open the bottommost drawer of his desk first, as if she were afraid to confront the real issue head-on. The drawer was still filled with the usual array of papers and objects. No one had bothered to clean it out.

So then she faced the top drawer, the one in question. She pulled it out slowly until it grazed her waist. She looked inside. She stuck her hand in and explored all the way to the back, groping first to one side and then the other.

She came to it. Her fingers locked around it, squeezed hard, and brought it out. She opened her hand and looked. It was just as Frau Behrman had described, a rather strange combination—a beautiful gold locket with a matching key chain. Miranda shuddered to consider the implications of this find.

There was one thing about the memento Frau Behrman had not mentioned. There was a single key on the chain. Maybe she hadn't known. It wouldn't be a key to the desk. The desk was unlocked, and one wouldn't leave a key for it *inside*. The same would hold true for the office. It might possibly be a spare key to his house, but what good would it do him in his desk drawer? He had no file drawer or instrument cabinet that locked.

She looked around the room. Aside from the opening to the corridor, there was a narrower door on the other side of the office. Miranda assumed it must be a closet.

She walked over and tried the door. It was locked. Taking a deep breath, she inserted the key and slowly twisted. It gave with the turn of her wrist. She opened the door, expecting to see a row of ratty coats or lab jackets.

Instead, what she beheld was a dark void, as if she'd fallen into Alice in Wonderland's rabbit hole. She took a step forward into the void. She didn't meet any resistance, so she took another step.

There was an eerie silence all about her. Dr. Behrman had a magic tunnel to some strange and mysterious realm.

She waited for her eyes to adjust to the darkness. Vague, half-distinct shapes started to emerge before her. She was at the head of a narrow corridor.

She walked slowly. The shapes became more defined. The corridor seemed narrow because it was lined with high shelves on both sides, shelves that went almost up to the ceiling. They were packed tightly with large glass jars, like the kind that held chocolates and jelly beans in candy shops. Only these jars were filled with—it was so dark it was hard making them out—but what was it now? She looked closer as she walked. These jars were filled with . . .

Brains.

Her heart tried to jump through her breastbone. Her stomach

heaved, and she didn't think she could breathe. The walls of the corridor were lined with brains—bloated, fraying, reddish gray hunks floating blindly in some cloudy liquid.

Her first, powerful instinct was to run back for the door and the safety of Dr. Behrman's office. She had to will her feet to remain where they were on the floor. It wasn't just brains after all. The lower shelves were stocked with larger glass jars, filled with all manner of other organs. She noted a pair of lungs in one, intestines squeezed into another, a row of livers next to a series of kidneys. She couldn't stop her shoulders from shuddering into a spasm that radiated down her back to the base of her spine.

With her hands held out in front of her, she groped until she came in contact with a hard, flat surface. By its feel it was wood, so she continued groping until she felt a doorknob. Please, God, that this one didn't have a lock on it.

She twisted the knob. It opened easily into another room. A burst of chilled air immediately gripped her. Bright overhead lights hung from the ceiling. Glass-fronted cabinets filled with instruments lined the walls. It had the typical dank, repulsive smell of a biology lab. There was a metal-topped counter with a sink in front of her, and beyond that was a steel hospital cart.

It suddenly registered that there was someone on it. His mouth was slightly open, as if he were about to say something to her, and he was staring straight up at the ceiling.

"Hello," she called out, trying to allay her own fears.

He didn't answer. Maybe he was unconscious, even though his eyes were open.

She came up right next to him, and her stomach seemed to collapse inside her as if it had been caught in a mangle.

The man's chest was completely splayed open, from just below his throat to his belly button. A metal device that looked like a canvas stretcher for paintings held the skin and muscle back. His ribs and breastbone had been sawed through and taken away. And right in the middle where his heart should have been was a gaping black hole. It was as though the organ had been sacrificed up to some ancient Aztec god. The arteries and blood vessels that should have connected to the heart just dangled in the maw, their open ends clogged with something thick and gummy, like a gutter downspout that hadn't been cleaned for years.

And still he continued to stare blankly up at the ceiling.

Miranda fought for breath. She nearly swooned. A wave of nausea swept over her.

Fighting to divert her eyes, she looked down at the table. The only time she remembered ever having seen a dead person before was when she was seven, when she had been escorted up a long flight of steps to see her grandmother lying in her coffin in the funeral parlor. But this time it was different. Here he was staring at her.

And someone had ripped his heart out.

She felt her own heart pounding violently in her chest. The face was pale and bloated with death. It could almost be a doll's head, so impersonal was the expression. Still, something about this man looked vaguely familiar to her.

She backed as far away from the cart as she could without leaving the room. The pungent odor from the table assaulted her nostrils. She wanted to run away, to get herself as far as possible from this death chamber, to forget she had ever seen it. But there is something powerful deep within every scientist, a compulsion, a force that has to explore, to know, to comprehend.

Timidly she inched closer to the corpse, as she had with her grandmother thirteen years before. An entire dimension of frightening memories came back to her as she recalled having tried to decide whether the stiff, humorless likeness bore any real essence of the woman she had known and loved or was really a fake, created by the perverse minds of foolish adults to tantalize and deceive her.

Against every natural urge she compelled her mind into rigid discipline. Who was this man, and where had she seen him? Did he work somewhere in the Kaiser Wilhelm? Someone she had known from school or the university? Was he a friend of Karl's?

Something about that fixed expression held a clue. If she had, in fact, seen him before, it had been with an expression similar to this one. But you don't see people with just one expression. Their faces change from second to second. She hadn't seen him dead before. That she would definitely have remembered. What was she thinking of?

She hadn't actually *seen* this man at all. The logic came to her suddenly. How can you remember someone's face in only one mode? You can't. But what about a person who doesn't change? It's obvious. His picture. She must have seen his photograph somewhere.

She began mentally cataloging all the possible sources. Books?

No. What would he be doing in a book? Advertising posters? She doubted it. Then she would have remembered an expression full of enthusiasm and life. Magazines? No. She hadn't read any lately. Newspapers? Yes. He must have been in the paper. Now that she had narrowed the source, she could focus in on the specific, just as she did with physics. She kept glancing fearfully over at the gleaming cart. She wasn't completely sure he wouldn't get up off the table and lumber across the room like a Frankenstein monster to kill her.

Then it came to her. It was an image of a man staring straight ahead without animation or character. It was over a small story about an athlete who had been stricken suddenly at the Olympic Village. Olympics. That was why she kept thinking of Karl. Yes. The athlete. What was his name now? Schmidt, or something like that. Rolf Schmidt. And what had happened to him? They thought it was . . . his heart.

Miranda felt the blood turn to ice in her veins.

Then she heard something. Her heart jumped again. Voices. Coming from the direction of the secret corridor. Coming toward her.

She panicked. Where could she hide? Could she wedge herself into one of the cabinets under the counter? She dashed madly about the room. The side of her arm grazed against Schmidt's cold, rigid hand. Her body went moist with perspiration.

She looked from wall to wall. There was one hope. Another door. A closet, maybe? If it weren't locked, she could hide there and hope to God the men coming into the room didn't need anything from it.

She grabbed the handle and twisted furiously. The voices grew louder. The door opened. She backed in and pulled it silently shut. She breathed a momentary sigh of relief.

The shock of recognition hit her like an open hand. She was in the main corridor of the biochemistry section. She snapped her head around with disbelief. Dr. Behrman's office was fifty or so feet down the hall and around a corner. And the door she had just pulled shut was labeled "Custodian's Closet." It was one of those you pass by every day without giving them a second thought. She tested the handle on this side. It was locked tight.

Still clutching the gold locket key chain, Miranda looked both ways to make sure no one had seen her. Thank goodness the hallway was empty. She wanted to scream and to keep on screaming, to purge the horror she had absorbed. Her legs were clammy and uncomfortable under her stockings and suddenly chilled. She wanted to change out of everything she was wearing.

She took a deep breath to regain her composure. Then she walked down the corridor back toward the physics section, as nonchalantly as she could manage.

Back in her office, she closed the door, then leaned against it for support. Still breathing hard, she willed the image of the gaping, mutilated corpse to go away. But it remained like an apparition in front of her—threatening, pursuing, haunting. There was no one left to rely on, no one left to trust. No one left to do anything. And yet something had to be done.

From her pocket she took the gold locket into her hand and held it in front of her for several moments before squeezing her tear-filled eyes tightly shut.

Döberitz

The weather continued cold and drizzly, a far cry from the golden sunshine of the Los Angeles games that had now taken on the status of cherished memory for David. He trotted by himself along the cross-country track that had been laid out behind the dormitory complex. He maintained a level of exertion that just kept him breathing hard. He had to plan his activities carefully so he didn't tighten up. Glenn Morris and Bob Clark were working out with the coaches today. David had always been a loner about training, and he thought he'd get more done on his own here at the Olympic Village.

Two solid days of practice. If he could just get them in, maybe he'd be okay. Two days by himself of hard training and no distractions. By Saturday afternoon it would all be over. The world could wait until then.

He wished it were that simple. The beguiling, maddening, challenging image of Miranda continued to haunt his every waking thought. Whether he was running, vaulting, hurling the discus, or putting the shot—and he had furiously pursued all of them today— her face imposed itself as an overlay on his mind.

He could stop kidding himself. There was no longer any question to him that she was all the British scientific people had cracked her up to be. So something had to be done. And there was just as little question that he was obsessed with her, body and soul. Not that he entertained any hope, especially after their "date" Monday night. He had his life, and she had hers. And then there was Karl. She was, after all, Karl's girl, not his. None of it was coming together. The "Miranda question" remained as much an enigma in his mind as the woman herself, like one of those mathematical theorems that by their very truth prove themselves to be false.

Somewhere amid the vast training facilities of the village, Karl was doing the same things he was. David wondered if the German was as nervous as he. It was a good bet he was, the way he'd been acting lately. Maybe David would join him in the steam bath after working out. Karl had said it helped him relax and keep his muscles from cramping, and he had become religious about never missing a day. Ali had seemed very curious when David had told her about it. She had wanted to know where Karl was going to be during the day. Maybe she was planning on including him in her list of interviews. Ali was terrific. She would always be special.

David didn't think he was missing much at the stadium today. There was such a large field for the pole vault that it would probably take all day to get through it. There were trials for the 110-meter hurdles. He thought the discus was today, and he particularly *did not* want to watch that, since he'd have to throw the discus himself on Saturday. And then there was the 50-K walk, a bunch of middle-aged men waddling around like ducks, that the English always seemed to do well in. They were so damn civilized it was a perfect event for them. They didn't even realize how ridiculous they looked. It gave him some satisfaction to imagine the aristocratic Hargreaves out there in his shorts, flapping his arms like a turkey and swiveling his hips from side to side.

The only really interesting event on today's schedule was the two hundred meters. Jesse Owens had a real shot of winning his third gold medal. That would be something to see, and David was sorry to be missing it. Real history in the making. At least what in sports passes for history.

He wondered how long anyone would remember what they did here in Berlin.

NINETEEN

As a rule women were not permitted inside the Olympic Village. But reporters were, and Ali's press pass appeared to be in order, duly authorized by the Reich Information Office and the German Olympic Committee. Not knowing how to resolve such a dilemma, the guard at the gate telephoned Wolfgang Fürstner in his office, who said that by all means the lady should be let through. Besides, she happened to be a particular favorite of Göring's.

She walked up the path from the main gate and looked around. This was quite a place, all right, even if it was in the middle of East Nowhere. A lot nicer than the dump they'd put the girls up in. If she hadn't been thrown off the team back on the boat, that place would have been enough to make it happen here in Berlin.

She oriented herself according to the village map the Olympic Press Office had given her. She checked her watch. Yep, just about right.

She found the German team's dormitory block and went inside. There was an attendant in a military uniform at the front desk. It seemed as though there were someone in a uniform at every front desk in this entire nation, as if the whole country were playing soldier. At least they all spoke English.

She flashed her press pass and her most captivating smile. "I'm looking for Karl Linderhoff, of the decathlon team," she told the young corporal. The best way to avoid suspicion was to tell the truth, though not necessarily what you wanted the truth for. "Would you know if he's here?"

"He is in the building," the boy stated formally. "I believe Lieutenant Linderhoff is in the steam bath at present. Perhaps you would care to wait for him in the reception area to your left. I will have him notified as soon as he is available."

"Thanks," Ali said, the winning smile still glued to her lips. "I think I'll look around outside for a few minutes." She nodded and turned toward the door, then stopped short, as if remembering something.

She turned back toward the desk corporal. "Would you have a little girls' room I could use?"

"I beg your pardon?" he said.

"A . . . you know . . . a facility."

A glimmer of recognition appeared in his eyes. "*Die Toilette.* No, I'm sorry, Fräulein. We have no lavatories here for women."

It was time for the winsome, poignant look. "Don't you think maybe you could find . . . something?" She struck a vulnerable but calculatedly sexy pose. "It's a kind of emergency."

Quite clearly this was one type of emergency this well-trained German soldier had never been taught to deal with.

"Couldn't you maybe help out a girl in a jam?"

The corporal looked around and frowned. "Very well," he said. "Come with me."

He came out from behind the desk and led her down the corridor, just past the steam room to the door marked TOILETTE. He knocked once, then opened it and called in, "*Achtung!*" He waited a short interval, then held the door open for her, clicked his heels together, and nodded sharply in the military style.

"Thanks," said Ali. "I'll remember this."

He nodded respectfully but made no move to leave, apparently intending to stand guard right there until she was finished.

"I think I can manage," she said. "I'll just lock the door on the inside."

This seemed to satisfy him. He nodded again. "Very well, Fräulein." With the door cracked open, she waited for his footsteps to disappear down the hallway.

As soon as she was sure he was out of sight, she slipped back out. The idea had come to her on a whim, but the more she had thought about it during the morning, the better she liked it. She glanced quickly in both directions to make sure the coast was clear, then stole next door to the steam room.

She opened the door just a crack, peered inside, and listened. A few low voices indulging the age-old ritual of male bonding. Security and solace in the crowd. There were four or five perfect bodies resplendent on the wooden decking, partially obscured by the swirling white mists.

Karl Linderhoff was sitting at the far end of the room, staring without expression into the clouded air, obviously lost in his own thoughts. His towel was casually balled up on the bench beside him.

That's just what I want, Ali said to herself. *Get to him when he's not expecting anything, when his defenses are down, when he's at his most suggestible. Now let's see how he reacts. If he's the man they say he is, he'll take this as a golden opportunity. At least he'll get into the spirit of the game. If not, well, that'll tell us something, too. And the others in the room will provide what science wizard David would call the control factor.*

She strolled in as blithely and nonchalantly as she could manage, then suddenly feigned a wide-eyed Betty Boop expression of surprise. "Oh, my goodness!" she called out.

Five naked men scrambled for their towels.

"How did I get in here?" she asked rhetorically, overplaying every motion as if she were in a silent film. "I'll just turn around and . . ." She turned to the closest man. "Say, you wouldn't happen to know where I could find Karl Linderhoff, would you?"

The man broke out into a wide grin. He pointed directly back.

"Thanks," she said, and gave him a comradely clap on his bare thigh. The others let go with a howl of catcalls, hoots, and whistles.

All except Karl.

She put her hands on her hips and motioned with her chin. "That him?"

The other men nodded delightedly.

She took a step toward him and said, "Hello, Karl."

He looked up toward the sound of the voice and froze. "Who— who are you?" His hands clutched ferociously at the edges of the towel now covering his midsection. His body seemed to go rigid. "How did you get in here?"

"I'm Alison Prescott. You remember. We met at the swimming stadium." She maintained the soft, controlled tone she had practiced. "I came to interview you. But as long as I'm here, it's so nice and quiet and relaxing, maybe this would be a good place to talk, get to know a little more about you for my story. Your friends can help."

"Tell her, Karl!" one of the others shouted out in German. Then to Ali: "I'm his friend. Ask me!"

"Show her what German men are made of!" another contributed.

Karl glared at them. "I don't know what you're talking about," he stormed. "Get out!" So much for sense of humor. He'd have to do better than that.

"Do interview with me!" the first man implored in broken English.

"I'll do it!" the second said, lifting his towel provocatively in front of him, as if proof were needed. Two more similar offers followed. Karl remained stone-faced.

Unperturbed, Ali came seductively closer. She reached out for his towel and deftly pulled it away, moving in on him in the process. The others howled with glee.

"You know, you're even cuter than I remember," she observed. *Okay, Mr. Acting Star, Mr. Former Class Clown, Mr. Ladies' Man. Let's see if you can live up to your own press.*

She sat herself down on the same bench and sidled up next to him, reaching out and placing her hand on his thigh. There was no question what effect that would have on any red-blooded American boy or any of the other hot-blooded German boys in the room.

This one quickly wrenched his leg away from her and grabbed his towel back in anger, though not before Ali had the time to gauge the effect she was—or, rather, wasn't—having on him.

"Don't you want to talk to me?" she asked, giving him a nice big silver screen pout.

He stood up, as if at attention. It was a rather ludicrous sight, she thought. "Get out of here!" he demanded again. The others protested vociferously.

Okay, fella, she thought. *You've had your chance to prove yourself. And one is all you get.*

Karl's eyes were full of some strange mixture of anger and fear. "Get out before I have to do something extreme."

She wondered what that would be but didn't think it would be the greatest idea to hang around and find out. And then there was the eager hospitality of the other young men to worry about.

The main thing was she had found out what she wanted to know.

She walked out of the steam room, then scampered down to the end of the hall. When she reached the next corridor, she slowed down and walked with dignity and her normal charming gracefulness back toward the building's reception area.

The corporal at the desk noticed her, then glanced at the wall clock. "Are you all right, Fräulein?" he asked.

"Great," she replied, walking fast enough so that he wouldn't notice she was drenched with sweat. "And thanks for all your help. Oh, it is getting kind of late, though. So when you see Herr Linderhoff, tell him I'll catch him later on!"

Dahlem

Three men stood assembled around the dissecting table in the room that, until very recently, had served as Abraham Behrman's personal laboratory. Two wore the long white coats common to the Kaiser Wilhelm Institute of Science. The third wore the black tunic of the SS.

Reinhard Heydrich had not previously met the young man at Rudolf Kiesel's side. He was intense-looking, with jet black hair, and could not have been more than about twenty-five.

"I have the pleasure of introducing one of our most promising protégés," Kiesel stated. "He took his degree in medicine from the University of Frankfurt and for the past two years has been a research fellow for the Institute of Hereditary Biology and Race Research. You will undoubtedly be hearing great things from him. Obergruppenführer Heydrich, this is Dr. Josef Mengele."

"A pleasure," Heydrich said stiffly. "Now, tell me what you have discovered. The *Reichsführer* is waiting for my report."

"Dr. Mengele, if you would . . ." said Kiesel.

"We have very carefully dissected and analyzed the heart," the young man explained. "There is per se nothing wrong with it. The condition of the muscle was excellent, far above the norm. No gross pathology that would cause a sudden and massive arrest."

"And yet it did happen," said Heydrich impatiently.

Ever so slightly and trying to hide his response, Mengele appeared to recoil from the rebuke.

"And according to my report, he was not even exerting himself when the attack occurred. If my information was correct, he was playing chess." Heydrich drew the last two words out to make his point. "If our athletes are going to die playing silly board games, then it doesn't say much for the condition of the Reich." He glared at Kiesel, as if personally accusing him.

Kiesel took on a professional tone to avoid the confrontation. "The problem seems more in the constituents of the blood itself."

"A clot?" Heydrich asked.

"Strictly speaking, no. And yet that is the nature of the effect. The fluid portion of blood is called plasma. Separated out, it is an amber-colored liquid that is mostly water. The remaining percentage of elements, including the red blood cells themselves, is referred to as the hematocrit. The hematocrit is the constituent of blood that actually carries the oxygen and nutrients and the chemicals essential to life. The plasma is merely the medium in which they are delivered. At a normal hematocrit level of forty-five, whole blood as a unit is three to four times more viscous than water. At a level of seventy the blood would be more than *ten times* thicker. And quite clearly it would lose its ability to flow through the arteries and veins."

"And what was Herr Schmidt's level?"

"Sixty-six."

"Meaning?"

Kiesel paused and cleared his throat. "Meaning," he said slowly, "that his blood had become so viscous it essentially turned to sludge. His heart, no matter what its condition, could no longer pump it through his system."

"That would seem to be a critical problem," said Heydrich sardonically.

Kiesel nodded. "It is one of the prime challenges we have set out for ourselves in the entire *Übermensch* program: How does one achieve maximum hematogenous and hematological efficiency without fatally compromising the basic delivery system? We knew all along it would be an extremely delicate balance." He indicated Schmidt's body on the dissecting table. "A balance we have clearly not achieved as yet."

"But will you?" Heydrich pressed on.

Kiesel shifted his gaze up away from the table. "The collection of specimens on the shelves just outside this room, most of them were collected during the Great War. I remember the first time I was honored to be here. Perhaps I was not much older than Dr. Mengele is now. But I'll never forget that Dr. Behrman led me past the collection and said to me, 'If we could take the best of all the individuals represented here and put them together into one body, what an extraordinary example of humankind we could produce!'" His gaze met Heydrich's once again. "Ever since then I have dedicated myself to fulfilling at least the spirit of that dream. And as you know, Obergruppenführer, we are close . . . so close."

"What will it take to go the final distance as we have promised the führer?" Heydrich asked.

Kiesel half smiled. "This building is among the great temples of modern science. And unfortunately it is a curious property of scientific research of any kind that the solution seems obvious only after the problem has been solved. But we are pursuing it diligently, trying to uncover the solution through our animal experiments. Now, keep in mind that animals do not always predict results in human beings." He turned to Mengele. "But if you would be so kind."

"We have a large population of laboratory rats that have been bred and developed under the *Übermensch* program," Mengele stated. "We began by extracting erythropoietin—a hormone which we have discovered increases blood mass—in large scale from the kidneys of donor rats. We felt we were well on the way to achieving the hemodynamic characteristics and elevated hematocrit levels we sought. We then carefully noted at what points the test rats would die of cardiac arrest, analyzed their hearts and circulatory systems through dissection, and began experimenting with the antiviscosity compounds. I don't want to confuse the issue for you, but since we had also introduced a nitrate compound to dilate the coronary blood supply selectively without affecting the other arteries, we had several variables with which to deal."

Heydrich waved him off. "Very well. The details are material to me only as they affect the ultimate outcome."

"I should think our Olympic performance thus far speaks to the efficacy of the program," said Kiesel. "The challenge ultimately, though, as Dr. Mengele suggested, is that we are dealing with such a profound number of variables. And of course, within the entire research team, there is only one individual who maintains the complete balance of variables within his own mind."

"Yes, of course," said Heydrich. "And we are dealing with that situation as effectively and speedily as possible. But this means that everyone else must redouble his efforts for victory." He took one of his characteristic pauses for effect. "I hope we all understand each other."

"Certainly," Kiesel assured him.

"Ah . . . excuse me, but there is one more thing we might mention," Mengele said, glancing over to Kiesel for tacit approval. "The rats in which we have implemented the complete program—it has been my department's responsibility to observe them very closely: performance, behavioral characteristics. . . ."

"And what about them?" said Heydrich, himself glancing over to Kiesel for confirmation.

"Well . . ." Mengele said, "we've been watching them around the clock in all situations. And it seems that some of the rats . . . well . . . they've gone crazy."

TWENTY

Thursday, August 6, Central Berlin

"So what is the status of our boy?" Stewart Menzies asked.

"I think he's the one keeping the secrets now," Arthur Hargreaves replied.

"Oh? How so?"

"I think he's already learned more than he's telling us. I think he knows that Miranda is our girl. But for some reason of his own, he's dragging his feet."

"Why would he do that?"

"Can't say exactly. As I told you, he's gone a bit cross on us. Could be he wants the illusion of being in control."

There was a pause in the conversation. Hargreaves became uncomfortably aware of the hiss and crackle of the overseas line.

"You don't think he's been turned?" Menzies slowly articulated. "I mean, German family heritage and all."

Hargreaves had searched his soul all night on the very point, but he was willing to stake his career on the personality profile. Science, even the soft sciences like psychology, had to be good for something.

"No, I don't think so," he said solemnly. "If anything, from what I've been able to gather from him, I think it might be more in the nature of his personal feelings for the girl."

"You mean he's sweet on her?"

"I shouldn't be surprised. The sexual angle was one of the cards we hoped to play."

"Yes, of course," said Menzies with seeming annoyance. "It was already a fine old tradition of spycraft when Mata Hari was still in nappies. But emotional attachment is another matter. It affects judgments. It goes against the rational. It's dangerous business, Arthur. And you'd better keep a tight rein on it."

Hargreaves sighed. "I suppose you're right."

"And we do have to see some results soon particularly if your suspicions are correct. When's Keegan's event?"

"Tomorrow and Saturday."

"And I imagine he's all at sixes and sevens, training full-time and all that."

"Yes, I'm sure."

"Well, we're taught that the Battle of Waterloo was won on the playing fields of Eton, so let's hope we're on the right track."

Hargreaves wasn't convinced.

"Look, give him the weekend then," said Menzies. "Let him run his race, or whatever it is he's doing. Then, Monday morning, he's full-time running for us."

Döberitz

"You must have heard by now," said Ali, the excitement still palpable in her voice. "Jesse won his third gold medal yesterday evening."

"It's the only thing people have been talking about at the village," said David. "I'm really sorry I wasn't there. And another Olympic record, too."

"I wouldn't have missed it for anything," Ali said, then looked at David and thought for a moment. "Well, almost anything. Anyway, he was absolutely beautiful. And Mack Robinson, too. If Jesse hadn't been running, Mack would have easily taken the gold himself. Between them the Germans didn't even have a chance."

It was both ironic and grimly interesting to David that anyone would think first of the Germans as the main competitors or the ones to beat. Two or three weeks ago it would have been unthinkable. Yet since the first events on Sunday a new reality had set in. A new Olympic age had dawned, and the Germans had become its deities. Every newspaper in the world was full of accounts of their stunning victories. If Adolf Hitler was staging these games as a means toward national respectability, he was certainly achieving his goal.

Ali had found a rather quaint old inn near the Olympic Village—*a future haven for camp followers*, David thought, *when they get around to turning the place into an army base.*

"They've got some nice rooms upstairs," she had reported before they sat down. "I checked. And they don't ask any questions. So maybe next week, when you're not in training anymore . . ."

But for the moment they were sitting across the breakfast table from each other. The early-morning hour was a hardship to Ali, who was still leading a full and active life on the other side of the clock. But today would be the crucial day of training, David knew, the last one before the event, and once he got started in earnest, nothing must distract him.

Whatever the distraction, it was nice to be sitting here with her. At this hour of the morning he could almost fantasize that it was a continuation of the previous night. He had always found Ali exciting. Now he also found her comforting, a touchstone from his past to give him stability and security against an imminent and unsure future.

She toasted him with her fluted champagne glass. "Hair of the dog," she explained before downing half the contents in a single gulp. She caught her breath and said, "You should have seen me last night."

David had mixed feelings about that. But he was encouraged by her excitement over Jesse Owens's latest stunning victory. Ever since they'd arrived in Berlin, she'd displayed nothing but cynicism and bitterness against anything having remotely to do with the American team and its despotic leader. David certainly couldn't blame her. It had been reported in the newspapers that she'd lost her final appeal for reinstatement. But now America was under challenge, and that was when patriotism always surged to the surface. Also, Jesse's accomplishment was so inspiring, particularly in light of the way the German leadership had been treating the "black auxiliaries," that even Ali's hatred for all things surrounding Brundage couldn't dampen or mask her response.

There was a quiet lull in the conversation. Ali said, "So are you nervous about tomorrow?"

"No," he responded. "Well, yes, I guess, when I stop to think about it. I try not to think about it."

"Typical David."

"So tell me what you've got."

Ali tried to open her eyes with her third cup of coffee of the morning. "I couldn't be doing this if *I* were in training," she commented. "Well . . . your suspicions about Linderhoff's athletic past have been confirmed. He sprang full-blown upon the track and field scene just about the time you first remember running against him." She reported her findings in detail and told of the people she had met and talked to.

David listened quietly, trying to absorb the full impact.

"I'll tell you something else," she went on. "That reputation of his as a comedian I mentioned to you?"

David nodded.

"Greatly overrated."

"How do you mean?" he asked.

She told him about the steam bath.

"Now that's something I would have liked to see."

"I'll bet you would," said Ali. The enticing mischief was plain in her voice. "Maybe we could arrange something."

"Your resourcefulness never ceases to amaze me."

"Call it a little homegrown experiment," she said as she used the end of her knife to massage a pat of butter slowly into her toast. She could make the simplest act into a sensual experience. It was one of her special gifts. "Then there's your friend's reputation as a stud. Also greatly overrated. I can tell you that the man has zero interest in the opposite sex."

"I find that difficult to believe," said David. "For one thing, he's got an absolutely stunning girl friend."

"Then I can't say much for her standards or expectations."

David felt the irrational need to defend Miranda but instantly thought better of it. He could already sense Ali's antennae coming out.

"David, the guy is definitely shooting blanks, so to speak. Something important is missing."

"How can you be sure?"

She held out her hand in front of her. "I was this close to him, standing face-to-face . . . ah, et cetera. No reaction whatsoever. None. And I was turning it on like you know I can do."

"I can't quibble with that," said David.

"Now maybe he used to be," Ali said. "Everyone says he was. But if that's so, Karl Linderhoff has become a different person."

David thought again about everything Miranda had said about Karl's abrupt change in personality. ("He's different lately. . . . And I don't know what to do about it. . . . I think he has lost his—his

desire for me.") And the man she had described as the gentlest creature in the world had hauled off without warning and hit her. Not
exactly the sign of a great sense of humor. But maybe David was
being unfair.

"You didn't exactly catch him at his best. You sort of had the
upper hand."

"In a manner of speaking," Ali said with a grin. "But that doesn't
alter the situation or his reaction to it."

"You know he's been under a lot of pressure. All of us have. You
might have just caught him on a bad day."

Ali's expression indicated she clearly wasn't buying this. "Bad day
or good, David, there are certain things in certain circumstances
where either you've got it or you don't. And this guy doesn't. At
least he doesn't anymore."

"But how can you be sure?" he asked.

"A woman can be sure. Trust me."

Dahlem

Miranda had been fretting all day about what to do. She hadn't
slept for more than a fitful few minutes all night. She wasn't getting
any work done, and several people had asked her if anything was
wrong.

She was sitting at her desk with her chin resting wearily on her
hands when she heard a single knock on her office door. She looked
up to see Karl standing there silently before her. Her heart jumped
in surprise.

His eyes were like magnets drawn to her. It was as if he were
afraid she'd disappear if he diverted his gaze for a moment. She also
noticed that his hands were trembling slightly.

She wasn't sure how to react. She hadn't been able to erase from
her mind for a moment what she'd found in Dr. Behrman's desk and
what she'd discovered in his lab. And after the way Karl had been
acting lately, she didn't know if she was thrilled by his sudden attention or wished he would just leave her alone. It made her nervous to
feel so out of control.

"I thought you'd be at the stadium or the village all day," she said.

"I had something important to do here," he replied tersely.

She raised her eyebrows and tried to smile. "That couldn't wait until Monday?"

"Ah . . . no." She had just been trying to make conversation, but he was looking at her as if she'd just asked him an embarrassing question in public or betrayed some deep, dark secret. His forehead was sweating. He seemed to be even more nervous than she was.

"Sit down," she said. He remained standing.

So what was on his mind? Why had he come to see her? Had he come to berate her again, to find more fault with her behavior? Or this time had he maybe come to say he was sorry for everything and that he really did love her more than anything? Miranda stared back at him and tried to weigh the possibilities in her mind.

Eventually the little girl who yearned to believe in fairy tales triumphed over the scientist who analyzed the hard data she observed.

"I'm very glad to see you, Karl," she said.

He did not immediately respond. The way he was staring at her made her feel as if she were undressed.

"Will you be coming to the stadium tomorrow?" he asked at last.

So that was why he had come. And now that she had finally heard the question, her first urge was to tell him that of course, she would be there if that was what he wanted, and none of what he had done to her in the last several days had really happened, and everything was now just as it had been, and he was the rock of her stability and the central focus of her life.

But that wasn't the way it was, and things had happened. And her second urge was to assert some vindicating streak of independence that would not allow her the warm luxury of crawling back into his lap so easily and being his kitten again. She wanted to punish him for the way he'd punished her.

The mere hesitation of her response seemed to prick up Karl's ears. When she did finally open her mouth and heard herself say, "I suppose so. I promised David that night at the symphony that I would," she saw the color rapidly drain from his face, to be instantly replaced by an almost purple shade of red that made the veins in his neck bulge out the way her father's sometimes did.

She hadn't had David on her mind. The tactic had come to her without conscious thought, and it made her realize in a flash of grim satisfaction what her sex had known by instinct since time began: that the pitting of one man against another has always been one of the most potent weapons in any woman's arsenal.

"What do you mean, you promised David?" Karl demanded in a threatening whisper. It made her feel weak in the backs of her knees, just as if she'd been called to account before her father.

But she was determined to stand her ground. "Just what I said." She then followed up her advantage. "I'll be there for both of you."

"Do what you like," Karl uttered. And he stormed out of her office in a way that had lately become painfully characteristic of him.

Miranda folded her arms on her desk and wondered if she had gone too far in trying to get back at him and had spited herself in the process. But the prospect of these two men competing against each other for two days of intense physical exertion had suddenly produced within her an intensely physical sensation. For the first time she found herself actually looking forward to going to the stadium tomorrow and sitting through the contest.

She didn't know whom she wanted to win.

Döberitz

Wolfgang Fürstner was in his office in the Olympic Village when his staff assistant ran in.

"Do we no longer bother to knock?" asked Fürstner.

"Excuse me, Captain," the assistant said nervously. "But there is someone to see you."

"And who might that be who can cause such a stir?"

"Obergruppenführer Heydrich of the SS."

Fürstner felt the blood draining from his face. "I see. Please send him in."

Heydrich came in carrying a black braided riding crop in his black-gloved hand. He did not wait to be offered a seat.

"I was hoping to receive a report from you by now, Captain," Heydrich said.

"There was nothing to report," Fürstner answered defensively.

"That in itself is something," Heydrich said. He crossed his legs and proceeded to swish the riding crop several times through the air. Fürstner found himself inwardly cringing. Heydrich gripped the crop by its two ends and flexed them down, as if to test how far it would bend before it finally broke. "But let us not waste time with word games," he went on. "You have been entrusted by the Reich with the day-to-day operation of the Olympic Village."

"Yes," Fürstner responded, still not knowing what to make of the exchange.

"Our athletes are a national treasure. We expect that they will be safeguarded as such."

"Safeguarded, Obergruppenführer? We have had no complaints about security here at the village. All procedures have been carefully reviewed and—"

"That isn't what I meant," Heydrich said testily.

"Then I'm afraid I'm not sure I'm following you."

"I wish for you and your staff to watch them carefully, see to their needs, observe their behavior. If you notice anything, I want to be informed with all the particulars."

"As I assured you in your office the other day, we haven't had any recurrences of the unfortunate incident with Herr Müller. I would certainly have told you if—"

"That was overt, gross behavior. By that stage it was already too late."

"Too late?" Fürstner repeated.

"Anything that seems out of the ordinary I want to know about. Not just in the future, but things that might have already happened as well. I want you to think back, question your staff, and tell me if you have observed anything with *any* of our athletes that you would not deem to be normal."

Fürstner sat and thought for a moment. "Nothing occurs to me, Obergruppenführer. "But if it does, I will inform you without delay."

"See that you do," said Heydrich. He reached into the breast pocket of his ribbon-bedecked tunic and produced a folded document. He handed it across to Fürstner, who unfolded it with carefully restrained anxiousness. "This is an authorization from the office of the *Reichsführer-SS* himself, granting you, as bearer, extraordinary powers and access. It cannot be questioned or refused, and it is in effect for the duration of the Olympic Games or until revoked by that office through me."

"Thank you for this vote of confidence," said Fürstner.

"It is only to facilitate your efforts to do your duty and to help us do ours." As always, Fürstner found something vaguely threatening in the *Obergruppenführer's* explanation.

Heydrich rose abruptly. Fürstner rose with him. Heydrich slashed the riding crop once against the side of his gleaming boot, as if for emphasis, then strode toward the door. "Remember, I expect you to question your staff on this matter," he said at the door.

"Yes, of course."

Heydrich stopped. "And one more thing, Captain. There is one athlete in your charge who bears particular watching. An American called David Keegan."

Fürstner felt himself go rigid.

"He seems to have a tendency to 'stray.'"

"Stray, sir? To what end?"

"That is what I wish you to find out for me. As discreetly as possible, of course." Heydrich offered another thin smile, then said, "As always, Captain, this meeting has been a sincere pleasure."

"Thank you, Obergruppenführer."

Fürstner listened for the sound of the outer door closing, signifying that his office was finally purged of Heydrich's presence. Then he sat down and put his hand up to his chin. What was the Gestapo chief telling him . . . or threatening him with?

As honored as he felt to have been singled out by Himmler's office, Fürstner found the entire matter deeply troubling, particularly the part about David Keegan. Had the Gestapo seen the two of them together at the Eclair? Even if they had, surely they couldn't misinterpret some old-fashioned German hospitality. And yet, if the Gestapo was suspicious of the American for something or other, then anyone who associated with him could fall under the same suspicion.

Keegan bore careful watching. There was no doubt about that.

TWENTY-ONE

It had been a good day of practice, the best David had had since he came to Berlin. He walked along the one of the village's many wooded trails completely alone, easing himself down from the bracing two-mile run that had capped off a full day's worth of activity. In spite of the exertion, his lungs felt as if they could take in all of outdoors, as if he could keep going forever. The cold, damp air didn't matter at all. In fact, no factor outside himself mattered anymore. He was peaking at just the right moment. He finally felt that elusive sense of perfect equilibrium within his own body with which an athlete knows that it's all going well.

This was the moment when he knew everything would change. Up until now he had been a team player, glorying in each American victory, his eyes misting over whenever he heard the national anthem played at a medal ceremony.

Yesterday he had turned inward, focusing all his mental and physical resources to the task ahead. And today he had turned selfish— no longer a team player, no longer an American athlete. From now until Saturday night all the competitors—himself, Glenn Morris, Jack Parker, Bob Clark, the guys he had trained with over the months and years—were single combat warriors, struggling for a prize that could belong to only one of them.

He saw a solitary figure coming toward him up the trail through the trees. A few more paces, and he realized it was Karl.

"How's it going?" David asked.

"Good," Karl replied. But he had that same tense expression and agitated manner that had become painfully normal in the past few days. "And with you?"

"Couldn't be better," David said, and wondered if maybe subconsciously he was trying to rub it in. "Have you been here all day?"

"Yes. I've been in the swimming pool most of the afternoon. The laps are good for maintaining the stamina without having to worry about straining muscles or joints."

"You've been where?"

"In the swimming pool. That's the nice thing about the Olympic Village. It's so big that you never have to run into your competition."

"Since when have you developed this affinity for the water?"

Karl looked at him as if he had no idea what David was talking about.

"What about last week in the—" David suddenly felt an inner chill and stopped. "You were swimming by yourself?"

"That's right," said Karl nervously, his eyes darting around. "But actually I've been looking for you. I'm going over to the Olympic Stadium for a little while. After concentrating here all alone for so long, I thought it would be a good idea to have the feel of the place in my mind today, instead of going in there cold tomorrow morning."

David considered this. He had wanted to stay away from all the other competitors, including Karl. He didn't want to get caught up in everyone else's anxiety. But there was a certain logic to what Karl said. You want your environment to feel comfortable. You don't want any last-minute surprises. And Karl seemed such a mess right now. If he could calm him down by being with him, maybe that was something one friend should do for another, selfishness or not.

He felt completely torn about Karl. Here was a man who could defend Hitler's indefensible behavior toward the black athletes, explain his unexplainable attitude toward Jews, and was capable of violence against the lovely Miranda. Yet he was so giving, so eager for friendship and acceptance—the best and the most frightening elements of the German character embodied in one man.

David remembered Tom's story about Jesse Owens and Lutz Long. That was really what the Olympics were all about. If he didn't do whatever he could for Karl, he knew he'd feel bad later on.

"Sounds like a good idea," he said finally. "I did want to see Glenn Cunningham run in the fifteen hundred meters, especially since we have to do the same race Saturday afternoon."

Karl seemed cheered by David's willingness. "I'm glad you're coming."

"Okay, then," David said, clapping him on the side of his bare arm. "Give me a couple of minutes to get changed, and I'll meet you at the bus."

David was struck once again by the smoothness of Karl's skin.

Grunewald

When David and Karl arrived at the stadium, the crowd was in the midst of a prolonged euphoria over the latest of the German victories. Gerhard Stöck, a blond giant, was the physical epitome of everything the Aryan supremacists held dear. He had just taken the gold in the javelin throw, upsetting Sweden and Finland, which, between them, had never lost it before.

The now-familiar strains of "Deutschland über Alles" rang through the arena, and the swastika was raised to the top of the highest flagpole. Stöck raised his right arm in a rigid National Socialist salute. The fiercely nationalistic crowd went wild again. Thousands of voices broke out into the "Horst Wessel Song." From the box of honor the Nazi brass saluted its approval. Word had previously come in of Josef Manger's win for Germany in weight lifting. And from the firing range came the announcement of twin German victories in the rapid-fire pistol competition.

Most impressive of all had been today's news from the Wannsee Golf Club, where the final event of the modern pentathlon had been staged in the morning. Gotthard Handrick, a lieutenant in the Wehrmacht and a good friend of Karl's, had shocked the world and become the first non-Swede ever to capture the title.

"That's incredible," David said when he heard. "No one gave you guys a chance in that."

"Discipline and will," Karl replied. "And the inspiration of our leader."

Was it the inspiration of their leader that had persuaded Karl to go in the water?

The two men got to the stadium just in time for the final of the fifteen hundred meters, the so-called metric mile.

So did Adolf Hitler. As the twelve runners were lining up, he appeared in the box, full of smiles and waving all around. As always, when he was in attendance, the führer's personal standard was raised on the flagpole opposite the one flying the Olympic banner. The crowd bellowed out its worshipful greeting. All activity came to a momentary halt.

The race turned out to be one of the greatest that David or any of the other hundred and ten thousand spectators fortunate enough to be there that day would ever see.

The field was perhaps the best ever assembled for this event. Luigi Beccali had won the gold in Los Angeles, and Galloping Glenn Cunningham held the world's record for the mile. And particularly with Hitler present, the Germans had high hopes for Fritz Schaumburg.

The gun sounded. John Cornes of England broke into the lead. After a lap he seemed to tire, relinquishing the pace to the powerful Schaumburg. Beccali began to make his move. Cunningham stayed with him.

From the back of the crowded pack, David recognized a familiar face. Jack Lovelock was a twenty-seven-year-old medical student from New Zealand who was now an intern at St. Mary's Hospital in London. But before that he had also been a Rhodes Scholar, and David had known him at Oxford. At five feet nine and 133 pounds, the curly red-headed Lovelock was all but lost in the throng. As he worked his way closer in among the others, he could be identified only by the all-black uniform of the New Zealand team, which made this gentle doctor look like the specter of death pursuing his fellowman.

Coming into the final lap, Lovelock boldly tried to make a move to stay with Cunningham. But Schaumburg and Erik Ny of Sweden muscled their way in front of him.

Ny shot out and took the lead. Schaumburg began to fade. A collective groan went up from the stands. Taking advantage, Lovelock battled his way up to Cunningham's heels. Beccali was confidently biding his time right behind them.

Archie San Romani, the darkest of dark horse Americans, suddenly came from out of nowhere to lead the pack. Like Beccali, had he been holding something back all this time?

Then, at the lower end of the backstretch, Lovelock began to surge. Pouring on everything, he charged ahead. Beccali and Cunningham charged after him, leaving the fading Ny in their wake. Into the final straightaway Beccali realized he had waited too long. He called on his last ounce of strength to get past Cunningham, but the American from Kansas pulled out his own reserves. He was sprinting madly toward the finish line.

But he couldn't catch Jack Lovelock. The diminutive New Zealander had paced himself perfectly and had known just where to make his move. He had known exactly what he would need and had saved it until now. As he closed in on the tape, he glanced over his shoulder to see Cunningham a safe distance behind. With that confident knowledge, he seemed to coast across the finish line and still beat the world time by a full second! So fast a pace did he set that the next four finishers were also ahead of the previous Olympic record.

As they came to a stop, Cunningham was shaking his head in amazement. The crowd was stunned. David was awestruck. He had never seen a race run with such strategic brilliance. All through the medal ceremony he couldn't get it out of his mind. And as he approached the Marathon Gate and walked out of the stadium with Karl, ghost images of the race remained with him, as a powerful dream can impose itself upon the waking emotions of the next day.

Little Jack Lovelock. He'd taken on the best in the world, kept his wits about him, and beaten them all. A Rhodes Scholar and man of science had won a gold medal. Now all eyes would certainly be on David in the morning. He was filled with admiration for Jack, who had always been a nice guy with a quick, easy smile. But he was also jealous, jealous as hell. Jack had run a hard, smart race. It was over now, and the prize was his. Now, when the guys got together in the pubs or meeting rooms at Oxford, it would be Jack Lovelock whose exploits they would recount, not his. It would be Lovelock's name that would be inscribed on his college's plaques of honor, not his.

Unless he also won. He had to do it. What he'd been trying to tell himself for a week now just wasn't true, and that was all there was to it. The gold medal in the decathlon *was* the most important thing in the world. Whatever else he accomplished in life, whatever other successes he enjoyed or failures he endured, this would be his claim to history. Even if he ended up winning the Nobel Prize for chemistry, how much sweeter it would be if the newspaper reported the recipient as "David Keegan, world-famous scientist and Olympic decathlon champion." This was his ticket into the history books. This was his stab at immortality.

And it meant proving something to himself. If he could do this and win, he could do anything. If he could overcome the competition, the fear, the fatigue. If he could just make himself believe. Because as any Olympic champion knows, the real battle is always with oneself.

And it all was happening tomorrow. His stomach clutched with tension. He hadn't wanted this to happen. He hadn't wanted to go into the competition feeling this way.

Then he looked over at Karl. The German seemed just as nervous as he was.

There was something else, though, David thought. Karl had suddenly gotten very good.

By the time they got to the transport area, the first bus for the village had already gone and the second had not yet arrived.

"I don't want just to stand and wait," said Karl, hands in his pockets and bouncing uncomfortably on the balls of his feet. "Let's take a walk."

"Suits me," David said. He felt like a spooked racehorse. All these people milling around were giving him the creeps.

They wandered off around the south side of the stadium, past the flapping banners of Coubertinplatz, and over toward the end of the railroad yard, where empty freight and passenger cars sat idly on spur tracks. Karl led the way.

"At least it's peaceful here," he said, but the look in his eyes was anything but placid.

"Thinking about tomorrow?" David asked.

Karl nodded. "I can't help myself. Do you think they're all feeling this way now?"

"I hope so," said David, trying to force a smile. And he couldn't help thinking back to the incident in the swim stadium's locker room, then imagining Karl doing laps by himself this afternoon in the village's indoor pool.

Karl looked off toward the darkness of the tracks.

"It's strange," David said. "Here it is, the night before the biggest day of our lives, and we're hanging around the railroad tracks like two small-town kids with nothing to do on a Saturday night." He stopped a moment and thought. "Do kids do that in Germany, too?"

Karl forced his own smile in return. "I imagine they do it everywhere." The only sounds were the occasional bird and the background noises of the distant crowd leaving the stadium. It was amazing how removed they could feel. Yet it truly was as if there were no one else within a hundred miles. For a long time neither man spoke.

"I guess we ought to go back," Karl said. "The next bus should have arrived."

They reversed themselves and began walking in the direction they had come. Just then David heard the commotion of feet and whispers. Someone else was whistling the familiar strains of "Horst Wessel."

"It's them!" David heard a voice call out in German. Karl suddenly tensed. David looked around to see a group of eight or ten young men advancing toward them out of the shadows. Their leader had a peculiar smile on his open, pale face.

"Something's wrong," Karl whispered. "Let's get out of here. Turn around. Follow me."

But as soon as Karl turned, two of the young toughs grabbed him by the arms. Karl tried to wrestle himself free, but two more held him firm.

"What's going on?" David demanded as the others grabbed him in the same way.

"This is them," the leader said confidently to his second-in-command.

"What's going on?" Karl asked with fury in his voice.

"You tell me what's going on!" the leader came back at him. "What business does a son of Germany have to share himself and his heritage with the enemy?"

One of the other young toughs spit in David's face.

"We know who you are." The leader continued to taunt Karl. "We know who you both are, and we know what you've been doing. You've been watched." Then he turned to David. "And we'll teach you a lesson in respect for your betters."

With that, he landed a fist squarely in David's gut. David doubled up in pain.

Karl tried to come to his aid, but those holding him wrestled him to the ground. One of them produced a balled-up rag, which he forced into Karl's mouth.

The leader kneed David in the groin and, when he doubled over again, hit him with an uppercut to the jaw. David spit blood. He tried furiously to break away from his captors but there were too many of them. Out of the corner of his eye he saw Karl struggling on the ground.

"Watch this," the leader said to Karl. "We'll show you how to deal properly with foreign vermin." He kicked David in the leg. "As lesson number one, one does not climb into bed with them! Do you understand?"

Karl remained rigid.

"I said: Do you understand?"

As Karl continued his stoic posture, the leader kicked David again. Karl said nothing. The young tough punched David twice in the stomach. David felt his insides heaving.

Reluctantly Karl nodded his head.

"I'm not sure I get you." The leader brought both fists down together on David's shoulder. David collapsed under the impact. The toughs holding him quickly regained their grip. The youths' leader continued to pummel him with both fists.

Karl nodded his head more vigorously.

"Good," the leader went on. "I think you're learning that *this* is how we deal with them!" He slapped David with all his might against the side of the head. Then he came back and sent David's head flying in the other direction.

David's knees buckled, and he fell to the ground. This time they let him stay put. They gathered around, and all kicked him. As best he could, David tried to curl up into a fetal position to defend himself from the attack.

"Take that home to your Hebrew swine friends!" the leader called out. "And send your black baboons back to Africa, where they can run with their own kind!"

The group that had been guarding Karl let go of him. Immediately he scrambled to his feet to rush them, but the others held their ground threateningly around David.

"Don't let us see you make this same mistake again," the leader warned, then once again looked down at David. "And another thing: Stay away from our German girls!"

A pang of fear stabbed through David's aching chest as the gang ran off together, disappearing into the darkness.

In another second Karl was hovering over him. "I'm—I'm so sorry," he said, cradling David's head with his forearm. "This is all my fault." He was close to tears.

David opened his mouth.

"Don't try to talk," Karl said. David leaned over and retched on the ground.

"I can't believe something like this could happen here in Germany. I'm . . . My whole country has been dishonored."

"It's not your fault," David gasped weakly. Every part of his body was on fire. He couldn't catch his breath. He wanted just to sit down on the pavement and cry, the way he had the first time he'd been picked on by a schoolyard bully. But that had been when he was six years old, and when he'd gotten home and looked himself square in the mirror, he had vowed that it would never happen again. And it hadn't. Never again.

Until now. Somehow he would get back at them.

Oh, God. What a time for this to happen.

Karl put his arm behind David's back. "You'll have to see if you can walk," he said. "I can't leave you here. Can you do it?"

With Karl's help and in agony, David struggled to his feet. Karl supported him as they trudged off back toward the buses. David wasn't sure he could support his own weight. As he limped along, he felt himself going in and out of rational thought. But during his lucid moments he kept replaying in his mind the taunts of the leader: "We know who you both are, and we know what you've been doing."

Someone had been watching him. Why they'd singled him out, he had no idea. What he'd done to bring on their wrath, he couldn't possibly imagine.

Everything hurt. Every step was an effort. But through his pain he recalled the other warning: "Stay away from our German girls!"

David wondered if Karl had heard that and whether it struck the same paralyzing fear in Karl's heart as it did in his own.

TWENTY-TWO

Döberitz

David propped himself up on his bunk and wondered if he looked as wretched as the grim faces of Karl, Tom, and Wolfgang Fürstner seemed to suggest.

"This is an outrage!" said Fürstner, pounding one fist into the other palm. "Everything we've worked for destroyed by the lawless acts of young hoodlums. I promise you we will get to the bottom of this."

"It's my fault," Karl repeated. He still looked shell-shocked.

"Stop talking like that," David said in a heavy whisper. He still tasted blood inside his mouth.

"We have to go to Brundage," said Tom.

David sat upright. "No!"

"Why not?"

"Just don't," said David wearily.

"Well, I am going to report it to the Gestapo," said Fürstner. "I have direct access to Obergruppenführer Heydrich. I can assure you that he won't let this lie quietly. I also have an extraordinary personal mandate from the *Reichsführer-SS* which cannot be interfered with. I warrant we will have the culprits within twenty-four hours."

"Wolfgang, do me a favor," David requested. "Don't do anything until after the decathlon's over."

"I don't understand," said Fürstner.

"I've been working for this . . . we've all been working for this for four years now. I don't want anything affecting it."

"I'd say something's already affected it," the deputy commandant remarked, "so I do not really understand your logic. And I particularly do not understand your refusal to go to the infirmary. Look at you. You're a mess. You could have serious injuries."

David closed his eyes and sighed. "I'm all right."

"Yes, I can see that."

"I don't want word of this to get out."

"So you're still playing Jack Armstrong, all-American boy," said Tom. "David, we're not at the Point any longer. You can stop trying to live up to your own image and just act human for a change."

David opened his eyes in the direction of the voice. "Thanks, Tom. That's helpful."

"He's right," Fürstner commented. "After what's happened, everyone would understand if you chose not to show up tomorrow morning. In fact, that's what I would do under the circumstances."

"Oh, sure," David said. He indicated Karl with his glance. "And make it easier for him."

For the first time since the attack a smile registered on Karl's face. Then he turned serious. "What else can I do for you?" he asked.

"Just twist your ankle during the hundred-meter dash tomorrow morning," David replied. "And just between you and me, it wouldn't hurt if you would trip Glenn Morris on your way down."

"Only don't tell Avery Brundage," Tom added. "He'd have our nuts."

"I think we ought to leave Lieutenant Keegan to rest," Fürstner stated. "He'll need it if he continues to ignore all appeals to reason." He moved toward the door.

Karl stood looking at David for a moment, then put his hand on David's shoulder. "I'll see you in the morning. David, I—"

But David waved him off. "Get out of here, both of you. I can get all the aggravation I need just from Tom."

"If you need anything, send for me anytime during the night," said Fürstner. "What I told you before about being at your complete disposal still applies, now more than ever." He and Karl left.

"Anything I can get you?" Tom asked when they had gone.

"I told you no."

Tom went back to his own bunk, folded his hands behind his head, and lay down. He stared up at the ceiling and asked, "So what are you going to do?"

"What choice do I have?" David responded. It didn't take him long to fall into a deep sleep.

Friday, August 7, Grunewald

In all the moments of his life set aside for dreaming about this morning, David had never imagined it would be like this. He had awakened with a hollow, gnawing feeling in his gut that he instinctively attributed to nerves. But as soon as he tried to move, sharp, stabbing pains like knife thrusts had ripped through his belly. His jaw hurt. His chest hurt. In fact, as he inventoried the effects of last night from head to foot, he discovered that very little of him had emerged unscathed. All he wanted to do was crawl back into bed.

He forced himself to his feet. Standing for a long time under the shower stream trying to revivify himself, he didn't see how he could possibly compete. Every deep breath was an effort. The pulsating water stung every inch of his bare skin. Yet he knew he would. This day had been too long in coming. Nothing would stop him.

During the bus ride from the village he'd said very little, and no one had come over to talk to him. This was in keeping, though. There isn't much to say to either condemned men or athletes on the morning their required performances are to take place.

There were so many things to think about. There were scores of competitors in the decathlon. The published schedule had listed ten heats for the hundred meters. The high jump would probably take several hours. But this was sizing up as the classic German-American confrontation. Besides David, the United States had qualified Glenn Morris, Jack Parker, and Bob Clark. Besides Karl, Germany had Erwin Huber and Helmut Bonnet.

Painfully walking out across the infield from the Marathon Gate and seeing the other competitors beginning to assemble, David suddenly felt as though he were moving underwater, with the concentrated pressure of the oceans bearing down on his shoulders and forcing the air from his lungs. The rest of his life was an abstraction. Over the next two days, within the confines of this concrete shell, would be determined who was the greatest athlete in the world. He could not imagine himself serving in the military, getting married, raising children, going on vacation, watching a movie, having friends over for dinner. All he could picture himself doing was running, throwing, jumping. He had become his task and in spite of his pain, there was no other reality.

From her vantage point in the stands Miranda watched the runners assemble at the starting line for one of the hundred-meter heats.

Karl and David had been assigned to this same one. Some of the athletes were still digging holes for their toes with little silver spades. Others were flexing up and down on the balls of their feet like Mexican jumping beans and shaking out their hands as if they were wet.

She had come to the stadium today for a specific reason, and she'd expected to be bored sitting through an entire day's worth of arcane and unfathomable athletic exercises. But as the runners found their places and lined up, she couldn't deny the primal thrill of anticipating these two men from different countries competing and straining and suffering before her, as if it were she they were actually fighting for, rather than some symbolic medal of gold. Her mind sailed. She pictured the eventual victor as the dusk closed in tomorrow evening, dirty and exhausted and bleeding, striding bravely toward the stands with the last ounce of his strength to claim her as his prize.

Karl was standing upright, pawing the ground first with one foot and then with the other. He looked like a bull about to charge. David was next to him, checking the alignment of his feet in the starting holes. As he bent over as if in pain, Miranda fixed her gaze on the taut muscles of his legs and buttocks, well defined against the thin fabric of his running togs. He stood up, extended his arms in the air, and arched his back, like a tiger stretching, and her heartbeat quickend.

The funny little man in the white suit raised his pistol and called out, "*Auf die Plätze . . .*"

The runners assumed their stances.

"*Fertig . . .*"

They tensed in anticipation.

Bang! The gun sounded, and they took off. It didn't seem possible to her that human beings could move so fast. Yet they all seemed frozen in space, as though the universe had just entered another dimension in which each segment of every movement existed in the same time and plane as every other. It reminded her of the paradox posed by the Greek philosopher Zeno, who described an arrow's reaching halfway to its target in a certain frame of time, then halfway the rest of the distance in half the time, then half that again forever.

Yet she knew from the study of physics and the experience of the eye that the arrow always reaches its target, and before Miranda had taken it all in, the runners all were approaching the finish line. She followed from the rear of the charging pack, through a throng of faces and uniforms she didn't recognize. Then she spotted David, in the thick of it with three other Americans. And then, out in front by a stride, she saw Karl.

He lunged forward, thrusting his chest out against the tape. He raised his arms in triumph, and Miranda heard the crowd behind her break into a wild cheer. Another runner in an American uniform followed right behind him, but it wasn't David.

How joyous she should feel now, she thought. Her boyfriend had just won an Olympic race in front of a hundred thousand people and the cameras of the entire world. Yet there was a hollowness inside her, a strange detachment and loneliness that made her empathize more with David's disappointment than share in the glory of Karl's success.

She tried to make out the expression on David's face. But his jaw was set in that typical, determined look he had, and she couldn't tell whether it was out of discouragement, frustration, or resolve to succeed next time. He still looked as if he were in pain. In any event, he walked over to where Karl was cooling down, surrounded by trainers from the German team, and offered his congratulations.

Arthur Hargreaves sat watching from the stands, dipping from time to time into a small bag of sweets. Against the chill of the Berlin morning, he wore a tweed cap, Norfolk jacket, and woolen scarf. In fact, his wardrobe had been chosen with the idea of making him look as nearly as possible the typical British tourist over for a holiday abroad. He felt so out of place at a sporting event that he felt need of this disguise as the only way of eliminating his self-consciousness and the irrational feeling that all eyes would be on him and his secret revealed.

He checked off the heat just run in his Olympic program. Young Keegan had lost the first event. But he'd run a spirited, gutty race, Hargreaves thought. And after it was over, he hadn't wallowed in self-pity or shown any signs of defeat. The expression on his face proclaimed that he was ready to put it behind him and move on to the next one. Hargreaves had no interest in games as public entertainment, but ever since his school days, he'd believed, like most of his class, that character will out on the playing field.

Karl Linderhoff had won it. Keegan had said how surprised he'd been by the German's good showings during practice. And now it had been borne out by the real thing. It was a fact that the team as a whole was doing far better than anyone would have thought. It wasn't just the chauvinism of the local papers either. Menzies had told him the press all over the world was handling it the same way. In a calmer moment it might even be worth having the boys back at the office take a look for themselves.

Suddenly, obliquely at first, Hargreaves noticed someone. He recalled to his mind's eye every detail of the photographs he had had on his desk and at home and in his briefcase for weeks. Yes, no question. There was Miranda Wolff, just one section over and about five rows in front of him. It was the first time he had seen her in person, and if anything, she was even more striking than her pictures. She must have to fight the boys off with a stick. The combination of that much beauty and brains in the same package was rare indeed.

Hargreaves observed her with fascination for several moments. She had her pale blond hair pulled back into a long ponytail that cascaded down her back and swept across her delicate shoulders every time she looked around. She had about her something of a—of a what?—of a serene, beatific aura, Hargreaves thought. She seemed somehow removed from the crowd around her and never took her eyes off the athletes on the field. He squinted and saw that she was actually looking at Keegan, following his every movement.

Maybe he is making some progress after all, Hargreaves concluded.

Heinrich Himmler was making one of his rare appearances at the stadium. He had rearranged an extremely complex and demanding schedule to be here both today and tomorrow. His seatmate in the box of honor turned out to be Rudolf Hess, but there was nothing to be done about that. Now that the progress of the games was reaching the critical point, Hitler was insisting that one of his most trusted personal representatives be on hand at all times.

There was another man sitting on the other side of the deputy führer. Hess leaned over to Himmler and said, "I would like to introduce you to a good friend from England. This is His Excellency the Duke of Hamilton, a firm friend of the Reich."

Himmler nodded his greeting.

"Smashing race," the duke offered jovially. "Your Linderhoff is quite a dynamo."

"Thank you," said Himmler.

"Left those Americans in the dust, he did."

"I know the führer will be pleased," stated Hess proudly. "The duke and I have had many pleasant and productive conversations this week. He is my personal guest in Berlin, and he's invited me to visit his estate in Scotland. If there is to be continuing peace between our peoples, it will be because of forward-thinking men such as His Excellency. I am confident that he and I can open up important lines of communications between our two countries."

The duke reacted with a dignified smile. For his own part Himmler couldn't imagine Hess communicating anything more challenging than Hitler's dinner order.

This time Hess leaned in toward Himmler and whispered, "So are things back on track?"

"By tomorrow evening we'll have a good idea," Himmler replied portentously. He crossed his legs and settled back in his seat to watch the rest of the day's events.

David lay on his stomach on a table in the locker room while the American trainer Rod Powell massaged the muscles of his back and legs.

"Where'd you get all these bruises, Keegan?" Powell asked. "Even you're not that clumsy in practice."

"Don't ask," David groaned, his chin resting on his crossed hands. "Just try to keep me from tightening up."

"I'm not a magician." Powell shrugged. "But I'll do my best." As if to prove the point, he then ground his knuckles into the small of David's back, making him yelp in pain.

David thought about the race he'd just struggled through. Karl had been every bit as good as David thought he'd be, with that sudden talent that had come from nowhere. He'd even seen Morris and Parker standing on the sidelines shaking their heads in surprise. He'd gone over to congratulate Karl afterward, but the German was off somewhere inside his own head. His eyes were a million miles away. He could have been in a trance.

The broad jump went better than David thought it would go. When he took his place at the starting line for his first attempt, he felt heavy and sluggish. But with every stride he felt his body getting lighter and lighter. Each step on the track signaled a sharper and faster takeoff to the next step. Finally every part of his body was working in concert with every other part. The rhythm was coming back. Remembering Lutz Long's advice to Jesse, he fixed his gaze on the takeoff point. He hit it perfectly and sailed through the air.

The frozen moment aloft was like a leisurely trip by balloon. There was plenty of time to think and strategize. *Tilt your head forward*, he told himself. *Angle your shoulders just so. Maintain your center of gravity. Have your knees flexed and ready for impact. Relax your ankles and calves to absorb the shock.*

Pain shot through his body as his feet implanted firmly in the dirt. But he pitched forward to squeeze out as much distance as possible. He stretched out his hands in front of him to stop his motion and then shot up when he had regained his balance, and trotted off. Altogether, a terrific jump, one of the best he'd ever made.

The other Americans did well, too. Clark reached 7.62 meters, and Parker wasn't far behind with 7.35. And when Karl's turn came, he leaped forward off his powerful stride well into the far end of the jumping pit. When the tape was pulled out, it showed his performance had matched David's almost exactly.

Without any sign of emotion Karl alone walked back toward the locker room. A sinking feeling came over David as he realized he would need his best effort just to stay in the running.

There was a break for lunch while efficient and serious-minded German crews gave every inch of the stadium one of its twice-daily scourings. The shot put began at three—simultaneous with the finals of the five-thousand-meter run. It was every bit the disaster David anticipated. Karl excelled at the spectacular hurl he had demonstrated the first day they'd practiced together. Not only did he display an incredible degree of raw power, but his control was almost superhuman. The judges measured and quickly announced an amazing 14.16 meters.

Morris was also outstanding at 14.10, and Parker managed to hold his own, so altogether the American performance was still reasonably impressive. But after three events the spellbound audience could already sense brewing a German victory.

The semifinals for the four-hundred-meter race were also taking place around the same time. When he finished his throws, David watched with interest because a similar run was the last event of the decathlon. What a luxury it seemed, from where he now stood, to compete in only a single event—any one of the ten decathlon activities would do—simply to concentrate on being the best at that one task, doing it, and then be done. He'd already run the hundred, done the broad jump, and put the shot. If any of those had been his single event, it would all be over, and he could relax instead of sweating through seven more competitions.

Why did he torture himself with ten events, a poor performance in any one of which could send his entire effort and years of training down the drain? Was it because he knew he was different, that he was somehow special, and that challenges which sufficed for ordinary people were never enough for him? Or was it perhaps that he was afraid—as with everything else in his life—that he wouldn't be good enough in any one thing, that the only way he could compete with other people was to resolve just to work that much harder and longer than they did? Unlike other Olympic challenges, in which you had to be very strong or very quick or very agile or very fast, the decathlon rewarded hard work and unrelenting determination. Those two areas were the ones in which David had always felt he had the best shot.

The fact was, if he'd been just a hundred-meter man or a broad jumper, he never could have beaten Jesse Owens. And if he'd been a shot putter, he wouldn't have had a chance against a performance like the one Hans Wöllke had turned in on Sunday. No, like it or not, the decathlon was David's event. Plodding hard work was his stock-in-trade. Gritty determination had gotten him where he was. And that was why he was now trying to convince a body that had been pummeled into submission fewer than twenty-four hours before that it could find enough strength, resilience, and coordination to make it over an ever-growing high jump bar.

The beginning of the men's four hundred proved unnerving. David came out of the locker room just in time to see Harold Smallwood being carried away from the track on a stretcher. He appeared to be awake and in great pain. He was lying down almost doubled over, clutching at his abdomen. He seemed to be gasping for breath. Visions of Rolf Schmidt and Horst Müller instantly flashed through David's mind.

He saw Dean Crowell standing near the American bench and ran over to him. "What is it?" he asked anxiously.

Crowell maintained his normally impassive gym teacher demeanor. "Just keeled over during the run," the coach replied. "He's been having pain all week. Doc thinks it's probably his appendix. He had an attack on the ship coming over, you know."

"Tom told me," David said. "What a tough break. I'm really sorry." But in the back of his mind, in spite of himself, the one he was sorry for *was* himself. He was sure he wasn't any different from anyone else, but his first thoughts were: *Why did this have to happen now? Why did I have to see it? Is it going to throw me off? And is it somehow related to what happened to the two Germans?*

"Smallwood's all man," Crowell continued, oblivious of any reaction from David. "Refused to let his condition stop him." There was something almost reproachful in his tone. "Chuck Middleman. There's another one. Been out here every fucking day in his cast, cheering the team along." And then there was the gym teacher back again when he said, "If we all showed as much dedication and guts as they have, none of us would have anything to bellyache about."

When David got to the jump area, several of the others were already there, stretching out, walking around, crouching down, and surveying the bar from all angles. Karl was standing several paces off by himself with the same intense look David had seen all day.

Unlike the previous three events in which each competitor gets one opportunity to give it his or her best shot, the high jump requires the athletes to keep surpassing themselves until they ultimately fail. An hour and a half were allotted on the schedule.

As his first turn approached, David focused all his attention on the real estate between the starting line and the landing mat on the far side of the bar. The stadium, the crowd, the other athletes—everything disappeared. The key to the high jump is approach and take-off. Once the jumper has left the ground, there is nothing he or she can do to increase height.

When his name was called, David moved to the starting line as if being pulled by magnetism. He visually marked off a target line two strides from the bar. He began running, his knees flexed and his arms swinging normally at his side.

Seven steps later he reached his imaginary target line. He brought his arms in close to his body, elbows down and trailing. He planted his left heel in the dirt. His leg straightened out, then flexed again as his body moved over it. His arms, still close to his body, shot forward and upward. His right leg came up to meet his arm. He was now airborne.

At the top of his arc he managed to straddle the bar perfectly, lying completely horizontally in the air. He lowered his right side and at the same instant turned his head toward the bar. This tipped his left side upward, clearing the bar. He landed agonizingly on his right shoulder in the pit and exhaled his long-held store of breath to relieve the pain.

The competition was strong. Everyone made his first jump, and the bar was raised to the next level.

Again and again the field cleared the bars. For the crowd excitement grew. For the athletes themselves there was only tension. Huber stayed in until 1.70. Bonnet managed 1.75. David finally went out at 1.80 meters, aching and spent. Morris got to 1.85. And Karl, employing a takeoff that made his legs seem like automobile springs, cleared the bar at 1.90. In the box of honor, Deputy Führer Hess and Reichsführer Himmler looked on with pride.

The last event of the day was the four-hundred-meter run. By this point in the competition decathlon contestants are physically exhausted and mentally spent. The only thing that keeps them going in this grueling final test is grim determination.

This race was divided into five heats. David drew the second heat, and again he was paired with Karl. Parker was also running with them. Clark was in the third heat, and Morris was in the fifth. From his experience the first day of practice David knew that he couldn't hang back and let Karl set the pace. Despite the way he felt, despite aching in every muscle in a body that proclaimed it just wanted to be left alone with time to heal itself from the wounds of last night's beating rather than have new injuries inflicted, he had to give it everything right from the beginning.

Someday, he said to himself, *my body will no longer hurt. I will not have to labor to breathe and struggle to think straight. But by then it will be too late. So I must behave now as if I did not hurt, as if nothing were wrong. I must sublimate. I must ignore everything physical. I must ignore everything mental. Then what is left? Something beyond, something I cannot even name. And that is what I must rely on.* He entered a bizarre dialogue with his body, urging it to stay with him for just four hundred more yards—one complete circuit of the track—and then he would let it rest. How he was going to keep it from knowing he planned on subjecting it to the same punishment tomorrow, he hadn't quite figured out.

Émile Binet of Belgium took the first heat in 52.2 seconds, not an insurmountable number. Still, running directly against Karl, David knew what he had to do.

The second-heat runners took their places. As soon as the starting pistol sounded, David took off like a flash. Instantly he was aware of the throbbing pain in his shoulders, stomach, and legs. But he refused to let it stop him or hamper his efficiency. If anything, he would use it as a prod to greater performance, the equivalent of a jockey's whip in the stretch.

A good runner learns never to look over his shoulder until the very end, and only if the race is clearly won. But out of the corner of his eye David could see Karl just slightly behind him, matching him stride for stride and coming up fast on the outside. David pushed himself to hold on to the lead. By the time they reached the first turn, David was giving it everything he had, and Karl was practically shoulder to shoulder with him. Jack Parker was several paces behind.

As Karl made his move from the outside coming out of the turn, David played the only strategic move he had, edging himself slightly to the outside. That would at least hold him into the second turn. If David could maintain his inside position coming out of it, Karl would have that much more distance to make up.

But as they came around the far end zone, he could almost feel Karl breathing down his neck. David couldn't try the same trick again; with his speed Karl would be able to outmaneuver him. He just had to run as fast as possible, knowing it would still take Karl into the final turn before he could pull out ahead. David felt as though a knife had been plunged between his lower ribs and were being worked in and out between every lengthening stride. The pain radiated into every extremity. And yet he ran faster still, deluding himself into thinking he could outrun the torment if only he moved fast enough.

Into the final stretch he was dead even with Karl. Parker was right behind them in case either one of them faltered. David tried to push himself that much harder, to squeeze another fraction of an inch out of every step. *Only another ninety meters to go*, he promised himself. *Only eighty*. For that much distance you could fly if you had to. You could walk on water.

Just as he had suspected, with about seventy meters left, Karl began to surge slightly ahead. David worked his arms viciously back and forth, desperately attempting to pull his body along through the air. Karl increased the force of his kick and thrust out his chest.

I'm going to beat him this time, David said to himself. *I refuse to let him win.* His teeth were clenched so hard his jaw ached. *Whatever he does, I'll do, too.*

But then, stride for stride, he began to falter. As David slipped back, Karl seemed only to gain strength and speed. David tried mightily to press that much harder with each step, to lean that much farther forward, to bend into the wind just a little lower—anything at all to buy back some of the disparity between them.

With fifteen meters to go, his lungs were burning, and his stomach now felt as if the knife had gone all the way through and come out the other side. And still he kept going. One last desperate lunge was all he had left. *This is it. Your last chance . . .*

David imagined he felt a blast of wind almost knock him over backward as Karl broke the tape two steps in front of him. He quickly found himself in a cluster with the other runners, crossing the finish line and slowing down to a trot. Karl jogged on ahead, his arms raised in triumph, accepting the shouted plaudits of the crowd, which knew it was seeing history rewritten before its eyes.

Sweating profusely and still gasping for air, David walked dejectedly back toward the American bench as Bob Clark, Helmut Bonnet, and the others began collecting for the third heat. He hadn't heard the official time yet, but Karl had to have cracked forty-nine seconds. That would have made David's time pretty good, too. But Karl had won. Karl had won.

David stopped once to bend over, let his arms hang, and place his head between his knees. When he came back up, he could see Karl at the far end of the field, surrounded by jubilant coaches, teammates, and Leni Riefenstahl herself, barking out orders like some general to her camera crew. David picked up his blue warm-up suit from where it lay on the back of the bench, and continued on toward the tunnel to the locker room. So much for day one.

He'd given his all, and it had not been enough. Tomorrow, from somewhere, he would have to find something more.

Just as he was about to disappear into the tunnel under the stands, a frantically waving arm caught his attention. He looked up to the railing above him. It was Miranda, in a blue wraparound skirt, knee socks, and a matching cotton sweater. Her hair was pulled back into a ponytail but was windblown from an afternoon outside, with blond wisps skewed about her forehead and neck. She was out of breath from fighting her way through the throng of people to get to him.

"Have you been here all day?" David asked, still surprised to see her.

Miranda nodded, but an urgency in her pursed lips told him she had not come over merely to console him over losing or to commend him for fighting the good fight. "May I talk to you?" she asked.

With the back of his hand David wiped the perspiration from around his eyes. "Right now?"

"Please," she said. "I need to talk to someone, and you're the only one I have."

David turned his head to see Karl still basking in glory at the other end of the field. Miranda had obviously seen him, too, but she was here, not over there with him.

"Let me just shower and change," David said. "Do you know where the athletes' entrance is?"

Miranda nodded gratefully.

When David came out of the locker room, she was waiting for him. She was smoothing out the tangles in her hair, an innocent, absentminded gesture that he found very sensual. The fetching smile she greeted him with was etched with gravity, which, if anything, made it more appealing.

"How are you?" he asked with concern.

She answered haltingly, "I'm . . . all right."

"Is anything wrong?"

"Yes, well, I'm—I'm not sure, but—" She'd had a chance to scrutinize him, and now she looked even more troubled. "What happened to you?"

"Nothing really."

"You have a big bruise over your cheek and a cut by the side of your mouth."

You should see me without my clothes, David thought. But he said, "It's nothing to worry about. Tell me about you."

She looked down at the ground as if studying her shoe.

"Let's take a little walk," he offered. He put his hand on the middle of her back and gently guided her down the concourse that ringed the huge stadium. As they walked, the flap of her skirt caught the wind, briefly revealing her shapely leg well up to mid-thigh. She hardly reacted but brushed the fabric down innocently with one hand, either unconscious of her own sexuality or so knowing of its effect that it had become second nature.

They walked in the direction of the Via Triumphalis, oblivious of the people beginning to empty out of the stadium, and she had nothing to say. He said nothing either for a while. He wanted to let her unburden herself in her own time and way. They passed by the roped-off display of the prototype of the new universal vehicle that Hitler had proclaimed would embody the dynamic spirit of the German *Volk* and fulfill his dream of an inexpensive car for everyone. But David thought the *Volks-wagen* looked more like a giant bug than a car, nothing like the stately Mercedeses that cruised up and down the Kaiserdamm. For all of Hitler's vision, David didn't see how the thing could catch on.

Finally, when they were halfway around the stadium, David slowed and took her by the arm. "Miranda, what's troubling you?"

She sighed in frustration, as if she didn't quite know how to begin. "I've seen something," she said awkwardly. "Some*one* actually."

"Who?" David said.

"An athlete. The one you tried to save."

"Rolf Schmidt?"

She nodded.

"But he died."

She nodded again. "I know. And I've seen him. I know where he is."

David put his hand on her arm again and pulled her toward the concrete side of the stadium, away from the flow of people. "Tell me what you mean."

She told him the story of her encounter with Dr. Behrman's secret lab, beginning with the gold key chain locket and ending with the approaching voices that had scared her away. She explained that Karl and the way he was acting had prompted her to seek out Dr. Behrman in the first place.

"But then, when I couldn't find him and I went to his house and his wife told me what had happened to her, I couldn't just go on as if nothing were wrong."

"No." David agreed. "And you've asked Karl about this directly?"

"Yes. But he won't tell me anything. He tells me it isn't any of my business." Then she told him of the packing crates she had seen in Behrman's office, all bearing that strange "K-208" marking.

David paused to take in the totality of what she'd said. The scientist does not jump to conclusions. He tries to interpret the data objectively and let them guide him. He thought back to the first time he and Karl had practiced together, with kindly old Dr. Behrman watching calmly from the sidelines. "If Karl works for Behrman, and Behrman has disappeared, and Karl tells you to mind your own business, and he's been acting strangely besides, then quite clearly Karl is somehow involved and knows something."

Miranda listened quietly while he talked.

"We'll confront him together," David said. "It's the only thing to do. I have some information about his past he may want to try to explain. He can't duck both of us. And if he tries, that in itself should lead us on to the next clue."

"When do we do this?" Miranda asked.

"Right after the decathlon. Maybe tomorrow night." To David that seemed an eternity away. "You meet me here tomorrow just like today."

"Yes. I will," she promised, then added, "I hate him for what he's done."

"Maybe he couldn't help it," David said.

He thought he saw her wrinkle her nose, rabbitlike, the way she sometimes did when she was thinking.

"What do you mean?"

"I don't know," David said. "It's possible that he may be in trouble. And maybe we can help him."

"Oh, there is one more thing," Miranda said. She reached into her handbag and took out a folded piece of paper. "I copied this down from something I found in Dr. Behrman's desk."

"What is it?"

She handed it to him. "A list of sports. From the Olympics, I think. So I thought it might mean something to you."

David unfolded the paper and studied the list, copied out word for word in Miranda's tight, precise handwriting. There was no explanation or background material on the page, only a list of events.

He scanned the column and read out loud: "Shot put, hammer throw, men's and women's javelin, women's discus, four-hundred-meter hurdles, ten thousand meters, men's and women's four-hundred-meter relay, pentathlon, decathlon—"

Suddenly it clicked. He lowered the paper for a moment. "Miranda, when did you first see this list?"

She wrinkled up her nose again and thought for a moment. "Tuesday morning."

"Are you absolutely sure?"

"Yes," she retorted a little petulantly. "Why? What is it?"

"What I read you is just the track and field section. But it goes on across the board—heavyweight lifting, thousand- and two-thousand-meter cycling, flyweight and heavyweight boxing, star class yachting, single, pairs, and fours rowing, single and double kayak, gymnastics, equestrian."

"I still don't understand."

"With a couple of notable exceptions, like the ten-thousand-meter run and the four-hundred-meter hurdles, every event listed here that's already taken place Germany has won."

"And if I found it Tuesday, then it was written before any of this could have taken place."

"Exactly. And in the two events I just mentioned that Germany hasn't won, the leading contender had dropped out: Horst Müller and Rolf Schmidt." He refolded the paper. "May I hold on to this?"

"Yes, of course."

"Have you told anyone else about this?"

"No. You're the only one I have to go to."

They gazed at each other wordlessly for a moment. Then she took the one step necessary to cover the distance between them. She laid both hands on his shoulders near his neck, so that her forearms rested on his chest. She kissed him on the cheek, then snuggled her head into the side of his chin. "I'll be hoping for you tomorrow," she said tenderly, another of those touching sentiments that doesn't quite translate properly.

David clasped his hands around her waist and pulled her tighter to him. For a moment they seemed to be holding each other up. Suddenly all his years of loneliness, of forced self-reliance and keeping his own counsel seemed to find their meaning in a young woman whose depth of loneliness and feeling was in every degree equal to his.

He pulled her head up and looked into her large, moist eyes, and this time he initiated the kiss, and this time it was firmly on the lips, and if anyone around them took any notice, he didn't care.

It wasn't until he raised his eyes and looked out above her blond head that he caught a particular movement he could not ignore. It darted like a flash of light behind one of the thick concrete pillars that supported the stadium.

"Excuse me just a minute," he said, breaking their embrace.

"Is anything wrong?" she asked.

"No. I just think I see someone I know."

"I'll leave you then," she said. "I have to be getting back, and I've kept you too long at a time like this."

"No, you haven't," he assured her tenderly. Everything within him was warring over whether to let her go or to prolong at any cost what they had just shared. But he had to move fast. "Okay, then. Tomorrow evening." He tried to keep the urgency out of his voice. "Are you sure you'll be all right getting home?"

"I'm sure. I'm a big girl even if I don't always act it." She smiled and said, "I'll be watching you all day tomorrow."

He let her go, yet continued holding on to the tips of her fingers until the distance between them finally pulled her away.

As soon as Miranda merged with the parting crowd, David turned on his heels.

Two columns down he thought he saw something. Stealthily he sprang from one to the next so as not to be seen. He insinuated himself into a throng of people emerging from the exit between the columns.

In another moment he was right behind him, a young man in his early twenties dressed in the uniform of the brownshirts. David matched his pace for several steps, duplicating the rhythm of his walk, swinging his arms in an identical arc. Then, when he was sure he had it down, he clamped onto the man's left wrist and easily bent his arm back into a hammerlock.

The leader of last night's group of young toughs turned his head with horror. With the press of people coming out of the stadium now, no one could tell anything was amiss.

"Don't say a word," David whispered to him in German, "or I'll rip your arm right out of its socket. Just walk where I guide you and keep smiling."

David directed him to the closest athletes' entrance. Right inside was the door to a locker room that he knew the five-thousand-meter men had used earlier in the afternoon and that would now be empty.

He dragged him inside and closed the door behind him. Without further ado, he grabbed the young man by his lapels and slammed him into the bank of metal lockers. The German collapsed to the floor.

David pulled him to a standing position and drove an uppercut into the edge of his chin, which again knocked him off his feet. "All right," he said calmly. "Now just who the fuck are you, and what do you want with me?"

The young man said nothing but spit blood onto the front of his uniform. Last night's look must have been a disguise. Not a bad one at that. But he'd overplayed his hand.

David picked him up again, drove him back into the lockers, and brought his knee up between the brownshirt's legs. The young man bent over, moaned, and made a weak retching sound.

"You know something, you're not quite as tough as you were last night. Amazing how much difference a day can make. A little more interesting when it's one-on-one, isn't it?" said David. The young man continued to be silent.

"Fella, I will break every bone in your body. And then I'm going to scoop you up and hand you over to Captain Fürstner at the Olympic Village unless I get some answers." David slapped the brownshirt's face first to one side and the other, three times in succession. Then he punched him hard in the stomach, just to let him know what it felt like.

"Why were you spying on me just now?"

"To see what you were doing," the young German answered sullenly.

"Makes sense," David said, nodding, "but doesn't tell me much." He gave him another hard one, aimed right below the rib cage. "How long have you been watching me?"

"All—all day," the young man gasped.

"Okay. Next question: Did you just happen to come upon us by chance last night?"

The brownshirt remained rigid, but David noticed a spreading wet spot in the area of his fly. This gave him some satisfaction that he was getting through.

David shook his head. "I ought to explain to you that you caused me no end of distress today, and to be perfectly frank, I regret to say that I'm not at my party best. I don't have much patience left, so unless you can be a bit more forthcoming and cooperative, even in my weakened condition, this is the part where I start kicking the living shit out of you. Does that make sense?"

The German nodded warily.

"I'll ask you one more time. The attack last night. Was it spur-of-the-moment or planned?" David took one step back and raised his foot in the direction of the brownshirt's groin in an effort to elicit a response.

"Planned," the German spit out.

"Okay. Now we're making progress. By you?"

The young man hesitated. David grabbed him by both arms and slammed him back into the lockers with an enormous clatter. "Don't push me anymore," David warned him. "Now, was it you who planned it?"

"No," the young man answered, practically weeping now.

"And what about staying away from German women?"

A look from David was enough this time. "That was part of the plan. To scare you off."

"Whose plan?"

"The one who asked me to do it."

David pressed on. "And who was that?"

Another siege of recalcitrance.

"If you ever entertain the hope of having children, I suggest you answer me," David stated.

The young man took a deep breath. "Karl Linderhoff," he stammered, then closed his eyes in defeat.

TWENTY-THREE

Döberitz

He was reeling, spinning, removed from the reality of the senses. It didn't add up. Karl had been a victim of the attack, just as he had. But then David realized that while the young tough had been punching and kicking him, his friends had been holding Karl down. They hadn't tried to hurt him. A perfect ruse to draw suspicion away from Karl.

How could Karl do that to him? As soon as he'd found out what he wanted, David had been all ready to fold the young tough in half and deliver him personally to Fürstner to deal with, no matter who was behind him, even if it was Adolf Hitler himself. Yet when he heard the name emerge from the German's bleeding lips, he lost all heart and motivation to do anything else. He had simply turned around and walked away.

He knew the brownshirt would eventually get back to Karl with what had happened. But he would get to Karl himself tomorrow night, with Miranda, as soon as the decathlon was over, and then they would have it out. And he'd at least had the presence of mind to warn the young man that if he said anything to Karl before that, David would personally see to his untimely demise.

David lay on his bunk, staring up at the ceiling. Tom had gone out somewhere, so he was alone. He had thought that Karl was his friend. How could he have been so wrong about him? He had thought there was something strong and deep between them that transcended the short time they had actually known each other.

Maybe Karl had some hidden agenda just as compelling as David's. And how much did Miranda have to do with it? The whole thing was too upsetting to think about, especially tonight. Tomorrow evening he would deal with it, with Karl. All he knew for certain was that no matter what, he couldn't just coldly turn Karl over to Fürstner or any of his even more imposing superiors. He owed it to their friendship to at least hear him out.

But there was something else that couldn't wait. It was a small act in the scheme of things, but it was something he could and had to do.

He got up, went out the door, and walked over to Dean Crowell's room.

"You're asking me to do what?" Crowell asked incredulously.

"Put Jesse Owens on the four-hundred-relay team," stated David.

Crowell draped his leg over the single armchair in the Spartan room. "Let me make sure I'm getting this straight, Keegan. We've already got three firm places—Sam Stoller, Marty Glickman, and your roomie, Quinn. The fourth is either going to be Foy Draper or Ralph Metcalfe. Are you suggesting we use Owens instead?"

"No. Use Draper, Metcalfe, and Owens. They're the fastest."

Crowell scratched the stubble of his beard. "Now I admit I ain't no Rhodes Scholar, son, but where I come from, that adds up to six . . . on a four-man squad. By the way, Keegan, what happened to you? Where'd you get those bruises? You out carousing or something the night before you had to run?"

"No, Coach." David sighed. "A little accident, but I'm okay."

"Does Brundage know about this?"

"No, I didn't want to bother him."

"'Cause I expected a little more out there from you today."

"I'll try to make it up tomorrow. But look, about the relay—"

"It isn't my decision. You know that Lawson Robertson's the head track and field coach. It's up to him."

"But you could talk to him. He'll listen to you."

"Sit down, Keegan." He motioned him over to the bed. "So who do you think we ought to ax? Quinn? He'll love you for that."

David paused for a moment, then said firmly, "Stoller and Glickman."

"Oh, terrific!" said Crowell, throwing his hands up. "The only two Hebes on the track and field squad. How's that going to look?"

David winced at the term. "Probably not great," he admitted.

"Anybody put you up to this?"

"Are you crazy?"

"Then why are you so hep on this?"

"Because I want us to win."

"And what makes you think we won't? We haven't lost this particular event since 1912."

"The Swedes had never lost the pentathlon either."

Crowell squinted his eyes. "What are you getting at, Keegan?"

David stood up and began pacing the small room. "I know I talked to you about this already, but the Germans are doing something. And somehow there're certain events *they know they're going to win*. How, I'm not sure. But they've got a list."

"You've seen this list?"

"I've seen a copy of it."

"Where did it come from?"

David shook his head. "It doesn't matter. You have to trust me on this. They knew in advance they would take the pentathlon. No one thought they had a chance. How could they have predicted that? They knew about the javelin, the shot, the hammer . . . all of them. And the relay is on the list, too." He didn't mention the decathlon. That would have to be his own battle to fight.

"Owens has already had his place in the sun," said Crowell. "He's coming home with three gold medals, for chrissakes."

"But can you imagine what it would do to the image of Aryan supremacy if he came home with four?" David pointed out. "Nothing else could do it. Look, Sam and Marty are good friends of mine. They're both great guys and real men. But we're a team. We're all in this together, and each of us has pledged to do whatever we have to for the good of the team, for the good of the country. And Jesse is the best. No question."

He realized—at least partially to his own horror—that he had begun to think like a general. Victory had become all-important. With what he had just found out, the games had become a war and victory had become an obsession. Victory at all costs. Even if it meant sacrificing individuals.

"And unless you do something radical, Coach, the Germans are going to win that race. They're going to win the women's relay, too. But there's nothing we can do about that."

Crowell pulled his leg back and sat straight. "You seem pretty sure of this."

"I am pretty sure," David affirmed.

"How can I believe what you're telling me?"

"All you have to believe is that unless you put Owens on the team, the Germans are going to win. They might win anyway."

"I think you're full of shit, Keegan. Anyway, how's it going to look if I do what you're suggesting? What's Brundage going to say?"

"Look, Coach, if you don't do anything, and the Germans beat you, how's *that* going to look? Everyone in the world, including Brundage, will be second-guessing you. You're going to look ridiculous, and you can't say I didn't warn you. If you put Owens on the team and you still lose, it's going to look like the right move because the Germans *were* so good, and then you're okay. And if you put Owens on the team and *win*, you're the hero. Your reputation is made."

Crowell scratched his chin again. "Okay, you've said your piece," he declared. "Now get out of here. You've got enough to worry about your own self tomorrow."

Saturday, August 8, Grunewald

David had been at the stadium warming up for almost an hour when Tom arrived and came over to him.

"Have you heard?"

"Heard what?" David said.

"Robertson's going to replace Stoller and Glickman. The coaches just made the decision this morning in time for the trials. The team's going to be me and Metcalfe and Draper and Owens. Word's getting out fast. Everyone's talking about it. I wonder what happened."

"I can't imagine," said David. "How are Sam and Marty taking it?"

"How would you take it?" Tom asked. "They come all this way, train all this time, work so hard, and give up so much to make the team. And where are you going to find two greater guys? Plus, either of them could have beaten the pants off the Germans."

"I know. It's really rough. Like Smallwood coming down with appendicitis."

Tom nodded. "But at least that was an act of God. This is an act of a somewhat less exalted being."

David had no argument with that. What it came down to was that once again he had had to wrestle with his conscience. And once again he was afraid that he might have won.

*   *   *

The track had been set up for the first heat of the 110-meter hurdles, scheduled to begin at 10:00 A.M. By the time David walked over to the staging area, activity was already in full swing. Serious-looking officials with clipboards were checking off numbers and herding athletes into position.

The inevitable moment arrived. David spotted Karl jogging and loosening up along the edge of the infield. Instantly his entire body tensed. His heart suddenly pounded against his breastbone. Everything was churning and surging inside him, like some rampant tornado swirling down to a single point. For the first time he had let come into sharp focus the anger over what had been done to him and the hurt of betrayal.

Unless . . . Had Karl somehow found out about David's own initial motives in befriending him—the fact that they were both pawns in a larger chess match—and was this his way of getting back? But that was crazy and irrelevant. Would his own crime have warranted being beaten senseless the night before the biggest test of his life? He had to stop thinking like this, today of all days. If he let it, it would drive him crazy. Whatever the unspeakable secret was, it would be his business to find out by tonight. One way or the other, he aimed to know. In the meantime, his only desire—stronger than ever—was to win.

Karl spotted him and came over. "David, how are you?"

"Okay," he replied.

"You don't look so bad. It was impressive the way you hung in yesterday in spite of everything."

"Thanks. You didn't do so badly yourself."

Karl shrugged magnanimously. "Just luck in a field this good. We'll have to see how it goes today."

"Yeah, we will," David said.

The hurdles are demanding to the one-event specialist. They are particularly taxing to the decathlon competitor. Few events in track and field require such an unforgiving combination of speed, agility, and technique. The impression given to the spectator is of the blinding speed of a sprint, combined in equal measure with the gravity-defying elegance of the long jump and the potential violence of a steeplechase. Because one is jumping over a series of barriers while running at full tear, it is easy to fall, pull a muscle, or sustain some other damaging injury which, at the beginning of the second day of competition, could be disastrous.

David, still hurting, knew he had to have a good run at the hurdles if he was to stay in the numbers. He watched anxiously as Émile Binet took the first heat in 16.0—good but not insurmountable. But in the second heat Jack Parker shaved a full second off that, pushing himself up closer to Karl and Bob Clark. David had never done better than 15.5, but by the time he lined up and dug his starting holes for the third heat, he needed the best run of his life.

"Auf die Plätze . . . fertig . . ."

He came off the line slowly and painfully but gathered momentum in the seven steps before the first barrier. He had a good takeoff, maintained his arms and legs parallel to the ground, and cleared the barrier in a single burst of energy. By the time he was past the second hurdle he had caught up to Tolama of Finland, and by the third, he was even with the Swede Olle Bexell. He came over the final hurdle ahead of the entire pack. Nothing could stop him. His legs were strong. He felt both relaxed and determined, and his only regret was that Karl wasn't running in this heat beside him.

He was sure he had broken the tape a full second before the next closest runner. And when his time was posted at 15.0 seconds, dead even with Parker and the best time he had ever run, he knew he still had a shot.

Now, more than an hour of standing around, watching and waiting.

The next three heats caused him no concern at all. The best anyone could manage was Clark in the sixth, with a 15.7. David's spirits soared.

Karl was leading off the seventh. David maneuvered himself in close to the finish line, giving himself the best vantage point for the entire race.

Karl came off the starting line like a shot, blowing away everyone else in the field. He was three hurdles out in front before the others seemed to realize what was happening.

His stride was quick and powerful as he came into the fourth hurdle; but David could see that his approach was too low, and he clipped the top of the crossbar, making it sway back and forth. This seemed to throw his rhythm slightly off going into the final leaps, and although he finished strong, it wasn't the blowout it might have been if not for this one small error.

He spotted David standing near the finish line and saluted him as he ran by, the way flying aces from the World War were said to have saluted opponents they hoped to down in battle.

Karl wasn't invincible. He had made this one mistake. But the rest of his race had been so solid that when his time was posted, he had equaled David's and Parker's 15.0. David had run the best time of his life, and all he had done was stay even.

It was an even greater blow than the results of the final heat, when Glenn Morris posted a spectacular 14.9 to wrest the lead away from Bob Clark. Morris, a car salesman from Fort Collins, Colorado, was a hell of a nice guy. The same thing David had thought about Karl, he realized. But there was something else, too: *Glenn is an American. And one of us has got to win.*

Of all the track and field sports, the discus throw most clearly evokes the image of ancient Olympia. Just as the broad jump requires the athlete to transform his body into a glider, or the shot put, into a cannon, so the discus demands that his body become a giant spring, with his arms as the powerful coils.

No one in the discus throw was close to Glenn Morris, not even Karl, who seemed mechanical and detached all through the event. His eyes maintained that fixed, glazed look that they had had throughout much of the first day of competition. He didn't even do as well as his teammate Bonnet, who was still nowhere close to the lead. David began to take heart that maybe Karl wasn't the superman he had begun to suspect.

But then there was the long midday break to sit and stew about it, with the pole vault not scheduled until three. That was also the scheduled time for the four-hundred-meter-relay trials, so during lunch the entire American contingent at the stadium was operating at a fevered pitch.

If the shot put takes strength, and the hurdles need agility, if the broad jump calls for balance, and the high jump for coordination, the pole vault requires all these, plus one more essential constituent: courage. No matter what else is said, it requires an enormous amount of courage to sail into that air from a running start on a long, thin stick and then fall through that air, unguarded and relaxed, from a height sufficient to break the back. It can also be grueling, with endless replays as new levels are reached.

There is also drama, as palpable as for any track and field sport. Unlike the throws and the broad jump, where the onlookers must wait for a tape to be brought out for an official measurement, the pole vault height is identified at the outset. It is a set barrier, a known frontier which the athlete must single-handedly conquer. And if he cannot do this, there is no more dramatic failure in the realm of the sport.

The first several rounds were uneventful. Going into this eighth event, the male athletes were playing cautiously, mainly concerned with not making mistakes. By the time the bar had reached a little more than three meters, the field began closing in considerably. The best either Morris or Parker could manage was three and a half meters, tightening the standards among the American contingent. Clark and Sweden's Bexell dropped out after failing to rise above 3.70. David felt as though he were hanging on by his fingernails. And there was still plenty of competition, including Peter Bacsalmasi of Hungary and Aulis Reinikka of Finland. Germany was still represented by Erwin Huber and Karl.

Huber was the first out, ending up with a 3.80. The Hungarian and the Finn cleared 3.90. Then it was David's turn.

He picked up the steel pole and checked his grip several times. His takeoff felt good. The pole had just the right spring; his arms were properly flexed. He knew he had enough lift to get over. If he could just swing his hips high enough and at the same time keep his sore back exactly parallel to the ground while he twisted his body around. He sucked in his breath as he pushed off from the pole and let it fall backward in front of the bar. He thought he could sense the top of the bar grazing the hairs on his bruised belly. But that may have been his imagination. David was always sure he was that close to failure. He sucked in to absorb the pain as he hit the mat and realized the bar was still in place.

Karl was next. All eyes were on Germany's last contender in this event.

His run and takeoff were a study in perfect form. The ease of his carry made it seem that the shaft weighed nothing. He absorbed the shock of his pole hitting the vault box as if it were nothing and then pushed off with unbelievable power. His body seemed to be sailing several inches above the bar. David could hear a collective gasp circling the stands.

On the way down, though, David sensed something wasn't quite right. Karl was coming down on his back, but one knee was too rigidly flexed. He hit the mat feetfirst, with his shoulders impacting a split second later. This forced his left foot under his thigh, appearing to turn his ankle severely.

David winced in sympathetic pain. Karl lay on his back on the mat for several seconds. That was clearly it for him.

But then he lifted his head. David watched his eyes travel over to the box of honor, where Adolf Hitler was standing and leaning over the railing with concern for his champion. In the intensity of the afternoon David hadn't even noticed Hitler's arrival at the stadium.

Karl looked to his leader, seemed to nod slightly, planted both palms firmly on the mat, pushed himself into a sitting position, then stood up and trotted off as if nothing had happened. The crowd erupted in a wild roar.

That's impossible, thought David. *I've seen that kind of injury on the basketball court. No one just sloughs it off like that. If he could walk at all, he should be in agony.*

David looked down at Karl's feet. Around the top of his drooping sock, there was already evidence of broken blood vessels and some swelling. David looked back at Karl's face and saw no evidence of serious pain. He just didn't see how the guy could keep walking on that ankle.

Could he be on some major pain-killing drug? No, that didn't seem possible. He wouldn't have been able to maintain the kind of timing and agility he'd displayed all day if he were. Like so many other things about Karl's performance here in Berlin, this just didn't make sense.

As soon as David took off for this next vault, he knew it would be his final one of the afternoon. Everything was wrong. He'd already surpassed himself once, and now he was completely out of his league. He snagged the bar painfully coming over, and it was all he could do to evade it and the falling pole and land on the mat in one piece. Bacsalmasi and Reinikka had already gone out right before him, so his confidence had been at low point to begin with. Karl also missed on his four-meter attempt; but his form was still perfect, and there was no evidence of the severe injury that David had seen happen with his own eyes.

There was a pause in the decathlon long enough for the qualifying trials of the four-hundred-meter relay. And then there were the finals of the three-thousand-meter steeplechase, a punishing, arduous course of eight laps around the track, involving a total of twenty-eight solid hurdles and seven water jumps preceded by hedges.

Since 1924 Finland had dominated it the way Sweden had the pentathlon. And although the Finns Volmari Iso-Hollo and Kaarlo Tuominen ended up one and two, Alfred Dompert of Germany came on so powerfully at the end that even Adolf Hitler was on his feet, cheering.

From the same seat she had occupied the day before, the javelin throwers seemed to Miranda like ancient warriors hurling their spears on the field of battle, all fighting nobly for their nations. But in Miranda's eyes there were only two. This concrete arena had transformed to the towered city of Ilium, and she was Helen of Troy.

It was deep into the afternoon, and her two champions were dirty and grim from competition. Each man gripped his spear with the fierceness and determination of having one chance to be used for the kill.

Karl was proud and aloof. He strutted across the lawn like a conquering hero, defying all to come within his domination. He had told her that when his time came to compete, he would be good. And in these last two days he had been. It is supposed to be easy to love a winner. She was troubled and confused about why she was now being pulled in such a different direction.

She had never seen such fire in gentle David's eyes. She could make out the definition of his bicep as he shuttled the javelin back and forth above his head. The hair under his upraised arm was matted together with sweat. Likewise, dark, wet ringlets matted down on his knit forehead. And as he planted one foot firmly on the grass to spread his muscled legs in the feint of a throw, Miranda pressed her own legs tightly together beneath her skirt.

The results of the javelin throw weren't good for the United States. Clark fell back, and so did Morris. Jack Parker and David were a little above the middle of the field. But all three Germans did well, especially Karl, who was now leading in points. A pall of resignation had descended over the American bench as everyone realized that with one event to go, Karl Linderhoff would win the 1936 decathlon.

This was the time that all the months and years of training prepared for, not in terms of techniques or skills, because that time had already passed. This was the time when each athlete had to face the totality of his pain and exhaustion, his anxiety and the realization that he had probably lost and had to be able to face all those demons down, knowing that the most painful and exhausting event of all was still to be run. The word "character" is much overused in sports. But if there are contexts in which it still does have true meaning, the final phase of the decathlon would be prime among them.

The fifteen hundred was divided into three heats. The first was won handily by Reinikka, who consequently put even greater pressure on everyone who followed. David was scheduled for the second heat, along with Karl. With David's point standing he was an extremely long shot. But he wasn't completely out of it. Glenn Morris had a better shot; so did Bob Clark. But if David could run the race of his life and no one did any better than Reinikka, then maybe . . .

As he stepped up to the starting line and began digging his toe holes, David had a strange sensation, or rather the absence of one. Since he'd been attacked Thursday night, through all the strain and punishment since then, this was the first time that nothing hurt. He had moved into that twilight world beyond pain, beyond exhaustion.

So it all came down to this. Not quite four times around the track. And whatever happened happened.

Before they got down into their starting stances, Karl came over to him and extended his hand. David took it reluctantly. Karl was no longer a friend. He was no longer a person. He was only a force of nature against which David was pitting himself. And David would do anything he could to catch him, to deprive him of this culminating win. It was immature, juvenile to want something this badly, but he couldn't deny that he did. And if he could somehow possibly attain it, no matter what else happened, his entire life would be different.

From his four-point stance David glanced over his shoulder at Karl's ankle. It was deep red and swollen way beyond its normal size. How could he even walk on it, much less spring off for the beginning of a mile run?

"*Auf die Plätze . . . fertig . . .*"

At the gun Karl shot out of the starting position as if nothing had happened, determined to set the pace right from the beginning. No matter how hard he pushed himself, David knew he couldn't keep up with Karl for a mile. This was too long a race for positioning or other strategy to make enough of a difference. If Karl could maintain this speed for several laps, he would win easily, and there would be nothing David could do.

He was vaguely aware of the screaming crowd in the background. He could hear the faint echoes of the metallic German voice calling out on the public-address system above them. Out of the corner of his eye he perceived the sea of tiny swastikas waving in the breeze as the runners rounded the final turn of the first lap. Still, there was no reality but the run, no sense of time but the rhythm of every stride, nothing actual on the face of the earth but himself and Karl and the red clay of the track.

After two complete laps he had almost managed to stay with the German. The rest of the pack followed behind. David pushed and pushed and pushed. He could feel the impact on his toes of every step, the dirt spraying up with every kick. Yet no matter what he did, Karl loomed just out of reach, always threatening to put on that one final burst of speed that would open a gulf between them that could never be closed. *How can he be running on that ankle?*

If he could somehow just hold the distance down for one more lap, David promised himself, then somewhere in himself he'd find the strength and speed for that final four hundred meters. *Just hold on. Just hold on. Make up a little space, and then just hold on.* If he could have sold his soul right then and there for five meters, he would have done it without thinking.

David sensed himself beginning to falter. His feet were like lead. His chest was heavy. He had to struggle for every gasp of air. His stride was ragged. He felt himself weaving from lane to lane.

And just then Karl began to make his move.

Just like yesterday. He's going to win, and there's nothing I can do about it. But I won't let him take it without a fight.

David was so intent on keeping up with him that he didn't even see the German go down. He had to swerve at the very last second to avoid him. Later he would swear that he had heard an anguished groan, but that might have been an unconscious embellishment of his imagination. At any rate he was so stunned he almost stopped running. The ankle had finally gotten to him, David realized as he quickly collected himself and instinctively surged ahead.

The lead was now his. The track was open in front of him. He thought he heard the collective moan of the partisan crowd, but it was still only background. All the conflicting thoughts forced their way back into his mind. That was a tough way to go out. But a lot of tough things had happened, and a lot less fair. And it wasn't his fault. What goes around comes around. A sense of cosmic justice settled in David's mind. He was meant to win this race.

Suddenly his whole body felt better, as if a great burden had been lifted. He picked up his stride, filled his lungs with air. The rest of the field had gained some ground on him in the confusion on the track, but David easily reached the finish line and broke the tape. He noticed Glenn Morris cheering from the sidelines.

The trainers closed in around David, but he pushed them aside. He fought his way through the small mob that collected on the track to get back to the spot where Karl was still lying.

But when David got close, he saw that Karl was flat on his back. His eyes were closed, and he didn't seem to be moving. And as far as David could tell before the closed ranks of German officials eased him away, they weren't working on his ankle at all.

TWENTY-FOUR

"Where is he? What's happened to him?" Miranda cried as David came out of the locker room. "No one will tell me anything."

"I don't know," said David grimly. "They brought him inside to the first-aid station, then took him away in an ambulance almost immediately. They wouldn't let anyone near him."

"What happened?" she pleaded. "You were right next to him in the race."

Behind him. He wanted to correct her, but it seemed a small and cruel point at the moment.

There was another small point, and David wasn't sure if Miranda knew . . . or cared. He had lost. He had left the track almost immediately, looking for Karl. But he had heard it in the locker room. As soon as the results of the third heat were in, Glenn Morris was proclaimed champion. From all reports he'd run an anguished and inelegant race, on the verge of collapse, yet panicked into trying to surpass himself and beat the 4:32 the stadium announcer had proclaimed he needed to win. It turned out to be a computation error, though. So even though Morris crossed the finish line a heart-sinking one and a third seconds slower, it turned out to be good enough. Bob Clark came out second in the points standing, and Jack Parker third. It was a clean sweep for the Americans, the first in history. At least David could take some comfort and satisfaction in that. For whatever it was worth, his own final standing was close to Parker's.

Would it all have been different if he hadn't been pressed into service by the British, if he'd been left alone to train without any distraction? Maybe. If he hadn't been beaten up the night before the competition began? Probably. Different enough to change the final standing? Who could say? Whatever the reason, the reality was that he had lost. And none of us has any choice but to play the cards we're dealt.

And would he have traded in this whole hand if it meant never having been dealt the "card" that now stood trembling before him, her face crossed with lines of worry? It was crazy, but in spite of everything, he wasn't completely convinced that he would.

In any event, the years-long quest for the Holy Grail was over. Sometime later on he would have to come fully to grips with that reality.

Later on but not now.

Döberitz

Miranda was feeling guilty and ashamed. Karl had been the love of her life, but she had sat in the stadium and hoped he'd lose, particularly when it was announced that he'd gone out in front.

But then this had happened. She felt ashamed for having turned against him and guilty for having wished this misfortune on him. A part of her almost wished they wouldn't find out where he'd been taken. Then she'd never have to face him.

David had brought her back to the Olympic Village with him, in a special car that the deputy commandant had provided. His name was Wolfgang Fürstner, and he seemed a kind, sensitive man. He was very gracious and nice to her.

She felt bad that David had lost, and she loved and admired him even more for the way he was reacting to it. Now the two of them were sitting in Captain Fürstner's office. It felt strange to be inside this all-male compound, and she knew if it weren't for Fürstner, she never would have been allowed.

He replaced the telephone receiver in its cradle and reported to David. "I spoke with the Olympic Security Office. You are apparently correct that Lieutenant Linderhoff was quickly removed from the stadium's medical facility, but they have no information as to where he has been taken. No one seems clear on who took him away, except that it was all very official. Perplexing, I'll admit. But you have to remember that we Germans are a highly bureaucratic people. Someone's always exercising his authority. It's a national obsession. Don't worry, though. We'll get to the bottom of it before long."

"Is there any way you can find out more?" Miranda pleaded.

"I've made calls to several of the likely hospitals," Fürstner explained, "but no one has seen him."

"Is it possible they wouldn't tell you for some reason?" asked David.

Fürstner opened his top desk drawer and took out a small black leather folder. It looked like a billfold. "I have special authorization from the *Reichsführer-SS*. If anyone were foolish enough to impede me, he would be doing so at his peril." He put the credentials back in the same drawer and closed it.

He noticed the tears forming again on Miranda's cheeks. He turned to her sympathetically. "Don't worry, Fräulein Wolff. We'll keep searching until we know something."

Miranda nodded in gratitude.

"In the meantime, I suggest that you let me have my driver take you home for some rest."

She started to protest, but David took her hand. "I think that's a good idea," he said. "There's nothing more you can do here." He rose and pulled her to her feet. "I'll see you first thing in the morning."

"Promise?" she said imploringly, holding on to his hand as though she were afraid to let go.

"Promise."

Fürstner smiled solicitously and pressed the button on his desk that would summon his assistant.

"Come on," said David. "I'll walk you out."

David watched her get into the car and then drive off. Just as it had last night, a part of him would have done anything to keep her from leaving. Another part needed desperately to be alone, to lick his wounds and sort things out.

When she had driven off, he walked slowly up the wooded path, back toward his room.

Sunday, August 9

The morning papers reported that the German decathlon contender Lieutenant Karl Linderhoff had suffered an allergic anaphylactic reaction during the running of the fifteen-hundred-meter race which had caused him to collapse and briefly lose consciousness. He was now resting comfortably at a Wehrmacht convalescent facility, where he was expected to remain for three or four days or until doctors were satisfied that he was in no danger of suffering further relapses. The German Olympic Committee and the German Commission for Sport and Recreation deeply regretted the loss of such a prestigious gold medal that appeared so close to hand but were grateful that no permanent harm had come to the athlete whose courage and fortitude had set an example for all of German youth.

Lieutenant Linderhoff himself was appreciative and deeply touched by all the expressions of concern, but his doctors were insisting on total rest with no excitement or distractions, however well intentioned, the reason for the secrecy surrounding his location.

The Tiergarten

Miranda had her sweater in her hands and was heading for the front door when her mother came into the entrance hall.

"You're out early for a Sunday morning," Hannelore Wolff commented. The expression on her face was as implacable as always.

"Yes, I suppose so," said Miranda.

"Where are you going?"

"Just out."

"May I ask where?"

"To the institute."

"On a Sunday?"

"I have some work I want to do."

"That can't wait until tomorrow?"

"It will be quiet there today."

"Have you any idea how long you'll be out?"

"Mother . . ." she implored.

Just then Professor Wolff came into the hall. "Let her go," he said calmly to his wife.

"Thank you, Papa." Miranda sighed, as if it had been a reprieve from torture. Hannelore folded her hands across her chest.

Otto took the sweater from his daughter and helped her on with it. "Miranda, when you see Karl, please tell him that we are thinking of him."

"Thank you, Papa," she said again. She tried to smile at him and said, "I will."

Dahlem

David met her at the *U-bahn* station, and together they walked over to the institute. The past two days still hung in the air like a heavy fog.

Every once in a while it would hit him again that he had lost, that his chance was gone. It was over, and there was nothing he could do about it. The sensation would come over him with all the discordant impact of a suddenly remembered bad dream.

"No word yet," David told her, "though Wolfgang was able to confirm the Wehrmacht part. At least we know now Karl's okay."

"I'd feel much better about everything if I got to see him," Miranda said.

Personally David wasn't exactly looking forward to the reunion. He didn't know how he could possibly face Karl again. A part of him almost wished they wouldn't find out where he'd been taken. Then he'd never have to see him.

But they had to see him, whatever the emotional costs. Otherwise, nothing could be settled. Karl was the only one who could lead them to the answers.

"In the meantime," David said, "I want you to show me this secret lab you told me about."

She nodded seriously, then shuddered at the possibility that the horrid body might still be in there on the table. "I'll try to get back in," she said bravely, clutching Dr. Behrman's key ring in her pocket.

They walked up the institute's circular driveway. "Try to look official as we go by the guard," she whispered to him. "As if you're some visiting colleague. It isn't unusual for the chemistry people to be in on weekends, but it is a bit for the physicists."

"I'll do my best," David assured her. And then, as they passed by the guard's desk in the lobby, he had the inspiration to say to her in German, "I'm grateful you agreed to see me on a Sunday. It's unfortunate, but I have to be back to give a lecture in Düsseldorf by tomorrow morning."

The guard nodded courteously and presented the log for them to sign. Miranda used her own name. David made one up. They walked down the corridor, up the stairs, and into the biochemistry section. Once again David had a vision of all the accumulated brilliance contained here on any given workday, not the least of it contained within the beautiful blond head of the woman walking next to him.

Miranda was getting good at casing the corridor in both directions. He wondered if she had any inkling of his own double-dealing.

They came to Dr. Behrman's office door. "This is it," Miranda said. She knocked lightly, then put her hand on the doorknob and twisted. The door held firm. "It's locked," she said with distress.

David tried it, too. The door wouldn't open.

Suddenly Miranda's eyes lit up. She quickly glanced up and down the hallway again, then took the gold key chain from her pocket. She tried to fit the single key into the door lock. The fit wasn't even close.

Crestfallen, she looked at him. "What do we do now?"

"How did you get out the first time?" he asked.

"Through the door marked 'Custodian's Closet.'"

"Show me where it is."

She led him down the hall and around the corner. "Try the key in this door," he instructed.

She inserted it in the lock and held her breath. Gently she twisted it. They heard the cylinder turn. She exhaled in relief and slowly opened the door.

The room was completely dark, but the overpowering, sour smell of formaldehyde was still there. They slipped in and quickly closed the door behind them. "Stand here for a minute," David said, hoping their eyes would adjust and pick up some light.

There wasn't much, but within a few minutes he was picking up a slight glimmer from across the room. "It's a corridor leading back to the office," Miranda informed him. "But there's a table in the middle of the room, so you'll have to feel your way around the outer edge."

Carefully David put out his hand and felt his way along a row of marble-topped counters until he neared the light glimmer. His hands touched a series of cold, rounded glass surfaces. Something grazed his forehead. He jumped. It felt like a spider web. But then it swung back and hit him again. He realized it must be a string. He groped for it with both hands. He found it again and pulled.

A single bare bulb came on. He blinked and gasped. The glass surfaces he had been touching were bottles filled with brains and other organs. His stomach tried to turn inside out at the shock. It was like some mad scientist's storage closet of spare parts. Actually, though, once he had recovered his senses, it was kind of interesting. It reminded him of the anatomical displays in the Pitt-Rivers Museum at Oxford, dating back to a time when scientists thought they could learn everything by merely collecting it.

With the glow from the corridor, David could see the light switch in the main room. He flipped it. The laboratory came alive with shadowy illumination.

Miranda had lingered by the far wall, like a child afraid to face the monsters she knew were at the bottom of the cellar steps. "It's still here," she murmured apprehensively. "The body, I mean." She raised her hand and pointed ominously to the examining table in the middle of the room. She inched closer, in a brave effort to show David she wasn't afraid.

Her scream made David's blood freeze.

It was Karl. His gray face was forever fixed in an expression of chilly calm. His naked body had been neatly slit open from just below his chin to the top of his groin in a dissecting procedure David instantly recognized from anatomy lab as the Virchow technique. Two surgical steel spreaders kept his viscera on permanent display. And the top of his skull had been neatly sawed off. His pinkish gray brain sat limply in the gaping cranial cavity.

Miranda gnawed on her clenched fist. Her eyes were instantly bulging with cold horror. Her face had drained of color. She clutched her quavering belly, and David knew she was going to be sick.

He rushed over and grabbed her around the waist as she lost all will to stand on her own. "Not here," he pleaded. "We can't leave any . . . evidence."

She swallowed hard. He could feel her whole body going tense.

After a while she nodded. "All right now." It came out a whisper. Tentatively he relaxed his grasp. Then her belly convulsed again, and she retched emptily into her hand.

"Oh, David," she wailed, and collapsed into his arms.

Nervously he held her for several minutes, stroking her hair and shoulders, trying to calm the racking sobs. When they had quieted a little, he held up her chin with his hand and said to her firmly, "Miranda, I just want to take you away. But we—I have to look, to find out. And you have to watch out for anyone else finding us here." He took her sharply by the wrists, knowingly hurting her a little in an effort to focus her attention quickly.

He positioned her over near the door. "Are you going to be all right?"

She nodded weakly.

Fighting back his own revulsion, he began examining the remains. If Karl himself could no longer provide them with any answers, perhaps his body could.

David knew enough physiology to recognize that Karl had been dead at least since last night. The report in the paper was a deliberate lie. He wondered whether Wolfgang Fürstner knew.

Mentally trying to distance himself from the slash down the center of Karl's body, David began with the obvious exterior features. In the background he could hear Miranda softly whimpering.

The first thing that struck him was the excellent musculature. Arms, legs, chest—Karl had been a superior physical specimen.

He picked up an arm and ran his hands along its length. Just as he remembered, Karl's skin was amazingly smooth. An adult male's elbows are usually bumpy and rough. Karl's were like eggshells.

Moving up the body, David realized to his horror that the eyes were open. He was supposed to be a scientist, a rational being, but it gave him the creeps to think of this dead person watching him.

There was something haunting about the eyes. He couldn't quite place what it was. They were widely dilated. But there was something else. Something about . . . Yes, it was the way the lids receded from the pupils, leaving gaps of white. It didn't seem to be a change brought on by death. It was frozen this way from life.

He turned away from the table for a moment. "Miranda. Face me. Let me see your eyes."

"What?" She still seemed dazed.

He stared into her face, then back to Karl's. Yes, definitely. Karl's eyelids were different.

The top of the skull was lying on the table, right next to Karl's right ear. With a shudder David picked it up and examined it closely. Just as he remembered. Karl's hair was thinning markedly. He was only in his mid-twenties. Could it really have been just the stress of the Olympics?

Now came the hardest part. David shifted his attention to the gaping body cavity. It is said that the only thing that makes a soldier capable of charging an enemy in battle is not taking the time to think about it. So before he became completely paralyzed by such normal human feelings as sensitivity and disgust, he took a deep breath and plunged in.

He concentrated on the vital organs one by one. The heart, not surprisingly, appeared strong and trim. There was almost no fat around it. No evidence of pathology. Lungs, liver, stomach—all looked normal. He kept having to stop himself and remember that this "lab specimen" he was examining so coldly had been running against him just yesterday, in the heat of passion, with the whole world looking on.

And now he was rummaging through the man's guts with his weeping girl friend standing by as guard. The whole thing was monstrous. He felt guilty for what he'd thought of Karl. He was confused and resentful of everything. He wanted to run away. But he knew he couldn't. He had to stay.

As delicately as he could, he pulled the large intestine down. *Please, Miranda, don't look now.* He pushed the outer curve of the stomach out of the way to view the kidneys. That was when he became perplexed.

The adrenal glands are two yellowish brown triangles that lie close to the upper end of the kidneys, alongside the spine. At least that was where they are supposed to be. David couldn't find Karl's. Suddenly he felt like the dumb kid in biology class.

Am I missing something? he asked himself. He lifted the lower portion of the stomach farther out of the way and palpated the entire upper lobe of the kidney. Nothing. Then he went to the other side, pressed up on the liver, pulled the duodenum to the right, held the pancreas out of the way. But he couldn't find the gland on that kidney either.

The adrenal is a complex gland that controls a number of different body functions, including the metabolism of nutrients and the fight or flight response. Karl's adrenals hadn't been removed. David saw no scar tissue. He simply couldn't find them.

He stood there contemplating the body for what seemed a long time. His heart continued racing. Miranda was still moaning softly behind him. Should they leave right now and call the police? Brundage? Fürstner? How could he explain what he was doing here? What if some of them were involved? Even if they weren't, at the very least Miranda would lose her job. No, for the time being they had to go it alone.

Maybe he could get some clues from the dissection itself. Was the guy who'd performed the autopsy looking for anything specific? David wasn't a doctor. He was only a biochemistry student. There was so much he didn't know. Yet he had to rely on what he did and come up with whatever he could.

His eyes traveled up the length of the midline incision. David had never done a postmortem himself and hadn't seen that many of them, but it seemed to him that the cut had been extended higher than usual. Usually it stopped at the sternum. Any reason for the variation?

What's up in the neck region of particular interest? The first things that came to mind were the trachea, larynx, and thyroid. He wrapped his fingers around the long, vertical muscles and exposed the windpipe. Not much you can do with the trachea. A person either can breathe or can't. The larynx looked okay, and Karl hadn't had any trouble speaking.

But then he saw the thyroid gland. It was shriveled up to a fraction of its normal size. The thyroid sits on each side of the larynx and surrounds the trachea. Its pinkish surface is granular and glistens, since it's made up of a jellylike material. Karl's looked like a dried-out piece of meat.

Strange about the adrenals, but this was even stranger. The thyroid helps control pulse rate, respiration, coordination and reaction time, contractility of the heart muscle, metabolism, and protein synthesis, among many other things. These all would seem to be necessary functions to an Olympic-class athlete. And yet this one looked as if it could hardly function at all.

He tried to fit it together. All the organs looked normal, but two glands of the endocrine system were hardly noticeable, in an otherwise tremendously fit athletic specimen. At least he was fit until he suddenly and unexpectedly dropped dead, David thought sardonically.

He glanced over at Miranda. She hadn't moved from her place, and the look of utter shock and revulsion hadn't left her face.

He had one more hunch to play out. Oh, God. He took a deep breath. He clenched his teeth and slid his hands into the skull. Now he felt as though he himself would puke.

Once he had his fingers around the brain, he gave it a gentle tug.

It came out easily in his hands. Its connections to the body had already been severed.

He picked up the jiggling organ in both hands and turned it upside down. He followed the two large blue optic nerves as they curved down to meet at the optic chiasm between the temporal lobes. Between it and the pons was the brownish gray pituitary, the so-called master gland of the body. In a normal adult male it should be about a half inch across. Karl's was so small David could hardly see it. He retraced his path to make sure he hadn't mistaken it for something else.

He looked nervously toward the door where Miranda stood guard. He didn't know how long they dared hang around here. Whoever had done the autopsy would obviously be coming back.

As carefully as he could, he stuffed the brain back into the skull the way he had found it. His fingers were wet and sticky. He didn't know where Miranda had found the strength to face this, but he was flooded with love for her.

"Okay," he said. An empty relief came over her grief-stricken face. He started to take her by the hand. She recoiled before he could touch her and they both looked down at his wet, glistening fingers. "Sorry," he said, holding the hands away from his own body. "Could you turn off the lights?"

As she went to turn off the lights, the conflicting evidence was already cascading through David's mind. The endocrine system, together with the nervous system, acts as the key integrator of biochemistry and physiology within the living organism. So how could it be that these three prime endocrine glands were so atrophied (he hadn't even found the adrenals) as to be essentially nonfunctioning? Yet he'd seen Karl's performance with his own eyes. It just wasn't possible. As his professor at Oxford would have said, it simply didn't correlate.

And what had killed Karl? What had killed Rolf Schmidt, for that matter? And what had happened to Horst Müller? What was going on with the entire German team? David was gripped by a spasm of unknown terror.

It made no sense. None of it did. He recalled sitting with Karl in the locker room of the swim stadium while he told David of his abject fear of the water. And then the day before the decathlon he said he'd been swimming laps all alone in the village pool. Could he have been lying to redeem himself in David's eyes? Maybe, but

David didn't think so. No matter what he did, he just couldn't get rid of that image of Karl sitting naked on the locker-room bench and spilling his guts out.

Suddenly another image came to David. He stopped short.

"What's wrong?" Miranda asked with alarm.

He visualized Karl's naked body that day and remembered the freshly healed cut along the edge of Karl's hip. "I'm sorry," he said. "One more thing."

"What is it?" she pleaded desperately.

"Please, just bear with me another few minutes. I don't have time to explain."

He went back to the remains. "Miranda, I hate for you to do this, but . . ." He gestured with his hands that he wanted her to help him turn the corpse on its side. She recoiled in horror. "Please," he said sternly. "Don't fight me now."

Reluctantly but bravely she did as she was asked, approaching the body gingerly, then gripping Karl firmly by the shoulder as David pulled him over onto his side. Tears squeezed out of her tightly closed eyelids. Her sobbing breaths were shallow and labored. David hated himself all the more for what this was doing to her. *Why don't you just slap her across the face the way Karl did? That would be infinitely kinder than what you're putting her through.*

He went to the glass cabinet. Unwillingly he wiped his hands on his pants, then opened the door and took out a scalpel. He paused in doubt. With Miranda still holding the body, he parted the legs enough to gain access to the hip. He took whatever pains he could to shield Karl's sex from her view.

He worked feverishly. Spreading the flesh of Karl's thigh with his fingers, David sliced through the still-fresh incision line. He felt some resistance, so he angled the blade to cut around it. He put down the scalpel and splayed the tissue.

Now he could see what had caused the resistance. It was some kind of tiny mass, about the size of a small olive. It had something of the consistency of an olive, too, only a little spongier. It didn't look like a cyst or tumor of any sort. In fact, it seemed that the large muscle mass of the thigh had been cut to implant it. David had no idea what it could be. But whatever it was, it adhered to the surrounding muscle.

He glanced up at Miranda. Then he picked up the scalpel again. He held the little sphere in place between his thumb and forefinger. Then he cut into its tough, fibrous shell. He pried it open. Inside, it was vascular and made up of long, thin, tightly coiled tubules which looked to be separated by thinner walls of some sort of interstitial cells.

The recognition, when it came, was just one more jolt. He suddenly got an uncomfortable, vulnerable feeling between his legs. Unless he'd totally misinterpreted, what he was looking at was a male gonad.

But it wasn't a "normal" male gonad. This looked like—was it conceivable and what was the point?—*fetal* testicular tissue, the sex cells of an unborn child! The anatomical location was perverse. But the structure and makeup were straight out of an anatomy textbook.

He had never seen anything so hideous, a corruption of nature, one of those things that make the whole world seem alien and hostile. Appalled by what he had seen and by what he had done, David pushed the implant back into the muscle fissure in Karl's thigh and brought the incision together with his fingers. He indicated to Miranda that she could let go of her burden. She did it with a low, anguished sigh. He didn't think she'd been paying any attention to what he'd been doing. He couldn't have explained what he had seen.

One more thing occurred to him. As subtly as he could, he lifted Karl's other leg. There was an identical incision low on the other hip.

They've given Karl an extra set of balls! Though he hadn't exactly been maximizing his own set, from Ali's report.

David tried not to let Miranda see that he was trembling. It was time to get out of here. She'd been tortured enough.

He looked a final time down at the body on the table. He had loved this man and then hated him. Now he had just cut him apart. But he was still no closer to understanding him. He closed his eyes briefly, in the closest he could bring himself to a moment of silent meditation. He brought his hand down to Karl's shoulder and touched him one more time.

I don't have any idea why you are lying here. By my gracious God, Karl, I am so sorry for all that has happened.

He opened his eyes and took a symbolic step away from the table. He couldn't wait to get to the men's room and wash his hands.

Grunewald

He hadn't wanted to leave her. He hadn't wanted to let her out of his sight. But she said she needed to be alone, and after what he'd put her through, he couldn't blame her. So he'd taken her home in a taxi, after securing from her the promise that she wouldn't say anything about what they'd seen, at least not until David could find out something about it.

He couldn't get the brownshirt's warning about Miranda out of his head. For whatever reason, he was the guy Karl had put up to attacking David. Who knew if he was tied up in all this? Or who else was. Or what "they" might do to her. There was danger here, and until he could figure out where it was coming from, the safest course was to give no indication, to act as if nothing had happened.

And he had his own "business as usual" to take care of. Today was the final day of track and field. Tomorrow the focus of the games shifted to the swim stadium, the tennis grounds, Deutschland Hall, and the yachting basin up at Kiel. But today, while the marathon was being run through the streets of Berlin, the stadium would witness both the women's and men's four-hundred-meter relays. What excuse could he give if he missed Tom's attempt to run for the Olympic gold, particularly in light of his own duplicity in the selection of the runners?

So he went to the stadium, where fewer than twenty-four hours before he had sweated and run and ached and suffered disappointment and defeat.

Sitting on the bench amid the frenzy of preparation, the stretching and warm-ups and baton practice, David was all alone with his thoughts. He didn't want to think about the decathlon. He couldn't help thinking about Karl. He had to analyze it all. He had to figure it out. *The truth shall make you free. Knowledge is the only road to salvation.*

The decathlon was over. Any time now, British Intelligence would be contacting him. They were probably watching him right now. But Hargreaves was a scientist. Maybe David could get him to help with the problem. No, not a chance. He'd tried that before. Hargreaves was too obsessed with his own "problem." And once the Englishman got hold of David, he'd no longer have the "luxury" of time for this, so he had to work fast.

First, he tried to list in his mind all the symptoms and physical traits he could remember. In no particular order, he came up with smooth skin and hair loss, wide-eyed stare and jittery nerves, tremendous strength and speed and agility—all apparently acquired rather suddenly—as well as an enormous appetite to go along with them. But when he'd examined Karl's dead body, he'd found the endocrine glands that should have been working overtime shriveled up to nothing.

And then there was the implant in Karl's thigh.

Tragedy had befallen three German Olympic athletes in the last two weeks. Two of them had ended up on the dissecting table in a secret laboratory connected to Abraham Behrman's office. In Behrman's desk Miranda had come across a list of Olympic events that was obviously a prediction of German victories. David had been perplexed by the old scientist's coming along with Miranda to watch Karl practice. If he could just take it one more step.

As he was thinking of steps, Chuck Middleman hobbled past the bench David was sitting on. The guy had terrific spirit. He'd been an inspiration to everyone on the team. David still felt bad for him. To train as long and as hard as he had, then not even to get a shot at it because of some freak accident—that was rotten luck. And by the time he got that cast off, those superb leg muscles would have shriveled up from disuse.

Shriveled up from disuse! It came to him like a jolt. Anything in the body will begin to atrophy or degenerate if it isn't used. The only thing that made sense was that Karl's endocrine glands had atrophied because they weren't needed. Why? Because something introduced from outside the body was doing their jobs for them . . . better and more efficiently than they could do on their own.

David's heart was racing as he went through the mental puzzle. A kind of conditioned negative response. And when you add the extra gonads, that could even explain Karl's lack of libido and interest in either Miranda or Ali. The exogenous substances had shut down his own system.

He hadn't been able to see it clearly until today, but now there was no longer any other logical explanation: Abraham Behrman was doing something to these athletes that was making them win.

And it was making some of them die.

The long-distance runners had left the stadium through the Marathon Gate. Now the attendants were preparing the track for the relays. The German women had shattered the world record for the four hundred two days earlier in their first trial heat. From the secret list, David knew the men's team would be equally strong.

He had already tangled with Brundage, and he'd already been put off by Hargreaves. He couldn't say anything until he had proof. But Karl Linderhoff was dead, and Abraham Behrman had disappeared.

Much to the delight of the capacity crowd, the women's relay had all the makings of a rout. Going into the final exchange, the Germans had a ten-meter lead over the Americans, their closest competitors. Hearing all the mad cheering, David didn't even bother standing up from the bench. The outcome was a foregone conclusion. As soon as the band played "Deutschland über Alles," he was going to duck into the locker room and stay there until the men's event.

But suddenly he heard a thunderous moan of amazement and disgust. He looked up. Heading into the handoff, Ilse Dörffeldt had been so eager to charge ahead that she'd missed the baton pass from Marie Döllinger. It clattered to the ground.

Realizing what she had done, she staggered to a grotesque halt. Tall, thin Helen Stephens, the American anchor, ran furiously past her for the victory! The British and Canadians galloped across for second and third. The astonished crowd couldn't believe its eyes.

The four Germans rushed together in a pitiful embrace, sobbing madly in a public display of their grief. They couldn't have lost on speed or agility. Everyone in the arena would testify to that. Yet they had fallen to something no one—not even the greatest biological scientist in the world—could have predicted.

And so, after this blow, it was not quite as much of a shock as it might have been when Jesse Owens led the American men to a new Olympic and world record in front of a hundred and ten thousand standing, cheering onlookers. Italy came in second. The best the stunned Germans could manage was third, a tenth of a second behind the Italians.

David leaped from the bench he'd been standing on throughout the race and ran over to the joyous victors. He pounced on Tom, then grabbed him by the legs and hoisted him high into the air.

"I knew you could do it!" he screamed above the tumult.

"Who would have thought I'd come away with the gold medal instead of you?" Tom said, still stunned with disbelief.

"That's because you're terrific!" David said to him. For a moment he could almost forget what he had seen this morning.

David's heart swelled with pride as never before as he watched the Stars and Stripes being hoisted to the top of the flagpole and heard

"The Star-Spangled Banner" played throughout the stadium. He glanced over at Coach Crowell, who was wiping away his own tear of pride.

In another few minutes David knew he would be back brooding and agonizing about the horror still unresolved. But he savored these precious moments as long as he could.

Maybe the Americans would have won anyway with the original team, David thought. Now they would never know. And Stoller and Glickman would have something they'd have to remember for the rest of their lives. He felt terrible for that. But the Americans had won; that was the most important thing. And he felt that he had finally done something for his roommate, after all that Tom had done for him for so long.

And there was something more, something that David cherished as much as he did Tom's jubilation and glory: With his fourth gold medal of these Nazi Olympics, Jesse Owens of Ohio had assured himself a lasting place not only in the record book of sports but in the history of nations.

TWENTY-FIVE

Monday, August 10, Dahlem

"The pathologists did a nice job of preparation," Rudolf Kiesel said, visually reviewing their work.

"Yes," Josef Mengele agreed. "There is something marvelous and fascinating about the human organism with all its functions visible and immediate. This many years after my first anatomy class, I still get an incredible thrill seeing the human body laid open like this."

"You'll go far," Kiesel predicted. "You have that natural curiosity and sense of wonder which cannot be instilled artificially. And you are fortunate to be a young man coming of age and professional maturity in such exciting times for science, in a climate in which it can flourish."

He leaned over the table and shined his ophthalmoscope into Karl Linderhoff's eye. "I thought it wisest to have the body brought here rather than out to Behrman. Of all the subjects in the *Übermensch* program, Behrman was closest to Linderhoff. In a way he was like a son to him. It would only exacerbate the current situation to require him to perform the initial examination. So I thought that we would do the investigation ourselves and then report the results. It will still be difficult for him, but perhaps he can be more objective that way."

"He is a Jew," Mengele pointed out, "not a race known for objectivity. Still, one cannot deny his brilliance. I could see that as soon as I became his assistant in the early stages of the rat experiments. I remember the demonstration we put on for Heinrich Himmler. I know the *Reichsführer* came away impressed by what he saw."

"Were it not for Abraham Behrman," Kiesel said solemnly, "none of this would be possible. Could you hand me a scalpel, please?"

Mengele went to the glass cabinet, found a scalpel and handed it to him. He then picked up his clipboard from the countertop and poised to record the observations Kiesel reported.

"Just a moment," Kiesel said, perplexed.

"What is it?"

Kiesel placed his arm under Karl Linderhoff's thigh and lifted. "Look at this. The pathologists have already begun the dissection. I left orders that they were only to prepare the body and then leave it for us."

"That is what I told them," said Mengele self-consciously.

"This compromises the purity of the investigation," said Kiesel, not quite able to hide his irritation. "Everything that happens at this point is critical. We have gone too far now to tolerate any mistakes. Let's begin."

The plan was for David to spend the morning at the Olympic Village, snooping around the German team and trying to find out if anyone knew anything and might possibly let it slip. He would also go see Captain Fürstner and ask if he had heard anything yet about Karl's whereabouts. One way or the other, David said, that should tell them something.

Then he would meet Miranda for lunch in the institute cafeteria on the pretense of a social visit and tell her what he had discovered. In the meantime, she was to go to her office and try to "act normally." He didn't want her to do anything that might arouse attention.

But that was a lot easier to say than to act upon. She'd spent all Sunday afternoon and evening by herself in her room, and she was certain her parents would find a way to punish her for what they must have seen as her insolent and sullen ways. She knew she couldn't tell them anything—even if she'd wanted to—but that left her only more alone with her anguish and confusion.

And now today, no matter how hard she tried to sit at her desk and concentrate on her work, she couldn't do it. The memory of yesterday, and the day before, and the day before that kept coming back to haunt her. It wasn't only her parents who'd be on her for the way she was acting. Dr. Hahn would fire her for sure when he returned from his trip if she was still behaving this way.

But this morning, no matter how she tried to discipline herself, she just couldn't sit still or concentrate. Every time she began to focus on her notes, she wanted to burst out in tears. Maybe it would be different after lunch, after she'd seen David. For right now it was hopeless.

So she got up and slung the strap of her purse containing Dr. Behrman's keys over her shoulder. She left her office, not knowing specifically where she was going, but knowing that she had to go *somewhere* and do *something*. Before she even consciously realized it, she was headed back to the biochemistry department. It had drawn her like a magnet.

She must have walked up and down the hallway a hundred times, trying to dissipate the churning energy that coursed through her.

In the middle of each journey she passed Dr. Behrman's office, shut up tight, with nothing but dismal gray showing through the glass transom above the door. She watched the office like a spy. How she longed to open that door and find him sitting there behind his desk as before, ready to welcome her, to stop whatever he was doing and listen to any story or problem. But she knew those days were over. His office was empty, save for those packing boxes marked "K-208." And the adjoining laboratory—a secret lair she had never known about—had become the scene of such grotesque horrors that even now she couldn't bring herself to believe she had truly witnessed them.

On her hundred and first trip down the corridor, she saw the light. Literally. It was shining through the transom above Dr. Behrman's door. The door itself was slightly ajar.

Slowing her gait while still seeming a casual passerby, she saw two men in gray overalls emerge from the office, carrying two of those packing boxes. Behind them two more men in lab coats came out. One appeared to be in his mid-forties. The other was much younger and had shiny black hair. For a brief moment his eyes locked with Miranda's. A chill of revulsion shot through her, as if she'd been a naked specimen.

The older man switched off the light in the office and closed the door behind him, locking it with a key.

"This should be the last shipment," he said to the younger man. "That will give him everything he needs to continue his work."

Miranda walked slowly, trying to pick up every word.

"Be careful," the man in the lab coat said to the one in overalls. "Some of that is breakable. And he has to have it by the time the latest bodies arrive."

"Don't worry," the moving man assured him. "It's going straight down to the loading dock. The truck's already waiting."

Now where is the loading dock? Miranda wondered as she bounded down the stairs. She knew she had a head start on the moving men, who would be using the service elevator. But she would lose it if she couldn't figure out exactly where to go.

She visualized all the roads leading up to the institute. One of them curved behind the building. And yes, she had seen trucks driving out from it. That must be it.

She took the stairs all the way down to the ground level and went out the back door. That would be faster than trying to find the loading dock from inside. Once out of doors, she followed the service road for a hundred or so feet across the rear of the building.

There it was. The road ended at the loading dock. And there was one small truck backed up to it.

No one seemed to be around, so she ran up to it. She was already out of breath. She climbed the concrete steps to the dock's platform. The doors on the back of the truck were open. There were already a couple of boxes inside marked "K-208." She heard the men approaching.

There was no time to think, only to act. She'd heard them say this was the last shipment. This would be the only chance.

She climbed into the truck's crowded cargo area, tearing her stocking in the process. When she glanced down, she realized the edge of the truck's fender had cut **her** leg, just above the knee. The space wasn't high enough for her to stand up in, so she ducked her head and scrambled to the back and crouched down behind the largest of the boxes.

A moment later she felt the floorboards vibrate. She heard the sounds of men carrying heavy loads. Then there was a thud as another box was set down right next to the one she was hiding behind.

"Hey, be careful with that," one of the men said. "You heard the doctor say it was breakable."

"Yeah, yeah. Okay," came the reply.

"Well, that should do it. Close 'er up and let's get out of here. We have another run down south of the city after this, and I don't want to get stuck in traffic."

She heard the men leave. Then there was a double slam of doors, and everything went suddenly black.

Panic instantly seized her. She was suffocating. She had to get out. Her mouth was dry. She was so frightened she wanted to cry. But she dared not make a sound. By now the vehicle was moving. There was some lurching as the truck drove off, then a lot of stop and go. Then they seemed to be on open road. She was stuck now. There was nothing to do but try to deal with it and make the best of it.

Resigned to whatever her fate would be, Miranda closed her eyes and tried as best she could to relax.

In a perfect world he would have awakened this morning with Ali next to him. They would have remained together all day, and between their passionate peaks of lovemaking, she would have comforted him in defeat and tenderly assured him that in every way that really meant something, he was very much a winner and a champion.

In point of fact, she had tried to call him and had left several messages since yesterday morning. But he couldn't bring himself to face her. At least not yet.

He remembered every detail of what had happened in Los Angeles. And he remembered how it had ended when he affirmed his commitment to the military and the reality of their separate lives hung in the gulf between them. Now his commitment, his obligation were all the greater. And after what had happened here in Berlin, he didn't know if he could face any more loss.

So this was not a perfect world. And instead of spending the day in one of those upstairs bedrooms in the quaint little inn Ali had found near the Olympic Village, David was on his way to the Kaiser Wilhelm Institute to watch over Miranda and report to her on what he had found out by mingling with the German team.

Or rather, what he hadn't found out, since this had turned out to be a very imperfect world. Everyone he talked to seemed to be buying the public statement. They all were concerned for Karl, but relieved that he was doing well, and were content to follow orders to leave him alone and let him recover in peace.

There had also been a message in his box that "Your friend from Cambridge called," but he had decided to ignore that one as long as he could. Anyway, he was pursuing their quarry. He was just doing it in his own way.

He was a little late getting to the institute. He hoped Miranda wouldn't be waiting long for him. But when he got to the cafeteria where they were supposed to meet, she wasn't there. It wasn't like her to get annoyed and go back to her office, but he decided to go up and check just to make sure. Anyway, there was a more likely explanation. She had probably become engrossed with her work and missed the time. Also, she could have been called into a meeting that she couldn't get out of.

But when he reached her tiny office, she wasn't there. He waited several minutes to make sure she hadn't gone to the ladies' room. Then he became bold, found the departmental secretary, and asked if she knew where Miranda was. She said she knew Miranda had been in, but she hadn't seen her for a couple of hours.

"Could she be in a meeting?" David asked.

"No," the secretary replied, adding that Dr. Hahn himself was in Paris for two weeks. "I frankly don't know where she could be. It isn't like her to wander off like this."

That was when David genuinely started to worry.

She didn't know how far they'd driven, or for how long. The darkness was disorienting and made her lose all sense of time and distance. The constant bouncing of the truck made her need to go to the bathroom. How much longer would it be? She hoped she wouldn't have an accident. What would she do then? In the middle of God knows where, maybe having to face God knows whom, and with wet pants besides.

The cut above her knee was beginning to throb. Her back and bottom and legs were already sore from her cramped position. Though that was nothing compared with what her parents would do to her if they ever found out about this. That was, if the police didn't put her in jail first. And the institute would certainly sack her.

Altogether something of a mess. *Well, Fräuleinchen,* she chided herself, *you got yourself into this.*

The constant rhythm of the road carried her along. The black interior of the truck had become her own alternate universe. Reality had ceased to exist outside it, like Einstein's ruminations on the borders of space and time.

Suddenly she sensed something different. The rhythm had changed. The momentum slowed. The truck turned a corner, throwing her against the large box and hurting her shoulder. The pace stayed slow, and the ride became even bouncier.

Stabilizing herself with her arms between the large box and the side of the truck, Miranda tried to rise and straighten up. Her head touched the roof before she made it all the way. Feeling her way in front of her and trying not to make any noise, she squeezed between the boxes, then dropped back to her hands and knees, trying to make her way toward the doors. Soon she could feel the floorboard, rough against her bare knee where the stocking fabric had been completely torn away.

She felt an open space beyond the boxes where she could get back to her feet. She groped the rest of the way until she reached the doors. She braced herself with one hand while with the other, she felt for the handle she remembered having seen between the two doors when she scrambled in.

It didn't seem to want to move. She strained on it until it finally budged. Then she pushed open the door, just enough to peer outside.

The light hurt her eyes. They were rolling down a country-looking gravel lane. Fenced-in fields were punctuated by occasional houses.

She secured her purse strap around her neck. Holding tightly onto the handle, she stuck her head out. The truck was moving much more slowly now, giving her courage to squeeze out onto the shallow deck in back. There were two hand grips, one on each side. If she stretched, she could just reach one of them. Holding on to it and the handle, she was able to close the door behind her.

Now she was spread-eagled out on the back of a moving truck, with no idea where she was. It was only a matter of time before someone saw her. And if the truck made another sudden turn, she'd be thrown off.

At the end of the lane the truck slowed to a momentary stop. *This is it*, she told herself. She strained to reach one foot down until she felt the bumper. Letting go of the hand grip and bending down to grab the edge of the deck instead, she pushed herself off the back. She stumbled and fell as she hit the ground, landing on the side of her hip. There was a jolt of pain. She got to her feet and dusted herself off before anyone could see her. Just at that moment the truck started up again, turned the corner, and quickly picked up speed. She realized her body was damp all over. She would be very embarrassed if anyone looked closely at her. But she knew she was lucky to be getting out alive.

Still slightly dazed, Miranda turned the corner in the same direction as the truck and walked down the block. Not too long ago this had obviously been farmland, just like the institute's compound at Dahlem. And unless she'd fallen asleep, as she was pretty sure she hadn't, she still had to be some reasonable distance from Berlin.

She continued walking. She still hadn't seen anyone on the street to ask where she was, and she didn't want to knock on any doors if she didn't have to.

Three blocks farther on, a double set of train tracks crossed the road, protected by an electric barrier. She decided it made the most sense to follow them.

After another block she heard a high-pitched whine that signaled an oncoming train. As it passed, the whine dropped significantly in pitch. If the Doppler shift was still in effect, she noted with relief, at least she had left her alternate universe and returned to the commonplace one.

Even more comforting, though, was the fact that the passing train had been one from the Berlin suburban electric railway. She followed the tracks another couple of blocks until she reached the small station.

The sign said ORANIENBURG, and the transit map on the wall indicated clearly that this was the end of the line.

TWENTY-SIX

"Where in the name of God have you been?" David demanded. He was trying to keep his voice down but knew he was still shouting.

"It's not easy to explain," Miranda said, wincing from his anger. She had come back to her office to find him sitting there, and what she saw in him was something she identified instantly from her childhood. It began with a look of gratitude and flooding relief, and as soon as it registered, it turned almost immediately to outrage and disapproval. And from there, the way she was conditioned, it was likely to become physical.

"You had me worried sick," he continued. "I didn't know what had happened. Didn't you remember we were supposed to meet?"

"Yes."

"Then where were you?"

"In Oranienburg," she answered defiantly.

"Where's that?"

"At the end of the suburban railway line. I didn't know it myself until today."

"How long were you there?"

"Long enough to take off my stockings and go to the ladies' room. Was that too long?"

He looked down at her legs and noticed for the first time that they were bare. She was also bleeding above one knee.

Her hands went indignantly to her hips. "So do I owe you an explanation, the way I do for my parents? Is that it?"

"Miranda, I don't know what's going on with you or what you've been up to. But you have to know you scared the daylights out of me."

"I scared the daylights out of myself, too," she said, "if that makes

290

you feel any better. Or maybe if you hit me, that would make you feel better. It's all right. I'm used to it."

David felt instantly ashamed. "No, that's not it at all," he murmured, reaching out for her. "I just care so much and—"

She added implacably, "And you don't think I can take care of myself. At first I thought it was just my father. Then Karl. Why don't men ever think women can do anything important for themselves?"

"You know I don't think that," he replied defensively. "I think you're brilliant. I think you can do anything."

"Except cross the street by myself?"

"I didn't say that."

She folded her arms across her chest. "And I don't need your forgiveness."

"I was just worried about you. I still am."

"Worried enough not to trust me?"

David exhaled slowly. "You've given me an impossible question."

"Science is full of impossible questions. So is life."

"Right. But I don't want anything like this to happen again. We've got to have a way to signal each other."

"What do you mean?" she asked.

He thought for a moment. "I know. Remember the large oak tree on the grounds? The one you said looks like an old man?"

Miranda nodded.

"If anything like this comes up again, leave me a note in its 'mouth.' That way I'll know what you're up to."

"If you insist," Miranda sighed.

"I do," said David. "Promise me you won't forget."

"I promise."

"Okay, then. Now tell me what happened to you."

She told him the whole story. About spying outside the lab and seizing the opportunity in the back of the truck. He listened without saying anything until she finished, though the color gradually drained from his face during her narrative.

David stared off through the window at Dahlem's rolling parkland. "Oranienburg. I know I've heard that name before. I wish I could remember where."

Neither one of them said anything for a long time, until Miranda broke the silence with "I guess I'd better do some work here before they decide they don't need me anymore."

David wondered if she had any idea just how absurd the statement was. He knew it was now his moment to seize. "Don't give them the chance," he said firmly.

She wrinkled her nose. "What are you talking about?"

"Leave, Miranda. With me. Leave Berlin. Leave Germany. Let me get you out of here."

Her body grew suddenly rigid. "I couldn't do that. My life, my work are all here."

"That's what you said last week. Hasn't enough happened since then to convince you this is no place for you?"

She was breathing hard. "I don't know what you're talking about."

"Of course you do. You told me yourself that you introduced Karl to Behrman. And you saw what they did to Karl."

"We don't know how it happened." She turned away from him.

"Yes. But we do know *what* happened." He grabbed her by the arm and made her face him. "Miranda, I held Karl's brain in my hands! His pituitary gland had shrunk to the size of an uncooked pea. I couldn't even find his adrenals. I don't even want to tell you what else I did find. But it made my skin crawl. I don't know why, Miranda, but this is what science has become in Germany. And if you stay, you can't avoid it, any more than your friend Behrman could. We can't deny it any longer. Something incredibly grotesque is going on, and he's behind it."

"You can't say that!" she sobbed. "You don't know that!"

"I know that he and whoever he works with wanted to win the Olympics so badly that they were willing to alter their athletes to do it, just the way you'd alter a racehorse or a pet dog."

"He wouldn't do anything like that. I'm sure of it."

"Miranda, you really are an innocent child. Grow up and face the world. You said he had no interest in sports, yet he showed up with you the first day Karl and I practiced together at the Maifeld. And then, where was it we found Karl's body? In Behrman's secret laboratory!"

"But I told you about the locket," she pleaded. "That means they've taken him away somewhere against his will. Somewhere near Oranienburg." With the back of her fist she stabbed away at her tears and tried to regain her composure. "Okay. As you say, I introduced Karl to Dr. Behrman. I'm responsible. Dr. Behrman must be in great trouble. And we've got to find him."

"Wrong, my dear. We've got to leave. We've got to run away."

"No," she said. The single word stunned him. David stared into her face. There were no more tears. Her voice was low and quiet, but steady and resolute, with the strength and toughness of steel. "We have to stay and find him. Before we think about anything else, that is what we must do. At least that is what *I* must do. With or without anyone else's help."

Döberitz

"Oranienburg? Yes, I suppose I've heard the name. Why do you want to know?" Wolfgang Fürstner crossed his legs, put his elbow on his desk, and casually rested his chin on the heel of his hand.

"I have to know if anything important goes on around there," said David.

"It's a suburb on the far northwest side of the city. It's about one hour's drive from here."

"I know that."

"The suburban electric railway runs out there."

"I know that, too."

Fürstner lifted his head and spread out his hands, palms upward, in a broad shrug. "Then what else do you want to know?"

"Wolfgang, don't play games with me."

"If you're asking me if that might be where they're keeping Karl Linderhoff, I would say it would be very unlikely. There are neither Wehrmacht installations nor convalescent facilities anywhere in that vicinity that I know of. But don't worry. I'm still trying to find out about him for you. I've gone through channels, and I hope to have the information very shortly."

"No, that's not it," said David.

"Then what?"

"It's—it's better if I don't say. I'm not sure myself."

Fürstner leaned across the desk. "Listen, David. As your friend, let me give you a piece of advice. I don't know exactly what you're digging for in Oranienburg, but I have been around here longer than you, and I do have some experience. Whatever it is you're after there, David, leave it alone. Do you understand what I'm saying? Take my word for it. Leave it alone."

Wilmersdorf

As he was leaving Fürstner's office in frustration, he recalled where he had heard the name. It had been the night the two of them had gone out on the town. Subconsciously that was probably what had made him go to Fürstner to ask about it. It was at the cabaret. Fürstner had asked the waitress something about a comedian who used to be there, and she had said something about Oranienburg. That was all he could remember.

He got to the Kabarett Éclair about ten. They were in the middle of another of their spectacular *Freikörperkultur* numbers. Only this time, instead of a tableau portraying the Brandenburg Gate, the beautiful, mostly nude, and acrobatic young show girls were depicting "Notre Dame Football." Even from the back of the room, David knew he had never seen the Four Horsemen represented to more stunning effect.

The club was already smoky and crowded. As soon as the act was over, the tuxedoed maître d' showed David to an empty seat at a long table in the middle of the grottolike room that seemed to be set aside for unaccompanied men. He ordered a beer from the waitress in fishnet tights. He studied her closely, hoping she was the same one who'd served them last week. They all were beautiful, and they all looked and dressed alike; but he didn't think it was she.

He engaged in amiable conversation with some of the men around him. One of them, a jovial traveling salesman from Frankfurt, picked him out as an American and took special interest in him.

"What is it that gave me away?" David asked, genuinely curious.

"It isn't your accent," the man said. "The way you speak, you could pass for a Berliner easily. And a high-class one at that. No, it's more the way you carry yourself."

David placed his elbows on the table and drew nearer. "What do you mean?"

"There's something about nearly all you Americans. It's—what would you call it?—a kind of innocence you always radiate."

There was a pause. "So what brings you to Berlin?" the salesman asked.

"The Olympics."

"Athlete?"

"Spectator."

"A good-looking, healthy young man like you should play sports, not watch them. That's what our führer teaches us."

"Never had much interest." David shrugged, proving to himself that for all his innocence he could still lie.

The highlight of the next show turned out to be the Brandenburg Gate number he'd remembered so fondly from his first visit. And the performer at the front of the chariot holding the reins was none other than Lorelei Bremmer. As soon as David saw her and her bare-chested companion victory nymphs, he felt himself growing hard. When she jumped, pirouetted, and contracted her glistening buttocks the same way he remembered from last time, he felt himself growing harder still. Then he remembered the epilogue to the performance, staged in her dressing room, and he just as quickly lost it, in spite of the fact that several of the girls were performing deep splits at the edge of the stage. How could he explain to her what had really happened that night?

Well, he'd have to think of something because she was his only hope.

As soon as the show was over, he asked for the telephone on the table. He picked up the receiver and said, "Backstage, please." The salesman from Frankfurt seemed impressed. Another moment, and he said, "Miss Bremmer, if you please." He waited again, wondering if he would lose his nerve, and if not, what he was going to say.

When she finally came on the line, the only thing he could think of was "Lorelei, this is David Keegan. I was . . . Oh, you do remember. Well . . . Lorelei, could I come back there and see you for a few minutes?"

She greeted him in the short red kimono he'd last seen her in, but the reception this time was somewhat different.

"What makes you think you can just come back here like this after what you did?" She erupted as soon as she opened the door to her dressing room. "Was that your idea of a joke, leaving me alone and unconscious on the floor?"

"Can I come in?" he whispered. "This is very awkward."

She didn't answer but turned and silently led the way into the room. David couldn't keep his eyes off those incredible legs as well as the hint of black silk panties peeking out from under the edge of the kimono as she walked.

He closed the door behind him and waited until she turned around. "Look," he said, "I can't tell you a whole lot. But what happened that night wasn't my fault. You have to believe me. I hope someday I can tell you, at least as much as I know myself. And I can understand if you never want to talk to me again. I wouldn't blame you. But I need to talk to you now. I have a friend who may be in trouble, whose life may be in danger."

She sat down at her dressing table, crossed one leg tightly over the other in an extremely sexy manner, and arched her eyebrows with reserve. "What is it you wish to talk with me about?"

He studied her face carefully as he said, "Oranienburg."

She blanched noticeably. "What about it?"

"What does it mean to you?"

"What makes you think I know anything?"

"I heard the name mentioned in this club the last time I was here by one of the waitresses."

"Ask her then."

"She isn't here."

"All I know is that it's the farthest northern suburb of Berlin," Lorelei said.

"I know that. And I know that the suburban railway ends up there. Everyone is very forthcoming with that information. But what else does it signify?"

She shrugged and said casually, "I'm not sure of anything."

David came up next to her and leaned against her dressing table. "I've been trying to reconstruct the exact circumstances under which I heard it. I can't, but I remember Wolfgang Fürstner asking about someone called Willi Zweig. He was supposed to be a comedian, I think."

There was a moment of utter silence. Then Lorelei said somberly, "Not 'supposed to be.' He was."

David held his breath.

"A brilliant man. The best. You've never seen anything like him. An absurd-looking little man with a nose and ears too big for his head. The tuxedo he wore every night made him look more absurd still. But in a minute he could have you roaring with laughter. And then, suddenly, you'd say to yourself, *What am I laughing at? This is the absolute truth, and it's no laughing matter.* I've never seen anyone who could look at life with such a clear, unclouded eye—every day of his life. Most of us, if we tried that for even one day, wouldn't be able to get out of bed in the morning."

"And what does Willi Zweig have to do with Oranienburg?"

She cast her eyes downward. "That's where he is. At least where he was. It's impossible to know any longer."

"He moved there."

"He was moved there." She turned her head away from him and wiped away a tear.

Throughout the conversation he had sensed the gradual stripping away of all the normal layers of comfort, complacency, and assumption. Now the truth was about to be laid bare, and he knew he could no longer hide from it. He put his hand on her shoulder. "Maybe you could tell me what you know."

She nodded. "I don't know why you need this information, and I don't want to know. And when you walk out of here, I want you to forget that we ever had this chat. You must promise me that."

David shook his head silently in agreement.

She began slowly. "No one on the outside knows much about it, but beyond the pleasant little village of Oranienburg is a detention center. That much is beyond dispute. They call it by the rather rustic, innocent name of concentration camp. But make no mistake, it isn't a meeting place for scout groups or junior guides or the back-to-nature people. It's surrounded by barbed wire. They bring dissidents there, and people someone has decided are enemies of the state.

"We don't know what happens to people brought there, but very few of them who go in ever come out again. One night the Gestapo took Willi Zweig away. Some of us heard he was in Oranienburg. But no one ever saw him again."

Tuesday, August 11, The Tiergarten

"When you took *three* glasses of orange juice at breakfast this morning, I assumed it was urgent," Arthur Hargreaves said as they walked past the lion pits. "That was why I risked phoning you up and having you meet me here."

"I think it is urgent," David affirmed. He'd never been able to figure out how the word got back to Hargreaves so quickly. The thought of being constantly watched still gave him the creeps.

"I think you'll find this zoo unlike any other you've been in," the Englishman commented cheerfully as they walked. "They've done a real first-rate pioneering job in creating outdoor enclosures for the animals that simulate their natural environments."

"That's very interesting," David said. "I'm glad to have the opportunity to see it, but—"

"It might not have had to come to this had you responded to any of my earlier entreaties."

"I called you when I was ready," David answered testily. "I thought that was the deal."

"Yes, yes, very well." Hargreaves sighed. "I don't mean to begin an argument. Tell me what's going on."

David stopped and turned to him. "I need you to help me pull off a rescue."

"Keep walking, please," Hargreaves said under his breath. "You're calling attention to yourself." David was amazed he could be so calm. But when David had complied, he said with some alarm, "Has anything happened to the girl?"

"No, that's not it. It's a professor she knows at the institute."

"You'd better explain."

David did so. The tigers had just been fed and were on a hill within their enclosure, huddling around a raw, bloody carcass of something or other. A fascinated crowd had gathered around the outside rail.

"Out of the question," Hargreaves stated when David had finished. "It would jeopardize all our work. You've done a good job for us so far. You've got her trust. The main thing now is to get her out as soon as possible. I'm sure this Behrman is an interesting chap, but we can't let this other problem interfere."

"That is the irony of the situation," David said. "But for this other problem, as you call it, she wouldn't trust me enough to go along with anything I proposed. The point is, something extremely spooky is going on that's actually changed the course of the Olympic Games. And Abraham Behrman is right at the center of it. He's the key."

"As I said, interesting. But not our problem. Our problem—yours and mine—is to get the girl out. In a nutshell. Plain and simple. End of brief."

"Okay, then," David countered. "Here's the reality in a nutshell, plain and simple: If we don't find the professor, Miranda refuses to go anywhere. Everything you're going through with me, I've already gone through with her—without letting on I was working for you or had any agenda or motives even a shade darker than the driven snow. If we want to get her out, we've got to get Behrman out first. That is the quid pro quo."

Hargreaves sighed again and put his hand on David's shoulder. "Let's take a look at the monkeys, shall we?" David complied. Two formidable gorillas were huddled against the back wall of the enclosure, staring off into space. "Well, if you're so convinced that Behrman is the key," the Englishman continued, "we might be able to arrange to have him removed from the scene. It wouldn't be easy, something of a risk. But in a stretch, if it were truly important to the project, we might be able to manage it."

"Do you mean what I think you do?"

"It is a possibility."

David wiped the air clean with his hand. "No. Unacceptable."

Hargreaves stared into the great apes' enclosure. "Monkeys always look so depressed when they're caged up, don't you think? Even in such an enlightened zoo as this one. More so than the great cats, which, I should think, would be more used to roaming and therefore feel its loss more acutely. But for some reason they always seem to manage to adapt rather better than the monkeys. Do you suppose it's because the monkeys are the smarter animals and actually know the score: that they'll be here forever?"

"No one who understands what's happening wants to lose his freedom," David responded. "He'd rather die first."

"I take your point," said Hargreaves, with a finger hoisted in the air for emphasis. "But Miss Wolff couldn't very well worry about his safety any longer if it became clear that he had, as Hamlet would have said, shuffled off this mortal coil."

"No," David repeated. "Absolutely not."

"In view of your terms, it may be the only way."

"So you've become just like them," David said.

"Alas, it is sometimes necessary in protecting what you believe in to deal on the same level as your enemy."

David shook his head. "I don't buy it."

Hargreaves gave him a patronizing smile. "You Americans are so touchingly idealistic."

David stopped again. "Fine. You're so smart, and you know all about me. You picked me out from all your other laboratory rats to run through your maze. You can predict exactly how I'm going to react to everything. Well, maybe you don't know as much about me as you think."

This time Hargreaves stopped, and he turned to face David. "You, is it? You Americans are also a rather self-important lot. All the time it's you. What about me? You've never expressed any interest or concern about why I'm here and putting myself through this. Admittedly we chose you, rather than the other way round, and we did put you through rather a bad time of it for a while. But there was a reason for it. Do you know, Keegan, in all the times we've talked, you've never once asked me a single thing about myself. Am I married? Have I any children? At my age and station, do king and country still stir a warm porridge in my heart?"

David found himself surprisingly moved as he listened and looked into Hargreaves's deep gray eyes. "All right," he said. "Are you married?"

"I am."

"Happily?"

"Quite."

"Children?"

"Two daughters, fifteen and twelve, in whom I take great delight."

"And the porridge?"

"Steeping hot. Which is why I was willing to leave the nurturing bosom of Cambridge and put up with this bloody assignment."

David was quiet for a few moments. Then he said, "I'm sorry."

"Apology accepted."

"Forget idealism. Now that we're talking on a human level, let's go all the way. This girl may be a genius, but she's also a twenty-year-old kid working over all our heads in some strange uncharted place that exists only in her own intuition."

"You don't have to tell me that."

"She's already been alienated from her family. Her only real father figure has mysteriously vanished. She's seen her boyfriend collapse in front of a hundred and ten thousand people and then found him lying on a table with his belly sliced open and the top of his head sawed off. One more shock like that will put her right over the edge. Even if she did agree to go work with you after that, she'd be useless, a basket case."

Hargreaves clasped his hands behind his back. "I take your point again. I don't like it. But I accept it. Which leads, I'm afraid, to the next dilemma."

"And what is that?" David asked.

"There is very little we can do to help you."

"You can't?"

"Sadly, no." He pulled David away so that they were far from any casual eavesdroppers and continued walking. "You know we have very little in the way of what they're calling in Spain a fifth column. That's one of the reasons we needed you for this mission. In other words, what you and Miss Wolff require cannot be achieved by force because we simply don't have it. And it can't be done by sneaking into this Oranienburg place because that works only in the movies. The people we're up against are too good for that."

"So it can't be done," David concluded grimly.

Hargreaves put the same finger up in the air. "I didn't say that."

"How then?"

"By magic."

"Magic? What do you mean?"

"Let me put it to you this way. Every good magician knows that by the time the audience starts following the trick, it's already over."

TWENTY-SEVEN

Wednesday, August 12, Döberitz

In trying to determine what their options were, Hargreaves had asked David if he'd been able to develop a close relationship with any Germans besides Miranda. When David told him about Wolfgang Fürstner, his eyes brightened immediately. When David further told him about Fürstner's special authorization from Himmler, he stood up and announced, "I think we may be in business."

According to the plan they had worked out, David immediately requested a meeting with the deputy commandant, which Fürstner granted for this afternoon. Its ostensible purpose was to press him on the subject of Karl. And it was one more thing David felt bad about. Three days after Karl's death David was still using him for his own purposes.

"I wish I could tell you more," Fürstner related. The two men were alone in his office with the door closed. "Believe me, it's as frustrating to me as it is to you. I can only imagine what Fräulein Wolff must be going through."

"Well, what's the problem, Wolfgang?" David demanded.

Fürstner shrugged helplessly. "It seems that whichever doctors are attending him have enough influence with the Wehrmacht brass to enforce the no-information rule."

"But what about your special authorization?" David asked, testing the waters.

"That kind of authorization is good for getting through barriers and ensuring immediate and unquestioned cooperation. But it can't work magic. Now, presumably, I could go to the office of the *Reichsführer* himself. But then I would have to explain why I required the information. And I couldn't very well say it was for an American

Olympic athlete and Lieutenant Linderhoff's girl friend. I must be rather delicate and circumspect about it. So you see the dilemma."

"Yes, I'm afraid so," David muttered.

"Still, I will grant you that this has become an extremely odd and perplexing affair. And I promise you I won't give up on it until I have an answer."

There was a knock on the door. It opened, and Fürstner's staff assistant appeared.

"Yes, Corporal?"

"Sir, excuse me, sir, but your attention is required in the reception hall for a few minutes."

Fürstner rose. "Excuse me, David. I'll be right back. I'm sorry for the interruption." He followed the corporal out of the office and closed the door behind him.

"Take your time," David called after him.

Now he was alone. Hargreaves's mysterious contact at the village had created the necessary diversion, right on schedule.

Immediately David got up and went behind Fürstner's desk. He opened the top drawer, found the small black leather folder, and placed it snugly in the inside breast pocket of his jacket. The logic he and Hargreaves had worked out was that it was unlikely Fürstner would have call to need it in the next day or so, so it was just as unlikely he'd even realize it was gone.

David closed up the desk and resumed his seat on the other side so that by the time Fürstner returned to his office, there was nothing for the two of them to do but exchange brief pleasantries.

From the calendar on the captain's desk David had noted that Fürstner would be at a reception in Berlin this evening until nine. The only physical obstacle was getting past Fürstner's apartment door. For that purpose Hargreaves had provided him with a rather sophisticated lockpicking kit and lessons on how to use it.

It was just starting to get dark. David was dressed in his team warm-up suit, probably the most standard item of attire at the village. He carried his red, white, and blue athletic bag with him. He would call no special attention to himself.

He walked down the path to Fürstner's quarters in the staff compound. When he reached the front door, he looked around to make certain no one was watching. He knocked on the door, and when there was no answer, he produced his lockpicking kit from the bag.

Since this was only a residence, it had not been fitted with a high-security lock. David opened the door within minutes.

Fürstner's apartment had only two rooms, a small living room connected by a tiny hallway to an equally small bedroom. Despite the fact that there was somewhat more furniture and a private bath, the living quarters were furnished in a manner just as Spartan as David's and Tom's own accommodations.

He quickly went into the bedroom and over to the single closet. When he first met the deputy commandant, David had noted that they both were nearly identical sizes.

David looked through the closet. In addition to the other standard articles of clothing, four uniforms—sets of tunics and trousers—hung against one side. David selected the one closest to the wall, folded it as neatly as he could, then stuffed it into his bag. He then arranged the hangers of the other three so as to call as little attention to the missing uniform as possible. By the time a normal person would notice anything amiss, the uniform would be laundered and back in the closet.

Tightly gripping the gym bag, David closed the closet door and left the apartment as easily as he had entered.

Wearing casual clothes and still carrying his bag, David walked past the guardhouse at the main gate, apparently in the direction of the bus stop. The guard on duty nodded as he went by. David purposely stayed in shadow so his face would not be visible. With the track and field events all complete, it wasn't unusual for the athletes to be wandering off any time of day or night, eagerly seeking the diversions that had been denied to them during so many hard and lonely months of training.

His actual destination was only a short walk away.

The inn Ali had found fitted the bill perfectly. There were quiet rooms available upstairs, and as she had reported, no one asked questions.

Miranda was already there when David arrived. She had checked into her room under a false name, according to his instructions. She had told her parents she would be overnight in Frankfurt at a conference Otto Hahn was hosting. Since he was actually in Paris, no one would be the wiser. And she planned to call in sick to the institute tomorrow morning. David didn't like the idea of involving her at all, and Hargreaves was dead set against it. But she had been adamant. Not being able to step in at this delicate stage, the Englishman had no choice but to accept it.

Considering the internal logic of the mission, she did have a point. Behrman wouldn't know David as anyone other than the opponent Karl had run against that morning, and there was no way to predict whether he could quickly convince the doctor to trust him. So despite the risk, Miranda would serve a purpose there. All she knew about the background of the mission was that a mysterious German "friend" was helping David with some of the details.

So far it all had gone amazingly smoothly, so much so that it still seemed like a game. Not until he actually found himself standing in Miranda's room did the immensity of what they were about to do hit him.

She was sitting on the bed with her blond hair hanging loose, one leg tucked under her and the other dangling over the side. She had just shed a white cardigan sweater, which lay next to her on the bed. Her white blouse, short plaid skirt, and knee socks made her look even more like an enchanting schoolgirl.

Tomorrow morning we are going to raid a Nazi detention center, she and I, he reflected as he gazed at her. And he thought his heart would burst with love and fear.

"You're sure you want to go through with this?"

She nodded. "Sure."

"Okay, then. Try to get some rest." He couldn't bear to leave her, even to go into the room next door. He drew her close and touched his lips to her forehead. She closed her eyes demurely. Then he let go of her shoulder and started to turn toward the door.

"Don't go," she softly pleaded, and, with the one hand she still held, gently pulled him back to her.

With what they were about to face, perhaps the sense of apocalypse was just as strong in her as in him. Perhaps she, too, was afraid of being alone. But at such times of danger, all is possible. And then he noticed the nipples of her perfect breasts penetrating and erect beneath the crisp white cotton of her blouse. A single glance up at her glistening and slightly parted lips and then into her dewy night blue eyes was sufficient to confirm the possibilities to him.

She was so unbelievably beautiful.

She wrapped her arms around his neck, then brought one hand

down to undo the buttons of his shirt. He found the clasp at the back of her skirt. He undid it, and it slid off her slender hips to the floor. Standing there in her blouse and knee socks and panties, she was at once poignant and slightly awkward, vulnerable and incredibly seductive. He hooked his fingers inside the white cotton underpants and gently brought them down her shimmering legs. They were already moist with her passion.

She was like a pent-up tigress, finally unleashed. Within moments they were on the bed, voraciously exploring each cherished detail of their bodies. Their clothing lay strewn around them in crumpled heaps. He felt himself tremble with the awareness of her exquisite and visceral sensuality. He took in the scent of her hair, her skin, everything about her and knew they would stay with him always. She purred with contentment as he licked the downy flesh of her thighs and tenderly kissed the soft tendrils of her yellow fleece. She had on nothing but her knee socks, but he stretched his free hand down to peel them from her calves and off her pointing toes. He would not be making love to a schoolgirl.

The thought quickly erased itself from his mind as she took him to her like some predatory cat. All the while her darting tongue played against his teeth and the insides of his mouth. His body pressed against hers as he wrapped his hands around her to clutch the soft rounds of her sensual bottom. He plunged into her, as if he could find refuge there, as if he could somehow lose himself within her mysterious depths. He had experienced nothing like her before. She gave him her body, her soul, her entire being, and by giving them, she possessed him completely. He could feel himself being charged with her pure sexual energy, released for the first time, as a supernova explodes into the far-reaching universe.

Afterward they were quiet and still. She rested her head against his chest as he stared up into nothingness. Everything had been so uncertain for him since he'd come to Berlin. But now, as he felt his heartbeat evenly resonate against her cheekbone, he was finally certain of two things: Everything was different now, and there could be no going back. And if he died performing this mission tomorrow, he would go to his death fulfilled.

She cuddled in close to him and stayed that way throughout the night. British intelligence would not be getting its money's worth out of the second room.

*   *   *

Wolfgang Fürstner returned from the French Embassy about half past nine. It was the third reception he had been to in as many nights, and the experience was beginning to pall. On top of that he had had too much wine to drink, and that always gave him a headache, a lot faster, for some reason, than the hard stuff. One couldn't refuse a glass of wine from the French, though. It might cause an international incident.

Fürstner loosened his tie on the way to the bedroom. It would be another early day tomorrow, another of the endless rounds of activity until the Olympics were completed. In a way he'd be relieved when the closing ceremonies were finally over with and the torch was doused.

He sat down wearily on the bed and pulled off his shoes. Then he stood up again and shed his green Wehrmacht tunic. He crossed to the closet, opened the door, and found the empty hanger on which the uniform belonged. He hung up the jacket, then stripped off his trousers and folded them neatly over the hanger in an intricate procedure that was second nature to every German officer.

He was about to close the closet door when he thought he noticed something. Four uniforms were hanging there, including the one he had just taken off. One was definitely missing.

Wolfgang Fürstner went back to the living room and picked up the telephone receiver.

TWENTY-EIGHT

Thursday, August 13

For one fleeting moment it was like waking into some mythic fantasy, a heroic adventure in a foreign land, a quaint country inn, his naked, golden-tressed Rhine maiden slumbering peacefully beside him.

Then his head cleared, and the familiar tight feeling gripped his stomach. It wasn't unlike the feeling he got before major track meets. But it didn't take long to remember that the stimulus was significantly different this time. There was a lot more to lose than a medal.

He turned to gaze at Miranda. Her hair was strewn about the pillow. A few errant strands were in her mouth. In her repose she was clutching tightly to the blankets. She still had about her the sensual glow of lovemaking, a radiant, life-affirming aura on the day they would together confront mortality.

A lot more to lose.

He didn't have the heart to disturb her. He leaned toward her, almost hovering over her. He sniffed her hair, her skin, inhaled the scent of her sleep. One more impression to keep in his memory.

She awakened within a few minutes. She opened her eyes slowly and smiled at him, a deeply dimpled, slightly crooked smile that retained the last vestiges of sleep. Then she swung her feet over the side and resolutely stood up.

Without any sign of self-consciousness she went to her purse and retrieved a fresh pair of panties, then gracefully stepped into them. She padded over to the bathroom. From the bed David admired the subtle girlish bounce of her hips and the leonine quality of her walk. Their clothes were still scattered about the floor.

By the time she emerged from the bathroom he was already

dressed. She dressed quickly. There was an unspoken urgency between them to get on with things.

They checked out and left the inn separately. They met behind the building in the parking lot. It had been cleared from an area of woods, providing natural seclusion.

The vehicle Hargreaves's people had provided was a long-wheel-base Opel delivery van. It was painted—quickly, David suspected—military green. There were no windows in the cargo area and none in the back doors. Hargreaves had already given David the keys.

He opened the back door. There was a military-style metal casket inside. Miranda shuddered when she saw it. Inside it they found the rest of his equipment: a shirt and tie, a cap, socks, and boots. A perfectly authentic ensemble unless they happened to strip-search him and discover he wasn't wearing regulation underwear. He comforted himself with the thought that if it reached that stage, he'd be a dead man anyway, so what was the difference?

He did a quick inventory. It all was here. Underneath the clothing, David found one additional item of precaution, a Schmeisser machine pistol.

A mirror had been provided to help David dress properly. An improper appearance for a Wehrmacht officer would give him away in a minute.

"I won't be recognized?" he remembered saying to Hargreaves during the planning. "After all, I performed for two days in front of more than a hundred thousand people."

"I hate to be the one to open wounds"—Hargreaves had sighed—"but *winners* are recognized. Jesse Owens—definitely. Glenn Morris—perhaps. I shouldn't worry in your case." It was good to know his loss was fitting into some sort of cosmic plan.

With Miranda helping him, he changed into his new identity. And when she held up the mirror for him so that he could adjust his cap and fix his tie, he was chilled by what he beheld.

He hesitated for a moment, then said to her, "I hate to do this to you, but—"

"Don't worry," she said. "It has to be done."

With a pained expression he held open the lid of the casket and helped her climb into it. "And don't you dare ask me if I'm comfortable," she warned as she settled in.

"You're going to be all right?"

"Yes. Let's get going."

Working against every instinct he possessed, he closed the casket lid and snapped the closures. He slammed the van's back door, laid his Wehrmacht cap on the dashboard, and assumed his position in the driver's seat.

Every good magician knows that by the time the audience starts following the trick, it's already over. Arthur Hargreaves's words rang continuously in David's mind.

Using German ordnance maps, David and Hargreaves had plotted out the most efficient route. Studying the Oranienburg area, they realized it had to be on a large site shown on the maps as a brewery.

A mile or two from the inn the route took them past the back of a small shoe factory. David stopped the van, got out, and placed the gym bag containing his street clothes in its large trash receptacle. Hargreaves had assured him someone would come to remove the bag before normal trash collection so that it didn't later turn up as evidence of their operation. That maneuver completed, he got back in the van and resumed the journey.

Whenever he had to stop for a light or traffic along the way, David looked around self-consciously. Could this stunt possibly work? Today was the thirteenth of the month. He hoped that wasn't a bad omen.

He wasn't crazy about the symbolism of the body in the coffin either. The whole idea was so gruesome and repulsive that he had spent a long time trying to come up with an alternative. And the escape, if it worked according to plan, would be even worse. But while Miranda had been hanging about Behrman's office, she had heard one of the men in a white coat talking about moving the equipment "by the time the latest bodies arrive." So this was the most logical plan.

Oranienburg

A laboratory had been set up in what had been one of the brewery's tasting rooms. The room had been constructed without windows, so that nothing from outside could influence the quality of the sample or the judgment of the sampler. For related reasons, it was deemed a perfect location for the lab.

Abraham Behrman sat on a high stool at the instrument counter, purposely doing nothing. Rudolf Kiesel noticed this as soon as he entered the room.

"They'll be delivering Müller's and Linderhoff's bodies soon," Kiesel reported. "I think it would be wise to conduct a simultaneous examination to compare effects."

"Then you do it," Behrman replied sullenly, not moving.

"But you are the one—the only one—who knows enough, who has it all in his head."

"And that is where it will remain," Behrman stated with finality.

Kiesel's voice quickly took on an icy edge. "Not withstanding my unending admiration for you, Herr Doktor, I cannot fathom your attitude to this work, which, after all, you originated."

At this Behrman stood up and placed his hands squarely on the counter. He leaned in toward Kiesel, a gesture which could have been construed as menacing had Behrman himself not been the prisoner. "The world may be fooled by all this Olympic revelry and German hospitality. But we know what is actually happening and where it is all leading. You know as well as I what is being done to all the so-called undesirables, to my people especially."

"Your people?" said Kiesel. "The Jews? The parasites of society? They are not your people. They are vermin, to be dealt with in the same way you would rid a house of pests. The princes of science, the elite of the universe—those are your people!"

"You've been taken in by the National Socialist lie, just as I was. Only I've had the honesty to see it for what it truly is."

"We're beyond politics, you and I. National socialism or Weimar democracy—what does it matter? It is only a transitory cycle. Science is the only eternal truth, the only thing that matters." Kiesel walked around the counter to be nearer Behrman. "I find your attitude strange and perplexing in a great scientist. We both are fortunate to be living in an extraordinary age for science. All the force fields of nature and history have converged here and now, for our benefit. Our ability to experiment on human beings, for instance, is one of the greatest gifts of all. It means that our research will progress ten times faster, possibly fifty times faster than in ordinary and less daring times. You are free to let your imagination soar, completely unfettered. You are free to do things scientists of other generations would not have dared dream of."

"And is this freedom the reason I am kept here against my will in this German corner of hell? Is it the reason they've threatened the safety of my wife and daughter if I do not cooperate? That is the real danger of national socialism to a man of science, my friend. It is not only a perversion of the soul but also a perversion of the mind."

"Extraordinary goals require extraordinary measures," stated Kiesel. "You, this project, our work are worthy of both." Then he left the room.

Abraham Behrman heard the door lock behind him.

The detention center was surrounded by barbed wire. Other than that, there was no indication the facility was being used for any purpose more sinister than the brewing of beer. David pulled up to the guardhouse at the main gate. There on the wall, in small formal capitals, was the only identification: KONZENTRATIONSLAGER DER STANDARTE 208. "Concentration Camp of District 208."

K-208. Now he was sure. Two hundred and eight. *How many of these facilities must already be in place?* David wondered.

As an SS corporal came out of the guardhouse, David leaned out the window of the van. In his best German, carefully practiced for accent and tone he said, "Captain Wolfgang Fürstner. I must see Dr. Abraham Behrman without delay."

With little deference or sign of respect the corporal asked, "May I see some authorization?" The SS had become a law unto itself within Germany.

David handed across the black leather folder. The corporal opened it and read:

DER REICHSFÜHRER-SS
Berlin

Issued to: Captain Wolfgang Fürstner, Wehrmacht

Effective: 6 August 1936–16 August 1936

The above-mentioned officer is acting under special orders of this office on business of critical importance to the Reich. He is to be assisted by all parties, military and civilian, without regard to rank or circumstance. Further, any measure he may deem necessary to institute or any order he may issue is to be carried out immediately and without question.

/s/ Heinrich Himmler

David watched as the unyielding expression on the corporal's face turned to one approaching awe. "The vehicle and its markings we can duplicate," Hargreaves had said. "The special authorization we can't. We've never seen one. We don't even know what it looks like. But that's the key, and you'll have to steal it."

The corporal handed the document back to him, straightened up, and gave David a sharp salute. "Building E, sir," he announced. "First left and then second right."

"Thank you, Corporal," David replied magnanimously. "By the way, I will need two strong men to carry the contents of this van into Dr. Behrman's quarters. After that we are to be left alone. Understood?"

"Completely, sir. I'll dispatch the men immediately."

"Good man," said David.

Inside the grounds Camp 208 resembled a smaller version of the Olympic Village. Neat rows of small buildings, some of red brick, some of wood. Storage facilities. Parade grounds. As the van reached Building E, an SS sergeant was already directing two prisoners in soiled gray uniforms up to the entrance. Fear had robbed them of any outward sign of emotion.

"The back of the van, Sergeant," David instructed.

He saluted. "Yes, sir," and motioned the two prisoners. Straining and stumbling, the two wretched men carried the metal casket behind the sergeant. David followed imperiously behind. Altogether it was like a strange funeral procession.

The sergeant led the group down the hall, then unlocked a door at the end. "In here!" he ordered the struggling prisoners.

The room was a large, well-outfitted laboratory. And sitting at a counter against one wall, looking considerably older and more haggard than the last time David had seen him, was Abraham Behrman.

"Right there on the floor will be satisfactory," David said sternly.

"Shall I have them open it for you, Captain?" the sergeant asked.

"This matter is strictly confidential," David snapped. He pointed to Behrman, who indicated a faint glimmer of recognition but then realized he must have been mistaken. "I am authorized by the *Reichsführer* to deal only with this man. Thank you for your cooperation. I will make sure it is noted. That will be all."

"Yes, sir," returned the sergeant. He saluted David, then turned to the inmates. "Get out of here, swine."

"Oh, and, Sergeant," David added, "leave this door unlocked. I do not wish to feel like a prisoner while I am here. I will lock it from the inside during my meeting."

"Of course, sir," the sergeant said as he left. David walked over to the door and locked it.

Behrman eyed his visitor with hostility and noted David's uniform with disdain. "Does the SS have the Wehrmacht doing its dirty work for them these days?"

"We would appreciate your quick attention to this matter," said David.

"Another specimen? I'm not interested."

"You no longer have a choice, Herr Doktor."

"We always have a choice," said Behrman.

"I think you'll have a particular interest in this one," David replied.

"Karl Linderhoff? Yes. Rudolf Kiesel told me. I don't know who you are. You owe me no personal consideration. But at least have the decency not to turn my stomach."

Paying him no heed, David leaned over and unsnapped the closures on the casket. "Doctor, I insist that you look." He pulled the lid off and wrestled it to the floor. A bit shakily and somewhat worse for wear, Miranda sat up in the coffin.

"Miranda!" Behrman's eyes looked as if they would pop out of his head. He looked from her to David and back again. "But I don't—" An anguished look came over his face. "My dear, what have they done to you?"

"It's not what you think," Miranda said hastily. "This is David Keegan. He's the man Karl ran against."

"The biochemist?" said Behrman, blinking back his disbelief.

"That's right," she said. David helped her out of the casket.

Behrman instantly embraced her. "Why were you in that box?"

"Dr. Behrman," said David, "we're here to take you away. We're going to get you out in this same casket. Miranda, too, I'm afraid, so it'll be tight. But as soon as we're clear . . ."

"Hurry!" said Miranda. "Let's get out of here."

"We can't yet," David cautioned. "It would look too suspicious. And then they'd come in to look for Dr. Behrman. We have to give him time to 'examine the specimen' before we take it out again."

"I still don't understand," said Behrman. He was holding her by the shoulders, refusing to let her out of his grasp.

"I became worried when I couldn't find you," she said. "We knew you were being held against your will."

"But how?"

She held up the gold locket.

He put his hands around her waist and clutched her to him again. Tears came to his eyes. "Oh, Miranda, I am so very sorry for everything. I am so very sorry for Karl, for what happened to him. For what I've done. All of it."

"Then you did go along with them," David solemnly stated.

Behrman dropped his hands from Miranda's waist. He turned to David with a look of regret tinged with disdain for the natural naiveté of an outsider. "Yes, I went along with them," he declared. "Yes, I let them support my work. Yes, I became one of them. And by the time I realized what they were actually after and what they were willing to do to achieve it, it was too late. Soon, I fear, an entire nation will be echoing those words."

"And you are responsible for the Olympic victories?"

"Yes. I and the people who have carried on for me. I am the father of *Übermensch*."

"*Übermensch*," echoed Miranda.

"That was the superman Nietzsche wrote about."

"And Hitler seized upon. Out of the mind of a maniac into the laboratory of the scientist."

"What did you do?"

Behrman smiled ruefully. "It isn't easy to explain, even to a biochemist. Though I suppose if it were, they would have gotten rid of me long before now and done it themselves. Are you familiar with the field of steroids?"

"I've read a little. Certain of the benzene ring compounds, including the sex hormones, adrenal secretions . . ."

"It's still in its infancy. But one of the things that's been learned is that the introduction of certain anabolic steroids into an individual's system will increase strength and muscle mass. Someday they'll probably be used by all athletes in competition.

"The significance of steroids was a tremendous medical discovery in itself. But it was only the beginning. We got to thinking. What if we went not to the product but to the source? What if we could somehow utilize all the potential power of the thyroid, the adrenals, the sex glands, the liver, the heart, and on and on? Then it might truly be possible to create an *Übermensch*."

"This is what you set out to do?"

"No," Behrman emphatically replied. "In science we seldom end up with what we set out to do. My original work was based on the growth hormone secreted by the pituitary gland. My theory was that if it could be isolated and synthesized, then dwarfs, midgets, so many of nature's innocent unfortunates might have a second chance, a chance at a normal life. But the more I learned, the more my imagination was seized. Have you ever read a novel by the English writer Mary Shelley? It is called *Frankenstein*."

"I've seen the movie," said David. He checked his watch.

"In it she wrote something that has stayed with me always: 'None but those who have experienced them can conceive of the entice-ments of science.' As you pursue your career, you will learn that to be true as I did. It becomes like an addictive drug. Working with animals, I began to experiment. Gradually, little by little, we built on our knowledge. Knowing that the thyroid hormone increases res-piration, metabolism, and protein synthesis, heart rate, and strength of contraction, and decreases time needed for thinking and reacting, I harvested thyroxine from donor animals and injected it periodically into my test rats, with astounding results. Then, we found that a substance from the kidneys increases red blood cell mass. I call it erythropoietin, meaning 'maker of red cells.' So by starving the kid-neys of the donor rats of oxygen, we made them hypoxic, forcing them to create more of this substance, which we also introduced into our test subjects. We also synthesized epinephrine from the adrenals and devised a suspension through which it would be released gradu-ally into the body. Many things we tried—a medical recipe of sorts—the sum total of which made mere steroids look like a daily dose of vitamin pills. And none of this was strange chemicals or drugs. It was all organic. A product of the body itself!"

"Incredible," David said quietly. His mind was racing to the next step of the plan. He was itchy to leave. Another few minutes for safety.

"We had unimagined success with our animal experiments. That was when we began our work with humans—to make them faster, stronger, smarter, give them greater endurance. And that is when we embarked on the road to hell."

David asked, "Where did the human donors come from?"

"From cadavers, very recently dead, obtained directly from the hospitals. At least, that was how it began, and that is what they told me. The *Übermensch* formula is species-specific. The substances must come from the life-form on which it will be used. I was content to use the dead to enhance the living. Then I discovered that my sponsors had not only been finding the *best* cadavers for me but were *creating new ones!*" Behrman spread his hands wide. "They are all around you, my generous donors—in this very camp and others just like it. The dissidents, the undesirables, the enemies of the state, the physically and mentally inferior, the Communists and Gypsies and homosexuals and Jews. My own people are providing the grist for the mill I have designed. Just as in the old days, this place is still a factory. But instead of beer, the new product is death."

Miranda gnawed her fist to suppress a wail of horror.

"But when you found out . . ." David said.

"That was when I balked. But I was in too deeply already. I couldn't leave. And I had a responsibility to the young men and women I had already treated with the *Übermensch* formula. But when they began to die, that was when I said, 'No more!' And that was when they brought me here and threatened my family."

"My God," Miranda cried.

David found himself trembling again. "But it doesn't make sense. If you were able to create such superior physical specimens, how could one die of a heart attack? Rolf Schmidt died right in my arms."

"It's a question of balance, like all things in nature. How to increase generalized performance levels yet retain homeostasis? If muscle mass is going to be increased, mobility must not be sacrificed. If you're going to increase respiration, you must guard against hyperventilation. Through the substance we isolated in the kidneys, we were able to increase substantially the red cell mass in the blood. That meant we were able to deliver far more oxygen to the entire body for each unit of blood. I think you can appreciate what this alone would do in terms of strength and endurance. But, then, how do you increase the hematocrit without making the blood so thick that it cannot flow? It is a question of balance, and in Rolf Schmidt's case the balance went wrong. When they examined him, they found his blood was so thick it had clogged an otherwise superb heart."

"They?" said David.

"They. I refused to cooperate. Yet I am the only one who understands the entire delicate balance. I was the one who was developing the agent which decreases the viscosity of the blood without affecting the hematocrit level. Take another example. The heart can function at peak performance of a hundred and seventy to two hundred beats per minute, but the coronary artery cannot supply blood fast enough at this rate for very long. We found a special nitrate compound that selectively dilated only the coronary artery without affecting the other arteries in the body. We know also the stimulating effect of epinephrine in increasing strength and performance under stress. We all have heard the stories of the mother who moves a heavy safe on her back to save her child caught in a burning building. Yet the stimulus is short-acting, even if additional substance is introduced from outside. But by employing plasma-binding proteins, such as albumen, that exist naturally in the body, we were able to alter the epinephrine-releasing mechanism so that it sustained itself over a period of hours."

"That would explain Karl's ankle," David said.

"What's that?"

"During the second day of the decathlon Karl turned his ankle. I was sure he was out of the competition. I didn't think he'd be able to walk. But then he got back up and ran another race right after that."

"Yes," said Behrman. "The effect of the epinephrine."

"I noticed other symptoms," David said. "Nervousness, dilated pupils, sweating. And then there was Karl's skin. It was so incredibly smooth, like a baby's."

"The increased thyroxine," Behrman explained. "The process isn't perfect. There are still side effects. Serious side effects. Particularly when combined with so many other factors."

"And that's what killed him," said David.

Behrman nodded slowly. "In one way or another that is what killed him. Whether it was too much epinephrine, or thickened blood, or acute renal failure, or thyroid storm. The specifics don't matter anymore . . . at least to me. What matters is that a young man I regarded like my own son, a young man Miranda introduced to me, is dead. And I am as responsible as if I'd put a gun to his head and pulled the trigger."

"But you had no way of preventing it," Miranda protested. Her face was wet. Behrman looked at her sadly.

"We saw Karl's body," David stated, "in the lab adjoining your office." Behrman merely shook his head.

David thought with bitterness about the twin incisions on Karl's body and his own revulsion upon opening one of them. "And what about the implants?" he asked.

Behrman grasped his hands together as if he were pleading. "I never agreed to the implants. As I told you, I was doing animal studies. That was how the idea came to me. But it was intended *only* for animals. It was long-term and theoretical, like Miranda's work with the insides of atoms. But they saw what I was doing, and it captured their imaginations, as the original ideas had captured mine. They forced me to accelerate my research. Things they shouldn't have even known about that I was doing, they were able to find out. I think my laboratory assistant—young Dr. Mengele—must have been reporting back to them."

David was chilled by the constant references to the unnamed "them," as if this perversion of science were a force beyond any human being's control. But he pressed on. "What about the women? Were they implanted, too?"

"Not in the same way," said Behrman. "No gonads. But the reticular area of the adrenal cortex was used in some. It was thought the results might be similar without the gender-conflicting effects the masculine tissue could cause. It had proved to be so in the female rats."

"And the extra gonads in the men also increased strength and muscle mass," said David.

"As well as provided testosterone to offset the osteoblastic effects of the thyroxine."

"So it wasn't nerves at all," said David, thinking out loud. "Karl's thinning hair. Actually a superacceleration of male baldness caused by a supersupply of the substance that triggers baldness in the first place. But, then, why weren't all the German men balding?"

"Because only a few were actually given the implants. A variety of different experiments and combinations was tried. As a competitor in an event as extended and demanding of a multitude of strengths and skills as the decathlon, Karl was one of the ones given the full treatment."

"Miranda showed me a list of Olympic events she found in your desk."

Behrman nodded again. "Only certain events were targeted for *Übermensch*. That was the only way to institute a control factor. That way all the other factors—higher motivational levels, the powerful influence of the führer, the advantage of being the host nation, and the desire to do well in front of friends and countrymen—could be discounted and the performance in the targeted events could be gauged directly against the performance in the nontargeted events."

"So far the results have been remarkable," David commented.

"This is what I gather," Behrman said.

"This is extraordinary," said David almost reverentially. "One of the oldest dreams could come true. You actually are on the verge of creating a race of supermen."

"But at what cost?" said Behrman sadly, turning his gaze to the pale and silent Miranda.

David was shaking his head in disbelief, unable to process all this so quickly. "And all of it just so Germany could triumph in the Olympics."

Behrman stopped short and looked at him incredulously, as if he had just made a joke in monstrously poor taste. "Is that what you think?" His voice was thin and strained. "That they would do all this to impress the world that they could win at some little games? That they could run faster, or jump higher, or throw a weight farther? Do you think this means that much to them? Do not question the depths of their viciousness, but neither question the height of their intelligence."

As he spoke, Behrman seemed to be gaining strangely in stature, like some fiery Old Testament prophet. "The Olympic Games, my friend, are nothing but an elaborate experiment. If *Übermensch* can be proved to work for Olympic athletes, it can work for the entire Wehrmacht. Every single soldier. It is only a matter of scale. There is an expression you might have heard: 'Today we have Germany, tomorrow the whole world!'

"We are not talking about games, Herr Keegan. We are talking about war. And war such as the world has never known."

Central Berlin

Heinrich Himmler sat with the others at a table in the study of the Reich Chancellery as his führer outlined his plan for greatness. And as he listened, Himmler thought about the time not many years back when the Reichswehr had been reduced to playing with phony tanks and wooden guns because the real things had been outlawed by Versailles. But with imagination and will they were already preparing for the greatest onslaught the world would ever see.

Himmler could pinpoint the exact date and time the seeds had been planted. On the morning of February 3, 1933, Hitler had called a meeting of his general staff. He told its members he intended to launch a war of imperial conquest to both the east and the west as soon as they were ready. And he asked for ways that the capability could be moved dramatically forward. That was where the germ of the *Übermensch* idea had begun.

The generals had told him it was impossible. Germany does not have the strength, they asserted. England and France will crush us at the first turn, they warned. But Hitler had the dream and the vision that none of the so-called professionals could share. Biding his time, he secretly built up the army and developed industrial capacity. All the while publicly yearning for peace, he privately prepared for war.

Himmler's thoughts raced forward to earlier this year, to March 7. That was the day Hitler sent his troops into the demilitarized Rhineland. It was specifically forbidden by the Treaty of Versailles. He had planned it only the month before, during the Winter Olympics at Garmisch-Partenkirchen. Once again the general staff was totally against the move, saying that the army was not ready and the French would surely resist them. General Werner von Blomberg was so certain of defeat that he committed the smallest possible force to cut down on needless German losses. And the fact of the matter was that at that point the whole thing was a bluff on Hitler's part. If the French had made a single move, Germany would have had to retreat.

But the French did not make a move, and neither did anyone else. At that very moment Hitler knew that he was right and all the generals were wrong. He had risen above conventional wisdom. He had transcended it. With a single roll of the dice, he had shifted Europe's balance of power in his own favor.

What others only dreamed about, Adolf Hitler turned into reality.

"Germany's future," Hitler was saying to the assembled gathering, "depends entirely on *Lebensraum*. We have a right to a larger share of land. It is our destiny. We must achieve it in Europe itself, in immediate proximity to the Reich. With the greatest possible efficiency. And at the lowest possible cost.

"Our first objectives will be Austria and Czechoslovakia." The führer continued, pacing back and forth before them. "Then Poland, Holland, Hungary, Belgium. France, England, and Russia will be the last to fall, but fall they will. And I want to move like lightning, as soon as the first thaw next spring, before any of the other countries are prepared for us." At this he turned directly to Himmler. "That is, if *Übermensch* is ready."

Himmler took off his spectacles to polish them with his handkerchief. "It all depends on one man," he reported quietly. "And now we have him where we want him."

Oranienburg

"So it all depends on you," David said.

"In all humility, yes," Behrman replied. "I am by chance at this moment in history an extremely valuable commodity. All the elements, the delicate balancing of biological forces—I am the only one who understands what has happened and has it all in his mind. I am the only one who understands how to utilize the data that have been obtained in order to correct the critical deficiencies in the experiments already conducted."

"Experiments like Karl and Rolf Schmidt and Horst Müller."

"And others you have not even heard of," said Behrman regretfully. "That is true. Without me, it would take them years to work through what I have already done and to reconstruct what I already know. Do you think there is any other reason they've been keeping an old Jew alive at such great expense here?"

"And what is this place?" asked Miranda. "I still cannot understand it."

Tears again welled up in Behrman's eyes. He had to be like a father having to explain to an innocent child the concept of death. "I cannot describe it to you," he said. "There is no place to begin. I will tell you but one thing that was told to me when I first arrived here . . . by a man who is now dead. There is a rule prisoners have among themselves. At night, if one of them is tossing and thrashing about, obviously having a horrible nightmare, no one is to wake him up—under any circumstances. Because whatever he is imagining in his sleep cannot possibly be worse than the reality he would be awakened to."

The tears were rolling silently down Miranda's cheeks.

"When I refused to continue my work, they decided they must proceed while they tried to persuade me, so they would not lose valuable time. There is an inmate in this very building. You will find him two rooms from here, and you will not believe what you see. The man who had been my own lab assistant—young Mengele—decided to remove his pituitary gland for transplant into an *Übermensch* subject, though I already knew from my animal work it was a futile exercise. He destroyed much of the prisoner's brain in the process. Now he is no more than a moaning vegetable. The camp commander decided the kindest and most efficient thing would be to exterminate the man. But Mengele thought it would be valuable to keep him for reference."

"My dear God," cried Miranda. David placed his hand comfortingly on her shoulder.

Behrman shuddered at his own memory. "Dr. Mengele also takes a special delight in working on dwarfs, the very people I set out to help with my work. He and his people have perverted everything that is sacred. If they are successful, future generations will forget that once medical science was used to comfort the ill and alleviate pain. And the word 'doctor' will be no longer a title of admiration and respect but an obscenity. What I have seen . . . How often I have wished to kill myself. Only knowing what would happen to my family, I have not had the courage."

Just then a small explosion burst from the direction of the door. The three of them turned to see wooden splinters flying across the room. The shattered door flew open, revealing Rudolf Kiesel, a Luger fixed prominently in his hands.

David immediately went for his Schmeisser.

"Don't even think of it, Lieutenant Keegan," Kiesel warned. No matter how skilled you are, I can kill both the doctor and the girl before you can get a single shot off."

"What is the meaning of this?" David demanded. "I am Captain Wolfgang Fürstner of the Wehrmacht, and I carry special authority from the *Reichsführer-SS*."

"You are merely a mannequin for one of the captain's uniforms," Kiesel replied. "The actual Captain Fürstner discovered it missing, along with his authorizing document."

"This is ridiculous!" David persisted, laying the Schmeisser on the floor and kicking it away from him. "I demand an explanation.

When the *Reichsführer* learns of this outrage, he'll have you strung up by your balls!"

But Kiesel continued, holding the Luger steadily on them. "Save your theatrics. The captain is a smart man, as are all German officers. The world will soon see that. When you came to him and asked him about Lieutenant Linderhoff and then about Oranienburg, he put it all together. He called here and asked for the one in charge of Dr. Behrman's experiments. That is how he reached me. And knowing the security of such a matter, he spoke only to me and pledged me to the security that you have violated. Now he is on his way over here."

He backed up to get a better aim on all three of them. "You might as well make yourselves comfortable as we all await his imminent arrival."

TWENTY-NINE

Holding the Luger with a steady hand, Rudolf Kiesel said, "Now that it's an academic point, how did you find out?"

David didn't respond.

Kiesel tensed up on the trigger. "That wasn't idle conversation, Lieutenant Keegan. It is important to me to know."

David remained silent.

"I'm sure you, being a soldier and a West Point graduate, have some heroic sense of honor, so the prospect of death will not sway you. But I assume the young *Fräulein* here is as important to you as the good doctor is to me. So unless you answer my question directly, I am prepared to blow her pretty head off."

David glanced over at Miranda. She remained cool and expressionless. He loved her for her strength and hated himself for his own frailty in loving her, which had given Kiesel this leverage.

Kiesel inched tighter on the trigger.

David took a deep breath. "You shouldn't go leaving bodies around where women can find them," he stated sardonically.

"Yes, I see." Kiesel grimaced. "We shall have to be more careful of such things in the future."

"But that only confirmed it." David went on contemptuously. "Running against Karl Linderhoff the past two weeks, I knew he was different. Seeing his body only made me see how different he was."

"A thoughtful observation," said Kiesel. "A pity we can't employ your impressive talents on *Übermensch*. And with as much as you've been able to discern, a pity we can't let you remain alive either."

Miranda gave a cry and went to David.

"Stay where you are!" Kiesel warned.

"All of you stay where you are!" another voice ordered from the direction of the splintered doorway. Wolfgang Fürstner strode into the room. He wore a uniform identical to David's. He carried a Schmeisser identical to the one David had thrown down. He was followed by four Wehrmacht troopers, wearing Olympic security detail insignias on their uniforms. Their pistols were also drawn.

He walked over to the man holding the Luger. "I assume I have the honor of addressing Dr. Kiesel."

"You do indeed," Kiesel replied proudly.

Fürstner motioned for one of his men to retrieve David's handgun from the floor. "I can assure you that the Reich appreciates your quick and confidential response."

"I came back here as soon as you telephoned," Kiesel said.

"It will be noted," Fürstner assured him. He replaced his gun in its black leather holster and walked over to David. Unceremoniously he ripped open David's breast pocket and removed the black leather authorization document. He calmly placed it in the corresponding pocket of his own uniform, then suddenly struck a furious blow across David's cheek with the back of his hand.

David recoiled as he felt Fürstner's heavy ring catch the corner of his mouth and draw blood. Miranda screamed.

Fürstner looked him in the eye and spoke with controlled rage. "You have disappointed me more than I can say. I trusted you. I extended the hand of friendship, and you betrayed me." He extended his hand outward in a different, less friendly gesture. "I don't know what your motives were, and I don't know what this is all about. But one thing I do know is that the Reich will not be made a fool . . . by anyone." He swept his hand in front of him. "Take them away. I have already given orders for Dr. Behrman's wife and daughter to be apprehended. Dr. Kiesel, I would appreciate it if you would be so kind as to accompany us to Gestapo headquarters. Obergruppenführer Heydrich is waiting to receive your personal report on this matter."

"Of course," said Kiesel.

The security officers led the three prisoners out of the building. As they walked, Miranda grasped David's hand and squeezed it hard. He had never felt so close to anyone.

Outside next to David's delivery van was a closed-top Wehrmacht troop carrier. David and Miranda and Behrman were ordered into the back seat. Facing them, two soldiers positioned themselves with their pistols constantly trained. In front of them sat Fürstner and Kiesel, with the third and fourth men taking up the front.

"Wolfgang, you have to understand what these people are doing," David pleaded.

"Shut up!" said Fürstner. "We have nothing further to say to each other."

But David persisted. "Why do you think you haven't been able to locate Karl Linderhoff? Because he's dead! They've already cut him apart!"

At this Fürstner turned around. "You can tell your story to the proper authorities in the SS. I'm sure they will be gratified to hear anything you have to say. I don't want to know any more than that."

They left the camp by the same route they had entered. Their view was limited by what they could observe out of the troop carrier's tiny windows. But as they passed the parade ground, they could see a rank of about thirty gaunt, ragged prisoners standing at rigid attention. In front of them, four more prisoners held a fifth man. He was on his knees, stripped to the waist, and almost limp in their arms. A black-uniformed guard was whipping him vigorously. His back was running with blood.

David, his gut heaving in disgust, appraised the reactions of his fellow passengers. Miranda winced in empathy at each blow and instantly broke out into uncontrollable tears. Behrman shook his head sadly, as if he'd seen it all too many times before. Kiesel and Fürstner didn't even seem to notice the display.

Once outside the gate they must have driven for at least twenty minutes. No one said anything, leaving David to the torture of his own thoughts. For years now, ever since he'd been a boy, whenever he'd faced any great challenge, he'd always tried to imagine the worst thing that could possibly happen. Then, no matter what took place short of that, it didn't seem so bad. Yet at the back of his mind each time he knew there would come an occasion when the worst thing he could think of would come to pass. He always wondered how he would deal with it.

They were on a sparsely traveled section of highway. The ride was uneventful. Then, suddenly, the driver pulled over to the side of the road. Within a minute two cars pulled up behind them. One was a black Daimler sedan. The other was a red Mercedes taxi with the Kaiserhof Hotel crown painted on the door. David looked around in confusion. Even Kiesel looked surprised.

"On orders of Obergruppenführer Heydrich, we are to change to these civilian vehicles so as not to call attention to ourselves as we approach Prinz-Albrechtstrasse," Fürstner explained.

He got out of the troop carrier. "Place them in the black car," he ordered. To Kiesel, he said, "I would be pleased to have you ride with me in the taxi."

As they were being herded into the new vehicle, David tried to size up the prospects. As soon as he could, he would have to make a move. In his own mind that was a given. The odds were never going to be good. That was another given. He would have to wait until they got as good as they were going to get. He would have to stay alert for the best opening.

Fürstner must have realized what David was thinking. He turned back to him as David was being forced into the back seat of the Daimler. "Your companions have a certain strategic value which necessitates their being kept alive. Your own is not so explicit. I've therefore given orders that if you cause any trouble, you are to be shot. Your body will be returned to the American Olympic Committee with the appropriate explanations. By the way," he added to the soldiers, "I want his tunic removed immediately."

Without letting him get up, two of the guards forcibly ripped the uniform jacket from David's arms and shoulders.

Then they were back on the road. The troop carrier made a U-turn and lumbered off in the other direction.

Twin pistols remained trained on David and his companions throughout the ride back into the city. He hoped the driver didn't hit any large bumps.

Central Berlin

The car took what seemed a roundabout route. They made their final approach to the central sector by way of the Friedrichstrasse, crossed over the River Spree, past the Comic Opera on the left and the Winter Garden Theater on the right. At Unter den Linden they turned right and proceeded down the wide, treelined boulevard. At the Adlon Hotel they turned left onto the Wilhelmstrasse. David knew it was only a few blocks straight down to Prinz-Albrechtstrasse and SS headquarters. A sense of resignation was sweeping over him.

But then the car made a sudden sharp turn to the right. Before any of them realized what was happening, they were on a narrow back street. It might even have been an alley. They went around another sharp corner and drove about half a block. They came to a wall with a gate in it, which opened just as they approached. They drove through, and the gate closed behind them. David felt his heart in his throat.

They came into a small, walled courtyard with the back of an imposing building behind it. The car lurched to a stop. The soldiers immediately got out. They opened the back doors for the prisoners and roughly dragged them out.

At that point David noticed the other car—the red Mercedes taxi—parked against the side of the building. The soldiers rushed them past it toward the building, and David had the fleeting awareness that this might be the last time he would ever see daylight.

They found themselves in a basement corridor. Wolfgang Fürstner was standing there, flanked by the soldier who had driven the other car. At his feet lay a large canvas duffel, the kind it would take a strong man to carry.

It was just Fürstner and the one other soldier. This was the best the odds were going to be. If he waited another moment, the others would be inside, and then it would be too late. If he could take Fürstner by surprise, get his gun, and take him hostage, he had a chance of turning the situation around and getting Miranda and Behrman out. He would improvise from there. This was the time to make the move.

The two other soldiers were already coming through the door when David was prodded past Fürstner. He mentally rehearsed his moves. Suddenly he lunged for the captain, drove his shoulder into Fürstner's chest, and sent him smashing into the wall. At the same instant he went for the leather holster, one hand unsnapping the catch while the other grabbed hold of the gun butt.

The other three Wehrmacht men drew their aim on him in instantaneous reaction, but by then David had the Schmeisser pointed at Fürstner's temple. Behrman and Miranda looked on in stunned disbelief.

"Make one move, and your captain's a dead man!" David shouted.

"I don't think the *Reichsführer* would like that very much." Then to his fellow prisoners he said, "Take their guns. Right now."

"David, this is unnecessary," said Fürstner.

David tensed on the trigger and grabbed him tighter. The other soldiers warily stood their ground. "Drop the guns," he insisted.

"No, you don't understand."

At that moment he heard another door opening, then footsteps from around the corner. "Whoever it is," David warned, "if they make a move, I'll blow your fucking head off."

"Put the gun down," said Arthur Hargreaves as he emerged into the hall.

It hit David like a jolt. *They've got him, too*, he thought. *The entire jig is up.*

"David, put the gun down," Hargreaves repeated sternly, as if speaking to an errant child. "He's on our side."

David pressed the barrel deeper into Fürstner's flesh. "What are you talking about?"

"Look in the bag," Fürstner said through clenched teeth.

"Do as he says," Hargreaves advised.

David motioned to one of the soldiers, who came over and unzipped the duffel. Inside, folded up into a fetal position, was Rudolf Kiesel. His eyes were closed, and his face was colorless. At the edge of the zipper opening David could just make out the top of his chest. Blood had spread out amoebalike across his shirt from a small black hole, the kind produced by, say, the bullet of a 9 mm machine pistol.

"What happened to him?" David demanded.

"We had a little disagreement in the car," said Fürstner.

"Don't you realize where you are?" Hargreaves broke in. "I'm not a prisoner. You have nothing to worry about. The mission is over. This is the basement of the British Embassy, and you're among friends."

The premature turn off the Wilhelmstrasse, the back alley, the courtyard: David ran the sequence back through his mind. He looked at Fürstner and drew the pistol tentatively from his head. Miranda and Behrman looked as confused as he felt.

David indicated the other soldiers, who were now putting down their weapons. "Then who are they?"

"Actors," stated Hargreaves.

"Actors?" David repeated incredulously.

"Yes. Recruited into the intelligence service from the resident company of the Birmingham Repertory Theatre. Quite an excellent group, you know."

"Where did you get the uniforms?"

"We have access to the same theatrical supply houses they do."

"Then why did I have to steal mine?"

"We couldn't take a chance on getting a specific officer's uniform wrong. Plus your stealing it created the logic for Wolfgang to report the crime and set things in motion."

"I have no idea what's going on," David stammered in frustration.

"Yes, well, put the gun down, and we'll go upstairs and try to get it all sorted out."

"This is the second time you've done this to me," said David as he held his wineglass out to the bottle of port Hargreaves was pouring. "I'm about to start taking it personally."

"Wouldn't want you to do that, dear boy," the Englishman replied. "It's all in the line of duty."

"So all the time you and I were planning the rescue, you and Wolfgang were already planning to come in the middle of it and 'capture' us?"

Hargreaves nodded. "Remember what I told you. Every good magician knows that by the time the audience starts following the trick, it's already over."

It was just David and Hargreaves, sitting in a small, ornately decorated reception room off the ambassador's office. Fürstner had quickly departed to return to his post. Behrman had been reunited with his family in another room, and Miranda was there with him, delighting in their love and gratitude.

"So Wolfgang is your agent," David said.

"Has been for some time," Hargreaves replied. "That was why he made such a point of befriending you early in the game. Who do you think's been monitoring your orange juice consumption each morning?"

"I can't believe what you put me through," David said, making no attempt to mask his resentment.

"Look, I wasn't happy about that," Hargreaves insisted. "One never is."

"Then why didn't you tell me? It would have been a lot easier just to have Wolfgang hand over his damn uniform and special authorization."

"Yes, I suppose it would have been. But there were several considerations. Number one, this was your operation, not ours. We tried to talk you out of it. Wolfgang tried to talk you out of it. Even Lorelei tried to talk you out of it."

"Lorelei?" David was stunned.

"Yes, she's with us as well."

"Then she did set me up that night in the cabaret."

"Good actress in her own right, don't you think? The point is we didn't want to do any of this, and under the circumstances we couldn't take a chance on compromising our one effective agent in place within the German power structure. I hate to have to be so hardhearted about things, but you were more expendable than he was. And if anything had gone wrong and you'd fallen into an unfortunate set of hands, those people are experts in getting out of you any information that you've got. Young men like you can tell yourselves you're going to be heroes and you're not going to crack. But believe me, eventually you will. That's why we couldn't take a chance on telling you. Plus we thought you'd give a much more convincing performance if you didn't know. People under stress tend to have mental lapses. We couldn't risk that. And then, if things hadn't worked out exactly according to plan and we couldn't get Behrman, we'd still have 'captured' Miss Wolff, as was our initial intention anyway."

"What if I'd done something extreme or desperate?"

Hargreaves rotated the glass in his hand and watched the purple liquid swirl around the inside. "We knew you'd consider it. Let's face it, you're one damn fine soldier. But from your psychological profile, we knew you'd never do anything to endanger Dr. Behrman or Miss Wolff."

"And Kiesel?"

Hargreaves reacted somewhat sadly. "As I said, this is war. Kiesel realized what was happening and tried to get away. Wolfgang shot him. At this moment he's reporting to Heydrich that Kiesel was a traitor. The rest of the account, like the best stories, is tinged with truth: Kiesel planned on smuggling Behrman out of the camp in a casket. The evidence will be right there. He conspired with an unknown accomplice who entered the camp disguised as Captain Fürstner. The real Fürstner got wind of the plot, surprised Kiesel and his accomplice in the act, and was captured by them. There was a car switch out of town, during which Fürstner was able to wrestle Kiesel's gun from him, but in the ensuing melee the other car sped off with Behrman and the accomplice in it. Within a few moments the Gestapo should be putting out an alert for that nonexistent automobile."

David shook his head in amazement, still trying to be angry for the way he'd been used, but knowing in Hargreaves's carefully reasoned logic that the end had justified the means. "What made Wolfgang turn?" he asked.

"I'd rather not say at this point," Hargreaves replied. "It's still a highly precarious situation, and I don't want to do anything to jeopardize it. Perhaps later on, when you're safely back in England or the States, then we can talk again. In the meantime, we've lived up to our part of the bargain. So I'd appreciate it if you would go to our young miss and get her ready to say bye-bye."

THIRTY

David changed out of Fürstner's Wehrmacht uniform. There was one thing he had to find out for his own sake before they left. After the tearful introductions had been made to Behrman's family, David took him and Miranda aside.

"Did Karl know?" David asked pointedly.

"Not everything, but more than some of the others," the old scientist somberly replied. "All the athletes were given regular vitamin injections to mask who was actually receiving the *Übermensch* factors. The ones on whom surgery was performed, obviously, had to be told the most."

"And Karl?" David pressed.

"He knew he was taking part in a bold scientific experiment that had some risk. And he knew he was serving his country. He did so willingly and with great character." Behrman sounded suddenly sadder and more despairing. "But in the last several weeks he grew increasingly distant. I could see what was coming."

"What was that?" Miranda asked with trepidation.

"It didn't happen all the time, but it happened often enough. We'd seen it first in the rats. Of course, the effects were exaggerated because of their smaller body masses, but the implications were clear."

Behrman was staring off into the middle distance, as if looking backward through time. "Of all the things we did, this was the hardest for me to face. Physics tells us there is no such thing as an isolated system. It's equally true for biology. We did a great many things to the body that had never been done before. The results, of course, could not be predicted. Through our manipulation of the neural axis, we had inadvertently succeeded in creating a laboratory-induced psychosis."

David thought not only of Karl but of Horst Müller thrashing wildly on the ground of the Olympic Village and of the mild-mannered Rolf Schmidt furiously upsetting the chessboard in the dining hall.

"Much of what Karl did in these last weeks, he was not responsible for," said Behrman. "He was not himself. He had delusions. He became paranoid. The dementia had already taken over. But when I remember him, it would be very sad for me if it were that way. I hope I can remember only the friendly, dedicated, and loving young man who consistently brightened up my laboratory . . . and my life."

"Thank you," said David solemnly. "It means a lot to me to hear this."

Miranda wiped away a tear of her own.

"I'm not letting her out of the building," Hargreaves stated firmly. "We've lived up to our part of the bargain. Now she has to live up to hers. She leaves the country at the same time as Behrman."

"She doesn't even know she's made a bargain," David countered. "After all she's been through, it would be a terrible mistake to rush her. Give me some time to ease her into the idea."

"Fine," said the Englishman. "Just don't leave the building."

"It won't work. You'll seem just as repressive as the circumstance we're taking her away from. All along, you've kept telling me I had to gain her trust. Well, I've done it. Don't ruin it now. I've got to get her into some familiar, nonthreatening situation before I tell her."

Hargreaves shook his head. "It's too risky. We don't know who may be on to her by now; who may be on to both of you, for that matter."

"If you want her mind as well as her body," David declared with finality, "you've got to take the chance."

The Tiergarten

Late in the afternoon David and Miranda strolled hand in hand along one of the shaded pathways in the far reaches of the zoo. The sounds of the animals were far away. To the casual onlooker they might have been two young lovers whiling away a leisurely summer day. And in point of fact David was already trying to figure out where they could spend the night together. They were near her apartment, but that wasn't very practical. Hargreaves desperately wanted her back at the embassy tonight, and wouldn't be terribly concerned about the sleeping arrangements.

God, she was beautiful in the dappled sunlight. Maybe they could go back to the inn at Döberitz.

She was just beginning to relax. "There's so much I don't understand," she said, and he could see her nose wrinkle and her forehead knit the way they did when she was thinking hard.

"What's on your mind?"

"Well, for one thing, why did we end up at the British Embassy?"

"Because the British were helping us."

"But why?"

"I asked them to."

"Why would they be willing to take such risks?"

David only shrugged.

"You're American. How do you know this Mr. Hargreaves?"

"It's a long story."

"Did you know him from Oxford?"

"No. I didn't."

"You met him here in Berlin?"

"That's right."

"He must be a very important man to have all those people working for him. Is he part of the embassy?"

"Not exactly."

"Then why is he here?"

David paused. They continued walking. "I guess you'd say for the Olympics."

She pulled him to a stop and looked at him quizzically. Suddenly a light bulb seemed to go on in her head. "He knew about Dr. Behrman's work."

"Not exactly," David repeated.

"Then they did this just for friendship?"

"It's a little more complicated than that," he confessed. He saw a park bench not far away. He wrapped his arm around her waist and guided her over to it. "Listen, we can talk about all that later. The important thing is we have to start making some plans. Sit down."

She obeyed but went on. "Another thing I don't understand: Why did Mr. Hargreaves seem so concerned when we left? He was worse than my parents on my first date."

"Hargreaves can be very nervous," David answered obliquely, putting his arm around her and drawing close.

"He was acting very strangely. And now you're acting very strangely. Why didn't he want to let you go?"

He realized her mind was moving faster than he could stop it. There wasn't any choice, so he said, "It wasn't me he was worried about."

She turned her body to face him. "What are you talking about?"

David took a deep breath and let it out slowly. "Miranda, it should come as no surprise that there are a lot of people who are very interested in you."

"What?"

He took another deep breath. "We didn't meet by chance."

"No," she said. "We met through Karl."

"And he and I didn't meet by chance either."

A troubled look came over her face. "I still don't know what you're talking about."

That was when he told her. Haltingly, but step by bloody step. From the initial encounter with Hargreaves through all the discussions about strategy and how to "get to her" up to the events of the morning. Throughout the narrative David watched as Miranda's face turned by degrees from stunned surprise to dismayed shock to an obvious, all-embracing sadness.

A terrifying stillness descended on her, and she sat there, open-mouthed, not saying anything for a long time. David agonized through the silence.

Finally she spoke, and by that time her expression had turned to outrage. "So I'm nothing to you but a subject. Is that it? One more laboratory specimen?"

"You know that's not true." He implored her.

"On Monday, when you were so upset with me for going off in the truck, I thought it was because you cared for me."

"Of course I do," David protested. "More than anything."

"But I see now you were only protecting your investment."

"How can you say that?"

"How could you *do* this? How could you use me this way? Everything that happened. The way you acted. The things you said." Her vexation reached a flash point as she ticked off the litany of her grievances. "None of it meant anything. It was all put on."

"No, Miranda," David said quietly. "It was by no means that. The way I feel about you is indescribable, and has been since the first time I laid eyes on you. I love you. It's that simple. In a way that I've never loved anyone before. If nothing else, last night should prove that."

Her eyes grew wider and blazed with heat. She opened her mouth to say something, but it was as if the hurt were so profound that words could no longer describe what she was feeling.

She got up from the bench and then hesitated there, as though she could plan only one step at a time. David put his hands on her upper arms, but she shook him off. She shivered with frustration and her own upset.

"I gave you everything," she cried indignantly.

"And I gave you everything in return."

She took one decisive step away from him. He followed her, and she took another. "I have nothing left. What can I believe any longer?" she asked plaintively.

What can any of us believe any longer? David thought. "I was an unwilling subject just like you," he said beseechingly. "We're both in this together. What else could I have done? And none of it changes the way I feel about you, any more than if we'd met in a restaurant or a movie theater . . . or right here at the zoo. If you'll just let rationality and logic sink in for a moment and think about it . . ."

Even in the paroxysms of her distress, the physicist in her could not ignore this appeal to reason. The transformation was instantaneous, and the effect was stunning. She stopped cold. The eyes grew deep and distant. David could visualize the wheels turning inside her head and gave thanks for her formidable intellect.

And then the process was complete, and her eyes returned to this world.

The first product of her reflection was a step in close to him, for which David offered up a silent prayer of relief.

Then she brought her hand back in a wide arc, and the impact of her slap resounded like a bomb blast throughout the park.

Central Berlin

"How could you let her just walk away?" asked Arthur Hargreaves incredulously. He paced around the embassy's reception room.

"There wasn't any choice," said David, absently rubbing the side of his face. He watched the Englishman circle.

"What do you mean, 'There wasn't any choice'? She slapped you in public, and you just stood there and let her walk off? You should have picked her up bodily and carried her back here if that's what it would have taken."

"Are you impugning my masculine pride or my judgment?"

"Take your pick," Hargreaves said. He started for a chair, then thought better of it and remained standing. He turned to David again. "I knew I never should have let her leave here."

"It's not like she's vanished into thin air," David pointed out.

"She'd better not have."

"If you'd forced her to stay at the embassy, do you honestly think that would have convinced her to come willingly work with you?"

"Well, you've done a first-class job of that, doing it your way, haven't you?" Hargreaves shot back.

"Look, Arthur, the burden I've been carrying here isn't exactly of my own making." It was the first time he ever remembered calling the Englishman by his given name.

"That's life, old stick."

"That's life?" David spread his arms out wide in a gesture of amazement. "Okay. You think I'm a fool. Miranda hates me. Karl had me beaten up. Avery Brundage considers me an annoying jerk. In the last two weeks I've betrayed just about everyone I've come in contact with in one way or another. All I wanted to do was come over here and try to win the medal I've been working toward for the last seven years, and you tell me, 'That's life'?"

"Well, it is," Hargreaves declared without letting up on him. "And we're all big boys here, in a less than perfect world."

David let out a sigh of exasperation. "Okay." He relented. "Let me try to talk to her tomorrow after she's had a chance to cool down."

"Right, you do that."

"First thing in the morning," David promised.

Hargreaves finally stopped moving. "Just remember one thing. She works *with* us if possible. But she's not to continue working *against* us. That decision has already been made. And one way or another it's going to be implemented."

THIRTY-ONE

Friday, August 14, The Tiergarten

He waited for her at the entrance to the *U-bahn* station and spotted her before she could get to the trains. He tried to read her temperament in her face and walk, but she conceded him no clues.

He came up alongside her, quickly gauged the number of steps they'd have together before she went in, and decided he'd better not waste any time on small talk.

"Is there any way I can persuade you not to hate me?" he said.

"I don't hate you," Miranda replied calmly, and offered him a conciliatory smile. "I'm grateful for what you did yesterday."

"Hargreaves tells me they're arranging to smuggle the Behrmans out of the country."

"That's very good," she said. "And I'm sorry I slapped you."

"It's okay. I can understand how you felt." They were almost out of steps. He asked, "May I talk to you for a few minutes?"

"I don't want to be late for work," she said.

"That's sort of what I wanted to talk to you about."

She stopped just as they were nearing the gate and looked at him expectantly.

"You can't go back there," he declared.

She wrinkled her nose slightly and asked in her innocent way, "Why not?"

"If you continue there, what do you think's going to happen to your work?"

"David, not here," she whispered sternly.

"Then can we go somewhere and talk?"

"No."

"When?"

"I don't know. Later maybe."

"Lunch today?"

"No. I'll be busy."

"Dinner."

"No."

"When?"

"I have to go to work."

He took her by the arm and pulled her sharply around. "Haven't you been listening to anything I just said to you?" People were starting to notice them.

"David, please," she said. "I don't think we should be doing this in public."

"Then let's go someplace private."

"It's impossible."

"That's ridiculous." He knew he was hurting her but wouldn't let go of her arm. "Three minutes—that's all I'm asking. Just come over here and walk with me. You've got to give me that."

She wearily nodded her compliance, as if finally giving in to a persistent child. He guided her from the station's entrance, back down the Hardenbergstrasse in the direction she'd come from. Only when they were sufficiently far away did he release her. With luck, the people who'd noticed them would think it was nothing more than a lover's quarrel.

When they were reasonably alone and out of the mainstream of pedestrian traffic, David said to her, "How can you even think of going back there?"

She looked at him almost blankly. "I have a job. It's where my work is."

"Do you think Abraham Behrman's going back?"

"He's safe. That's all that matters."

"And what about you?"

"Let me worry about that. It's not your concern."

"Of course it is. I care about you intensely."

She lowered her eyes briefly but said only, "Anyway, my work is different from his."

"But you've seen what's happened to science. All science. It's nothing more than a weapon now. You can't separate out what you do and say it's not. That's just sticking your head in the sand. Did you think what Kiesel's people are doing is just an aberration?"

"That's biology," she stated insistently. "Physics is different. It's pure. It's abstract."

"What do you think they're going to do with it?"

"That's not my affair."

He was dumbfounded. His voice was growing in stridency and desperation. "Miranda, I can't believe I'm hearing you talking this way. How can you deny it?"

"My work is very important to me. It's my life. The institute is where I belong. It's the only place I can find peace." She turned back in the direction of the station. He quickly followed.

"Doesn't what you saw in the camp yesterday mean anything to you?"

"We'll talk about that later."

"We'll talk about it now!"

"David, I'm telling you. This is not the time or place. Please believe me."

"Aren't you ever going to grow up?" For the first time he empathized with her father in wanting to beat some sense into her. And if he thought it might have done any good, he would have strongly considered it right here.

They were back at the *U-bahn* entrance, where she turned again to face him. "That's all," she announced with finality. "I have to go." There was an air of icy determination about her that he just couldn't crack.

"Miranda, I love you," he said. "I don't want ever to be without you."

"Please, David," she begged, "this is difficult enough as it is."

"You don't know what you're doing," he said with exasperation, seizing her once more by the arm.

"I know exactly what I'm doing." She rebuffed him, turning instantly cold. "And if you don't let go of me, I'm going to scream as loudly as I can."

He stared intensely into her face as he slowly released his grip. She held his gaze for one beat longer.

"I'll call you in a day or two," she said as she turned and walked briskly into the station. He heard the crowds scrambling. A train was just pulling up.

But as he watched her emerge onto the platform, then thought about facing Hargreaves, he knew that a day or two would be a day or two too late.

Central Berlin

"Right. That's it then," Arthur Hargreaves announced from behind his desk. "She's made her position clear. There doesn't seem to be any more legitimate hope of getting through to her. David, we thank you for all your efforts. Sorry it didn't work out better. We'll take it from here."

"You can't be serious," David proclaimed, standing there before him, ashen-faced.

"I can't afford not to be serious," Hargreaves said in reply. He closed a file folder in front of him. "Well, it hasn't been a total loss. We picked up an unexpected bit of good fortune in Behrman. And we certainly couldn't have done that without you. The boys downstairs have been talking to him all day. Extraordinary stuff. You should feel very good about that. We should have listened to you earlier."

"Then listen to me now."

Hargreaves raised his hands in a gesture of helplessness. "You've done your best. I'm not saying you haven't. But she's just not buying it. And we can't take a chance that she'll come up with the Great Rapture and deliver it directly to Adolf while we sit on our knuckles."

David shifted uncomfortably in his chair. "What are you going to do?" he asked with trepidation.

Hargreaves leaned back in his own chair. "As you said yesterday, you've borne enough of the burden in this already. Don't try to take on any more of it."

David rose to his feet.

"We really do value all that you've done and appreciate all your sacrifices. We'll let your own people know how good you've been about it, and we'll make it up to you in any way we can."

"I'm sure you will," David muttered.

"We'll want to do a full debriefing in a day or two, okay?"

"Sure. Whatever you say."

"Oh, one more thing, Keegan," Hargreaves called after him. "Don't go do anything stupid now."

Dahlem

It was difficult getting back into her work after all she'd been through, but Miranda knew she had no choice. With the door closed and all the drawers of her battered gray file cabinet pulled open, she sat at her desk, meticulously going over every paper and work sheet she had produced in the past six months.

She pushed herself relentlessly, working through lunch, not once getting up from her desk until she realized rather uncomfortably that she had to go to the bathroom. She hurried back directly and resumed her labors.

By the middle of the afternoon every part of her body ached, from tension, fatigue, or mental strain. She had developed a piercing pain at the bridge of her nose from constantly converging her eyes on a single focal point. Her desk chair under the best of circumstances was only barely adequate, having reached the venerable stage of seeing service to junior staff members in a final rotation before the scrap heap. Consequently, her bottom was just plain sore from the continuous sitting, only partially alleviated by the periodic shifting of one leg and then the other under her.

And still, she pushed herself.

Hard by her stack of working papers was a second stack of clean sheets, onto which she carefully copied out all of the formulas and equations from the originals so that even a detailed examination of the new pages would reveal them to be, in fact, just that.

But on every one she made a single change.

Döberitz

David lay on his bunk, staring up at the ceiling. He was alone. Tom had been spending each day at the stadium, and as a gold medal winner he had become something of a celebrity.

Everything inside David was churning. Each Olympics was apparently destined to end for him with the same double loss: both the medal and the woman of his dreams. The mere suggestion of what Hargreaves's people intended to do filled him with dread.

How could such a brilliant girl be so completely dense?

He'd done everything the Brits had asked of him, and where had it gotten him? Where was it about to get Miranda? No matter what, how could he just lie here and be party to it in the name of the greater good?

He loved this woman. And more important, he had been loved by her. He thought back to the night before last at the inn. *How do you turn away from that?*

You don't. It was as simple as that. He sat bolt upright at the bold and simple clarity of the epiphany. So far he'd gone along. He'd always gone along and done what he was told and what was expected of him. In high school. At West Point. Now here.

But there comes a time when it doesn't work to rely on anything outside your own heart and gut. There comes a time when you have to be your own higher authority.

As of this minute he declared himself a free agent. No more following orders. From now on he followed his own instincts, regardless of the consequences. And he knew immediately what he had to do.

He had to go back to her, to explain to her what was *really* happening. Fuck Hargreaves. Fuck everyone. And if she still insisted on turning a blind eye, he would then do whatever it took.

Central Berlin

The young brownshirt sat stiffly and nervously in the presence of Reinhard Heydrich.

"Your name, please," the *Obergruppenführer* demanded, even though it had clearly been presented to him with the accompanying dossier.

"Oskar Klemt, sir," the young man intoned, his forehead beading with perspiration.

Heydrich didn't bother looking up from the dossier. "It goes without saying that you will be completely candid with me," he advised. After the report yesterday from Fürstner he was in no mood for any nonsense.

"Yes, of course, sir," the young man said.

"Good," said Heydrich, finally glancing up and letting their eyes meet for just a second. Himmler had given him a simple and direct mandate: Find Behrman and his family before it became necessary to inform Hitler of the turn of events. Messengers of bad tidings were not rewarded in the Third Reich, as Heydrich himself had made clear to Fürstner.

Rudolf Kiesel's wife and brother had already been brought in for questioning, but so far the exercise had yielded nothing. Then there was always the chance that Fürstner himself had been involved in the plot with Kiesel, in spite of the several hours of questioning he had undergone yesterday. With what they'd turned up in his background, it was not outside the realm of possibility. Heydrich had decided to let things play normally for a day or two, lull him into a sense of security and trust. That way, if there were any skeletons hanging in the closet, the closet door would remain unlocked. At any rate they still needed him for another few days.

"So then," Heydrich resumed, "I am to understand you undertook certain activities on behalf of Karl Linderhoff."

"Yes, sir," Klemt stated, clearing his throat conspicuously and pulling at his tight uniform collar. "But then, after the second day of the decathlon, when I couldn't get back in touch with him, I thought I'd better contact your office."

"A wise choice," Heydrich commended him. "Now, this attack which Linderhoff had you stage against the American"—Heydrich scanned the dossier—"David Keegan. Its purpose was to adversely affect his Olympic performance?"

"I'm sure that was part of it, sir."

"But also?" Heydrich prompted.

"He was upset over the way, ah, the interest his, ah, his lady friend seemed to be taking in the American."

"Yes, of course. Now then, perhaps you could tell me what you know about the young lady."

Dahlem

It had taken her all day, and she was teetering on the brink of exhaustion. But the work was complete. Now there was only one thing left to do.

She had spent the past two hours hunched closely over her desk, one by one memorizing the original versions of her papers. Now she gathered them up and shoved them into the extralarge handbag she had brought for the purpose. Then she rose from her desk, took her sweater from its hook, and left her office.

She paused for a moment in the doorway and stared back at the tiny cubicle. She took in all the minute details, as if saying good-bye to a friend she knew she'd never see again.

In the corridor outside the central biology lab there was an incinerator chute designed for the disposal of caustic chemicals, small animal carcasses, and worn-out materials. As a practice the cleaning crew also used it to get rid of anything that could be fitted through its cast-iron door, leaving less to carry down to the refuse cans.

When the coast was clear in both directions, Miranda pulled open the heavy door and began methodically feeding the papers through in small stacks. It took only a few minutes to empty the handbag of many months' work.

She was on her way out of the building when two men in matching black leather trench coats came up to her and stopped her.

"Fräulein Wolff," the first man said, placing a hand on her wrist, "please come with us."

By the time he got off the *U-bahn* train at Dahlem, David had decided exactly what he was going to do. He would go straight up to her office and tell her in no uncertain terms why her life was in danger and that she had no choice but to come away with him. Once she was safe, then she could do what she wished, and if she never wanted to see him again after that, that was the way it would have to be. But until then there was no more time for discussion, argument, or trying to break through that frustratingly childish side of her nature. If she wouldn't come willingly, he'd gag her, put her over his shoulder, and carry her out.

When he got to her office, it was locked. He banged on the door, but there was no answer. He went right to the departmental office.

"Excuse me, please," he asked the woman behind the desk in his most conversational German. "Could you tell me where I might find Fräulein Wolff?"

She looked up at him starkly, as if he'd just invoked the dead. "She's not here," the woman informed him. She was trying carefully to restrain her emotions, maintain the sense of business as usual, but the terror was not far from the surface. "She, she left."

"By herself?" David insistently inquired. If Hargreaves had touched a hair on her head, he would hunt him down to the ends of the earth.

"No," she replied, her voice shaking. "With the Gestapo."

"Dr. Hahn's been informed and is on his way back from Paris," the woman added, as if this might somehow get the situation back under control.

Panic-stricken, David headed down the hall. He slowed instinctively as he passed two wary-looking men in business suits who did not look as if they belonged there.

He clambered aimlessly down the stairs. What was he going to do? He had to do something. Should he go back to Hargreaves? Maybe Wolfgang could help.

Suddenly he realized where he was going. He raced out the back door of the building and into the lovely park where he'd first walked with Miranda. There he found the old, dead oak tree, the one that Miranda loved. He peered into the gaping crevasse.

Wedged way at the back he found something—a single wadded-up ball of paper. Thank God she remembered. Urgently, he unfolded it, desperate for her message.

But there was no message. Instead, the page contained nothing but the set of equations Miranda had written out for him in this very setting.

Why would she do this, unless she were trying to tell him something and couldn't risk spelling it out? He was sure it was the same formula because he had committed it to memory as an indication for Hargreaves of what she was actually up to. And Hargreaves had been impressed. No, *overwhelmed* would be a better word. David could practically see him salivating as he wrote it down. And here they were, the same equations again on this work sheet.

Only she had changed them.

THIRTY-TWO

Central Berlin

"How could we be so stupid?" David lamented. He pounded on Hargreaves's desk with helpless frustration. The British scientist sat there, anxiously chewing on the end of a pencil.

"We thought she was hiding her head in the sand," David went on, "when what she was really doing was *covering her tracks!*"

"And the reason she didn't let you in on this—"

"Was the same reason you didn't. She must have realized we could be under surveillance, and if she told me anything, it could tip *them* off, too. It's the only logical explanation. What I thought was the action of a petulant child was actually an act of supreme courage."

The Englishman stared grimly out the window.

David continued to rant. "So she actually was intending to leave with us. It's just that she *did* understand what was happening and didn't want to give them the benefit of her research. And you were going to have her killed!"

"I never said that."

"You didn't have to. You were ready to kill a young woman who was willing to risk her life for your precious cause!"

"Yes, well, that is a chastening thought," said Hargreaves soberly. "And later, when there's time, we'll all atone for misjudging her. But at the moment we have a disaster on our hands."

"How about some more of your magic?" David proposed.

"I'm afraid that bag of tricks is empty," said Hargreaves, shaking his head. "Obviously we can't have Wolfgang Fürstner go snatch her out of the hands of the Gestapo."

"He can at least find out where they've taken her."

"Perhaps. But I wouldn't be overly optimistic on that score. After

349

what is undoubtedly being viewed as the fiasco with Behrman, any involvement on Fürstner's part is going to be suspect. Apparently Heydrich's already revoked his special authorization."

"Well, we can't just sit around and do nothing," David said.

"We don't intend to," said Hargreaves. "Time is definitely of the essence. It won't take them long to break her if that's what they've set out to do."

David shuddered.

"Keep in mind, we've got as much at stake as you do."

"I would question that," David replied sullenly. Then he turned toward Hargreaves and leaned over the desk. "So what are you going to do?"

"Well, as you suggested, the first thing we've got to do is find out where she's been taken."

"And how are you going to do that?"

"It isn't going to be easy," Hargreaves admitted. "It's not exactly as if we had direct access to the German command structure."

"Then we'll have to find someone who does," David declared.

Wilmersdorf

"Well, you've got some nerve showing up here!" Ali exclaimed as she opened the door of her suite at the Hotel Bristol. She was wearing a blue silk dressing gown printed with peacock feathers. "After all the messages I left for you that you just ignored!" Her hair was still wet, and she looked as sexy and sensational as always.

"I don't have any excuses," said David. "Actually I do, but you probably wouldn't be interested." He stood there awkwardly in the hallway. "Can I come in?"

"All right, but make this snappy, Keegan." She turned and led him into the room. "I have a big night ahead of me."

She went into the bedroom and sat down at the dressing table. "Dr. Goebbels is throwing the biggest party of the Olympics tonight," she said, trying to get a reaction. In the vanity mirror's reflection David could see her applying pink base cream to her cheeks. She even put on her makeup like a movie star. "Two thousand people invited to an island in the middle of the river."

"I bet it'll be nice," said David as she dipped into her eye shadow.

"I bet it will be. So what's on your mind?"

"I need your help."

She didn't bother turning around. "So what else is new?"

"It's life and death."

"I don't know who's more dramatic," she commented as she applied her lipstick, "you or I."

"Ali, I'm serious."

She put the lipstick down and turned to face him.

"I think I'd better tell you what's been happening since I last saw you."

Central Berlin

"So far we've drawn a complete blank," Hargreaves reported dismally. "We've got everyone here working on it, and I've thrown it back to the staff in Fifty-four Broadway for analysis."

"You said it yourself," David said urgently. "There isn't any time for analysis."

"If you have a better suggestion, I'd be happy to entertain it. Perhaps you have some resources we don't have," Hargreaves testily replied.

David didn't respond.

"There's been talk in London of trying to do a diplomatic deal."

"What do you mean?"

"Make her into a cause célèbre," Hargreaves explained, "this prominent scientist who wants to leave for intellectual freedom. God knows there's plenty of precedent among German scientists. Try to embarrass them into letting her go. They might be particularly susceptible to that approach during the Olympics, when they're trying to put a good face on for the world."

"So what are we waiting for?"

"The obvious problem is that if they don't already know what a resource they've got, they will as soon as we start calling attention to her. And then they'd never let her out, no matter how much diplomatic stink we created. Whatever the case, we've still somehow got to figure out where she is."

In the midst of crisis the everyday details of life and bureaucracy have to go on. Heinrich Himmler recognized this truth, and his devotion to its principles was his special gift.

Reinhard Heydrich had been entrusted with the urgent task of locating Abraham Behrman. But in the meantime, if the führer's plan was to go forth on schedule, none of the associated arrangements could be let slip. This was why Himmler had called in Gruppenführer Theodor Eicke and his eager assistant Adolf Eichmann.

They sat next to each other in Himmler's office, across the conference table from the *Reichsführer*. He always thought of the two men together. It must have been the similarity of their surnames. Since July 1934, Eicke, the energetic forty-four-year-old Alsatian, had been chief inspector of the concentration camps and overseer of the SS's prestigious Death's-Head formations. In just two short years he'd done an exemplary job of streamlining their efficiency and organization. And his political loyalty was without question. Directly before taking over his current post, Eicke had personally dispatched Hitler's rival Ernst Röhm as the deposed SA chief sat sweating in his prison cell at Stadelheim following the Night of the Long Knives.

Eichmann, just barely thirty, was slight and gaunt, with small pig eyes. He was neither dynamic nor flamboyant, but he had a dedication to organization and an eye for the details of bureaucracy, and in him the *Reichsführer* saw much of his younger self.

Together Eicke and Eichmann had been given the task of assuring a continuous supply of suitable donors for the *Übermensch* program.

"Thus far the number of individuals already in the camp system has proved sufficient," Eicke methodically reported. "However, as soon as *Übermensch* shifts into its next phase—the strategic one—Herr Eichmann's computations suggest that we will need a dramatic increase in our head count."

Eichmann took over with a deferential nod to his superior. "Jews, Gypsies, homosexuals, and mental deficients all can continue to provide a rich stock without unduly upsetting the sensibilities of the ordinary German people."

"Very good," said Himmler. He was trying hard to maintain his concentration on this critical issue in spite of his larger concerns. "Of course, we shall never be rough or heartless where it is not necessary," he felt compelled to comment to the two men. "We Germans, who are the only people in the world who have a decent attitude to animals, will also adopt a decent attitude to these human animals. But it is a crime against our own blood to worry about them." He addressed his two visitors with admiration. "Both of you know what it means to see a hundred corpses lying together . . . five hundred, or a thousand. To have gone through this and yet to have remained decent, this has made us hard."

The *Reichsführer* rose from his chair and escorted the two men from his office. "Thank you both for coming," he said cordially. "Please be assured that your efforts have not gone unnoticed."

As they left, Reinhard Heydrich was waiting to enter. Himmler could now turn his attention to the more pressing matter. Soon, he would have to leave to attend Dr. Goebbels's party. Much as he hated such social chores, it wouldn't do to be conspicuous by his absence.

"The rescue of Behrman was unquestionably an inside job," Heydrich reported.

"Unquestionably." Himmler quietly agreed.

"The problem is we don't know how far inside. So while that remains a problem, my inclination is to get her out of here."

"As you wish," said Himmler.

"I'm going to move her to someplace safe. Tonight."

"And one more thing," Reinhard Heydrich said to his adjutant as he strode purposefully back to his office. "There is an American Olympic athlete called David Keegan. We cannot make a scene violating the neutrality of the Olympic Village, but as soon as he next comes outside, I want our men waiting at the gate to bring him in."

Wannsee

The party was staged on the Pfaueninsel—Peacock Island—a magnificent nature preserve in the middle of the Havel where, a hundred and forty years earlier, Friedrich Wilhelm III had built his summer palace.

For tonight, though, the army engineers had built an elaborate pontoon bridge to convey the two thousand invited guests from the mainland. Once on the island, they were greeted by scores of young ballerinas dressed as Renaissance pages and carrying torches to conduct them to their dinner places. The trees were festooned with Japanese lanterns and sparkling butterfly lamps, and the lilting music of several dance bands permeated the mild summer air. Waiters in tailcoats circulated throughout the crowd proffering glasses of the finest French champagne. Propaganda Minister Josef Goebbels, the party's host, was suave and gracious in a white gabardine suit that highlighted his impressive tan. His wife, Magda, was resplendent in white organdy.

Ali arrived wearing a low-cut evening gown of blue silk, set off by a shawl of gauzy white lace draped around her shoulders. She had taken pains with her appearance, even more so than normal, and if she did say so herself, she looked smashing.

That opinion was heartily endorsed by her patron, Hermann Göring, who found her immediately. He was impressively decked out in his blue air marshal's uniform with all its ribbons and decoration. He rushed over to her and took her hand in both of his. While clicking the heels of his shiny boots together, he brought the hand to his lips for a gracious kiss.

"I am totally at your service," Göring proclaimed. "What can I do to assure the pleasure of so beauteous a lady?"

You could tell me where your friend Himmler is keeping this Wolff girl, Ali thought, all the while offering a dazzling smile for public consumption. *But something tells me that ain't exactly the sort of thing you had in mind.*

The plain truth was that David had given her a pretty tall order. While she may have temporarily become a favorite of Göring's and the darling of the Nazi brass, it was unlikely any of them were going to give away state secrets in exchange for a dazzling smile or whatever else they could read into it.

Still, the stakes were too high simply to shrug it off and go about business as usual. Whatever she might have felt about herself and David, however peeved she might have been, she couldn't close herself off from what he'd told her. So this party that she'd looked forward to as the height of the Olympic social season had suddenly taken on a deadly urgency.

"You must promise me a dance early in the evening," Göring asserted, plucking glasses for them from a waiter's silver tray, "and another when you have become slightly drunk."

She flashed him a naughty, flirtatious smile and said, "I swear, you'll lead a girl to ruin if she gives you half a chance."

Ali mingled with the crowd of Berlin's elite. Everyone was here: Hess and Himmler and Ribbentrop; Carl Diem, Theodor Lewald, Henri de Baillet-Latour, and all the Olympic big shots. She spotted Avery Brundage. For a moment their eyes met, and she noted with satisfaction that he was the first to look away.

That son of a bitch.

Charm and wit were in abundant supply. Small talk reigned supreme. Dinner was served. Everyone said it was the most lavish affair of its kind they could recall since those impetuous days at the height of Weimar prodigality. Dr. Goebbels seemed intent on proving to the world that Nazis really were just as human and fun-loving as the rest.

Yet as the evening crept on, Ali despaired of finding any way to help David. If a life were on the line, she would be willing to do anything she possibly could, to trade all her charm and wiles if it would make any difference. But if she were to make a mistake and tip off the wrong person, that poor young woman would be in an even bigger mess than she already was.

She gave Göring the promised dance, practically smothered by his enormous girth, but by this point it was a strain to keep up appearances. Her declining mood was matched perfectly by the face of the white-haired man in a blue uniform she spotted standing far away from the center of the festivities. "Who is that?" she whispered in Göring's ear.

"Oh, that's Canaris, admiral and chief of the military intelligence service," Göring answered with disdain. "Quite a sourpuss, isn't he? But what can you expect from a man who won't even join the party?"

"Why is he such a big deal then?" Ali asked, intrigued. Canaris was already a legendary figure.

A big grin spread over Göring's face. "He's a war hero," he said with a mocking laugh. "Just like me!"

After the dance Ali made her way over to where Canaris was standing alone. He looked as dour as ever. "Having a good time?" she asked coquettishly.

"No," he responded with disarming candor. "I never do at these things."

"I like your uniform," she purred, running her fingers from the braided gold epaulets on his shoulders to the four gold stripes along his sleeve.

"Thank you," he said flatly, "though it's not so admired these days as the flashier uniform of the SS. That one is designed even to flatter the appearance of a weasel, of a toad."

She made her eyes as big and admiring as she could. "But I understand ~~you~~ are referred to as the Fox and your headquarters has become known as the Fox's Lair."

"I've been called a lot of things in my career," Canaris commented dryly.

"My name is Ali," she suddenly stated in an effusive burst of friendliness. "Alison Welles Prescott. I'm a swimmer. Well, I was a swimmer. I guess I'm a journalist now."

"Yes, I know."

"You do?" she said, showing manifest delight.

"It's part of my business to know."

Ali tried to control her eagerness. *Tread softly*, she told herself. "Do you know a lot?"

"What needs to be known."

Now how can I get him to trust me? "And can you find out what you don't know?"

"Sometimes," said Admiral Wilhelm Franz Canaris.

The explosion of fireworks lit up the sky and sounded like an invading army as Ali and the admiral left the party together.

THIRTY-THREE

Saturday, August 15, The Tiergarten

It was early in the morning. David and Tom waited nervously along the perimeter of the park in an automobile secured by Wolfgang Fürstner. He had also provided such assorted items as a pair of Mausers and ammunition, a folding Hirschkrone paratrooper knife, and several lengths of piano wire.

David had brought Tom in yesterday afternoon. He was the one person David knew he could count on. "And all this time I thought you were just . . ." He was stunned by David's revelations and only rebuked his roommate for not calling on him sooner. They had both spent the night away from the Olympic Village, in a small dive in the heart of the red-light district, where no identification was required and no questions were asked.

"How long do you think she'll be?" Tom asked.

"She called an hour ago and said to meet her here." David looked at his watch. It was just after 7:00 A.M. "I hope she's okay."

Just then Ali emerged from the dense trees and walked quickly over to the car. It was obvious she hadn't had much sleep. She climbed in the back seat. David turned around. "Well?"

"They've taken her to a castle called Wewelsberg in Westphalia about a hundred and fifty miles from here," she breathlessly reported.

"A castle? Are you sure?" said David.

She nodded, rubbing her eyes. "The word came directly from one of Canaris's best contacts in the SS."

"Why there?" asked Tom.

"It's an SS stronghold. Himmler wanted to create a proper home for his Teutonic Knights. Round table and everything. They've been rebuilding it on the site of an ancient fortress." Fürstner had provided them with maps of the entire country, which David was now digging out. "The closest town is called Paderborn," Ali added.

A scowl came over Tom's face. "How do we know what Canaris tells us is true?"

"He's old school," Ali explained. "He hates Himmler and the SS and all that they stand for. And he's a direct rival of Heydrich's. He'd do anything to discredit them in Hitler's eyes, as long as it doesn't implicate him. Admittedly it's totally self-serving."

"There's a certain comfort dealing with self-serving people," said David. "If you understand their motives, then you know you can trust them."

"Shouldn't we tell Hargreaves what we're doing?" said Ali.

David shook his head. "I'm sure Wolfgang will do that for us. Anyway, I'm not going to wait around for some committee in London to sort itself out and decide what the best policy is. The main concern of the British at this point is to make sure Miranda doesn't keep working for the Germans. Well, they've got that. My concerns are different. I'm not going to let them wait for the SS to do the rest of their job for them." He paused, then asked Ali, "So what else did Canaris tell you?"

"His service has been putting together a dossier on this place and what goes on there ever since Himmler started building it. I think the original idea was to prove to Hitler that Himmler was crazy and obsessed with all this knights and armor mumbo jumbo. Anyway, he thinks they're probably keeping her in a cell in the old dungeon area of the castle. Most of the space down there has been turned into a basement for the kitchen and storerooms, so a corridor connects the two." Ali brought out a large sheet of paper and unfolded it to reveal a draftsman's diagram. "Canaris gave me this."

"That's sensational!" said David, leaning over to give her a huge smacking kiss. "You always come through."

"We do our best," said Ali.

"That is great," Tom said. "But how do we get in? If you'll remember from your military history, the chief purpose of castles is to keep people *out*."

"Yeah," said David. "The only way the siegers at Harlech finally got in was by bribing the gatekeeper. I have a feeling this one might not be so easy to crack."

"True," said Ali, then waited a beat before adding, "Unless, for instance, you happened to know that the local bakery delivers bread and rolls every morning at exactly five o'clock so they're fresh for breakfast."

David and Tom looked at each other, then simultaneously turned to Ali. "Are you sure?" they said in unison.

"I didn't stay up all night for nothing," Ali contended. "By the way, Keegan, you owe me!"

They dropped her off at the Bristol, and it was as painful as any parting either of them had known.

"You take care of yourselves," she insisted, doing her best to draw out the moment before she'd have to leave the car and send them on their way.

"We will," David promised. "You're clear on the rest of the plan?"

She nodded, blinking back her tears. "I'll be praying for you every minute. And I'm not exactly a religious girl."

"Thanks," said Tom dryly. "We'll definitely need it with this screwup running the show."

"Well, just try to keep him out of trouble," Ali said imploringly.

"Yeah, well . . ." She leaned over the back of the seat and the three of them hugged tightly and wordlessly. Then she got out of the car, and David and Tom drove off into the Berlin morning.

"You know," said Tom as they reached the city limits, "it's not that I don't trust you. But I think I'd feel a whole lot better about this thing if I were working with someone who'd also won a gold medal."

Westphalia

She woke up in a small room with only a bed, a wooden chair, and a toilet. Her head still felt fuzzy. The walls and ceiling and floor were all of stone, and there was a drain in the center of the floor, as if it had been a shower. The only opening in the walls was a locked wooden door with a tiny window, and when she got up to look through it, all she could see was blackness.

She sank back down onto the bed. She remembered very little after those two men had stopped her as she was leaving the institute. In fact, she remembered nothing from then until two minutes ago when she woke up. She wondered how long she'd been sleeping.

She thought she should be hungry, but her stomach felt tense and queazy. The toilet across the room was something of a reassurance. Her head was taking a long time to clear. Her right arm was swollen and sore a couple of inches above the elbow. She didn't remember hurting it.

Miranda looked around the room once more and sighed. She crossed her legs under her on the bed. She leaned back against the cold stone wall and stared blankly at the opposite one as she waited forlornly to see what her fate would be.

She didn't know how much more time had passed before she heard the door open. A rather pale and thin but pleasant-looking man in a gray business suit came in.

"Mind if I sit down?" he asked. He looked to be in his late twenties. Miranda was taken aback by the request and only shrugged her consent.

"My name is Walter Schellenberg. Is everything all right?"

How do you answer a question like that?

Without waiting for a reply he said, "I'm sure you're confused about what's happened and where you are."

Miranda nodded apprehensively.

Schellenberg's eyes were sympathetic. "I thought as much. Those two fellows who picked you up can do as they're told well enough," he said, "but they're not exactly long on sensitivity. By the way, would you like something to eat?"

Miranda shook her head no.

"Well, I've already asked to have some food prepared. It'll be here for whenever you feel hungry. I want you to keep your strength. Are you shivering? You look as if you're cold. I'll have some blankets sent in, too. Good. Now, as to substantive matters. You may be feeling a little light-headed. It's nothing to worry about. You were given an injection to help you relax and sleep. The way you feel is a perfectly normal reaction. Also, your parents have been informed that you're safe and that everything's fine."

"Is it?" she asked.

He looked at her as if stung by her lack of trust. "Yes, of course. You're here for your own protection."

She gave him a quizzical glance.

"There have been several attempts made recently on prominent scientists, particularly at the Kaiser Wilhelm Institute. We're very concerned about that. Perhaps you heard about Dr. Abraham Behrman's disappearance?"

Miranda nodded again.

"We'd like you to tell us what you know about that so we can help protect you."

"Where am I?"

"A secure house where none of the people who might wish to harm you can get to you."

"Where?"

"Someplace safe. I can assure you, we're working diligently on Dr. Behrman's case, and we won't let the same thing happen to you. I want you to help us make sure we can keep that promise."

This was all very confusing, particularly in her current state. She didn't know what to say but was relieved she was being treated so courteously. She'd already scared herself half to death conjuring up all sorts of horrible things that might be done to her.

There was a knock on the door. "Enter," said Schellenberg. "Oh, here's the food. Excellent."

A man in a white kitchen suit wheeled in a cart filled with covered silver platters. "Good. Just put it over there," Schellenberg instructed. The man bowed his head once and then left. "You sure you wouldn't like anything now?"

"No, thank you," said Miranda.

"Very well then." Schellenberg crossed one knee comfortably over the other and clasped his hands in his lap. "Now, you work for Dr. Otto Hahn. Is that right?"

"Yes."

"Very good. A highly respected scientist. And I know he thinks very highly of you, too. We have a copy of your personal record. Now, what can you tell me about Dr. Behrman?"

That came from nowhere. "Just that he's a very nice, kindly man," she said. "I like him very much and wish he hadn't gone away."

"Of course. Do you know where he went?"

"No."

"What about Karl Linderhoff?"

"What about him?"

Schellenberg gave her a knowing wink. "I understand he's your, ah, boyfriend. Is that right?"

"I guess you could say that."

"And you knew that he worked with Dr. Behrman?"

"Yes, certainly."

Schellenberg paused for a moment and gave her a look of concern. "Miranda . . . may I call you that?"

"Yes," she said anxiously.

He uncrossed his legs and addressed her straight on. "I'm on your side. I want you to know that. I want to do everything I can to help and protect you. But there are other people here who are very upset about what's going on and don't have a lot of patience. You and I have a good, strong, trusting relationship. But unless those other people see some progress from us soon, they're not going to let us continue working together." He shrugged helplessly. "And then it's out of my hands. I'd hate for that to happen."

Her gut was suddenly turning to water. She hoped she didn't need to use the toilet in his presence. "What do you mean?"

He waved her concerns away with his hand. "Let's not think about that," he said kindly. "I'll try to hold them off as long as I can. I'm just going to need a little help from you."

Twenty minutes later Walter Schellenberg emerged from the cell and said to the aide waiting for him in the dark corridor, "We're not going to crack her with kindness, I don't think. At least not in the time we've got."

"Drugs?" asked the young man in uniform.

"Not reliable enough. And we've been told we can't take a chance on destroying her memory. Let her sit and stew for a while. Then tell Obergruppenführer Heydrich she's his whenever he's ready."

Lower Saxony

It was hard going through the rugged German countryside. Tom did most of the driving while David followed the maps. Other than refuel the car once, they didn't take the time to stop.

As they were approaching the Harz Mountains near Blankenburg, it started to rain. By the time they were up in the narrow, winding mountain passes, the skies had opened up. A couple of times they nearly ran off the road. When David looked down at the sheer drop below, he wished that he hadn't. It would be quite an irony to fail the mission because they'd ended up at the bottom of some ditch.

"Is this what Clausewitz meant by 'friction' when he wrote about his theory of war?" Tom asked. "No matter how prepared you are and how well you plan, there's always going to be some unpredictable friction that creeps in during the actual battle that you couldn't plan for and had no way of predicting and that can alter the entire outcome."

"Try not to think about it," said David. "Just keep driving."

Westphalia

She was left alone again for a long time, during which Miranda picked at her food. It was a gourmet meal—ham and turkey and goose, salad and rolls, and wine and cider. But no matter how much she tried to tell herself that she needed her strength, she just couldn't eat.

She'd done her best not to tell anything important to that Schellenberg fellow. He seemed like a nice man, and he had treated her well. But it wasn't as if he'd offered to let her leave. And there was always that veiled threat that if she didn't cooperate and tell them what they wanted, the "others" would come in, and they wouldn't be quite so "reasonable."

But there was a secret she had to protect. In her type of scientific research you can take one small wrong turn, follow it along for months, then end up long, long afterward at a complete dead end. That was what she was counting on to happen when they found her "new" notes. And after what Dr. Behrman had told her and what she had seen in the camp, this was a secret she was willing to die to protect.

Though it certainly would be lovely if it didn't come to that, she thought wistfully. What a glorious, impossible fantasy it now seemed to be able to run away with David. She got a warm, moist feeling just thinking about it . . . and him.

It was true that it had been a shock when he told her that he'd been "assigned" to her by the British. And the slap she had given him had been genuine. She had felt like an object, cheap and betrayed. But with a night to think about it, she had realized that he'd had no choice. None of them had. Not David, not she, not Karl. And no matter what she did as she lay in her bed that night, pounding the pillow in frustration and anger, she couldn't deny what had happened between them, the way he'd touched her soul as nobody had before and the way she'd touched his in return.

She felt so wretched that her last meeting with him had had to be the way it was. But she couldn't have risked telling him all the things she felt and what she planned to do. If she had, he might be here in the cell right next to her. Still, it was horrible to reflect that now he would leave Germany thinking she hated him and she would never get the chance to say how very much she loved him.

The door opened again. This time it was a guard in a black SS uniform. "Obergruppenführer Heydrich will be here shortly to continue the examination," he announced. "In the meantime, you are to remove your clothing so it can be searched."

Miranda was struck dumb by the order. Her eyes widened in fear. What could they possibly expect to find? "Everything?" she gasped.

"Everything," the guard stated bluntly.

"No, I won't!" she cried adamantly. "Bring Herr Schellenberg back here."

"If you do not follow instructions and cooperate, I am to do it for you," the guard informed her.

She waited for him to leave or turn his back or look away. But he stood there staring straight at her, and the expression on his face indicated he didn't expect to wait very long.

Trembling, Miranda began taking off her clothes. She laid each article folded as neatly as she could on the wooden chair. It seemed important to do it this way. It was the only dignity she could preserve. Dispassionately the guard evaluated each item as she placed it on the chair. He finally appeared to raise his eyebrows with interest as she sat down on the edge of the bed to peel off one stocking and then the other, and when she stood up again to remove her bra and panties, she glared back at him as if he were the personification of all that was evil in the world.

She stood with her hands folded in front of her. Of course, the guard found nothing. When the examination seemed to be complete, she asked, "May I get dressed now?"

"Remain as you are until told otherwise," the guard ordered.

Now she understood the sole purpose of the exercise. It was to humiliate and weaken her, to further unequalize the equation, to make her feel vulnerable and defenseless. Well, it had certainly worked. She felt all those things.

On his way out the guard removed the food cart.

*   *   *

Somehow, they made it. In spite of mountains and rain and crazy German drivers. They crossed the Weser at the gabled city of Hamelin, where the Pied Piper was supposed to have driven all the rats into the river. When the townspeople didn't ante up the reward he'd been promised, he played his pipes again and lured all the children out of their houses to come away with him, and they were never seen again. With slight modifications tailored to the existing circumstances, David decided that that would be a very valuable talent to have around now.

They arrived in Paderborn around dusk, after hours of negotiating the narrow lanes cut through the verdant Westphalian foothills. And when they finally saw the massive Romanesque tower of Paderborn Cathedral materializing before them, they knew that the opening phase of their mission had been successfully completed.

"The *easiest* phase," Tom was quick to point out.

The first thing they did was to find a hardware store, where they purchased rope and the other supplies they might need. Payment was no problem as David still had a large number of reichsmarks left from Hargreaves's "expense account".

"If we get out of this alive, I'm going to cash in every pfennig he gave me and spend the winter in St. Moritz," David said. "They're going to have one monumental accounting mess."

"Yeah, that'll show 'em!" said Tom.

There didn't seem to be a huge choice of eating possibilities in town, but they looked around until they found a fairly crowded Ratskeller where no one would take any particular notice of them. David was careful to speak only German, to which Tom would nod and mumble from time to time as if he knew what David was saying. The food wasn't particularly good, but then they weren't particularly hungry either. They ate because they knew they had to and didn't know when they would next get the chance.

The next several hours were devoted to recon. For the first time both men were trying to make practical use of all the strategic theory they'd been taught at the Point. "Time spent on reconnaissance is never wasted" was the catchphrase of military science.

Leaving the town of Paderborn, they located the bakery. It was a small shop along a row of quaint half-timbered buildings. The smells of baking bread and cakes were almost tempting enough to lure them inside. Out back of the place they found what must have been the delivery vehicle, an aging Opel pickup with a closed back to keep the bread warm.

Then they drove southwest toward the castle itself, set in a rugged area between dense hilly forests and the vast Westphalian plain. The romantic, mystical region was dotted with medieval fortresses and fabled ruins. But Wewelsberg was different. For one thing, it was much larger than the rest. It had been built by a knight called Wewel von Buren who had used it as his outpost of armed resistance against the invading Huns, a piece of symbolism that couldn't have been lost on its modern patron, Heinrich Himmler.

David and Tom got out of the car and stood silently on an overlooking hill. The castle loomed before them, imposing and threatening against the gray night sky, the dark, unspeakable territory lurking deep in the murky heart of every fairy tale. Just to look at it sent a chill through David.

But there was another way the castle was different. Despite the age of its foundation and battlements, Wewelsberg looked "new" and "lived in." Inside, modern men the same age as he and Tom, of the same profession were going about their business as if living in a castle in this day and age were a perfectly normal occurrence. Inside—and he prayed Canaris was right about where—was Miranda. It was a bizarre anachronism to think that this citadel of thirteenth-century warfare held a woman whose mind might hold the key to the warfare of the twenty-first.

His own mind recoiled from imagining what they might be doing to her in there. "Boys like you can tell yourselves you're going to be heroes and you're not going to crack," Hargreaves had said to him. "But believe me, eventually you will." But it wasn't he who had to be the hero. And for the moment all he could do was sit by helplessly and wait.

Sitting naked and shivering on the bed, Miranda tried to steel herself for the next confrontation. How should she act? Did it show more or less composure to try to cover herself with her hands? Should she be meek and docile or bold and defiant? And when it actually happened, would she even be strong enough to make that determination, or would she fall apart in uncontrollable terror?

She didn't have to wait long to find out. The door opened again. A tall man with straight blond hair and sharp, angular features strode into the room. He had narrow, haughty eyes and thin lips that seemed to her unmistakably cruel. He was wearing a black SS uniform, which didn't do anything to alleviate the impression of cruelty. Under one arm he carried a black leather riding crop, and Miranda wondered whether he intended to use it on her.

"I am Obergruppenführer Reinhard Heydrich," he announced in a very businesslike manner. Instinctively she rose to her feet.

"We don't have a lot of time, so I'll come right to the point. We need certain information about you and your relationship to the Jew Dr. Abraham Behrman and what you might know about his disappearance. We will obtain this information in the most efficient manner available to us. What that manner is will be up to you."

Miranda fought for self-control.

"You were known to be associated with Behrman's assistant, Karl Linderhoff."

"Yes, that's right," she said timidly. *Stick to the truth wherever possible,* she told herself.

"What did he tell you about their work together?"

"Nothing."

"You were also known to be close with the Jew."

Miranda nodded.

"You were seen repeatedly outside his office on various occasions."

"I was worried about him and wanted to know where he was."

"You'd do better than to worry about the fate of Jews," he advised her. "And did you find out where he was?"

"No."

"You were also seen associating with an American athlete, David Keegan, on repeated occasions at the Kaiser Wilhelm Institute and the Olympic Stadium."

"He was a friend of Karl's."

"And you were also seen entering the Behrman house in the Grunewald and speaking with his wife."

This last comment sent a stab of panic through her heart. She clenched her fists for courage.

"What did you speak about?"

"I asked her where her husband was. She said she didn't know."

"And why were you so interested?"

"I was worried."

"Tell me about this David Keegan."

"I've told you everything I know."

"Quite frankly, Fräulein Wolff, I don't think you have, and I'm losing my patience. What have the two of you been talking about?" Heydrich swished the riding crop through the air.

He took a step toward her, and Miranda tensed herself to be hit. Instead, he continued to the door, opened it, and signaled whoever was outside to come in.

Two uniformed guards entered and brought in a large iron receptacle. It looked like a caldron or cooking pot. In it was an iron fireplace poker heating over glowing coals. Miranda shuddered. The two men carried the pot by its wooden handles to protect their hands from burning. The poker also had a wooden handle.

Miranda's eyes went wide with crazed fright, and her heart pounded wildly in her chest. She had counted on a beating and had bravely convinced herself she could withstand it. Even if they beat her till she bled, she would not tell them anything. She recalled the times as a girl she'd been whipped by one or the other of her parents and had refused to cry out of sheer obstinacy and pride. But what these people apparently intended to do to her had been beyond her very imagining, and despite all her self-preparation, she was completely unprepared to deal with it.

"The choice is yours, Fräulein Wolff," Heydrich intoned.

But there was no choice. About that she had already firmly resolved. So she fainted.

When she came to, Walter Schellenberg was hovering over her, kneeling down and cradling her head in his hands. Reinhard Heydrich stood some distance away, impatiently leaning against the doorframe. He continued slapping the riding crop against the side of his leather boot.

"Miranda, please," Schellenberg was saying desperately, "tell them what they want to know. They're serious, and they won't stop until you tell them. I beg you."

"I've told everything I know," she said as calmly as she could manage and wondered what it must feel like to have a red-hot piece of iron held against the skin.

Schellenberg rose and addressed Heydrich breathlessly. "Please, Reinhard, I know she's going to cooperate. She's in shock. Just give her a little time." He was wringing his hands. He looked back beseechingly at Miranda for confirmation, but she just closed her eyes to block it all out as long as possible.

She opened them again to see Heydrich looking back at him with disgust. Then he signaled the two guards to remove the caldron. Schellenberg followed him out of the cell, saying, "I know we can work this out reasonably." He turned to Miranda and begged, "Please don't make a liar out of me."

As soon as they were gone and the door was closed behind them, she collapsed into the fit of hopeless sobbing that she hadn't wanted them to see.

When the heavy oak door was shut, Heydrich clasped his hands behind his back and began walking down the hall. "Good work," he said to Schellenberg, who walked next to him.

"You, too. I'm convinced she knows where Behrman is, and one way or another she's going to tell us soon. I wouldn't be surprised to hear her pounding on the door and begging to talk."

"Yes, I'm sure you're right," Heydrich agreed. A rueful smile crossed his lips as they continued walking. "Still, there is something about being in a castle that inspires one with the castle builders' own methods. In a way, it would be a shame not to be able to use them."

Schellenberg nodded, then said, "You should know in your planning, though, that the Reich Scientific Office is quite interested in Fräulein Wolff in her own right. The führer, as you know, doesn't set much store in this atomistic theory. He's much more interested in ideas he can grasp, like bigger, stronger soldiers. But the scientific people do. So whatever it takes to break her, they'd like something left when we finish."

THIRTY-FOUR

Sunday, August 16

Miranda spent a cold and sleepless night. At least she thought it was night. She'd lost all sense of time and couldn't be sure. Fretfully she huddled under her only blanket, waiting for her tormentors to return. Every sound outside the door sent a chill down her spine and simultaneously made her break out in an icy sweat. She squeezed her arms tight against her body to keep warm as she pictured what they would do to her. She finally understood the purpose of the drain in the floor.

Her clothes remained folded on the chair where she'd placed them, a constant reminder of the rewards that could await her—that she'd be allowed to get dressed again, and fed, and not be hurt, and treated like a normal person as soon as she exercised good judgment and came back to her senses.

All her life till now had receded into a hazy, distant memory. She wondered if her parents and brother would be worried about her and what, if anything, they'd actually been told. It was almost comical how little they knew. She supposed that was her own fault. She had come home after the rescue of Dr. Behrman, and they'd asked her how her day had gone. She'd just shrugged and said, "All right," and they must have thought she was just being her normally sullen, brooding self.

For the first time she missed them. Missed everything that had been and everything that now never would be. All the years of possibility, all the opportunities, all the excitement and new experience that would cease to exist for her.

It had taken all night, but Miranda had finally faced the prospect that she was going to die.

*   *   *

Erich Heuer loaded the last large sack into the back of the truck and then climbed into the cab. Helga was already inside waiting for him. She was in the middle of a yawn that she turned into a smile of greeting when he sat down beside her.

He was just coming on his shift, and she'd been baking all night. She would ride with him while he made his deliveries. Then he'd take her home and come back to the store in time for opening. This brief overlap was the only thing that made these predawn mornings at all bearable for him.

Her hair was flecked with white specks of flour, and as he drew close to her on the seat, all the delicious bakery smells still clung to her. As long as he'd worked there, and as much as he'd never gotten used to getting up this early, Erich could still associate those smells with sweet and pleasant things.

Like Helga.

"Someday soon I'd like to roll you in dough," he said as they drove off.

"You're impossible!" she declared, dismissing him with a brush of her hand.

"I'll bet you'd love it," he came back. "You can't fool me. In fact, as you sit there every day squeezing the dough between your fingers, you must be thinking of me and where you'd like to put it."

"Honestly!" said Helga. "Where do you come up with these things?"

"I know where I'd like to put it!" he announced waggishly as he reached over and stuck a hand up under her skirt.

"Stop that!" she shrieked, squirming and slapping him away. "You'll get us both killed!"

He withdrew his hand, but only as far as the lower part of her thigh above the stocking, where she graciously let it remain. "You can't convince me you don't like it."

"You only have one thing on your mind." She playfully scolded him.

"And you don't?"

She assumed a tone of great propriety. "There is a time and a place for everything."

"Just tell me the time and the place and I'll be there," Erich promised.

She rolled her eyes in a "boys will be boys" expression.

On the road through the woods that led to the castle a car was stopped ahead of them. It was just at the place where the rock had been cut away, and there was only room for one vehicle to pass at a time.

Erich slowed the Opel to a stop. He leaned out the window to see what was happening. What a place for a car to get stuck.

The driver got out and walked back toward them, shaking his head. He came over and leaned on the window. "Sorry," he said, looking in. "I don't know what's wrong. All of a sudden the thing just died."

"Well, look," said Erich, "I'm in a hurry. I've got deliveries to make. So we'll just have to move it somehow out of the way."

The man nodded, and as Erich opened the door to get out and help push, he suddenly saw a gun pointed at his head.

"All right," the man said. "Get out slowly and keep your mouth shut."

Helga yelped in terror as they both noticed another man at her window. He was also holding a gun.

"I have no money," Erich pleaded. "We have nothing of value."

"That's a matter of opinion," the man responded. Erich looked to Helga, horrified.

"No, we're not going to do that," the man said impatiently. "But if you don't cooperate, we are prepared to kill you, so you decide. Now get out."

The two bakery colleagues did as they were told. The two men were speaking to each other urgently in low tones in a language that sounded like English. They opened the trunk of their car and brought out ropes, with which they tied the two of them up, hands and feet. They also gagged Helga.

"You're next," the man said, "but first, you're going to give me some information."

"Whatever you say," Erich spluttered, "only don't hurt us."

"I want you to tell me exactly what happens when you make your delivery to the castle. Step by step. Who you see. Where you go. Everything."

Erich nodded in dread.

"Then, if it turns out you're telling the truth and I come out safely, then we let you go. If not, my friend here will kill you both. Very simple. You understand?"

Erich indicated that he did.

* * *

Ten minutes later, with the pair bound and gagged and safely in the trunk, Tom said to David, "It should be pretty straightforward. Down the steps to the kitchen, down the hall to the cell, open the door, back up and out. If it all goes well and according to plan, you'll both be out safe and sound in seven minutes."

"Let's hope so."

"Now I'll ask you one more time. Are you sure you won't let me go in with you?"

"I'm sure," said David appreciatively. "With two people, that's twice as much chance for detection and twice as much chance something will go wrong. Besides, I need you here and ready to move as soon as we come out."

"I feel you're doing all the hard parts."

"No, I'm not," David assured him. "Remember what we've been taught. This is a team effort, and the only thing that counts is the result."

"I knew you were going to give me some dumb Olympic analogy," said Tom. They stared at each other silently. Then Tom said, "Good luck, David," just as he might have before an athletic meet. "Time to go out there and do it!"

David drove across the lowered drawbridge of Wewelsberg Castle and felt as Jonah must have felt when he descended into the belly of the whale. The heavy oak and iron grillwork of the medieval portcullis raised as the delivery truck pulled up into the gatehouse. David was relieved that the guard simply waved him through. But that, he decided, was no more than the equivalent of the whale's swallow. When it came time to get out, Jonah had had considerably more difficulty. The portcullis slowly descended behind David's truck. Now, even if he had wanted to, there was no turning back.

The deserted inner courtyard was a large triangular expanse. It was covered in paving stones that violently jounced the Opel's badly sprung suspension. The castle's walls and towers were black against the dark sky, and it took David several moments to adjust his eyes. He could see occasional human silhouettes against some of the narrow windows. All in all, it was weirdly quiet and peaceful.

Stay calm, he warned himself. *Do this by the book.* He took a couple of deep breaths.

He brought the truck over to the doorway set in the corner of the far wall, just as the delivery boy had told him. The two walls cast overlapping shadows which turned the area into a murky void. David carefully angled the vehicle so that the back would be right up against the door.

He opened the back door of the truck, pulled out the first sack, and hefted it onto his shoulder. He carried it down the spiral stone staircase that led to the basement level. The kid said the standard procedure was to bring the delivery straight into the pantry. The only open door he'd pass along the way was the one into the kitchen. This first trip would be a good scouting run.

It turned out to be just as the kid had described it. As he walked past the kitchen door, he called in a brief, guttural greeting to the two cooks. Without turning around from their stoves, they waved back. David continued on to the pantry, set down the sack of bread amid the pile of stores, then went back into the corridor.

He looked down in the opposite direction. It seemed to go just where Canaris had said it would. Then he reversed himself and climbed back up the stairs.

The second trip seemed almost routine. The cooks hardly even noticed him. He didn't bother saying anything to the kitchen workers.

When he got to the pantry this time, he put down the sack next to the first one. But this time he quickly looked around, then opened it and removed from the top what he would need for the next phase of the mission. He undid his buckle and slipped the Mauser's leather holster onto his belt. Most of the other supplies fitted into his pockets. The two lengths of rope he wound around his shoulder.

Returning to the darkened hallway, he followed it in the opposite direction. He stayed close to the damp stone wall in case anyone happened to pass by.

As soon as he made the first turn, he knew he must be in the right place. A bored-looking guard in a black SS uniform was slowly ambling the length of the corridor. In the middle of his circuit was the wooden door that led to the cell.

David paused a moment to steady his nerves. He peered around the corner and waited until the guard turned his back. He removed a length of piano wire from his pocket, put on his gloves, and formed the wire into a loop. Then he quietly came up behind the guard, quickly falling in to match him stride for stride. He began making up two strides for each of the guard's one, and soon he was right behind him.

With all his energy directed into one decisive movement, David lunged for the guard's back. The instant he made contact, he clamped his hand over the man's mouth and deftly slipped the wire loop over his head.

"One tug and you're a dead man," David whispered in German. "Now give me the keys."

The guard tried to protest, but David pulled the wire loop tighter as a warning. With a wrenching gasp the guard also saw his own pistol now pointing at him. He frantically fished through his tunic pocket until he produced the key ring.

"Right," David said, then turned the gun around and struck the butt across his adversary's temple. He caught the man under the arms as his knees buckled, and as he laid him out on the floor, David could see that he was out cold. He unwound the two lengths of rope from his shoulder and efficiently tied the unconscious man's wrists and ankles. He fitted a gag tightly in place. Then, as a final flair, he connected the ends of the wire noose to the ankle binding, making it impossible for the man to struggle to his feet without choking himself. *That should keep him for a while.*

David stood up, removed his gloves, and fumbled with the keys until he found one that fitted the iron door lock. He pulled the latch, and the door groaned on its hinges.

He held his breath as he pushed the door open. There was Miranda, naked, wet-faced, and cowering behind the room's only bed.

"David!" she gasped.

Thank God. He wiped away his own spontaneous tears of gratitude. She had already rushed into his arms before he could inquire, "What are you doing like this?"

"Don't ask," she said as he could feel her whole body tremble against his. He couldn't fight the erotic surge as he felt her nakedness next to him.

"Well, hurry up and put your clothes on."

"There's nothing I'd rather do," she assured him.

While she was getting dressed, David dragged the guard into the cell. She buttoned her skirt, then sat down to put on her stockings.

"Forget the damn stockings!" he exhorted her. "Let's get out of here."

She got up immediately and stuffed them into the pocket of her sweater. David took her by the hand and led her out. He locked the door after them.

"This way." He pulled her along down the corridor.

As they neared the kitchen door, he said, "Now get behind me until we clear it."

That hazard passed, they climbed the circular staircase to the waiting truck. Its back doors were still opened as David had left them.

He helped her in and closed the door immediately after her. He climbed into the cab and started up the engine. Everything according to plan, just as Tom said. *Two more minutes, and we're out of here.*

Just as David was about to put the truck in gear, he saw an SS guard on patrol with a German shepherd. They crossed the courtyard together and stopped in front of him. The guard raised his hand in a friendly wave, then moved his head around to get a better view into the Opel's cab. David grinned back at him.

"Where is your girl friend this morning?" the guard asked. "We don't get to see many pretty faces around here." He squinted into the front window. "Wait a minute! You're not Erich."

"No," David admitted. "Erich's sick today."

"I don't think I've ever seen you in town," said the guard. The German shepherd growled menacingly.

This must be what Clausewitz meant by friction.

"Wait another minute!" said the guard. "I know. You must be Erich's cousin from Düsseldorf! The one he said was coming."

"Yes, that's right," said David, smiling with relief.

"He's never mentioned a cousin to me," the guard said severely. He blew his whistle. The castle seemed to come suddenly alive.

Oh, shit, thought David. His first instinct was to make a run for it, to throw the truck into reverse, turn around, then drive like mad straight for the gatehouse. But the portcullis blocked the only exit. Castles were designed for a specific purpose.

The guard gripped the door handle and pulled it. Through the open window, David dropped him and his dog with two shots from his silencer-equipped Mauser. He raced around to the back of the truck and ripped open the door. "Come on!" he said to Miranda, yanking her out.

There was nowhere else to turn. They couldn't possibly scale the walls. They couldn't let themselves be surrounded in the courtyard.

So they raced back through the courtyard door, back down the staircase, and past the kitchen. The cooks looked up at the turmoil.

"This way." David led her past the pantry, around the corner, and back toward the cell.

"What are we doing?"

"Improvising," he said as they turned a second corner.

There the corridor ended abruptly at an iron-studded door.

David tried it. It was locked. Maybe one of the keys would work, but he didn't have time to try. He pulled the Mauser out of his belt and aimed it directly at the lock. "Stand back!" he said, and fired. Ragged pieces of oak splintered out at them. David rushed in and jerked the door open.

They found themselves in a large, quiet room. They were still underground, so there were no windows and it was dark. But there were angled holes in the vaulted ceiling that channeled in the moonlit sky with an eerie glow. David kept his gun drawn and listened warily for sounds. Nothing.

"This place is creepy," said Miranda, gasping to catch her breath.

They were surrounded by stone pedestals almost as tall as they were. On each one rested a black metal urn emblazoned with a red swastika. It was obviously some sacred burial crypt for the SS. There were no other doors, but a staircase chiseled out of the solid rock led up one wall.

"It's our only choice," said David. He grabbed Miranda's hand again and pulled her along.

They reached another door at the top of the stairs. David tried it. This one wasn't locked. He pressed the latch. It opened into a massive dining hall. It seemed half as big as a football field and was ringed on all sides by a carved wooden balcony. A wooden staircase along the side wall rose more than twenty feet to meet it. Flags, crests, and full suits of armor belonging to the original Teutonic Knights lined the other three walls. In the center of the room was an immense round table, straight out of King Arthur.

As had become his instant habit, David immediately looked for a way out. There was a double set of doors at the far end of the room. He and Miranda made a dash for them but halted suddenly as they saw a contingent of SS guards rush through at them.

David braced into the firing position and pulled off two shots in quick succession. The first two men fell to the floor. The other three fanned out to either side of the room. Dragging Miranda by the hand, David rushed forward and dived for the table. Shots from the invading troops rang out. Several ricocheted off the wall and buzzed above David's and Miranda's heads.

With his outstretched foot, David kicked over four of the heavy chairs and formed a barricade. From that position he could shoot in both directions and keep the invaders at bay.

It went on like that for several minutes. But he knew time was against them. They were pinned down, and SS reinforcements would arrive any moment. He would have to make a decisive move quickly.

He estimated the distance between themselves and the stairs up to the balcony. He didn't know where it led, but it was the only possibility. It was flanked on each side by a standing suit of armor. Both the helmeted mannequins held spears. One of them also carried a studded mace with a wooden handle by a heavy metal chain. He made a quick mental note and rehearsed the next step in his mind. The underside of the stairs would at least provide some minimal temporary protection.

"I'm going to try to make it over there," he said to Miranda. He handed her the Mauser. "I want you to take this, and as soon as I move, I want you to start firing at those men. Got it?"

Miranda nodded.

"Ever used one of these before?"

She scrunched up her face into a deprecating frown. "Sure. All the time. Especially in my work."

"Well," David said, "I can't think of any better situation to practice in."

"Thanks." She picked up the gun with both hands and tried to aim.

Four more soldiers rushed in, followed by two officers. They were wearing open shirts without tunics, obviously having been quickly roused out of bed.

David knew he couldn't wait any longer. In the split second it took the new men to get their bearings, he sprang. Miranda opened fire on the incoming troops. Out of the corner of his eye he could see one of them clutch his shoulder and drop his gun. *Okay, Miranda, keep it up.*

David scrambled to his feet and lunged in the direction of the balcony stairs. Too late he realized his path was blocked by one of the upturned chairs and two long side benches. *More friction*, he thought. Enough to cost him his life.

There was no choice. Instinctively he planted his right foot firmly on the floor, leaned forward, then launched into the hurdling position. He cleared the heavy chair easily and touched the floor in time to spring over the first bench. As he sailed over the second, it felt as natural as if he'd been on the track. It was over in a split second. He came down and caromed into the wall before the guards could draw aim on him.

Flattening against the closest suit of armor, he indicated to Miranda to run behind the overturned chair, then crawl under the benches.

"When I give you the signal," he whispered. He gripped the armor chest plate with both hands, nodded in her direction, then sent the metal body suit cascading into the expanse between himself and the table.

As soon as he did it, Miranda jumped to her feet. She ran behind the chair and quickly squirmed under the two benches like a marine on an obstacle course. She came up and darted into his arms.

More shots rang out and pinged off the armor before the guards realized what David had done. The clattering metal wreck had created enough of a diversion to get her safely across.

Together they huddled behind the staircase. That gave them about another five seconds of protection, David decided. "Who are those two?"

"Heydrich and Schellenberg," Miranda said.

So that was the Blond Beast.

Just at that moment Heydrich gave a signal, and the troops in front of him who had just come through the door began advancing.

David grabbed the gun from Miranda and fired point-blank in their direction.

The Mauser clicked weakly. Out of ammunition. And the only weapon he had on his person was the knife. *Fuck*. Not much use at this range and no match for a bullet.

He looked desperately around him. Without hesitation he grasped the spear from the second armored figure's hand. He cocked his arm back and hurled it across the expanse of the room. It sailed through the air with a singing whine and embedded solidly in the chest of the leading attacker.

The impact sent the man crashing into the two men behind him, whose shots wildly hit the ceiling.

As the fourth regrouped to fire, David took the mace from the other hand of the suit of armor. He pivoted around once and flung it straight at the attacker's head. It hit him squarely just above the right eye. A horrible scream and the sound of cracking bone echoed sickeningly throughout the great hall.

Not exactly an Olympic record, but not bad either considering the hammer throw wasn't one of his sports.

But he knew this had bought him only a few more seconds. In any battle of force they were destined to lose. What could he do to change the equation?

Time to play the one ace in the hole.

"Heydrich!" he shouted in German. He grabbed Miranda sharply by the arm and wrenched her into a semicrouch. At the same time he brought his knife up to her neck. She let out a whimper of fright.

The room grew momentarily quiet.

Maintaining the knife at her throat, he came around from behind the stairs and tentatively took the first step. "If any of you come an inch closer, I kill the girl!" David yelled. "Don't play me for a fool. We know who she is and what she does. I'm warning you! I'll kill her!"

He brought the knife up below her chin and pressed the razor-honed point into the skin, deep enough to draw blood. It trickled down her neck for the whole room to see.

She screamed frantically, "No! Don't let him do this! Help me! Don't let him kill me!"

"Good work," David whispered to her. "Just stay with me."

"Hold fire!" Schellenberg blurted out.

"Smart thinking," David called to him. Without taking his eyes off them, he began marching Miranda roughly up the stairs. From his position across the room Heydrich glared at them. Schellenberg had a worried, confused expression.

Even if they kill me, maybe this will be enough to keep Miranda alive, David hoped.

They reached the top of the staircase and hurried along half the length of the balcony toward the doorway. The soldiers below stood cautiously at bay. David could see that the door led to a crenellated battlement atop one of the walls.

They emerged onto the wall walk between the great hall and one of the castle's corner towers. Stone merlons projected up at regular intervals along the wall. The sun was just coming up.

David leaned over between two of the merlons and looked down to a jagged rocky outcropping that jutted out about fifteen feet to a moat. But there was no way to reach it without being smashed to pieces on the rock.

At the top of the tower David spied a large red swastika banner atop a flagpole. Its hoisting rope flapped against the pole in the morning wind. The rope was their last chance. If it was long enough, they could use the flagpole as an anchor and scale down the wall.

They raced the length of the wall walk till they reached the opening into the tower. They bounded up the flight of spiral stone steps to the top and from there out onto the tower's parapet.

There they came face-to-face with a guard still on night watch. Immediately he drew his pistol. David drew his knife.

"Charge a gun and move back from a knife" was what the Army taught in hand-to-hand combat.

So David charged, lunging and parrying to keep his opponent from gaining the offensive. David rushed the guard and grabbed his wrist. He squeezed hard on the nerve, forcing him to let go of the pistol. With his elbow David knocked it away and sent it flying over the wall. But at the same time the German had enough presence of mind to go for the knife.

The two men struggled for the weapon, exchanging advantage several times as they knocked each other into the crenellation. As they staggered out into the center of the tower once more, the guard used his superior position to force David to the ground. He bent David's wrist back, and David felt himself losing his grip on the knife's handle.

The guard seized it from him and brought it up in an arc of attack. As David stared into the man's eyes, he knew with a certainty it was the last thing he would ever see in this world.

Then, just as the knife was descending toward his chest, David saw the guard suddenly gasp for breath. His eyes bulged wildly, and his arms began flailing in the air.

David looked up in astonishment, and there he saw Miranda. She was behind the guard, her knee wedged into the center of his back for leverage. And wrapped tightly around his neck was a garrote formed of her two stockings. She was tugging with all her might, and she held him in that position long enough for David to retake the knife.

He plunged it into the guard's rib cage and ripped straight up. Blood gushed in a fountain and splattered both of them. The man convulsed briefly, then collapsed onto the stone pavement.

At the same moment David was overcome by revulsion for the killing and an impossible love for Miranda for making it possible.

They could hear the soldiers from the dining hall already clambering up the stairs after them.

Still clutching the knife, David went to the flagpole. He cut the rope where it looped at the bottom pulley. But as he grabbed the pole for support, it swayed back and forth. *Shit*, he thought again. *It isn't fixed in its receptacle so they can take it down during storms. Or maybe it's that the castle's still under construction. Whatever, it's not going to hold.* He pulled up on the flagstaff, and it came out in his hands. *Double shit.* The soldiers were getting closer. He knew they must be on the wall walk by now.

Then another idea struck him. He leaned over the tower and judged the distance to the moat. He fingered down to the end of the pole. It might give them just the leverage they needed to get beyond the rocks.

"Miranda," he ordered, "grab on to my shoulders, and hold tight. When I say 'three,' we're both going to push off as hard as we can. Got it?"

"Yes."

He aimed the end of the pole at the base of the wall where it met the floor. That would have to serve as the vault box. *Okay*, he told himself, *you don't need height, only distance. But you get only one shot at it.* He hoped the moat was deep enough to absorb their impact.

"Ready?" he said to Miranda. *Auf die Plätze . . . fertig . . .* he thought. "One . . . two . . . *three!*"

Together they pushed off. The pole began its steady rise, carrying them over the wall. When it reached the apex of its arc, David swiveled his hips and kicked strongly away from it, giving them the distance they needed to clear the rocks. With that he let go of the pole. Miranda held on to him for life. They fell straight down and splashed into the muddy moat, touching bottom hard before floating back up to the surface.

David grabbed her in a rescue hold and paddled through scummy water over to the side. He hoisted himself out, then her. They scrambled up the shallow bank and darted into the nearest stand of trees.

A phalanx of soldiers had by now taken up positions along the wall walk. Bullets kicked up the ground David and Miranda had just covered. It would only be a matter of minutes before Heydrich sent the dogs out.

From the relative safety of the trees David stopped long enough to look around and get his bearings. He oriented himself to the castle's gatehouse. Okay. The rendezvous point he'd established with Tom would be just on the other side, before the road comes out of the forest.

"A little farther," he urged Miranda.

They ran through the woods. Breathlessly. Beyond exhaustion. Beyond fear. Beyond even conscious thought. They ran because they knew they had no choice. Because stopping would mean certain death. It was the same discipline as grinding out the fifteen hundred meters at the end of the decathlon when every fiber of your being told you to quit. David only hoped Miranda could call up something similar in herself.

After about half a mile she stumbled and fell. David helped her up. He leaned over to lift her onto his back.

"No, I can make it," she panted. She took his hand, and they set off again, his heart bursting with love and admiration.

Tom was waiting at the rendezvous point. The motor was already running.

He hustled Miranda into the back of the car.

"Where are the other two?" David asked him.

"Still in the trunk."

"Okay, let them out."

"You sure?"

"Yeah."

Tom opened the trunk. The pair of terrified lovers sat up. "By the time they find these two," David went on, "we'll be safely across the border in Holland."

The two men helped Erich and Helga out of the trunk. "Thanks for the use of the truck," said David. He shoved a wad of reichsmarks into Erich's coat pocket, then left the two, still bound, lying on the ground beside the road.

As the car sped off, David turned to Miranda. "Are you okay?"

She nodded, still breathing hard. "I think so."

He pulled her to him and buried her head in his arms. "Remind me to take you on my next mission," he said, then grew more serious. "You saved my life up there."

"My mother always told me to keep a spare pair of stockings with me," Miranda responded. "I guess she was right."

"How's your neck?"

"It's all right."

"The bleeding's stopped. By the way, I'm sorry I had to do that."

"I know," said Miranda. Then she added with a wry smile, "Well, I guess you paid me back for slapping you."

Tom glanced over his shoulder. "You did that to her?" he asked incredulously.

"Heat of the moment," David explained.

"We're not really going to Holland, are we?"

"No. But I figured telling them would be the most efficient way of letting Heydrich think we are."

Tom looked over his shoulder again. "I take it from the wetness of your garments, your general dishevelment, and the fact that you somehow seem to have misplaced the truck you drove in with that things did not go exactly according to plan."

"You take it correctly," said David.

"So what happened?"

"In a word, friction."

THIRTY-FIVE

It didn't take the SS long to find the baker and his girl friend. They were brought straight to Reinhard Heydrich, who conducted the interrogation personally. It didn't take him long to establish that Keegan and Fräulein Wolff were headed for the Dutch border, some 125 kilometers to the northwest. Even with the head start, it would take them several hours to reach their destination. Heydrich immediately put out an order that all frontiers, ports, and border crossings were to be carefully watched, not only with Holland but throughout the country.

David, Miranda, and Tom sped through the rural Westphalian roads, back through the fairy tale town of Hamelin, and on to Hanover. They abandoned the car on a residential street and took a taxi across town to the station. There they caught the first through train back to Berlin.

By this time their clothes had dried, but there was little else they could do about their appearance, so they decided they'd call the least attention to themselves by booking third-class passage. They weren't terribly upset when they found that no one wanted to sit anywhere close to them.

Once safely on the train, Miranda went into the lavatory compartment to wash her face and comb her hair. It seemed to her an enormous luxury.

Not trusting to let her out of his sight, David waited patiently outside the compartment door. Standing there, he could reflect for the first time on what he had done. He had come here to triumph honorably over the Germans in the Olympics. He hadn't been able to do that last weekend, but today he had managed to kill five of them.

Or was it six?

When they returned to their seats, Tom was waiting pensively. He asked, "What are you going to do if we get out of here alive?"

David and Miranda looked at each other for a moment, and it was obvious that they were thinking the same thought.

"First thing: Tell about the camps," said David.

Miranda nodded in accord. "Once the world knows the truth about what's going on, the horror will have to be stopped immediately."

Central Berlin

Ali was waiting for them as planned at the Friedrichstrasse railway station with a car and driver provided by Arthur Hargreaves. The Englishman had asked if he might come along, but Ali thought it would be best if he didn't.

She sat fidgeting nervously in the back seat, hoping that all had gone well. She knew she couldn't take much more of this suspense.

Finally she saw them, looking much worse for wear, but alive and safe and apparently unharmed. There were no words to express her joy and thanksgiving.

Westphalia

So far there had been no reports from any of the borders or frontiers. Something was wrong. Reinhard Heydrich summoned his aide to his office at Wewelsberg, the one right next to Himmler's.

"Have my airplane prepared at once," he ordered brusquely. "I'm flying back to Berlin."

Wilmersdorf

It was warm and sunny in Berlin, with only a slight overcast to the sky. It was some of the most pleasant weather they'd had here during their entire stay.

The car took them to the Hotel Bristol, where they went immediately up to Ali's suite. David's and Tom's team uniforms were hanging in the closet next to hers. All their other clothing and possessions were already packed up at the Olympic Village.

Miranda took the first turn in the bath, stepping out into one of the hotel's luxurious cotton robes and fresh underwear Ali had lent her. She combed and brushed her hair.

"Well, you certainly cleaned up nicely!" said Tom as she emerged from the bathroom with a glowing smile.

While David and Tom washed, Ali handed Miranda her uniform.

"It's a good thing I didn't burn this as I wanted to," she said. She positioned Miranda in front of the full-length mirror and brought out her sewing kit. "A couple of places we'll definitely have to take this in," she observed.

By the time the men had washed up and put on their own uniforms, she had Miranda completely pinned up. "What do you think?"

It was strange to David to see his blond Rhine maiden dressed in the blue blazer and white flannel skirt of the American team. "Could you do up mine while you're at it?" he asked Ali. "This thing never has fit right."

"You can't afford me," she retorted. She quickly dismissed him and Tom from the bedroom. Miranda took off the blouse and skirt again, and Ali went at them with needle and thread. The German sat by patiently. Then she climbed back into them and put on the blazer.

Ali stood back and scrutinized her work. "Good enough." She opened the bedroom door for the men to see.

Miranda fixed the white linen cap on her head at the properly rakish angle and posed for their approval. Ali kissed them good-bye and wished them luck. "I'll be looking for you there," she said.

The car was waiting for them at the front door.

Grunewald

Late in the afternoon the last event of the three-day equestrian competition was finishing up at the stadium, giving Germany yet another stunning triumph with all three medals. The arena was packed far beyond capacity for this concluding day. In a showing of nationalistic zeal German authorities had decided to let in an additional twenty thousand people.

The crowd was primed. The games had been a spectacular success. With all events completed, Germany had done better than the United States, Italy had done better than France, and Japan had done better than England. What more vivid proof could be needed of the benefits of the fascist and totalitarian systems over the tired and depleted democracies in proclaiming a bold and enduring destiny for the future?

Now, as daylight waned into dusk and the orange sun began its slow descent between the twin portals of the Marathon Gate, all that remained were the closing ceremonies.

The outpouring of emotion was overwhelming. The Olympic bell began its steady tolling. An assemblage of uniformed trumpeters sounded a slow fanfare. Spotlights converged in the sky above the stadium to bathe it in an otherworldly glow.

The Count de Baillet-Latour ascended the podium. The Belgian's voice rang out over a hundred loudspeakers as he declared, "We proclaim the closing of the eleventh Olympic Games. And in accordance with tradition, we call upon the youth of every country to assemble in four years at Tokyo, there to celebrate with us the twelfth Olympic Games!"

The Berlin Philharmonic played Beethoven's "The Flame Dies" as white-robed girls carrying laurel wreaths suddenly appeared, leading the final procession of athletes still remaining in Berlin. Joyously they marched around the concrete oval, following their national flags but waving in friendship and the spirit of international brotherhood to the appreciative and loving crowd.

Few could have realized it in the intensity and excitement of the moment, but those who later took the time to study Leni Riefenstahl's brilliant film might have noticed an extra, uncounted woman, marching with the American team. Her long blond hair was tucked up under her white linen cap, and on close examination her blue blazer appeared somewhat large and less than properly fitting. But this was no time for such nit-picking. The greatest international spectacle in the history of the world was coming to a magnificent and glorious conclusion.

The Olympic flame was doused. Tendrils of black smoke wafted up into the evening sky. As the führer waved to the assembled multitudes and the athletes filed for the last time through the Marathon Gate, the crowd broke spontaneously into the stirring strains of the "Horst Wessel Song":

Bald flattern Hitlerfahnen über allen Strassen,
Die Knechtschaft dauert nur noch kurze Zeit!

Soon Hitler flags will flutter over every street,
The days of slavery are almost over!

It had become a steady, disciplined, rhythmic chant of "Sieg heil! Heil Hitler! Sieg heil!" by the time Reinhard Heydrich arrived at the stadium in his Mercedes staff car.

With four SS aides behind him and three companies of Death's-Head regulars in the Maifeld, Heydrich rushed over to the staging area where the buses were loading to take the first contingent of American athletes to the Berlin train station. From there they would head directly to Hamburg, where the SS *President Roosevelt* was waiting to carry them back home. Those who wished to remain a little longer to enjoy the marvelous German hospitality could wait for the larger SS *Manhattan*, scheduled to sail on the twenty-sixth.

"I would like to speak with some of your athletes," Heydrich demanded of the coach who seemed to be in charge of the logistics.

"What about?" the man asked.

"Official business of the Reich," replied the *Obergruppenführer*.

"I'll have to see about this," Heydrich was told.

And within another minute or two he found himself face-to-face with Avery Brundage, president of the American Olympic Committee and defender of all that was sacred in amateur athletics.

Brundage listened to the request impassively. "Absolutely not." He ruled with a wave of his hand when he had heard enough. "Politics has no place in athletics, and I will not have these games sullied by any such stain."

"This is not a request," said Heydrich angrily.

"I agree," said Brundage. "It is nothing! Olympic athletes are accorded full diplomatic status, and I will use all avenues of international law to assure that this practice remains inviolate. Now, I insist that you leave my athletes alone this instant! Or do you care to create an incident that will destroy all that your proud country has achieved in these last weeks and proclaim Germany once again a pariah among nations? I, for one, do not wish to see that."

Heydrich's already thin mouth grew thinner with rage. "This will go to the highest levels of the Reich," he vowed. "You have not heard the last of this!"

"Nor have you, sir," Brundage retorted. And as Heydrich and his men stormed off to their cars, the American team leader turned to his coaches and said, "All right, let's get these buses moving!"

As the driver of the first bus prepared to pull away, Ali arrived, having just come down from the press box. She was wearing the same lavender-colored dress she'd had on for the opening ceremonies, and as always, she looked absolutely gorgeous.

"I saw you all out there," she said to her three friends. "You looked pretty sharp to me."

There was a big hug and kiss for Tom, then an even bigger one for Miranda. The two women wept in each other's arms. Then Miranda and Tom climbed into the bus, and it was time for David.

"I wish I knew some way to put it all into words," he said achingly.

Ali shook her head. And when her eyes had cleared, she put her finger tenderly up to his lips and whispered, "Don't even try. I know."

He flung out his arms and squeezed her to him as tightly as he could.

"Just like L.A. four years ago," he said through his own tears. He had let her go but held her hands in his. "I can't believe this has happened to us again."

"I know." Her eyes were still moist. "Four years," she said, shaking her head slowly back and forth. "But cheer up, Keegan. Maybe I'll see you in another four at the next Olympics!"

EPILOGUE

There were no Olympics four years later, nor were there any four years after that. By the time the games were to have commenced in Tokyo, the entire world had been plunged into conflict.

When the final tally of the 1936 Summer Games was complete, Germany had, in fact, "won" with a total of thirty-three gold medals, twenty-six silver and thirty bronze. The United States was second, with twenty-four gold, twenty silver, and twelve bronze.

With the disintegration of the *Übermensch* program, the war of national conquest Adolf Hitler had decreed was actually held off two more years, giving the Allies an opportunity to become at least slightly better prepared for the Nazi onslaught.

Gradually the German nuclear effort began to lose momentum. Research proceeded down many blind alleys, and the brilliant promise it had shown in the mid-1930's was never realized.

David went with Miranda back to America, where he assumed his active-duty commission in the U.S. Army. Shortly after the United States entered the war, he was assigned to London, where he directed special Allied intelligence operations into Germany. Many of them are still classified. He resumed his scientific career after the war.

Miranda was allowed to go to London with David. She was detailed to the secret Tube Alloys program, the British equivalent of the Manhattan Project, where she worked closely with Arthur Hargreaves.

Abraham Behrman refused to continue any of the research related to *Übermensch*. He settled in England and devoted himself to his original effort, continuing to contribute important work in the field which eventually led to the successful large-scale treatment of children with growth hormone deficiency. Unfortunately a number of tragic cases in the late 1960's of children suffering from dementia and organic brain disease traced to human pituitary derivatives led to a suspension of the program. Today, with the advent of safe, genetically engineered hormone stocks, the treatments have happily been resumed.

The Olympic Village did become a German army outpost as its designers had intended. Concentration Camp 208 was closed during the consolidation of 1937, and its inmates were transferred to the larger and more efficient camps at Dachau, Buchenwald, and Sachsenhausen.

Despite the reports of David, Miranda, and numerous others, nothing was done about the concentration camps. And by the time Dachau was liberated in April 1945, more than eleven million individuals, including nearly six million Jews, had been exterminated.

Throughout the Second World War and for many years afterward David wondered what Karl Linderhoff would have become had he lived. Would he have remained a "good German" after the meaning of that term had begun to erode and alter radically? Would he have been willing to take part in the atrocities which David witnessed firsthand? The questions always plagued David, but he continued to take comfort in the things Dr. Behrman had said that afternoon at the British Embassy in Berlin.

For reasons best known to herself, Ali Prescott decided to remain in Europe after the Olympics. She gave up her promising film career and pursued journalism seriously. The next time David saw her was on her wedding day in London. She married the Viscount DeVere, a widower considerably older than she, with grown children. Despite her new status and title she independently continued her career as a correspondent during the war, though rumors persisted of other secret exploits in service of the Allied cause.

Professor and Frau Wolff both survived the war, although he lost his teaching position for refusing to pledge his adherence publicly to the Nazi cause. Miranda saw them again after the war, in Berlin. And when she asked her father if they had known what was happening to the Jews and other officially undesirable persons, he replied: "No, we didn't know exactly what was happening to those people or where they were being taken. But we knew that *they were being taken, and they weren't coming back!* What else did we need to know?"

* * *

As for the others:

Avery Brundage remained president of the American Olympic Committee. He became vice-president of the International Olympic Committee in 1945 and president in 1952. At the 1972 Summer Olympics in Munich, Brundage insisted that the games go forward after eleven Israeli athletes were murdered by Palestinian terrorists. He married a German princess and lived for several years at her family's castle. He died in 1975 at Garmisch-Partenkirchen, Germany, site of the 1936 Winter Games.

Wilhelm Canaris continued as chief of military intelligence throughout most of the war. While taking no active role in resistance, he used the apparatus of the Abwehr to spread its activities. In July 1944 he was implicated in the ill-fated bomb plot to assassinate Hitler. Upon his arrest Walter Schellenberg, by this time an SS *Gruppenführer*, was appointed head of the combined intelligence services. Canaris was executed at the Flossenburg concentration camp on April 9, 1945.

Wolfgang Fürstner committed suicide on August 18, 1936, two days after the Olympics concluded. The German press reported his death as the result of an automobile accident, but foreign journalists discovered that he was of part Jewish background and knew that as soon as the games were over, he would be removed from his position and subjected to the same treatment as other Jews.

Martin Glickman, who, along with Sam Stoller, became one of the two Americans denied the opportunity to compete in the Berlin games, returned to Syracuse University and became a star football player. He went on to become a distinguished sports broadcaster in his native New York City, as well as consultant to several networks.

Otto Hahn was awarded the 1944 Nobel Prize in chemistry for his work on the fissionability of uranium and other heavy elements. At the time of the award he was being held in military custody by the U.S. Army. Upon his release in April 1946, he became president and director of the Kaiser Wilhelm Institute. He died in 1968.

Rudolf Hess remained deputy führer until May 1941, when he left

Germany alone in a Messerschmitt 110 on a self-proclaimed peace mission with England. He landed in Scotland, where he hoped to negotiate a peace plan with the Duke of Hamilton, whom he had met at the 1936 Olympics. He was declared a madman in Germany and incarcerated in England until the end of the war, at which time he was sentenced to life imprisonment by the Nuremberg Tribunal. Eventually he became the sole inmate of Spandau Prison in Berlin. He took his own life in 1987 at the age of ninety-two, whereupon the prison was torn down.

Reinhard Heydrich continued as chief of the Berlin Gestapo. After the invasion of the Soviet Union, he took charge of extermination operations for all the occupied eastern territories. He was the principal architect of the Wannsee Conference in January 1942, which formulated the key strategy for the Nazi Final Solution. Shortly thereafter he was appointed Reich protector of Bohemia and Moravia. In June 1942 he was assassinated in Prague by Czech resistance fighters. By way of reprisal, the Czech village of Lidice was destroyed, and its entire adult population executed.

Heinrich Himmler ruthlessly consolidated his power to become the second most powerful man in Germany. When Germany's defeat was assured, he attempted to negotiate a favorable peace with the Allies. He was captured by the British while disguised as an army private. When his true identity was discovered, he committed suicide in a military prison.

Eleanor Holm divorced singer Arthur Jarrett, shortly after returning from Berlin. She married Billy Rose upon his divorce from comedienne Fanny Brice and toured with his Aquacade. In 1938 she appeared with decathlon winner Glenn Morris in *Tarzan's Revenge*. The following year she starred in Rose's Aquacade at the 1939 New York World's Fair. Her subsequent divorce was heralded in the popular press as the "War of the Roses." She moved to Florida, where she continued her athletic pursuits and became an interior decorator.

Josef Mengele joined the Waffen-SS and served as a medical officer in France and the Soviet Union. In 1943 he was appointed chief doctor at the Auschwitz concentration camp in Poland, where he pursued heinous and perverse tortures on inmates in the name of medical research. He had a particular interest in dwarfs and twins and hoped to continue his work toward the perfection of a master race. After the war Mengele escaped from a British internment hospital and fled to Buenos Aires. Following the capture of Adolf Eichmann in 1960, Mengele became the most wanted Nazi fugitive, traveling among Argentina, Brazil, and Paraguay. He is believed to have drowned in a swimming accident in 1979.

Stewart Menzies became head of MI 6, the British secret Intelligence Service, upon the death of Admiral Hugh Sinclair prior to the outbreak of World War II. During the war he was known by the code name C and oversaw the cracking of the Nazi Enigma code. He was still intelligence chief when a band of pro-Soviet double agents led by Harold "Kim" Philby infiltrated the British intelligence establishment. He retired from the service in 1951 and died in 1968 at seventy-seven.

Jesse Owens went back to Ohio State and then into business and eventually became secretary of the Illinois Athletic Commission. He left in 1955 to take part in a goodwill tour of India for the U.S. State Department. He made a return trip to Berlin, where he met the widow and son of Lutz Long, the German athlete who had befriended him and who, as a pilot, died in the first week of World War II. Throughout his life Owens continued to speak on sports and the Olympic movement and remained a symbol of racial equality and athletic grace under pressure. The records he established in Berlin held up for more than two decades. In recognition of his stunning achievement his name was inscribed on the Marathon Gate, where it remains to this day.